Things Made Up And Written Down

Mark Weaver

ISBN: 979-8-480-99961-7

TO ALL THE WILD FRIENDS I GREW UP READING, WATCHING, AND LISTENING TO
and who were with me when I wrote this book:

To The Young Man of Providence
To Carl and the Pale Blue Dot
To Professors Feynman, Hawking and Quatermass
To the Good Doctor from his Gentle Reader
To Neil, Edwin, Michael, Yuri and Valentina
To Laika, who went first and didn't come back
To William, Patrick, Jon and Tom
To Thunderbirds, Stingray, Joe, Scarlet and XL5
To UFO, Space 1999, Survivors and the Tomorrow People
To the Double Deckers and Catweazle
To Timeslip and Children Of The Stones
To Harold, Charlie and Buster
To Stan and Ollie, Bud and Lou, and Moe, Larry and Curly
To The Whirlybirds, The Aeronauts and The Flashing Blade
To Daktari, Animal Magic, Skippy, Lassie, Flipper and Tarka
To Blue Peter, Magpie and How?
To The Clangers, The Herbs, Florence and Dougal
To Noggin the Nog, Ivor the Engine and Captain Pugwash
To Crackerjack, Jackanory and Vision On
To Pogles' Wood, Bagpuss and Tales of the Riverbank
To Black Beauty, Champion, Follyfoot and White Horses
To the RA concert party of Tin Min, the Home Guard of Walmington-on-Sea and the regulars at the Café Rene
To Robinson Crusoe, Belle and Sebastian and Lizzie Dripping
To TC and Benny, HK Phooey and the HB Bunch
To The Banana Splits, Swap Shop and Tiswas
To Marine Boy and Voyage To The Bottom Of The Sea
To Jaques Cousteau and One Of Our Submarines
To DM and Penfold and Willo The Wisp
To Hullabaloo and Custard
To Roobarb and Custard (no relation)
To Andy Pandy, The Woodentops and Play School
To the Flower Pot Men and Watch With Mother

To The Three Musketeers and The Count of Monte Cristo
To The Man In The Iron Mask and Squire Haggard
To Casey Jones and Bonanza
To The Lost Islands and The Beachcombers
To the driver and passengers of the Mystery Machine
To Dick and Muttley and Penelope who was usually in peril
To Camberwick Green, Trumpton and Chigley
To Paddington Bear and The Wombles
To The Muppet Show, Basil Brush, Sooty and Potty Time (which isn't what it sounds like)
To Jennings, The Railway People and The Borrowers
To Bill, Tim, Graeme and Kitten Kong
To DP Gumby and the Parrot Sketch and Spike's Q
To Swallows and Amazons and Three Men In A Boat
To Viv, Neil, Rik and Mike, Edmund, Percy and Baldrick
To Mowgli, Baloo, Winnie the Pooh and Tigger Too
To The Fall and Rise of Reginald Perrin
To The Whistle Test, Rock Goes To College and TOTP
To Chris Foss, MC Escher and HR Giger
To EE 'Doc' Smith, AE van Vogt and Philip K Dick
To Pelham Grenville, Bertram and Reggie
To Robert Sheckley and Stainless Steel Harrison
To Arthur, Ford, Marvin, Trisha and the big Z
To Douglas for getting drunk in a field in Innsbruck
To Patrick Moore, Jodrell, Parkes and Goonhilly
To John Ronald Reuel
To James, Jacob, and Kenneth for Connecting, Ascending and Civilising
To William and George, who taught me about running and gave me the idea for this bit
To Richard Coeur de Lion and Alexander the Great,
To Robin the Hooded Man and Hereward the Wake
To Dante, Salvador, and Vincent
To Swamp Thing, Daredevil and Elektra and Moon Knight
To Nikola Tesla and Thomas Edison
To Messrs. Theremin, Pearlman and Moog
To Jon-Tom and Mudge, wot
To Alice in Wonderland and Fat Freddy's Cat
To Rjinswand and Zweiblumen, GNU TP
To Fafhrd and the Gray Mouser

To William, Gideon, Edward and Othniel
To Harry, still waiting for Rosabelle believe
To J Tiberius K and the crew of NCC-1701
To Tom and Jerry, Trixie and Dixie and Tintin
To Clark, August and Two Gun Bob
To Space Invaders, Tempest and Elite
To The Adventure Game and The Great Egg Race
To Tomorrow's World
To Dr. Moreau, Dr. Frankenstein and Dr. Jekyll
Thank goodness you never went into practice together
To King Kong, Godzilla, The Land that Time Forgot and She
To Stranger in a Strange Land
To The Silver Locusts and The Centre of the Earth
To Diamonds Shining Crazily and Lambs Lying Down
To Mouselow, Melandra and Treasure Trap
To 633 and 617 Squadrons, James Bigglesworth and D Dare
To The Ancient Mariner and The Once and Future King
To Kind Hearts, Pimlico Passports and Ice Cold Alex
To The Thunderbolt, Genevieve and the Lavender Hill Mob
To Butch and Sundance, Bonnie and Clyde and Ned Kelly
To The Rochdale Cowboy and Fred the steeplejack
To Compo, Foggy and Clegg
To Jack and Joan romancing and Fred and Ginger dancing
To Sykes and Hattie, Marty F and Eric and Ern
To Kes, Billy Liar, the Iliad and the Odyssey
To The Shadow of the Torturer and The Lord of the Flies
To Thieves' World, AD&D and CoC
To the staff at Fatty Owls
To Pierre's monkeys and Johnny Dangerously, once
To Columbo, Ironside and Magnum
To Bo, Luke and Daisy, Richie and Joanie
To Mindy and that guy from Ork
To Mickey, Davy, Peter and Mike — here we come
To the Mary Rose, the Vasa and the Marie Celeste
To Robert Harbin, Ali Bongo and Charlie Cairoli
To The Amazing Randi and Magnus Pyke
To Count Dracula, The Mummy and The Werewolf
To Charles B, Alan T and 'one more thing' Steve
To Love Among The Ruins and The Starry Night
To The Six Million Dollar Man and Whoops Apocalypse,

To Randall and Hopkirk (deceased)
To The Man From U.N.C.L.E and The Champions
To Valerian, Scarlett and Rael and Tiger Lily
To the sonic assassins and their Hawklord
To Omni, New Scientist and Astronomy Now
To Peter and James, Turner and Sparrow, LJS and Jim
To Westley and Buttercup, as you wish
To The Bash Street Kids, DTM and Gnasher, Dan and Minnie
To The Canterville Ghost and Dorian's picture
To Charles Dickens, the Brothers Grimm and Hans Andersen
To Zorro, The Lone Ranger and Ivanhoe
To Tarzan of the Apes, Fu Manchu and Ming the Merciless
To The Old Man and the Sea and The Loch Ness Monster
To V and the Wizard of Northampton
To Roj, Vila and Kerr
To The Golden Shot, It's A Knockout and Screen Test
To Zirk, DR and Quinch, Halo and Axel Pressbutton
To Galloping Gourmets, Fanny Craddock and Clement Freud
To Not Having A Clue, Just A Min and Call My Bluff
To Messrs. Milligan, Bentine, Sellars and Secombe
To Number Six, 007 and 2001
To Tutankhamen, Athelstan and In Search of Michael
To Them!, The Earth Standing Still and Forbidden Planet
To Mission Impossible, The Avengers and Sapphire and Steel
To The Time Machine and The Prisoner of Zenda
To Dr. Jones the archaeologist, Mark, Harrison and Carrie
To Silent Running, Altered States and Soylent Green
To Dark Star and Ice Pirates
To Androids Dreaming Of Electric Sheep
To Friends Come In Boxes
To Le Morte D'Arthur and Tirant Lo Blanc
To The Anglo-Saxon Chronicle, Beowulf and Geoff C
To Maya and Smartie, Primrose, Pleiades, Tigger, Baggins, Biscuit,
Loki, Minky, Lichfield and Little Kit

AND WITH LOVE TO

Mandy for putting up with this nonsense

'In the midst of life's journey I found myself in a dark wood, for the right path was lost'

— Beginning of Dante's Inferno

'...inside every old person is a young person wondering what happened'

— Terry Pratchett

This isn't the beginning of the story, but it's a good enough place to start.

I promise to tell the truth, the half-truth, and nothing like the truth.

— The Author

Chapter 1

Circling The Drain

Am I circling the drain? Am I gradually, slowly, and inexorably getting sucked down the plughole?

I stand shivering in the half-light cold drizzle misery, forty-two minutes into my commute on Chinley railway station's needlessly long platform on a dismal early morning in November. The thought has been stalking me for longer than I care to remember. Always there, always at the edge, going away from time to time, but always coming back. Now it is nagging more frequently, more insistently, with more of a sense of urgency. Am I circling the drain?

But what if I am already down the plughole? What if I am so caught up in the mundane day to day existence of holding down a job, paying the bills, and doing what is expected of me that life isn't passing me by — it has passed me by and I've been so wrapped up in my own small world that I haven't even noticed?

What happened to the hopes and dreams of the seven-year-old me, the fourteen-year-old me, the twenty-one-year-old me, and all the other years' me in between them and the me who turns fifty-one in a month's time? There is a part of me that is slowly realising this isn't a dress rehearsal for the real thing. This is the real thing and time is running out.

There is a platform announcement. It always comes just before the express train to Cleethorpes barrels through.

'The next train on platform two will be the seven forty-eight Northern service to Sheffield, calling at Edale, Hope, Bamford, Hathersage, Grindleford, Dore, and Sheffield.'

Minutes after the Cleethorpes train has done its barrelling, the local stopping service from Manchester comes ambling in. The dozen or so waiting commuters move closer to the edge of the platform, eyeing up where the train will stop, where the carriage doors will be, and then huddle around waiting for them to open. There is always a pause while the conductor releases the deadlock allowing the doors to open. It always happens. Always. It would seem that people can't be trusted to open doors for themselves on the railway.

I think back to when I was a teenager, catching the train to Manchester from Dinting railway station. Middle of nowhere Dinting at the junction between end of the line Glossop and the now end of the line Hadfield, formerly just another station on the long since closed Woodhead line in the Peak District. Those carriages had individual compartments and heavy, manually opened doors that you could open even if the train was moving, if you were so inclined. What the hell happened that you now need a conductor to check each time if it is safe to let you on or off the train? Maybe that's not the reason. I will have to find out.

I get in the front carriage and find a seat. There is always a seat at this time in the morning at this point in the commute. Chinley doesn't really have a rush hour. A few stops further up the line and closer to Sheffield and it will be standing room only. I close my eyes and concentrate on the thought.

Am I circling the drain?

I am going to sit at a desk on the eleventh floor of an office block where you can't open the windows and stare at a computer screen for eight hours. I know the names of the people on my row, the row in front of me and the one immediately behind. Beyond this I could walk past people in the corridor and not know who they were. I am too busy doing my job to have time to look up from my desk. I don't get up to go and talk to people, they are too busy doing their jobs. I have somehow become a corporate drone doing my bit to keep a small wheel in the big company machine turning. Some are double or triple hatting — management jargon for doing more than the one job they were originally hired to do. Redundancies, staff turnover, and positions not being filled means 'temporarily' covering another position gets you another hat to wear, and then another, and temporary becomes just the way it is. Before you know it you're a hat rack wondering what the hell happened and why there isn't enough time in the day or days in the week to do everything that is expected of you.

But I digress. Am I circling the drain? I know the answer is yes. What I don't know is what it means, and what I can to do about it. In an intuitive way I know it means that unless something changes I am just going to keep going on as before, the same old sequence of the same old things. Days turning into weeks turning into years, and before you know it you're staring down the barrels of your fifty-first birthday thinking of the reasons — or excuses, your call — for how you've ended up here. It all seemed so much easier when I was a kid, or is that the effect time has on memories? Is the golden glow of childhood just the cherry picked highlights, with all the intervening boring bits edited out onto the cutting room floor of middle age?

I have a thought. A fleeting, elusive, not particularly well thought out thought. Half-formed and ethereal, at the edge of vision, on the edge of crystallising into something tangible. I try to grasp on to what I can and try to remember to remember. As quickly as it came, it goes. I feel both a sense of loss for the thought and relief it has gone in case it was a Big Thought. The kind of thought that turns your world on its head and makes you look at things very differently. I'm not ready to expose my soul to the harsh, unblinking eye of self-criticism just yet, especially the criticism of the seven, fourteen, and twenty-one year-old me's.

I used to believe the only criticism that was worth listening to was your own. Now I know that not to be true. There are two reasons. The first being that if you set the bar too high, with anything less than perfection not being good enough, then you have set unrealistic expectations you are never going to live up to. Here's an example: I once got 98% in a Biology exam. Did I think, 'Well done, great result'? No. I thought, 'What did I do that was so stupid I fucked up and missed 2%?' This was when there was no such thing as 'geek chic'. Being a swot got you beaten up. This colours your whole thinking. The second reason is that criticism comes in two flavours — constructive and destructive. 'That's crap and you are crap' should rightfully be ignored as it is an opinion. Whoever says it can go screw themselves. 'That's crap because X, and here's what you need to think about to make it better' may just have a grain of truth in it, or it might not. At least is it something you can consider even if you ultimately reject it.

The thought fleetingly surfaces again. It is elusive, but this time there is a picture in my mind— a small, grainy, black and white photograph. I can't quite make out the three people in it but I instinctively know who they are. They are me aged seven, fourteen, and twenty-one, and I know they are disappointed in me.

Am I circling the drain? Yes. What am I going to do about it? That photograph. The answer is in that photograph. I just need to figure out what the question is.

My thoughts are interrupted and my attention is back in the train. The conductor is checking tickets. As Chinley is an unattended station and doesn't have a ticket machine, or anything much else for that matter — one unheated shelter with a leaky roof and that's all the amenities you've got — you buy your ticket from the conductor. Sometimes they don't make it all the way down the train. This time the conductor has made it to where I'm sitting. I ask for a return between Chinley and Wakefield, even though I'm not going as far as Wakefield. Why? Because it is cheaper to go to Wakefield via Sheffield than it is to go to Sheffield. The conductors don't tell you this. Well, that's not quite true. One did, but only one. I'm wondering if it was his last day on the job as I've not seen him again. I pay cash as I always do — I have the exact change ready — and put the ticket away safely in my wallet. I think about asking the conductor what's the deal with opening the doors, but it's too late. He's already heading back down the carriage to do the doors as we're about to pull in to the next station. More people board the train. We are not at the standing room only point yet, but the available seats are rapidly filling up. I don't see the conductor again for the rest of the journey. By the next stop we've hit standing room and by the time we've picked up the passengers at Dore the train is packed. Not just standing room only but pressed together, with personal space no longer meaning anything. I hesitate to use the cliché 'packed like sardines' as these people are neither dead, filleted, nor covered in tomato sauce, but they are packed tightly and some of them look like they have dead eyes. I wonder if I look like I have dead eyes. I wonder if they are wondering if they are circling the drain. I'd like to think that if you are aware enough to ask the question it means the answer is no, but if that's the case, why do I answer yes?

The train pulls in to Sheffield. There is a pause while the conductor opens the doors and then everyone gets off. Last on, first off means that I'm one of the last to get off. It's not a problem as I'm not in a rush to get to the office, and at least I had a seat for the journey.

The walk up from the station is quite pleasant even though it is still drizzling. The water in the cascade of pools and steel sculpture/waterfall wall at the front of the station has been turned off, but it still trickles in the falling drizzle. Then up past the mobile coffee stand with the third best coffee in Sheffield. The sign doesn't say which came first or second. Third is just a fancy way to say runners up, which is just a fancy way to say we lost. We're not the best. I wonder what they are going to do about it and what is their plan to become the best, not just in Sheffield, but the whole of Yorkshire, or are they going to settle for third? Then I catch myself. It is 98% in Biology thinking all over again. I need to stop doing that.

Written on the wall of the university building behind them is a poem by Andrew Motion. It has a line:

To speculate
　　What if...?
　　What if...?
　　What if...?

When I get to the office I'm left waiting in the foyer on the ground floor as the elevator takes a long time to arrive and I don't feel like walking up eleven flights of stairs. It eventually arrives and a couple of minutes or so later I get to my desk. No 'Hello' or 'Good morning' to the people that are in today as each one of them has a headset on and is in a teleconference. It's going to be another of those days where there are people about but you are isolated, like being alone in a crowd only in an office. I take my laptop of out of my bag, connect it up, and turn it on. While it is booting up I unlock my desk draw and take out a Post-it note and draw the photograph from my thought. It isn't very good and looks something like this:

* * *

I take the Post-it note and put it in my wallet for safekeeping. I want to remember the thought and explore what it means. By now my computer has started and I'm logging on to the network. I put my thoughts aside as work needs to be done and I put my attention to the tasks ahead. By the time I look up again the day has gone and it is time to be packing up and catching the train back. This is how each day goes. Head down, concentrate, do what needs to be done. Day in, day out.

When it was lunch time I used to eat at my desk, until I heard the term 'deskwiches' a couple of years back. It made me stop and think. What was I doing? There and then I resolved there would be no more deskwiches for me again — ever. Instead I would get up and go away from my desk to eat. Where I am now the staff restaurant is on the twelfth floor. I used to take my lunch up there for a while when I was new, but that didn't last long. Now I just don't do lunch but work through because I have so much to do. I don't know which is worse, but at least I'm not eating deskwiches. The closest thing I have to a break these days is grabbing a coffee when I can and then back to the grindstone. Queuing for the coffee is the break. Is it any wonder why I think I'm circling the drain?

Don't get me wrong. I enjoy my job. I won't bore you with the details, but suffice to say I find it interesting and challenging. Challenging in a good way that is. I'm on a good salary, with a good company — even if it does have a tendency for ending up in the news for all the wrong reasons — so what have I got to complain about? How can I put this? When I was younger I didn't know what I wanted to do when I grew up. I was pretty clear about what I didn't want to do, but that's not the same thing and isn't helpful. You don't have a target to aim for, only an end point to avoid. I fell into what became my career completely by accident. Bills needed to be paid, so I took a temporary three month position, enjoyed it, found out I was good at what I was doing, and that was it. Then came a temporary six month position, then one for a year, and before I knew it I'd picked up qualifications in what was to become my field and I was off. That was three decades ago. I've been in this game a long time now.

But while I enjoy what I'm doing, I never really answered the question about what I wanted to do when I grew up. If you were to ask the seven-year-old me, the answer would be easy: astronaut. That's what happens when the moon landings take place when you're that age. Ask the fourteen-year-old me and you get a different answer. Realising that since there was no UK space programme and you needed to be an American to be an astronaut the answer changes: fighter pilot. Ask the twenty-one-year-old me and you get the now familiar answer: I don't know.

In *Logan's Run* (the book, not the film), the crystal in my palm would have gone black at twenty-one. Maybe that's what happened to my dreams. The crystal flickered from red to black and the light went out as the reality that life didn't owe me a living finally dawned on me. Then came marriage, children, and jobs — not necessarily in that order — and the crystal stayed resolutely black. Maybe the nagging doubt 'Am I circling the drain?' and the photograph are signs that maybe, just maybe, there is still a flicker of hope in there somewhere. I have to keep that flicker alive, that tiny, glowing ember which could so easily be extinguished. I don't even dare hope it could ever become a raging fire. For now I just have to care for that ember. Protect it, care for it, nurture it. It is the most precious thing in the whole world because it is mine and I have no idea what it is. One thing though is for sure. I am beginning to feel like I'm an artist trapped inside the body of someone who has to pay the bills.

I take the Post-it with the picture out and look at it again. I am going to talk to each of the me's and get to the bottom of this. I don't know how I'm going to do this or what the outcome will be, but I figure it has to be worth a shot and you've got to start somewhere.

Chapter 2

The Conversation With The Seven-Year-Old Me

How does fifty-year-old me talk to a seven-year-old me? I don't mean what to say, but how do I bridge a forty-three year gap in time? Without really knowing what I am doing, I take two chairs and put them facing each other as though two people were going to have a face to face conversation.

I sit in one chair and try to get myself in the right frame of mind for this, but I'm not sure what the right frame of mind is. I try to imagine the seven-year-old me sitting opposite me. The chair stays empty. I just start talking.

'Hello. Are you there?'

I feel rather silly doing this, but keep going.

'Hello. I'm you from the future — your future. I wanted to talk to you.'

The chair remains empty. I close my eyes and can picture a small boy sitting there. He is wearing a striped white and blue T-shirt, charcoal grey shorts, long grey socks pulled up to the knees, and brown sandals. In his hand is a model aeroplane, a 1:72 scale Airfix *Spitfire* to be exact. He holds it out to show me.

'Did you make that?'

He nods. I knew he was going to do that. He is, after all, me — just a younger version of me. I have his memories, but what does he have that I don't? Youth? Everything being new? Potential? Enthusiasm? These are obvious things, but there is something else. Something I don't know, but he does. Something I have forgotten over the years and don't remember or even know that I've forgotten. This is a variation of Donald Rumsfeld's unknown unknowns. An exquisite lapse of memory. I've forgotten that I have forgotten.

'It's very good.'

There is an awkward silence. I don't know what to say to myself. I get flashes of thoughts from science fiction movies and books about time travel, and meeting yourself, and paradoxes, and changing history, and all the problems that can cause. Marty McFly in *Back To The Future* fading into non-existence as a different future unrolls. But this isn't time travel. It is imagination. It is a thought experiment.

'I'd like to talk to you about something.'

'Sure,' he replies.

Is that what I'd have said at that age? Sure? It's what I'd say now, but back then? Maybe I'd have said okay. I put the thought aside and carry on.

'I want to ask you what you want to be when you grow up.'

I wait for the answer: astronaut. What I get takes me completely by surprise.

'I want to be a film maker.'

In a flash I can see it as clearly as though it was yesterday. I am six. I'm outside the front door of our house, by the lounge window with the low pane of glass my sister once put an armchair through when she tipped it over, but that doesn't happen for a few years yet. There is a papier-mâché model on the ground. It is a lunar landscape, complete with craters and a small mountain at the back. It is painted grey with poster paint and dusted with coal ash. There is a plastic Airfix model of the lunar lander beside a crater and a small figure of an astronaut on the surface exploring. This is what it looks like before the astronaut gets out:

I remember I always wanted an astronaut helmet, but never got one. The closest I got was making one out of a cardboard box and tinfoil, but I was never happy with it because it had corners rather than the rounded curves of real helmets and didn't have a plastic visor you could swivel up either.

Then I remember the camera — my dad's Standard 8 mm cine camera on its rickety tripod. I'm six and I'm making a stop-motion film about an astronaut on the lunar surface. Move the figure, take a frame, move the figure, take another frame. I don't remember where I learned how to do this, whether someone told me — my dad? — or I read it or saw it somewhere. I don't remember asking questions about how to do it. But there I am. I have made the set and arranged the shot. Click, move, click, move. I know the camera is my dad's, but I don't remember asking to borrow it. I do remember my mum getting the film from the Chemists, and the yellow and black Kodak box containing the silver tin with the precious spool of film inside.

Then I remember what happened next. The film wouldn't re-wind in the camera. I'm in my bedroom with the curtains drawn. The room isn't in complete darkness, but it should be dark enough. I'm under my bed sheets so it is as dark as I can get it and I have closed my eyes, just to be sure. I am doing everything by touch. I can feel the catch on the side of the camera where it opens and click, it pops up. I open the door and can feel the film inside, only rather than being on a spool it is in loops where it hasn't wound on properly. My heart sinks. Now I understand why it won't wind back. It never even made it past the lens, so not one single frame of my moon landing was ever filmed. I pull back the covers and I'm sitting on my bed in the dark. I don't think I cried. Big boys don't cry. The film slowly ruins as the light seeps in. I can feel the sense of complete disappointment again. Was this my first big dream dashed before it even began? Disappointment that crushed the life out of ever trying again? So why say that I wanted to be a film maker at seven if the dream died at six?

There is nothing to say that any of this has to make sense, that any of this is what really happened. What six-year-old doesn't have a vivid imagination? But at what age does the system beat it out of you? Six-year-old me needs some kind words, some encouragement, but the best I can manage is, 'Don't worry kid. It all works out.' What kind of encouragement is that?

Maybe I can talk to fourteen-year-old me more easily. I try to clear my thoughts, but the upset six-year-old is haunting me. There is more than disappointment behind those eyes. I think back to my harshest critic being myself. I started that at six? I need to clear my mind. A long walk and fresh air is needed.

* * *

I don't sleep well that night. When I close my eyes the six-year-old me is there looking at me. In his hands, my hands, he… I… am holding a coil of film. But it is his eyes I can't look at. I don't know what to do. I need to put something right, but I don't know what and I don't know how. A part of me has died. It died a long time ago and I've only just found out about it. I don't like it. It is unsettling. What other hidden memories will I uncover? Nothing good, that's for sure, so why am I drawn to do this again? The answer comes back immediately in the form of a question.

Am I circling the drain?

I sleep fitfully.

Sunlight filters softly through the curtains, but what should be a gentle start to the day is nothing of the sort. I awake with a start. I am at the edge of the park on Newshaw Lane where it runs alongside the road where Green Lane joins. Someone has just thrown a penknife at me. I don't know who it is or how old I am other than I am young. Junior school age, maybe first or second year. That would make me eight or nine. The blades of the penknife glint as it spins through the air in an arc, missing me by a wide mark. It was not a good throw and the boy who threw it has run off. I don't know him. He started running away the moment it left his hand so I didn't get a good look at him, but I'm pretty sure I don't know him. I go to where it is lying in the grass and pick it up. It is a cheap penknife and both of the blades have been extended. The handle is made of pressed metal covered with imitation ivory. There is a slight S curve to the handle. The blades are blunt. It looks something like this:

I fold both blades back inside then try to open them again, but they are stiff. I use my teeth to get a grip and they catch where the fingernail slot is. I chip the tip of my lower right canine. It is still slightly blunt to this day. Now I remember why.

How do I remember this? I remember the knife, but I don't remember what happened to it. Another long forgotten memory has surfaced. I wonder what else I will remember, or make up and have masquerade as a memory. How do you know memories to be true? They are recollections about past events, subject to the vagaries of what is recalled, what is left out, either deliberately or by happenstance, and time. Distorted, deleted, and altered. Does time really heal or does it edit memories? Do we remember less with time, or does it lay dormant until triggered by some chance event or thought or smell? Isn't smell supposed to be a powerful trigger for memories? I seem to remember watching something about taking 'memory boxes' into old people's homes, with items from bygone days to reminisce over, and racks of glass vials containing scents like freshly mown grass, or the air after a thunderstorm to trigger memories.

I have another memory I've forgotten about. I am in the front room of my paternal grandparent's house — a typical two up, two down terraced house in Stalybridge, Cheshire. The front room was the best room, but I don't ever remember it being used when we went to visit. We were always in the back room, whose door handle was an amber coloured glass bar with speckles of glitter set inside which promised something magical lay beyond. The radiogram, piano, and laundry rack on pulleys hanging from the ceiling for drying clothes counted as we didn't have any of these things in our house.

There were other differences. The toilet was outside in the back yard and was called the privy. It had whitewashed walls and a nail on the inside of the door to hang the toilet roll on. The toilet paper was always hard and scratchy, and if not Izal Sanitised then something very much like it. It makes today's extra soft, cushioned, colour coordinated toilet paper positively decadent in comparison, but that is not the memory. On the mantelpiece above the fire in the front room was a small glass bottle of smelling salts. I would unscrew the top to sniff at the pungent substance within. Whatever it was could give tomcat piss a run for its money. As a child I had no comprehension of why anyone would need smelling salts. I still don't.

One time I stayed over the night. I can't remember the reason. My grandfather was still alive at that time so I'd be maybe five or six. As I was getting ready to go to bed, a porcelain bowl under the bed was pointed out to me.

'What is it for?'

'In case you need to go in the night.'

Go? Go where? It didn't make any sense.

'The back door will be locked so you won't be able to use the privy.'

Then the realisation dawned on me. There was no inside toilet and no way of getting to use the outside one without waking anyone up to be let out to use it. I was supposed to urinate and defecate in this chamber pot and then put it under the bed until morning? I found this quite appalling and made sure that my bladder and bowels were both thoroughly empty before going to bed that night. I even passed on my usual bedtime drink. Thinking about it now, I guess that's what happens when you have grown up in a different age with different expectations regarding plumbing arrangements. If you've never known anything different, then that's just how the world is. Stepping into that house was stepping back to a different generation, a world where the bath was made of tin and hung on the back door, where you had to take a candle down to the coal cellar, and where the radiogram was the source of news and entertainment. Now that I think about it, I don't ever remember seeing a television set there.

Chapter 3

The Conversation With The Fourteen-Year-Old Me

This time I don't bother setting up the chairs. I get one chair, sit in it, and close my eyes. In my mind there is nothing there. No pictures, sounds, sensations, or anything. Just blackness. I can hear background sounds within the house and indeterminate faint, muffled sounds from outside. I breathe more deeply and slow my breathing down, waiting for the fourteen-year-old me to appear. I begin to realise it isn't blackness I picture in my imagination, it is night. The air is still and I am in the back garden of my childhood home. There isn't really any light to see by other than the crescent moon high in the sky. The orange-yellow glare from the sodium street lights is blocked out by the house. I become more aware of my surroundings. The air is cold and there is dew on the grass. I can see it glistening in the moonlight as my eyes become more adapted to the dark. I am also aware that I am not alone. In the shadows is a fourteen year old boy in a thick coat and woolly hat, and holding a pair of binoculars.

'What are you doing?'

'Looking at Andromeda.'

'Can I see?'

'Okay. Find the W of Cassiopeia. Use the right hand V of the W as a pointer and go down about twice the distance and you should see a fuzzy blob.'

He hands me the binoculars and points up in the general direction of the constellation.

I orient myself and put the binoculars up to my eyes, then lift my glasses up to my forehead and try again. Enjoy your good eyesight while you can I think to myself. You've only got a few years left before you're in specs. Then I catch myself — imagination, not time travel.

The familiar faint blob comes easily into view. I've done this many times before and this is my imagination after all.

'Have you got it?'

'Yeah.'

'The light you're seeing left there two and a half million years ago.'

'Where did you learn that?'

'Patrick Moore's *Yearbook of Astronomy*.'

The thought occurs to me that if you wanted to find out about that sort of thing back then, it was either through books at the library or the occasional TV programme like *The Sky At Night* or Carl Sagan's *Cosmos*. Pocket money rarely ran as far as astronomy magazines and even when it did it was too specialised for the local newsagent to carry. There was no internet back then, or mobile cell phones, or personal computers. Thinking about it, there was a lot that hadn't been invented, developed, or made commercially available that we now take for granted. Nowadays if Wi-Fi isn't available it is as uncivilised as there being no clean water or electricity. Back then it is just how it was.

I think of how I would explain Wi-Fi to my fourteen-year-old self, or Bluetooth, and why it matters, or seems to matter, but don't. There's no point. This is all inside my own head. It is an interesting thought experiment, but not for now. Maybe another time.

'Aren't you going to ask me your question?' he asks.

'How do you know I'm going to ask you anything?'

'Because I'm you and this is a conversation we're having inside your head. It's pretty obvious really.'

Was I really that precocious or am I overthinking this?

The scenery shifts and I'm in the fourteen-year-old me's bedroom. It is a small room and the bed just fits along the short wall with the window, with no space at the head or foot. It is pushed up hard against the radiator under the metal framed window. It is a cold room, even with the radiator. Ice forms on the inside of the window in the hard Peak District winters.

There is a stack of paperback books piled on the floor against the wall, maybe thirty or forty of them. In my mind's eye I run down the titles. They are mostly science fiction, mostly Asimov, and mostly from the second hand book store on the indoor market in Glossop. There is no bookcase, no shelf. In fact, apart from the bed and books there is only an old wardrobe in the bedroom. Well, that's not quite true. On top of the wardrobe is a stereo. That might be stretching the description a little. It is a radio cassette player from a car, which has been built into a wooden case. When I turn it around, the back is open for ventilation and inside is a transformer to convert it from car battery power to 240 volts AC mains electricity. I think this was one of my dad's home electronics projects, but I can't be sure. The radio didn't work particularly well, which isn't surprising given that it didn't have an aerial.

Fourteen-year-old me looks at me earnestly.

'You need to be quiet now. No laughing out loud under any circumstances. I mean it.'

He is kneeling on the floor in front of the battery powered radio borrowed from the kitchen. It is made of heavy grey plastic and has a long telescopic aerial and a big dial on the front. There are plastic stickers, diamond shaped, showing where the stations for Radio 1, 2, 3, and 4 can be found. I'm tuning to Radio 4 and I know what is coming up next. As the announcer says, 'The Hitchhiker's Guide To The Galaxy by Douglas Adams, starring Peter Jones as The Book...' the fourteen-year-old me hits play and record on the cassette recorder.

Then I remember why there is to be no laughing, or any other noise for that matter. I am recording it using a portable cassette recorder with an external microphone placed directly in front of the radio speaker so any other sounds that get made also get picked up.

I watch the younger me listening intently, covering his mouth — my mouth — to stifle any sounds that would spoil the recording, not that it would have made much difference. The cassettes I was using were cheap and the sound quality truly awful, but it didn't matter. I would listen to those tapes time and time again, becoming almost word perfect and able to recite whole chunks of each episode from memory. The hiss of the recording was almost part of the magic. I think I still have those tapes somewhere. I imagine they would be quite unplayable now as the magnetic tape will have degraded, and anyway I don't have a cassette player. Just one more piece of technology that has outlived its time, along with VHS, LPs, and floppy disks.

I don't need to ask the fourteen-year-old me a question right now. I'll save it for another time as I've got what I needed for now. The memory of listening to something totally wonderful for the first time.

Chapter 4

Mind The Gap

It is another day and another commute. The cold grey drizzle of yesterday has been replaced with a cold, clear day. It is still twilight as the sun hasn't risen yet, but it will be bright when it does. Frost coats the world with a dusting of ice crystals, which sparkle in the early light.

The train is late and the platform announcer can't decide quite how late it is — six minutes, then nine, then eight. It finally comes creeping into the station like a drunk husband trying to avoid awkward questions twenty minutes late. There is still a delay while the conductor releases the doors for opening. There is still no news about why the conductor has to release the doors. I watch closely this time. The train stops. The rear-most doors, where the conductor is, half-open to let the conductor peer out down the length of the train. Then the doors are released and opened fully. People leave the train. When the way is clear, new passengers get on.

Instead of going to where I usually sit at the front of the train, I head for the back and watch as the conductor looks down the length of the train, closes all the doors apart from the rear-most ones, which remain half open, peers out and looks down the length of the train one last time, then closes the rear-most doors fully. Two buzzes to the driver and the train pulls away.

Is it that the train might have missed the platform and passengers are going to step out into nothing and plummet to their deaths, or the gap between the carriages and the platform is too wide and people are going to plummet to their deaths? I figure the risk of death by plummeting must be very high, which is why they must do the check.

As I've boarded at the door control end of the train, the conductor comes to check my ticket fairly quickly. I get the usual Chinley —

Wakefield return and after paying the fare with the exact change I ask what the deal is with the doors.

'It's procedure,' the conductor says. 'We've got to check no-one has got stuck in the doors and that the lights are on.'

He moves on to check the ticket of the person in front of me, but then comes back and quietly, almost conspiratorially, says to me, 'To be honest, it's a bloody pain because you've got to do it at every stop. Procedures, huh?'

I don't ask anything more, but I'm now wondering why you would need to check if anyone was trapped in the doors when the train arrived at a station as they would presumably have been trapped there since the previous stop and hadn't been noticed on the previous check. I can understand doing it before the train departed, but not after. I guess it is just easier to follow the same procedure each time than a more complicated two-step procedure — one for arrivals and another one for departures. I think back to the manually operated train doors when I was a kid. There was no central locking. There wasn't even a handle on the inside. If you were inside the carriage, you had to slide down the window in the door and reach through to the brass handle on the outside to open it. Back then you could have opened the door on the side away from the platform and jumped down onto the track, or into an oncoming train if you were so minded. I guess back then you took more responsibility for looking after your own safety, and if you got it wrong it was your own stupid fault. These days you'd probably have a claims company after you to sue the railway company. I sometimes wonder what happened to the world and despair. It is the same thing with take out coffee with the lids which say, 'Caution. Contents Hot'. I mean, really? Who would have thought that coffee could be hot. I'm only surprised the warning is in English and not in pictogram form for those that can't read. I wonder what the sign for that would look like. It would need to be more specific than just the exclamation mark inside a triangle, which I take to be a more general 'caution' warning. I wonder if it would look something like this:

Looking at that makes me realise I am not a very good graphic designer.

Is it wrong to wonder what the compensation would be like for spilling hot coffee over yourself as a result of being trapped in a train door? Whatever happened to the days when you would have been told to not be such a clumsy pillock?

The rest of the journey passes the same way it always does, getting busier as the train gets closer to Sheffield, but this time I am imagining people getting trapped in the doors and being dragged along the platform, their horribly mangled corpses falling down the gap between the platform and onto the track when the doors open. I stop to get a coffee from the third best place for it in Sheffield and look at the words on the building behind.

'What if...?'

What if I stopped being so morbid? I've got a lot to do at work so I head to the office. Same route there, same routine with the lift, same performance plugging in the laptop and booting it up. Same sort of queries waiting for me, same old, same old...

Am I circling the drain?

And we're back to where we started. Another day, another week, another year. I need to talk to the twenty-one-year-old me and find out

— or is that remember —what was going on with him.

Chapter 5

The Conversation With The Twenty-One-Year-Old Me

Before I close my eyes to catch up with this incarnation of myself I spend a few moments recalling what I can about being twenty-one. I was in Preston studying for a degree. The course? Well, it started out as Combined Sciences at Preston Poly and without changing courses or institutions I left Lancashire Polytechnic with a degree in Combined Studies. Now it is called the University of Central Lancashire and I've no idea what they call the course. The sciences then studied which were combined? Physics and astronomy. The fourteen-year-old had made it from the binoculars in the back garden.

So what has the twenty-one-year-old me got to say for himself? I close my eyes and I am not where I was expecting to be inside the Jeremiah Horrocks Observatory, but in the Great Hall at Peckforton Castle, home of the legendary — or infamous — Treasure Trap.

For those who don't know what Treasure Trap is, or to be more accurate was since it folded long ago, was one of the first live-action role playing games. The idea was to go to the castle — a real one built in the middle of the 19th century as a medieval style castle for a wealthy landowner— and become a warrior or wizard or some such hero, and together with other intrepid adventurers go exploring the castle. This usually took place in semi-darkness and involved fighting monsters and plundering treasure. The plots usually weren't very complicated and tended to be along the lines of wander around in the dark with no real idea of where you are or what you are doing, find the monsters, kill them, don't get killed yourself, then rob off with the treasure. All good, clean, wholesome fun which taught me a few invaluable lessons in life:

1) Never run into a dark room without first checking there is not a ten foot deep pit with sharpened spikes at the bottom just on the other

side of the door. This is not a situation you typically find in everyday life, but it is one to be aware of nevertheless. Similar useful tips include don't put your hand inside a hole in a wall without at least first poking around inside said hole with a long stick to check for traps, and don't kick down a door when bursting into a room. While it might look good in the movies, the reality is it usually takes a lot more than just one good kick to break down a sturdy castle door, by which time the monsters on the other side have had more than enough time to put down their plastic cups of tea and be ready to slaughter you when you finally get in. It is much easier and way more effective to have an expert quietly pick the lock and sneakily let everybody in.

2) Candles blow out easily in draughty castle corridors. It is much better to take a paraffin lantern as these tend to stay in and give better light, and you can put them down without them falling over, which happens a lot with candles.

3) Putting damp straw on a smouldering fire in an enclosed space makes a lot of smoke. This is very good if you are a monster and want to make life difficult for a party of adventurers and stay alive yourself, even if you are taking in so much smoke into your lungs your life expectancy is going down faster than someone on a forty a day habit — death from swords, daggers, maces, pole-axes and fireball spells notwithstanding.

I am alone with the twenty-one-year-old me in the Great Hall. He is standing in a pool of light from one of the huge leaded windows along the wall opposite the fire place so big you can stand inside it.

'Do you know what I'm going to ask you?'

'Yes,' he replies.

'And?'

'Let me ask you a question first. Why are you asking?'

I am a little surprised the twenty-one-year-old me has asked this. Would I really have asked? It doesn't sound like something I think I would have said at that age. Am I putting words in my mouth? This is a construct which is all in my mind after all. I put this speculation to one side and answer the question.

'Because I've lost something that was once important to me and I can't remember what it was.'

'And you think I can help?'

'Yes.'

'That's not why you're asking,' he says.

'It isn't?'

'No. Why are you really asking?'

I'm beginning to think student me must have taken some kind of critical thinking and questioning seminar recently.

'I'm fifty, almost fifty-one, and I'm wondering what I've done with my life.'

'You mean being a multi-millionaire-rock-musician-racing-driver-test-pilot-movie-star is wearing a bit thin?'

'Not even close.'

'Harsh. So what have you done?'

'Got married, had kids, held down a good job, nice house, nice car, two cats...'

'And that's not enough?'

I feel uncomfortable. We must be getting closer to the nub of the matter. I answer honestly.

'No.'

I think a moment and then add, 'Don't get me wrong. I don't want to seem ungrateful. I've done well, but it's just...'

...it's just that it's not about what I've got. It has never been about material possessions or having things. There is a Seasick Steve song, *I Started Out With Nothing And I've Still Got Most Of It Left*. Only I started out with nothing and I've done quite nicely. That must make me seem like a smug bastard, but it's not how I think. For me it has never been about having things for the sake of having them, for show or for status. It has been about what it has allowed me to do.

'If it isn't about what you've got, what is it about?'

The answer surprises me. I was about to say something about having experiences, but what comes out is, 'I don't want to die without having told my story.'

'What story is that? The story of your life?'

'No, that would be a pretty dull story.'

'So what is it?'

'You don't know, do you? Seven-year-old me knew. What happened between then and now?'

'What are you on about?'

'There was a kid. You used to know him. He built a movie set on his front door step and was making a film of a moon landing, aged six. Fast forward a bit and the same kid was reading everything he could get his hands on and had read the *Iliad* and the *Odyssey* by the time he was eight. The same kid who would spend hours leafing through the two volumes of the Oxford English Dictionary, revelling in all the words, in the richness of the language. The same kid who discovered whole new worlds of fiction, who found so many genres, so many writers, and you know what happened next?'

'Tell me,' the twenty-one-year old me says.

'It was crushed out of him by the people whose job should have been to encourage him, to put him on the right lines.'

'You can't blame it on the teachers we had.'

'Can't I? Up until now I might have agreed with you, but what kind of message does it send to someone when he is told that Shakespeare will be too difficult for him so he is going to be put in the lower set and given less difficult texts to read? Streamed at eleven without them even knowing he'd already got Homer under his belt. And no, that wasn't a Simpsons reference.'

'Simpsons?'

'Don't worry. You'll find out, but that's not the point. Instead of being guided and nurtured, you get school reports like '[redacted] should spend less time trying to be off-beat' for English. Your confidence gets slowly chipped away. Then several things happen around the same time. You start to believe the criticism of your teachers and you become increasingly self-critical. You write a story for school. Instead of 'Here is where you could have made it better' you get 'Nobody is going to want to read that'. You get dismissed out of hand. Then along comes something so amazingly, wonderfully, breathtakingly original that you think, 'I'll never be able to do anything like that' and you stop even trying. You turn on yourself. You get 98% in an exam and you don't think, "Neat — great result", but "Why did I screw up on the 2%?" The sciences become more and more appealing because with them you are either right or wrong. Equations don't lie. Experiments either support the theory or they don't. Then you're told you're not good enough for Shakespeare, but here, you can read these other books instead. They'll be, uh, easier for you. Looking back, the seeds were being planted right there.'

'You seem pretty angry about it.'

'Too damn right. I've got stories inside my head that I need to tell, and this time I don't give a fuck if nobody likes them. You know, I wrote a novel when I was in my early thirties. I had a full time job and two kids, and yet I managed to get 80,000 words down on paper. It probably wasn't very good, as the rejection letters I received bore out, and in the end I put it away in a drawer and put down my pen. I've not looked at it since then. A few years ago the urge to write got the better of me, so I wrote a radio script. Just a half hour script, and I submitted it to the BBC. It got rejected. I wrote another one, but had no confidence in it and just put it away. There was no point getting another rejection letter. But I find the need to write keeps coming back. It won't go away. Sure, I can suppress it, sometimes for years, but it is still there. I can keep busy at work, be so frazzled and worn out at the end of the day that I don't even think about it. But then the itch starts, and it grows, and it won't go away. Then I start to resent work because it is getting in the way of what I really want to do, which is to write. But 'really want to do' won't pay the bills, it won't put food on the table or keep the roof over my head. So the resentment builds and I start to think, am I circling the drain?'

The twenty-one-year-old me looks deeply unsettled at this outpouring of years of built up frustration and anger spilling out of me.

'Don't worry kid. It's not your fault. You keep doing what you're doing and it will all work out.'

'But what can I do differently?'

'You can't. That's the whole point. You do what you do that gets me here. Here is my problem, not yours.'

The twenty-one-year-old me still looks unsettled.

'But what I do now is what happens to you later. My future is your past.'

'Look. Don't sweat it. You've got some great things coming up. You're going to have a ball.'

It's true. There are some great things coming up. There are also upsets and disappointments, but I'm not going to mention those. He doesn't need to know. He'll find out soon enough.

Chapter 6

Discovery Channelled

It is a strange feeling to trip headlong over something you have long wanted which had been hidden in plain view, and an even stranger feeling to end up on your back on the floor and realise you were the one to put it there in the first place and forgotten about it. The combination of shock, surprise, elation, and pain makes an unusual cocktail, although one which does not come with a cherry on a stick, a slice of lemon, ice cubes, or an umbrella. I feel a sense of relief at having identified what has been eating away at me, but there are other emotions in there too, all mixed up so that I can't easily identify them. Anger at myself for having suppressed something so fundamental to me and delight at having rediscovered it. Frustration, sympathy, rage, isolation, fury, and many others. Then one that gives me the deepest chill of all. Fear. Fear that if I could do that to myself, what else could I do? Fear of failing. Fear of rejection. Fear of not being good enough.

But this time I recognise the symptoms. This time it is different. I am still scared, but now I'm staring right back at the face of the person who scares me the most — myself — and I'm not blinking.

Sometimes a person can be their own worst enemy and not even realise it. A person can have their finger pressed so hard on their own self-destruct button and so believe in the lies they tell themselves that the reason they are doing it — self-preservation — is the ultimate price to be paid.

I'm reminded of Maslow's hierarchy of needs. If you don't know what that is, it looks like something along these lines:

I had to look the names of the levels up on the Internet, but the basic idea is that the most fundamental needs — food, water, shelter — are at the bottom of the pyramid. You can look the rest up for yourself. This isn't a text book. The point I am trying to make is that I suppressed something very basic in me. I did it for the noblest and the basest of reasons. Being the family man, the breadwinner, the sensible, grown-up one. Reliable, dependable, but scared of rejection, afraid of failure, concerned not to rock the boat and bring the house of cards tumbling down. I look at that last sentence again. It is a mixed metaphor, and besides, what would I be doing building a house of cards on a boat in the first place? It is a displacement to move me away from my fear behind all this. I try and I fail. But so what? Big deal. I've failed before with writing. I've got the rejection letters to prove it. But if I try and fail and bring down everything around me? Now that is a big deal, so I take the easy way out and bury my dreams. That's not seven-year-old me talking. That's not fourteen-year-old me or twenty-one-year-old me. It's someone who thinks he has more to lose than he has to gain and takes the easy way out by quitting while he thinks he's ahead. By burying his dreams for fear of not being good enough, according to his own ridiculous standards. 98%. But I told you, not this time. I'm staring back. I'm not blinking.

So, what does this tell me? That deep down at a visceral level I'm a story teller, a wordsmith, a writer? I recoil at the thought of how pretentious that sounds. For fuck's sake I'd better not blink if I'm being serious about this.

'How can you be a writer if you haven't written anything?'

Don't blink.

'But I have written things.'

'That went nowhere.'

'True, but I learned from the experience.'

Don't blink.

'You wasted all that time.'

'I showed that I could make time if I believed enough in what I was doing.'

Not blinking.

'Nobody read it.'

'Someone read it, if only enough to reject it.'

Still not blinking.

'But your writing had no effect on them.'

'Wrong. The effect was that they didn't take it up. I provoked a reaction in them, even if it wasn't the one I was going for. Even if it was indifference, boredom, or outright hostility for how bad it was, I got a reaction.'

'Why put yourself through that again? You'll only get rejected again.'

'Quite possibly, but you're not taking into account something fundamental which I have only now realised. I'm not writing to become a bestselling author. I'm not writing to become rich and famous. I'm writing because I need to write. I need to express myself, and for the first time I don't give a fuck what anyone else thinks.'

There. Not blinking. Staring you down.

This is cathartic. I need to write, so I get my laptop and clear a space on the table. The word processing software displays the top part of a blank page. My fingers are poised over the keys and... nothing comes out. The page stays blank. I type in the first two words — CHAPTER ONE — then stop. I don't have any words. I've got nothing. I go and get a cup of coffee. Maybe with a coffee I'll start writing.

Two cups of coffee and doing the washing up, putting a load of laundry in to wash, and cleaning the cooker hob later I am no further forward. Maybe I should write longhand this time around. Pen and paper. Old school. How it was before computers, word processors, and typewriters. Somewhere in a drawer is my fountain pen. It is a nice one given to me as a leaving present by colleagues at a place I used to work. After a bit of rummaging around I find it, still in the black leather presentation case with its companion ball point pen. I click the cap off and unscrew the barrel of the fountain pen. The gold nib is still bright, although the ink has long since dried out. I'm going to have to give it a thorough clean.

I also find the bottle of ink I got for the pen. It is still in the cardboard box it came in and still has the faded price label from twenty odd years ago. It is barely legible, but I can just make out the price of £1.99. I wonder how much ink costs these days? I open the box and take the glass ink jar out. Parker Quink permanent black ink. The sides are black all the way up to the lid, so I can't tell how full it is. I give it a shake. It sloshes, so there is at least some ink in there. Holding it up to the light I think it is about half full. I try to take the lid off, but it is stuck fast. Using a fountain pen is not going to happen straight away.

I find an old plastic takeaway container in the cupboard under the sink and put the disassembled pen in it, then run some water over it. Blacks, blues, and purples leach from the pen, bleeding into the clear water. I put the ink bottle in a bowl in the sink and submerse it, leaving it to stand.

Meanwhile, I'm quite taken with the idea of getting a second fountain pen and a different colour of ink to write with. Alternating between the two will allow me to see how much I've written in a day. I go back to my laptop and start researching fountain pens. I hadn't realised how much choice there was — from a few pounds up to several hundred and more. I wonder who would buy a fountain pen costing the best part of a grand and what they'd use it for. You could buy a second hand car with that kind of money. I figure that the kind of person who would buy a pen like that wouldn't be the kind of person who would buy a car like that. I read a number of reviews and in the end settle on a more modest number, admittedly with a gold nib, and head out to the stationers to see if they have one in stock. Sure enough in the display cabinet is the very pen I am after. The assistant takes it out for me and I hold it as though I was writing. It has a nice weight and feels good in my hand. I ask if it has a converter — the refillable reservoir for use with bottled ink — or comes with a cartridge. The assistant doesn't know so I quickly unscrew the barrel and check. It is a converter, which is what I wanted. I say I'll take it.

This then leads to the assistant going through every single box underneath the display cabinet to find the right one for the pen. The reason? All the pens come in almost identical, featureless white boxes with the only clue to their contents being a serial number on the side, which he doesn't know. He opens each one in turn to find the one I'm after, and as it turns out it is in one of the last boxes he checks. While he is doing this I choose another bottle of ink. The choices in stock are limited — black which I already have if I can get the lid off, blue, and royal blue. I choose the royal blue, which costs £4.69. That's inflation for you. I also pick up a hard back A4 spiral bound, lined notebook. I now have everything I need.

By the time I get home the stuck ink bottle and my old pen have had a good soak. I dry the ink bottle off and try the lid. It goes with a crack as the dried ink gives way, having been softened by the immersion. I wipe the neck and lid clean with some kitchen paper, getting splotches of ink on my fingers in the process.

Next I rinse the various parts of my old pen under the cold water tap until the water runs clear. Then I blot the parts dry with kitchen paper.

I fill my old pen with black ink and my new pen with the royal blue ink. Now I have to make that all important first decision. Which one to start with? I pick up the new pen, open the new notepad and begin to write. Or rather don't begin to write.

The pristine white page defies being despoiled with any kind of mark. The pen is poised, but I can't make the nib make contact. The opening words remain tantalisingly out of reach, unformed, and with no idea behind them. I don't know what to write. After all the soul searching, the wrestling with my unconscious, the re-realisation that I am a writer, I am without words. I don't have a story to tell. I am a phoney, but one that is not blinking. Then I have an idea, not about what to write, but about using a problem against itself. I vaguely remember something about if you're being rushed by a 17 stone guy in a judo outfit, make the fact that he is 17 stone his problem, not yours. If you don't know what to write about, write that you don't know what to write about.

I'll teach that blank piece of paper not to be so damned intimidating. I write the first word — Bollocks — then follow it up with Fuck. Bastard. Twat. Arse. Bollocks. Then I draw a smiley face underneath. The page looks something like this:

Now that I have broken the deadlock, the second thing I write has to be better than the first, but I'm in the mood for breaking rules. This time I write a worse second sentence. It was a dark and stormy night. Then worse still. It was a dank and wormy night. I wonder how much worse I can get it. It was a Damp and Foamy Light!!! Three exclamation marks — the sure sign of a diseased mind. Excellent. I wonder what other writing rules I could break. Do not ever use one word sentences. Period. And never start a sentence with and. Don't put things in parentheses (ever). I am starting to enjoy this too much. I draw a line under this and start properly.

I don't know what to write about so I am just going to write. I don't know what I'll write, how long I'll write about it, but I'll write it anyway. In two sentences I've written 'write' five times. Write, write, write, write, write. That's an average of — who cares? I can work out the percentages later. Write, write, write, write, write. Just keep putting one word down after another. Here's a thought. Instead of it being the same word, maybe I should start using others. Oh, what the hell. Write, write, write, write, write. I am heartened and intensely relieved that this will never be published and see the light of day. The damp and foamy light of day. This is so liberating. ~~Dear god never let this be published. And by god I mean Zeus or Odin.~~ There. I've crossed something out. I'm having fun. I am being playful. This is what it is all about. Having the freedom to let the words flow, the ideas bubble out and be committed to the page, abstract thought made real through abstract symbols. Pigment on flattened sheets of plant fibre. We started out drawing hands on cave walls with ochre. We've come a long way since then.

I wonder what our Stone Age ancestors would have made of a book. Being anatomically modern humans there is no reason why, given an appropriate upbringing and education, they would not have been able to read and write.

The Hand On The Wall

I place my hand on the wall, over the handprint which has been there for millennia, a shadow in ochre, a silhouette in time.

Okay. So whose hand is being placed? It is told in the first person, but who is 'I'? Where is the wall? How did 'I' get to the wall? How did 'I' know the handprint was there in the first place or have 'I' just discovered it? Who made the handprint in the first place? Was it a man, woman, or child? What led them to make it? What significance did it carry? What happened after they had made the handprint? Who else has placed their hand over the handprint? There are so many questions, and that is just from one sentence. Should I have just said wall? It could be interpreted as a brick wall and that wouldn't work with the prehistoric hand print I had in mind. Should I have said rock wall or cave wall? Cave wall implies a cave, but rock wall could be inside a cave or outside on a cliff. Am I overthinking this?

Not blinking.

If I am placing my hand in the present, it is a contemporary story, but it doesn't have to be. Millennia would also have passed between the palaeolithic and, say, the Roman period, in which case it is now a historical story.

I, Marcus Aurelius, place my hand on the wall.

In a flashback I remember my maternal grandma calling me Marcus Aurelius. I'm young, maybe three or four, so we're talking mid to late 1960s and she is vacuuming the carpet in her house in Guildford. It is an upright vacuum cleaner and has a cloth bag on the outside at the back of the handle to collect the dust. When it is turned on it inflates like a bagpipe and makes an equally terrifying noise. She lets me stand on the vacuum cleaner head and cling on to the handle and ride it while she moves it backwards and forwards. There is no way this can make cleaning the carpet any easier for her, and after a short while she says, 'That's enough for now, Marcus Aurelius.' I hop off and she gets on with the job in hand.

Where was I? Hand? A Roman in a cave putting his hand over a cave painting of a hand. What is he doing there? Exploring? Escaping? Is he alone? Are others with him? There are a lot of possibilities.

What if…?

What if the handprint were on Mars? That shakes things up. This is now science fiction. Is it an astronaut in the near future wondering how an ancient handprint got put on a rock wall on Mars? Is it in the far future and some distant descendant of the human race has discovered a handprint made by one of the first colonists to arrive on Mars? Or is the 'I' the Mars Rover extending a robotic arm over the handprint it has discovered and Mission Control are going crazy about the implication there was once intelligent life on Mars.

On balance it seems like a reasonable first line to play around with the ideas that spring from it. I might give it a crack and write a short story using it as an opening, but I'll also see if I can come up with another angle to explore. I don't know what that is at the moment, but here goes. Opening line again please.

The Hand On The Wall

I place my hand on the cave wall, over the handprint which has been there for millennia, a shadow in ochre, a silhouette in time. The rock feels cool to my touch, as it has felt on the previous occasions I have come here. This time will be my last. The years have caught up with me since I first came here. The first time there was apple blossom on the tree outside the cave. Now snow lies on the ground and there is a biting wind, but inside the cave it is cool and still. Then I do as I have done every time I have come here. With my hand resting on the wall I turn off the torch. The blackness is oppressive, not merely dark. Even the dark in the countryside, away from street lights, where the pale moon casts shadows and the faintest stars are beacons to guide the way isn't this black. This is absolute dark. The void where nothing else exists, where time is meaningless. Only my hand on the wall connects me with the universe. It is the anchor preventing me from being dragged from existence and devoured. I cling to the handprint and the humanity that put it there. Has one minute passed? An hour? A year?

Am I imagining it or can I hear voices in the distance? High and ringing, like children's laughter?

'Dare you to go into the cave.'

'No way. My nan says a bogeyman lives in there.'

'I heard it was a troll what eats your bones and makes soup out of your eyeballs.'

'Ew...'

'Dare you.'

'Why don't you go first?'

'I don't want to get eaten. You go.'

'You're okay with me being gobbled up?'

'Better you than me.'

'Lets's go together.'

Then silence. Still the darkness. The ever present darkness, disturbed only by the briefest flickers of light across the millennia. I wait. For minutes, hours, or years? Time is meaningless in here. Were the voices in my mind? Memories of days gone by or were there children there? I turn on the torch and my eyes scrunch up in the fierce brightness. I am still touching the cave wall, my hand still over the handprint. I let go. Was I dreaming? I look at the handprint one last time, silently acknowledging the person who put it there, now long dead yet in some way still here. I leave the cave.

It has fallen dark outside. The snow is still falling and the wind still blows. The footprints I left have long since gone.

I go and get a cup of coffee to give myself a few minutes away from what I've written before reading it again. First of all I tell myself, 'Don't blink'. This is the first thing I've written in ages so my 98% not good enough asshole of a self can shut the fuck up for a while.

How did it go? Well, I got some ideas down. It may not be great literature, but I got pleasure from doing it. I got some dialogue in. I wasn't sure how I'd do that to start with, but a point seemed to come where other people and not inner thoughts were needed. I wasn't sure about putting 'he said' or 'she said' in so I left them out. Were they boys or girls? What ages? It is ambiguous. I think it is the better in this instance to leave those details to the reader, but, I think there is a lesson for me as a writer that to start it ambiguously and let the reader come to their own conclusions, but then later turn it on its head and say something completely different would ruin it for the reader. There is a difference between writing a twist in the tail and screwing it up for the reader by not letting them know important details at the right time.

The bit about apple blossom and snow at the beginning just kind of popped in. I didn't know about the footprints, or rather the significance of the lack of footprints, at the end when I wrote that part. I just liked the idea of apple blossom at the beginning and the snow seemed a good contrast with it. Spring and winter. There was something about the blossom of youth and the winter of old age there too. Was that a bit heavy handed? Clichéd? Purple prose? I don't know. I don't think it was, but then what do I know? I can feel Mr. 98% looking over my shoulder. Please excuse me a moment while I tell him to fuck off.

Right. Back again. Where was I? Were the children real? I don't know. I don't even know who the person inside the cave was, other than they were old. I'll leave that to the reader's imagination too.

I think it might be fun to have the children go into the cave, only to have something lurch out of the dark at them. Put some flesh on the bogeyman's bones. Doing that would have taken the story in a different direction and that's not what I wanted to do with this. I'll file it away for use at some time later, maybe expand it into something a bit longer, or maybe not. I think it stands well enough as a vignette, a snapshot of a moment in time. We'll see.

Chapter 7

The Secret Diary Of [Redacted], Aged 50 3/4

It is 07:34 and I am in the railway station car park at Chinley again. In a few minutes I will walk down to the station itself, cross the iron footbridge, and wait on the platform until the train arrives. For now I sit in the car alone with my thoughts. Rain drizzles on the windscreen. I started this morning listening to the Today programme on the radio, but the news was so depressing. The world is in a great mess. Wars, conflict, political deadlock, catastrophes — man made and natural, financial turmoil, murders, the list goes on. I tuned in to a classical music station for a little light relief, thinking something more cultural might help. It didn't. I then tuned in to a rock music station and within a couple of minutes the dirge it was playing got too much to bear. I finished the drive in silence.

I'm thinking about what I will write while I'm on the train. Usually I will listen to a podcast or maybe an audio book, or read something — a magazine or a paperback — but not this time. I am going to try to write while on the train. Well, write until I get to Hathersage or maybe Grindleford and the train starts to fill up and I'll probably have someone sitting next to me by then. As I'll be writing longhand, with my notebook resting on the bag balanced on my lap, I'm not sure how I'll feel with someone looking at what I'm writing while I'm still writing it. It's curious. What makes being read while I'm in the act of writing so different from being read when it is written? Is it the idea of it being the raw thought, unedited, maybe, probably, going to get changed? Or is it that the person might be thinking, 'What drivel' as they read what is being written — but if that was the case they could still think it even after the ink had been long since dry on the page. I guess the only difference is that they could put a face to the writer and make a mental note not to sit next to such a moron again. Or deliberately pick them out to see what other drivel was being penned. Is that Mr. 98% speaking again? I've told you before. I'm not blinking.

I check the car's lights are off and the wing mirrors tucked in before locking it and going down to the station, past the bungalows with their neat front lawns and net curtained front windows. The train is bang on time and hurries in to the station. It makes me think. Sometimes it arrives almost apologetically, as if trying not to draw attention to itself. Other times it seems to march in as if to say hurry up and get on, I haven't got all day. Other times still it ambles, races, trips, slinks, shuffles, sprints, glides, crawls, and lopes. I wonder how many different ways to describe how the train arrives I can come up with. Probably too many. I might write a list someday, but not today. I have my thought that I want to write down.

So, the train hurries in to the station as though trying to get out of the drizzle as soon as it can. All the seats where I can sit by myself are taken, so I'm forced to sit next to someone. No writing this morning. Instead I alternate between looking out of the window and closing my eyes and thinking about my thought, which is this. Does what I have written so far seem a little like a diary, along the lines of *Bridget Jones's Diary* or *The Secret Diary Of Adrian Mole*?

[In the interest of narrative accuracy, that last paragraph was written on the train back from Sheffield. The person I was sitting next to got off at the first stop, so I've been able to write for almost the whole journey, which isn't bad. Swings and roundabouts, and it makes up for the lack of writing this morning.]

I can't say I have read *Bridget Jones's Diary*, only seen the film, or at least part of the film. Well, probably more like ten or fifteen minutes of it if I'm being honest. I read Adrian Mole ages ago and remember that I enjoyed it. I don't remember reading any of the sequels. Maybe I should. Anyway, in the spirit of the books — one which I haven't read and one that I can't remember that much about — here are some key points.

Units of alcohol consumed: unknown. I had a glass of red wine last night. Quite a big glass, but I didn't measure it. Make that 2½ units. Actually I had two glasses. Make it 5. Then add the doctor factor where they don't believe how much you drink and add half as much again. We're now up to 7½ units. Or do they double it? Make it 10.

Weight: unknown. I don't remember the last time I weighed myself. As long as my clothes still fit and I don't need to let my belt out I figure I'm doing okay.

Weight change increase: unknown. See weight above.

A piece about pining over Pandora: I don't know anyone called Pandora. Wasn't that the name of the planet in Avatar? It was an okay film. Great special effects, but shame about the plot. It would have been nice if it had had one. I wasn't madly in love with the planet.

Length of thing: unknown, presumed average. I assume I must have measured it when I was younger, but have no recollection of so doing. How do you measure it anyway? Anatomically they don't attach to the body at 90° so what is the correct methodology to follow? Upper surface? The side? Follow the curve around at the tip or extrapolate from a projected tangent?

Note to self: do not research this on the Internet. That way dodginess is certain to lie. Consider deleting last few sentences, then re-consider. Something about artistic integrity and writing what makes you uncomfortable and not blinking. There is a quote about this sort of thing I remember reading fairly recently on Twitter #writing #amwriting.

Another note to self: try to remember what it was as it was more eloquent than 'artistic integrity and writing what makes you uncomfortable and not blinking'.

Postscript: this is exactly what private browsing options on Internet browsers are for. A foray to some of the dodgier corners of the web, i.e., the vast majority of it, and a discreet moment in private with a tape measure and a working knowledge of the appropriate methodology reveals that I am comfortably above average. Smug married.

Chapter 8

Marlowe And I

I've just found the quotation.

'The best work that anyone ever wrote is the work that is on the verge of embarrassing him, always'
  — Arthur Miller

The next quote I read is,

'When in doubt, have a man come through the door with a gun in his hand'
  — Raymond Chandler

I feel embarrassed — partly about what I've just written and partly because if that is the best work I can come up with then I'm in trouble. Do I have doubts about whether I can make it as a writer? You bet.

At this point I am surprised as a man comes through the door with a gun in his hand. I look up from my desk. He superficially resembles, but is legally distinct from, the private detective Philip Marlowe so as to avoid any copyright issues with the estate of the late Raymond Chandler. This one is named after the Elizabethan playwright and poet Christopher Marlowe, who has been dead for long enough for copyright not to be a problem. The gun he is carrying is a sixteenth century matchlock pistol if that helps.
  'Come in Mr. Marlowe. I've been expecting you.'

'How did you know I was looking for you?'

'As the narrator, I'm omniscient.'

'That's a fancy word for a know-it-all.'

'Blame it on my upbringing. I read too many dictionaries as a kid.'

'That kind of behaviour can get a fella into a lot of trouble.'

'Like having a gun pointed at him?' I motion towards the antique pistol Marlowe is levelling at me.

'Exactly. So have you got what my client wants?'

'You mean the Big Boss?'

'That's the guy.'

'What's he paying you?'

'Seventy five a day, and another hundred and fifty for a result.'

'And if I won't give it to you?'

Marlowe waves the gun at me. 'I can be very persuasive.'

'The manuscript is in the drawer here. I can give it to you, but there's something the Big Boss needs to know.'

'Do tell. I'm all ears.'

I take the manuscript out of the drawer and rest it in front of me on the desk. Marlowe reaches to get it, but I pull it back.

'It's the only copy. He'll be happy to know that, but what he won't like is that if he takes it I'll write another one — only this time I'll write it with even greater disregard for anyone's sensibilities. I'll be even more open, even more scathing, and I'll make sure that he is full square in the cross-hairs.'

Marlowe lowers the gun.

'I'll be back. Don't leave town anytime soon.'

'I've got no plans.'

I am about to put the manuscript back in the drawer, but as he is part way through the door, Marlowe turns back to me.

'You know, I could have just shot you and taken it.'

'You are many things, Mr. Marlowe, but you're not a killer.'

I pause and look at the inch thick wad of paper in front of me.

'You can pass a message on to the Big Boss while you're at it. Tell him from me — I'm not blinking. He'll know what it means.'

I read back from 'I look up from my desk' and start to wonder. Does this fit here? Should I just cross it out? Where was I going with this idea? I don't know.

Just then the door opens again and Marlowe walks back in with the gun pointing straight at me. He has a determined look on his face.

'I was half way down the stairs when a thought struck me like a blackjack in an alley.'

I don't like where this is going.

'What does it matter to me if you write another one? I get paid for delivering this one.' He gestures with his gun. 'Hand it over.'

'And if I refuse?'

'Then I'll give you lead poisoning with this here bean-shooter and take it anyway.'

'You make a persuasive argument, but I decline. You're no killer.'

'I wasn't when Chandler was writing his Marlowe. But you? You're different. You'd have me pull the trigger.'

Would I? I'm panicking. I'm not blinking, but maybe this would be a very good time to blink.

'I'll give you a count of three.'

Three. That's not very long. My mind races looking for an answer.

'One.'

He wouldn't shoot me. I'm the one holding the pen, even if he is the one holding the gun. Without me there is no story. The pen is mightier than the sword, but is it mightier than the gun?

'Two.'

Seriously, I mean I'm the narrator. Without me the story ends right here. He can't shoot me.

'Three.'

I'm not blinking.

And with that, Marlowe pulls the trigger. I've never been shot before. I don't know what its like, but I soon find out. The last thing I see before the world goes black is Marlowe taking my manuscript.

As endings go, that is not very satisfactory on several counts: A) I am dead. I am not happy about that. B) as stories go it sucks. C) I can't think of a C, but it needs one.

Take two.

'You can pass on a message to the Big Boss while you're at it. Tell him from me — I'm not blinking. He'll know what it means.'

Marlowe leaves. I hear his footsteps fading as he walks away. There is a pause and I hear him coming back. I figure he has changed his mind or thought of something. Either way I don't want to be here when he gets back so decide to make myself scarce. I can't leave the room without running in to him, but where to hide? There is an old wardrobe in the corner of the room. I hadn't noticed it before. It's an obvious place to hide, way too obvious, and probably the first place Marlowe will look after he doesn't find me hiding under the desk. I quickly grab the manuscript and climb inside the wardrobe. It is full of clothes on hangers, which will help to hide me. I pull the door to from the inside just before Marlowe enters the room and hold my breath and try to make absolutely no sound whatsoever. I hear Marlowe open the desk drawer, then slam it shut. Guess what buddy? No manuscript there. I clasp it closer to my chest.

Just then I feel the back of the wardrobe give way with a sharp crack. I must have been leaning on it too hard. There is no way Marlowe could have missed it. I'm going to look foolish hiding in a wardrobe. Maybe it will just be easier if I give him the manuscript and have done with it, but I told you, I'm not blinking. The hero has to find a way out of the sticky corner he's got himself — or herself — trapped in. Not with a 'and with one bound, Jack was free', but a really clever, unexpected way out. Only I'm buggered if I can think of one. I run through the options in my mind. Marlowe is actually deaf and our earlier conversation was because he can lip read. He hasn't heard the crack and will just leave. Likelihood: zero. Believability: also zero.

I know. The wardrobe has a secret door at the back. The likelihood is zero and the believability is also zero and it is a bit too CS Lewis, but I can re-write it so that it has always been there and drop in a reference to having secret escape routes earlier in the plot.

Okay, so even though Marlowe has heard the crack I can still get out. Moving quickly I swing the panel hiding the secret door to one side and step through. Just then the wardrobe door opens and it is light inside the wardrobe. Marlowe is there with his gun, but I'm already running down the passage.

Passage? Since when was there a passage and not a small hiding hole? Without thinking I burst through the door at the other end, and am unpleasantly surprised by the sudden drop and the spikes at the bottom of the ten foot deep pit. Treasure Trap 101. I should have known better.

Take three.

'You can pass on a message to the Big Boss while you're at it. Tell him from me — I'm not blinking. He'll know what it means.'

Marlowe leaves. I can hear his footsteps fading as he walks away. There is a pause and I hear him coming back. I figure he has changed his mind or thought of something. The door opens again. Marlowe walks in with his gun pointing straight at me. He has a determined look on his face.

'Back so soon, Mr. Marlowe?'

'I was half way down the stairs when a thought struck me like a blackjack in an alley.'

I have a plan this time. 'And what would that be?'

'What does it matter to me if you write another one? I get paid for delivering this one.' He gestures with his gun. 'Hand it over.'

'And if I refuse?'

'Then I'll give you lead poisoning with this here bean-shooter and take it anyway.'

I pause as though weighing up my options. I once acted in one of the school plays in a leading role. I can't remember if I was any good. Probably not, but I'd better be good now. If not I'll be wearing a Chicago overcoat real soon.

'You make a persuasive argument.'

I reach for the drawer to get the manuscript.

'And no funny business.'

It hadn't occurred to me that I could have a gun in the drawer, but even if I did he would still have the drop on me. I get the manuscript out. It is an inch thick wad of A4 paper inside a large manilla envelope.

'It's all there. Every last word.'

I push it across the desk to Marlowe.

'You can still tell the Big Boss that I'll write another one. Tell him I'm not blinking.'

'I've been hired to collect a parcel, not pass on messages.'

I shrug. You win some, you lose some.

Marlowe picks up the manuscript and leaves. I wait until the door closes and I can hear him going away. As he leaves the front of the building I'm slipping out of the back. Having pulled the old switcheroo and given him an envelope full of blank paper it won't be long before my little ruse is discovered. I need to lie low for a while until the heat dies down. Maybe I'll take a short break away by the seaside. Being out of season it won't cost much and I've got a few days leave at work I need to take. I've not done this before — going away just to write or taking time off just to write. This could be interesting.

Chapter 9

Family History And Herstory

We used to go on holiday to the North Wales coast when I was kid, staying at caravan sites all along the Lleyn Peninsula. It took a while for the penny to drop that this was where some of my family on my dad's side had come from, and that didn't occur until long after I was a kid. This has got me thinking. I've lived all over the UK, moving from naval base to naval base until around the age of four or five. That's what happens when your dad is a submariner in the Royal Navy. Portsmouth, Plymouth, Dumbarton, Helensburgh, Rosyth, Guildford. If you know anything about the geography of the British Isles you will know that Guildford isn't anywhere near the sea. Sure, it has got a river running through it, but it is hardly deep enough to sail an Oberon class attack/patrol submarine up and down.

Guildford was a stop over with my mum's mum while quarters opened up elsewhere. I don't remember much about staying there, although I do remember some of my time in Scotland. These are just snatches of memories, images, snapshots. My first pet, a hamster, whose name I will not divulge in case I may, or may not, have used it as a password re-set question for an online account. Peeling a bag of prawns caught in Loch Lomond. Part of me wonders whether I should research the Loch Lomond prawn population in case some pedant points out that there never has been one. Remind me to reword it to a bag of prawns bought in Loch Lomond, or a bag of prawns bought from a travelling purveyor of seafood on the shores of Loch Lomond. There. Problem fixed.

Where was I? Ah yes, memories of Scotland. The last one was crossing the Forth Bridge when we were moving back to England after my dad had finished his service in the navy. Even then we didn't stay put for long and soon ended up in the Peak District village of Hadfield.

It is a place you have probably never heard of before, or if you have then you probably wouldn't if the BBC hadn't chosen it as a location for the dark comedy *The League Of Gentlemen*.

As a kid it was the arse-end of nowhere. I have come to realise, after raising kids of my own in a completely different place, that wherever you grow up is the arse-end of nowhere. This is just the natural order of things. For all its many faults for not being somewhere wonderful and exciting and full of really wild things, it was a wonderful and exciting place to grow up. I just didn't realise it at the time.

Looking back now, I had so much freedom. Sure there was school to go to, chores to do, and the usual day to day stuff, but when it was my time, in summer in particular, the freedom to roam was unlimited. There were just two rules. Tell someone where you were going, even if that changed and you ended up going somewhere completely different, and be back before dark. Other than that I could pretty much go anywhere. Down to the river to play alongside the Etherow and on to the reservoirs to walk along the dam walls; up to Bankswood; on to Castle Hill, also known as Mouselow, where a Bronze Age hill fort looked out across the valley to the square outline on the next high land which was where the Roman fort once stood; down to the ponds that fed the calico print works now long since gone at Dinting Vale, and the now overgrown woods where Beatrix Potter's grandfather's house once stood, the remains of collapsed walls still visible. I was given a cannonball found in a field on one of the farms, but it later turned out to be one of the steel balls used to grind the pigments used for dying and printing. It is very heavy and would make a great paperweight if it didn't keep rolling off the desk; on further still and onto the moors, beautiful and wild on a summer's day and bleak and unforgiving in winter. Even in summer the weather on the moors could change rapidly and weren't to be taken lightly. People have died of exposure up there and it would be all to easy to add one more name to the list and a newspaper headline in the local paper would be your memorial. Fifteen minutes of posthumous fame and then next week you'd be the wrapping round someone's bag of chips. This was back when chips were wrapped in newspaper.

When anyone from outside the area would ask me where I came from I'd answer Manchester. I've never lived in Manchester, which was half an hour away by train, but at least people had heard of Manchester even if they had no idea where it was. To begin with I didn't answer Manchester, but the conversations would go something like this.

'Where do you come from?'

'Hadfield.'

Blank look. 'Where's that?'

'Near Glossop.'

Still a blank look.

'It's near Manchester.'

'Ah, Manchester United. <Insert name of current big name player here>.'

Then it would usually go off into some rambling discussion about football, which I would have no idea about since I don't give a damn about it. I have been to precisely five football games, not counting the ones I played in at school. Stalybridge Celtic once when my dad took me, Manchester City once when I went with a friend, Reading against Gillingham twice, both times on Boxing Days, when a friend of my dad's could get tickets because he worked for a company that sponsored one of the teams, and once to Nottingham Forest when my son's school gave away free tickets.

Now if I am asked I say I come from London because everyone has heard about it and nobody gives a damn, unless they are American and would love to visit the old country because their ancestor came from <insert place name>. For Americans I say Hadfield, skip over the blank expression, and move on.

This brings me back to where I really come from. The truth is I don't feel like I am from anywhere. I don't have 'roots' in the way that someone who has lived in one place for all their life has or whose ancestors have lived there for generations might. My lot are wanderers and explorers who don't seem to stay in any one place for long.

This raises a question about how long do you need to live in a place before you can call yourself a local or before the locals would agree that you were a local? My grandfather was born and raised in London. His middle name? St. David, which is a bit unusual. David by itself? Fairly unremarkable. St. David? Odd.

He happened to have been born on 1st March, St. David's Day, so there is a connection there, but lots of people are born on 1st March and don't end up with a middle name of St. David. Approximately 1/365th of the population, or 1/366th in a leap year, if you don't account for seasonal variations in the birth rate. Either way you have a better chance of being born on 1st March than you have of winning the lottery, and the chances are your middle name isn't St. David either.

His father, Percy, was a Londoner born and bred, but his mother, Kate, was Welsh born and bred. She was disowned by her family for a long time for 'marrying a foreigner', and there is the connection to the family holidays in Wales. Revisiting the ancestral stamping grounds in Penrhyndeudraeth where my dad was taken as a child to visit 'The Welsh Aunts', who seem to have borne the same fearsome reputation as the aunts in any novel by PG Wodehouse; to the blacksmiths to pump the bellows — a tiring and seemingly never-ending labour — where grandfather worked the metal for the mines; and to visit Portmeirion just up the road where some of the relatives appeared as extras in *The Prisoner*, or so the family stories go.

I think about my mum's side of the family who were clustered around the Potteries in Burslem (Stoke-on-Trent. It's not really near anywhere else you might have heard of if you haven't heard of Stoke, so to confuse the Americans let's say it is near London) until she moved to Guildford as a girl — and there is the Guildford connection. Why the move to Guildford? Because back then the air was cleaner and her brother had respiratory problems. The doctor's advice to my grandma? Get him out of the Potteries or you'll bury him there. So that was that. Leave family and friends behind to give your child a fighting chance for life. And she did. Granddad had a job at the Cooperative Dairy and got a transfer. Then war broke out. The end of the war for him came on the slopes of Monte Cassino in Italy in 1944. Charlie from the Potteries now lies at rest in the corner of a foreign field that is forever England. His regiment? Welsh Guards.

The connections that have led me — or you, or anyone else on the planet for that matter — the chance connections are just so astounding when you look back and think what if they had stayed? My mother wouldn't have met my father. What if Kate hadn't gone to London because one of the other girls from up the street hadn't gone.

What if...?

And so on. I am amazed that any of us are here at all. Welcome to the world. We live here. It's a wonderful and exciting and full of really wild things place. Go out and explore, just tell someone where you're going and be back before it gets dark*.

* * *

58

*There are different degrees of darkness, the first of which is civil twilight. This is where the sun is less than 6° below the horizon. Next comes nautical twilight which ends when the sun is 12° below the horizon and navigation at sea using the horizon is no longer possible. Then comes astronomical twilight which ends when the sun is 18° below the horizon and the sky is dark enough for astronomical observations. This still isn't dark to a kid playing outside. Childhood twilight ends and proper darkness begins when your mum calls you in for your tea because it is going cold and she was expecting you hours ago.

Chapter 10

Trouble Is My Business

I am sitting on a wooden bench on the sea front at an undisclosed location on the Lleyn Peninsula. It is cold, wet, and miserable, and before the Welsh Tourist Board get all up in my face about this I will go on to explain that this is perfectly normal and acceptable as it is the middle of November and exactly the sort of weather you can expect at this time of year in this location. The sea and sky are both the shades of grey that battleships generally come in. Battleships, or targets as submariners have been known to call them.

The bag of chips I am eating are not wrapped in newspaper but plain white paper. I can't remember when chips stopped being wrapped in newspaper, or the reason for it. It can't have been the cost as old newspapers would have been free, brought in by helpful customers in return for an extra scoop. I reckon it was probably something to do with health and safety or hygiene regulations (Purveyors of Deep Fried Potatoes Orders 1976) or some such thing. I don't remember there being a spate of fish and chip paper poisonings that led to this state of affairs. I could research it, but what would be the point?

The chips are actually quite good — bought from a proper, old fashioned chippie or 'fish bar' as the genteel folk of Cheshire would have it. They taste all the better for being eaten outside, with the driving wind and the smell of the sea adding to the tang of the vinegar and saltiness of the salt. I look at those last four words again. Saltiness of the salt? What else would salt be apart from salty? Is there any other word which would describe salty? I could look it up in a thesaurus, but reckon that any word I found wouldn't be worth using so I leave it as it is. Salt is salty, okay? The saltiness of the salt is the phrase I am using. Get over it.

My mind starts to wander. An idea is starting to form. Here we go…

I start to make notes in my pocket notebook. They are jumbled up and don't make sense, but I put down the thoughts anyway before they fade away. A few words spoken, a name, something that happens, a feeling. It isn't making sense and there is no story to it, just glimpses of an imagined whatever the hell this is. A character is starting to emerge, but not the one I first thought it would be.

I keep writing. Ideas. Images. I've got lots of pieces of the jigsaw, but I don't know if there are any pieces missing and there is no picture on the lid of the box. There isn't even a box. The initial excitement of making things up, the giddy rush of enthusiasm stops dead. What was just in front of me starting to take shape has gone in an instant. The potential for what could be turns out to be as ephemeral as the briefest of mayflies. What I could see out of the corner of my eye has vanished when I looked straight at it. I can't do it. I can't make a story out of this nonsense. It's too hard. I don't even know where to start.

There is a metallic click and instinctively I freeze. There is a gun pointed straight at the side of my head. An antique matchlock. Guess who.

'The Big Boss wasn't amused at the pile of blank paper you sent him.'

'Really? I thought he'd quite like it. That was the second instalment of what I was going to write, only I hadn't gotten around to writing it.'

'He's not interested in what you're going to do. He's more interested in what you've got now.'

'What I've got now is not a lot. I've hit a wall. You can tell him he was right. I can't do this.'

I slump on the bench and stare at the ground in front of me feeling completely dejected. I've driven three hours, found an out of season guest house that wouldn't be a great place to stay even in season, sat in the rain for over an hour getting colder and wetter the longer I've been here. All I've written are some garbled ramblings, incoherent thoughts, and outright gibberish. I really can't do this.

Marlowe lowers the gun.

'I thought you were the guy who wasn't blinking.'

'Yeah, well I blinked okay.'

There is a pause. I turn my head to look at him.

'Here's what we're going to do. Give me your manuscript and stay here. I'll be back in an hour.'

I reach into my bag and pull out the spiral bound A4 notebook I have been writing in and give it to Marlowe. He quickly flicks through it to check it is the real deal.

'An hour. Don't go away.'

I am alone again on the sea front with just my thoughts for company.

'Why did you do that?' asks a small boy by my side.

I startle at his presence. Damn seven-year-old me for asking awkward questions.

'It's a long story kid. You wouldn't understand.'

'Did you do it because you were frightened?'

'No, it wasn't because of that.'

'Even though he was pointing a gun at you?'

'No. There are some things worse than that. It wasn't the gun.'

'What was it then?'

I can't lie to myself. Well, I can and I've been pretty good at it on occasions, but not now. This isn't the time or place. I'm having that uncomfortable sensation you get when you know you've just got to face up to something, even though it is going to be unpleasant and you know you're going to let someone you care about down.

'The truth is I can't do it.'

'Can't do what?'

The seven-year-old me is looking lost.

'I can't write. I thought I could, but I can't. There, I've said it.'

I feel very cold and empty now I have said those words and it isn't the weather that is causing it. I watch as a tear forms in the corner of seven-year-old me's eye and trickles down his cheek. I can feel myself welling up too. There is a lump in my throat.

'I'm sorry kid. I'm no good.'

'But we were going to make films and tell stories and have adventures.'

So there it is. The broken dreams of a child and I am the one who broke them.

'There is nothing I can say which is going to make this any better.'

I try to regain control over my emotions. After all, isn't that what I always do? Drive the feelings down and bury them where they can't hurt? Be the grown up, the logical, sensible one? The absolute bastard who doesn't shed a tear while others are in pieces? I can feel the resolve in me start to stiffen.

Seven-year-old me is standing in front of me, staring with hatred through tear stained eyes. Fourteen-year-old me is standing behind him with his hand on his shoulder, not saying a word. He doesn't need to. I get the message. I close my eyes and wish for this to go away.

There is one last voice. One last thing I hear and I don't know who says it.

'You did this.'

I think it is me.

And breaking another rule of grammar I'm on the bench in the rain on the sea front again. Alone. Bollocks to not blinking. Bollocks to writing rules.

Less than an hour later, Marlowe comes walking back up the promenade, his raincoat flapping in the wind. At least it has stopped raining, even though the clouds still look threatening.

'I'm glad you're still here. I did wonder if you'd bail on me and I'd have to track you down again.'

'How did you find me here in the first place? I could have been anywhere.'

'Some places are more obvious than others. Besides, I'm a PI and it's my job.'

Ask an obvious question…

'I've got something for you.'

Marlowe hands me a carrier bag with something in it.

'What is it?'

'Photocopy of your manuscript. When I came into town I saw a newsagents near where you're staying that did copying and had an idea.'

'I don't understand.'

Marlowe sighs. 'Gee, you know for someone who is supposed to be smart you can be real dumb. I get paid on results, so no manuscript for the Big Boss means no reward for me.'

'I still don't understand.'

'I'm doing you a favour here buddy. The Big Boss gets his manuscript, I get my hundred and fifty, and you get to keep your big mouth shut.'

'Because I could have taken that copy at any time.'

'Now you're getting the picture.'

'Mr. Marlowe. Can I ask why you're helping me?'

'Who says I'm helping you? I'm helping myself.'

'But why take the copy and give it to me? Do you think I can write?'

'Buddy, I'm a fictional character inside your imagination. What do you think?'

'I don't know. I thought I could. I keep thinking I could, but then I freeze. I don't know where to start. I get stuck on the first sentence, the first scene, and the page stays blank.'

'Then start on the second one.'

Terrific. That's right up there with 'Just put one word after another and keep going' and 'If you're afraid you can't write, the answer is to write'.

I'm reminded of something JB Priestley once said. 'Write as often as possible, not with the idea at once of getting in to print, but as if you were learning an instrument'.

There are some truly horrible notes coming from what I've been practicing. Some time between the age of seven and fourteen I learned to play the euphonium, one of the larger brass band instruments, and got good enough to not to be chased down the street by an angry mob when me and a friend would go out carolling door to door at Christmas. Maybe I just need to reset my expectations, and there is the manager in me coming out. Reset my expectations? Do I also need to have a mission statement and set myself milestones and deadlines? Now that I think of it, maybe that's not such a bad idea. Okay, not the mission statement thing, but setting some goals that will lead to knocking out a half-respectable tune. That's a very mixed metaphor, but you know what I mean.

I need to go and find that seven-year-old again and have a talk to him.

Chapter 11

Another Conversation With Seven-Year-Old Me

Seven-year-old me is in his bedroom sitting on the floor with his back against the door to stop anyone from coming in. I know he is because that's what I used to do. I can hear him sobbing. I sit on the floor with my back against the door on the other side.

'I just wanted to say I'm sorry.'

'Leave me alone. I hate you.'

'Will you let me in? I just want to talk to you.'

'Go away.'

'It will only take a moment. I promise.'

There is movement on the other side of the door and it snatches open. I am not prepared for the sight of the blotchy face and red, streaky eyes of the small boy in front of me.

'Promise? You make a big thing about keeping the promises you make to other people, but you don't keep the promises you make to yourself. You say, 'You shouldn't make promises you can't keep' and then you go and break them when it's you. I had hopes and dreams and you broke them, and you keep doing it every time and I hate you.'

I can't disagree with what he's saying because I know it is true. I can't bluster my way out. I can't bullshit this kid — he's me — and I can't talk my way out of it either. Fuck. I'm going to have to be honest with myself.

'You know the thing about you? You're right, and that's what makes what I'm going to say so hard for me. We did have dreams. You had dreams and I let you down. I wasn't good enough. I tried my best, I really did, but things change as you get older. It gets more complicated. You get all grown up and you get responsibilities, more and more of them, and before you know it, before you even realise, those dreams have faded and you don't even remember you had them.

You get dressed each day and you go to work and you come home and you do that every day and before you know it you're old and your life has passed you by. We didn't get to climb the temple at Machu Pichu, we didn't touch the statues on Easter Island, and we didn't swim with the fishes on the Great Barrier Reef.'

'But why not?'

'Anything I say will be an excuse and you don't deserve excuses. I'm sorry. I'm truly sorry. I let you down.'

He kneels on the floor next to me and puts his arms around my shoulders and hugs me. It is too much and I break down.

Later, much later, he asks, 'Is there anything we did do?'

I wipe the tears from my eyes.

'Yeah there is. We flew aerobatics in a two-seater training aircraft near Southwell Minster, and we went swimming with sharks, and we went to the top of the tallest building in the world.'

'So we travel?'

'Yes. Most of it is with work and most of it isn't as glamorous as it sounds, but yes, we travel.'

'And are there flying cars and moon bases and spaceships?'

'No flying cars or bases on the moon just yet, and the spaceships haven't changed that much, but there is an International Space Station, which is pretty neat, and we put rovers on Mars, and landed on a comet.'

I don't know who I am cheering up — him or me.

'And you find someone who is really great and have two kids of your own. That comes as a bit of a surprise I can tell you, and you do your best to raise them.'

'Am I a good dad?'

'You do your best and you don't always get it right. Sometimes you get it badly wrong. They will sorely try your patience and they will push you to your limits and beyond, but you always love them, even when they are breaking your heart and you are helpless to watch as they make their mistakes. It will kill you inside and you will go through some horrible times, but you make it and so do they.'

'Thanks for being honest with me.'

'You deserve it. You know, I was on the point of giving up back there. Putting the manuscript back in the drawer and putting it away forever. Now I'm going to carry on.'

'What will you write about?'

'I don't know and that scares me. The easy thing would be to not face up to it. All I need to do is put down my pen to make it go away. It would work for a while, it always does, but then one day I will find myself at a railway station waiting for a train, or catch myself staring out of a window when I should be working, and I will ask myself a question which will chill me to the bone because I know the answer. I will ask yourself 'Am I circling the drain?' and the answer will be yes. Yes I am, and you know who put me there? I did. The only way out is to pick up the pen and write. Write like my life depended on it. Write like the ink is running out and I have got to get every last word down. Write like today is my last day alive, because one day it will be and anything left unsaid will stay that way.'

'Now I'm scared.'

'Don't be. I'll be scared enough for both of us. I need you to stay strong for when I waver again, and I will waver.'

And with impeccable timing, the ink starts running out of my pen, but I don't feel like dying today. I refill it from the bottle and check the pen for tomorrow is full and ready to write.

I don't know what I will write and that scares me, but not as much as the alternatives.

Chapter 12

The Writer's Toolbox

It is the following day and I still don't know what I am going to write. The page is blank, the words unthought and unformed, let alone unwritten, but I have a plan. A few years back I picked up a copy of *The Writer's Toolbox* — 'creative games and exercises for inspiring the "write" side of your brain' — which I have now got in front of me. The box lid is open and the hourglass from the box is standing on the desk. I've used it a few times before when I got stuck so I figure I might as well give it a go now. At least it will be writing, even if what gets produced doesn't fit anywhere and doesn't get used for anything.

I draw out a First Sentence stick and turn the hourglass over.
* * *

I put tulips under all the pillows, and then set fire to the house.

WTF? What kind of lunatic would do such a thing? What kind of lunatic would put a First Sentence stick like that inside a Writer's Toolbox in the first place? I turn the hourglass back over and the few grains which had run through begin to run back. Is it cheating to want to draw another one? I suppose it is and there is probably a good reason why you are supposed to start with the first one you draw. Probably something about putting you on the back foot, put you outside your comfort zone, and getting the creative juices flowing. Well, there is a reason it is called a comfort zone and as far as I'm aware my juices don't come from tulips. They are probably poisonous anyway. You don't find Tulip Salad on restaurant menus for a very good reason. But, in the interest of having a go I'll do it. I turn the hourglass back over again and write out the first line.

I put tulips under all the pillows, and then I set fire to the house.

You might ask why I chose tulips, and the answer is fairly easy. The flower shop was all out of roses, it being Valentine's Day. At least they were red.

The hourglass runs out. I don't know how long it was supposed to be, but it wasn't very long, maybe less than a couple of minutes. I only got four sentences down and one of those was the opening line from the stick. There's a timer on the clock on my phone, so I draw the next stick, a Non Sequitur, and being careful not to look at it until I turn it over, turn the hourglass over and start the timer.

He was skating on thin ice — that's all I can say.

I'll say. Setting fire to the house was letting him off lightly. If I was being vindictive I'd have set fire to the house with him in it, smothered under the pile of pillows I'd put the tulips under. Where did he get the idea I like pillows anyway? One or two to rest your head on at night, but the quantities he would buy them in?

'Happy birthday. I've got you a present,' he'd say and guess what, it would be a pillow.

'Happy Christmas.'

Guess what.

'Happy anniversary.'

A pillow.

Pick an opportunity to be given a present and take a wild guess what I'd get. Go on. I dare you.

Frilly edged lacy ones, scented ones, patterned ones, large ones, small ones, antique ones, novelty ones, heated ones, ones with Bluetooth and speakers in them, feather ones, foam ones, soft ones, hard ones…

I look at the hourglass. The sand in it has got stuck and the timer is at seven minutes fifty-four seconds, fifty-five, fifty-six. I tap the top of the hourglass to get the sand flowing again, realise that I have lost my train of thought and watch it run out without writing anything else down. Right. Reset the timer to zero, give the hourglass a good shake, draw another Non Sequitur stick, don't look at it, set the hourglass down and restart the timer.

'There you go, making up lies again.' That's what they told me.

Hold on. I hadn't finished with the pillows. It would have been nice to have been given something more suitable, more appropriate. Jewellery, perfume, anything but pillows, and yet every time, pillows. I'd tried dropping subtle hints, then less subtle ones, and finally come out with 'If I get another pillow from you I'm going to burn the house down and every single last pillow in it.'

'Oh you don't mean that,' he said. 'I know how much you love your pillows.'

The hourglass is empty. Two minutes and forty-eight seconds. I hadn't even got to the bit about making up lies. Do I restart? Do I draw another stick? The instruction book is no help, so I flip a coin. It comes up heads, so I draw another stick. I look at what it says.

You could make a living doing this sort of thing.

I suppose I could, but I had never thought about it until then. I think about drawing another one, but hey, what the heck. Go with it. I restart the hourglass and timer.

I'd never considered arson as a career, but I guess someone has to do it.

I could be the Tulip something or other. What's a good word that begins with T that goes with fire? Time is short. I'll figure it out later. But thinking about it, is it really a career, and even if it is I expect the pay wouldn't be that good or the jobs that regular. The only people likely to hire you were ones wanting you to do an insurance job, and by definition these are probably the people with the least amount of money to be throwing around because if they were, they wouldn't be needing you to pull an insurance job for them. And besides, you wouldn't exactly be able to advertise. It would be word of mouth, and how often would you get people idly dropping it in to a conversation that they were thinking of hiring an arsonist and did you happen to know anyone good?

Five minutes eighteen? What is it with this hourglass? Does time run twice as fast in one direction? I'm going to draw one final stick, 'The Last Straw', to finish this off. Hourglass set, timer ready, stick drawn.

The lemon sherbet that melted all over the counter.

…was the thing that set me off. He'd left it out of the fridge despite what I'd said, and guess what was in the fridge in its place? A meringue pillow with 'I love you' written on it in red icing sugar with love hearts and red roses around it.

    I gathered the pillows, every last one, piled them over the tulips I'd bought, and doused them with the Chanel Number 5 I'd bought myself knowing I'd not be getting any from him.

Three minutes and sixteen seconds. This isn't right. I'm going to run some controlled timings to establish the mean, mode, and median times this damned hourglass comes up with. The Toolbox is going back in the cupboard for now.

One day later and I've not done the testing on the hourglass. I figure the sheer randomness of how it measures time and how it is so wildly inconsistent is part of its attraction as a writing tool. By not knowing if you've got two minutes or ten minutes (assuming it got stuck) means that the next stick can come at any point, so you've got to keep writing. As long as I never use it to time boiling an egg I'll be all right. I look back over the exercise I've done and the bit I skipped over when I couldn't find a word beginning with T to put with Tulip. Then it occurs to me — the Tulip Torcher. That would be the name my arsonist went by. The calling card would be a bunch of tulips left at the scene, except in the case of insurance jobs when it would be a dead giveaway that it was a fraud. I think they will be black tulips.

I type 'black tulip' into a search engine — not the obvious one in case you're wondering, but an alternative that doesn't track you and target you with advertising. It takes me to a Wikipedia entry which has four entries. A plan to evict all Germans from the Netherlands after the Second World War; an 1850 novel by Alexandre Dumas; a strategic formation to protect cargo planes in the Afghanistan War (although which one isn't specified as Afghanistan has had a lot of wars over the years, starting with Alexander the Great, although I doubt he used cargo planes); and a Soviet military transport plane which was taking away corpses of personnel lost in the Afghan-Soviet war (1979-1989). There is also a film set in Afghanistan; a restaurant in Florida; a flower shop in the United Arab Emirates; a hotel in Istanbul; a tattoo shop in Taunton; and an antique shop in Denver, Colorado.

I wonder if there is a character in this? The Black Tulip. Not at all like the Scarlet Pimpernel (type of flower, *Anagallis arvensis*, a member of the Primula family) — and there she is — Anna Gallis — dressed from tip to toe in black.

But who is Anna Gallis? Did she smother him with what would be his final gift of a Laura Ashley number with a floral motif and matching duvet cover? But wouldn't that make her more Black Widow than Black Tulip? I ditch that approach.

Anna, Anna, Anna. Who are you? I mean, who are you really? Heroine of revolutionary France? That looks like a drugs reference, and if actresses aren't actresses but actors, shouldn't Anna be a hero? Is she the pilot of the Antonov flying out of Afghanistan? A daring jewel thief? An international art thief stealing back what was stolen from her family by the Nazis? She is not young, not the mid to late twenties I had first thought, but more mature — less conspicuous, less obvious. A black, skin tight bodystocking clad individual climbing over a wall at night is highly suspicious, but a middle aged woman in everyday clothing? It would be unusual, but easier to explain that one away. It doesn't draw attention in quite the same way. There is more room for a plausible excuse, more reason to believe an explanation. Is she widowed or divorced? Maybe her husband disappeared in mysterious circumstances, no body found and no trace of where he went or what happened. I'm beginning to get an idea of someone who is not your archetypal art thief.

There is a vignette, a series of images, a sequence of scenes. The Black Tulip has located a house where part of the collection of Viktor Klein is housed. Is that a good name? It will do for now. Viktor is long dead and it is his reclusive son Otto who now lives there. It is an ordinary, nondescript house in the suburbs of... where? Somewhere in Europe? Maybe Germany or Austria. Not France, where the Black Tulip's family lived before fleeing in haste when the country fell, leaving almost everything behind.

As it is an ordinary house there is little security around the property. Yes, a burglar alarm and good locks on the doors and windows, but not any kind of high-tech laser grid with 24/7 security guards like you would find in a James Bond or Mission Impossible type film. Its protection is its anonymity, but rumours swirl in the art world. Even a mild mannered, innocuous art gallery receptionist gets to hear things, piece things together. Stake out the place, learn the owners' movements, and when the time is right, move in. The head mounted video camera will help later when there is more time to analyse the footage.

Does the Black Tulip have a specific target in mind for this first incursion or is it a reconnaissance mission? Maybe she sees paintings that she recognises, or maybe one catches her eye she has a hunch about, but isn't sure. Does she take anything this time or carefully conceal that the house's security has been breached so the owner remains unaware for now?

The owner comes back earlier than expected. The Black Tulip hears a noise and freezes, but gets out in the nick of time. The owner, Otto, a balding, overweight short man notices one of the pictures not quite hung straight and puts it level. He is suspicious for a moment, but passes it off. Anna has got away with it this time.

At some point there is another scene. Otto comes back. Everything is normal, as it always is. He pauses to admire the Rembrandt. Is that a bit too obvious? How about the Vermeer? Did the Nazis like Vermeer? Anyway, he pauses to admire one of the paintings of a well-known artist. Then he notices a gap on the wall. One of the paintings has gone. Just one. It is not the most famous or the most valuable. In its place is a flower, a black tulip.

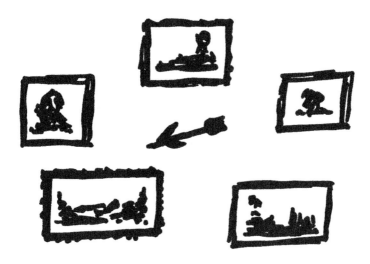

This next part is out of sequence and needs to be put somewhere above. As Otto is coming back to the house he passes a lady in the street. She is not one of the neighbours. He knows who these are and knows them just well enough to say 'Hello' and 'Good morning' to them when he sees them, even though he doesn't stop to talk. He never stops to talk. He is known for keeping himself to himself. She wishes him a pleasant afternoon and then crosses the road. She is wearing a headscarf. Otto notices that it is a print of van Gogh's *Starry Night*. That is what catches his attention, that and the canvas shopping bag with *Sunflowers* on it. If only you knew what I've got, he thinks to himself. That's it — the painting he stops to admire is a van Gogh. The Black Tulip hasn't stolen that — it is not hers to take back. She has got what belongs to her in that shopping bag. The flower is her calling card. It says you are on notice. I could have taken anything I wanted to and yet I didn't. I am selective. I am principled. There is nothing you can do about what I've done. You can't report it to the authorities, because that would lead to the awkward situation of explaining exactly how these other stolen artworks were acquired. No, you're just going to have to accept that someone knows your secret, took something at will, and could come back at any time.

Having got what rightfully belongs to her, she stops at a public telephone and places a call to the local police. Or does she? There are other families in her situation and don't they deserve justice? But there are other Otto Kleins out there and by exposing one and bringing him to justice does that make the others harder to be tracked down and harder to recover the other missing paintings from her family? If she doesn't inform on Klein, does she just leave the tulip or is there a note with it? If there is, what does it say? I don't know. I'm going to have to write something about Anna, get to know her — how she thinks, how she acts. I get the feeling she has dark secrets of her own and will surprise me with what she does. I like her, but there is an edge in there and I wouldn't want to cross her.

Otto has a story too — born into a world not of his choosing and trapped by his heritage. His mother died young. He remembers a picnic with her in a field with long green grass that waved in the wind. They had strawberries. His father was often away on business for weeks at a time. When he did see him there was never a hug. The succession of nannies who raised him were each as starched as the last. But how he and his father loved their art. That was their common bond. The art was theirs and theirs alone, but now it was his prison. A burden he can't share, one that can only be lifted when he dies. Now is the slow, patient, passing of days until his release. The alternative — the questions, the police involvement, his collection being taken away from him, the inevitable media spotlight being thrust on him — is too much to even think about. No, better to keep quiet, keep himself to himself, not attract attention, and in the evenings, over a frugal supper of bread and cheese, to gaze over a Matisse, or a Chagall, or a Klee.

The phrase 'frugal supper' makes me rethink Otto's appearance. He is not balding or overweight, but a frail, grey haired old man in wire rimmed glasses with a haunted look in his eyes.

There is another scene. I don't know if it is connected or not. I don't get the sense it is connected, but who knows. It might come in useful at some point. Here it is:

The flight of steps headed up to the top of the passage had been well worn, the edge of each step rounded by the steady action of countless footsteps, but the wear had happened long ago. A pair of heavy wrought iron gates fastened by rusted chains and a sturdy padlock barred the way to anyone who came this way now, not that anyone ever did. The newness of the padlock stood in marked contrast to the chains and gate.

A more discerning observer may have noticed the well oiled hinges of the gate, but this was not immediately apparent to the casual eye. Typically what first drew the attention was the small painted wooden sign, now faded peeling, which simply read, 'Closed until further notice'.

The 'Closed until further notice' sign doesn't seem very Otto, unless maybe it referred to the gallery that belonged to his father Viktor. Ha! There was an art gallery. That would explain how his father got involved in looted art. It would explain the sign and why the gates were in the condition they were if Otto was using the passage on a regular basis. It would change the location from the suburban setting I had thought Otto's house was to somewhere with more of a labyrinthine, walled feel to it, like the old quarter of a large town or city. Buildings closely packed on top of each other, winding passageways and narrow streets. Maybe this was where Viktor holed up when the war was over after all. I can see Anna picking the lock — which means that somewhere along the line she has acquired the ability to do this. Why was that? Does she fasten it behind her by hooking the padlock through the chain but not closing it, or lock it again to avoid being followed and interrupted, but have to pick it again when she was leaving? If she needed to leave in a hurry she would be trapped.

Now I can see Otto returning. He is standing at the gates, puzzled and worried about why the padlock is undone. He was sure he had locked it behind him when he left. He is always so particular, so careful. He goes through the gates and closes them behind himself, reaching through the bars to turn the sturdy key in the padlock. He gives it to good tug to make sure it has locked properly. Then he slips the key on its chain back into his overcoat pocket and slowly climbs the stairs, one at a time, to the old shop at the top and his apartment above it.

Yes, it is connected. This is where Otto comes back unexpectedly and Anna only just gets out in time. I need a cup of coffee so go downstairs from where I'm writing to get one, only to be given The Encouraging Talk by the Mrs.

Chapter 13

The Encouraging Talk

Don't get me wrong. I love my wife dearly and I am lucky that she is so supportive and caring and is tolerant enough to put up with me being self-indulgent and disappearing off to write at any spare moment I can, even if it means that lawns don't get mowed, carpets vacuumed, rooms decorated, or any of the myriad domestic chores, small or large, either get put off or plain just don't get done. The Encouraging Talk is the worse possible thing that could happen right now. It is a complete, utter, and total disaster.

Why? Because the only good that can possibly come from it is that it leaves me exactly where I am now, and anything else will either have me questioning myself, my abilities, my motivation, or any one of a number of things which will set me back. My confidence in doing this is already molecule thin, supported only by an imaginary seven-year-old version of myself and a fictional character I have appropriated who is working to his own agenda. I already have the Big Boss to watch out for, so any encouragement — however well-meaning — will be coming from someone loving and supportive and who would say loving and supportive things regardless of what it was I was writing, which is hardly objective. Anything other than this will have me doubting my abilities and lead me to a crisis in confidence and me putting down my pen. Either way it is a draw-lose for me and a lose-lose for the Mrs. I try to explain this in the nicest possible way, but I think I'm coming across as either a complete jerk or a tortured artist. To me the two things are one and the same right now.

There are times when I have got the page in front of me and a pen in my hand and the words just won't flow. The ink will not leave the pen because I can't make the words uncongeal in my mind. But then some kind of magic happens. I find a place to start, two or three words start to fit together, then a sentence, then another one, and another, and then I'm off. Getting those first few words down is like trying to open an artery, but then there's a spurt and all hell breaks loose, at least for a little while until the bleeding shuts down. I don't have any red ink. Perhaps I should try writing in that colour for a while to see what happens. As well as black (original) and royal blue (new) I now have turquoise, purple, and green inks. I am deliberately saving the purple ink for purple prose when I need to get that out of my system. I got the green because I thought it would look nice, but now I vaguely remember something about crazy people writing in green ink. I have no idea where that is from, so I'm saving it for when I want to play around with crazy ideas.

Note to self: it was something about writing to publishers in green ink, so if it ever comes to that stage, remember to stick to black or blue.

Coloured ink was going off on a tangent. Where was I? Ah yes. The Encouraging Talk. There are probably writers out there who do share what they are working on with their family and friends, who do genuinely appreciate the comments they receive, and for whom The Encouraging Talk is exactly that — encouraging. Something which says, 'I have every confidence in you, that what you are doing is worthwhile, that you will succeed.' But that's not me. I don't even feel quietly envious of them; it is more like frank incomprehension. Maybe that makes me the odd one out, the misfit, the loner, but that's the way I'm built. I wonder why that is. I have a horrible feeling it is something to do with me.

That didn't quite come out the way that I meant it to. I mean, of course it is something to do with me, but what I am trying to say is that it is my inner critic, Mr 98%, the Big Boss — call it what you will — but it is that internal voice which says, 'Who are you kidding?'

Actually I am being kind to my inner critic here. The reality is that it can be a nasty piece of work. The language is harder, more bitter. You have no idea as to the viciousness I can lay into myself when I am being critical of me. With friends like that, so the saying goes, who needs enemies? Maybe you are beginning to get an inkling of why The Encouraging Talk is so hugely discouraging to me. Oh dear lord I am being a tortured artist, or as I said earlier, a complete jerk? Actually I was being nice there too. What I really meant was a completely fucking ridiculous pretentious twat. Whatever happened to 'I'm not blinking'? I think I blunk. Ha! Break rules.

* * *

I wait for Marlowe to appear again with a gun. It is a while before I realise I am going to have to do the next bit myself. I wonder whether the younger incarnations of myself are going to put in an appearance any time soon, but they seem quiet for now. Is that a good sign? I don't know. I don't have enough information. Anna and Otto seen quiet for now too. I don't want to do another Writer's Toolbox exercise either, so instead I just write out the first thought that occurs to me. It does not make sense.

It is unusual to put gravy on your cornflakes, Ptolemy decided, but there are days when putting gravy on your cornflakes and then adding a garnish of thinly sliced jalapeño pepper was not just required, but practically mandatory. Today was such a day.

My pen stops dead after 'such a day' as I sense my inner critic looking over my shoulder. There are no words spoken. There doesn't need to be. The half-remembered look of disapproval one of my English teachers would give me is enough, and the words of an old school report come back to haunt me.

'[redacted] should spend less time trying to be offbeat.'

What I've just written about the cornflakes and gravy is offbeat, but then that is precisely the point. Is it crap? Maybe. Probably. Yes, but where is the encouragement to do something better?

'That's interesting' is a kinder way of saying, 'What the fuck? What do you think you are doing?' Why was it never anything like, 'What was it that you were trying to achieve?' Then after whatever the reply was, follow it with, 'Here is something you might want to think about for the next time', or, 'To make it even better, you could try…' but no. Nothing about what I should have been spending more of my time doing. No. Go straight for the kill. You stepped out of line, Sunny Jim. You didn't follow the rules, and now we're marking you down.

I get it now. How could I have been so blind? But at that age you don't think about it like that, or at least I didn't. I was raised to respect authority figures without question. Do as you are told. Don't step out of line. Conform. What the report was really saying was, '[redacted] must not be creative. [redacted] must not learn to think for himself. [redacted] must not ask awkward questions. [redacted] must be more like us. Any form of rebellion will be crushed. There is no place for free thinkers, idealists, or radicals. They agitate. They cause trouble.'

So, bit by bit, they chip away at your confidence to be yourself, to be different, to think differently, until the 'model pupil' is produced, thinking the right thoughts, behaving the right way, conforming. Uniform, vanilla flavoured, part of the system.

'All in all you're just another brick in the wall'
— Pink Floyd

Love the album, love the song, and only now do I realise what an excellent job the school did turning me into a brick. Such an exquisite touch to do it so well that I didn't even realise it had happened.

Chapter 14

Tranquility Base Here. The Eagle Has Fallen Off The Swing

Looking back on my childhood, I am thinking about who my earliest role models were. Taking my family as given (I was going to say, 'Taking my family for granted', but that sounded wrong) I was initially stumped, but then I started to remember who had influenced me. First and foremost were the Apollo astronauts, in particular the crew of Apollo 11.

I was five and a half, and I remember staying up to watch the launch of the Saturn V rocket from Cape Kennedy to the Moon. The next day I was in the garden playing on the swing and tried to see how high I could fly. As high as the Moon? I didn't have a rocket, but I was going to give it my best shot. With each kick of my legs the swing went higher and higher. There comes a point when you are swinging so high that you are either looking straight down at the ground or straight out to the sky. It was at that point the metal stakes holding the swing to the ground started to come loose. I didn't care. I was going to the Moon. What was the worst that could happen? Quite a lot as it turned out. The stakes pulled free at the top of one particularly vigorous swing and the whole thing fell forward. I flew through the air and landed heavily on my back, knocking all the wind out of me. Fortunately no real injury was done. It is funny the small details you sometimes recollect. I can clearly remember that I was wearing wellies.

At that age, being an astronaut seemed a perfectly reasonable ambition to have. I was not aware in the slightest there was no British astronaut corps. I knew there was a man on the Moon. It had been on television. If he could do it then so could I. All I needed to do was swing harder and not worry too much that I didn't have a space helmet. They were only made of plastic and had a big hole at the bottom so you could put them over your head, so it couldn't have been a big deal if you didn't have one. Words like 'vacuum' and 'asphyxiation' weren't in my vocabulary or worldview at that age. In my imagination I landed on the Moon and walked around on the surface collecting rocks and encountering the occasional Clanger-like creature from time to time. I would later make a film about it.

Following on from the Apollo astronauts, anyone else automatically fell short of the mark, with the exception of other astronauts, or rather cosmonauts as they were known in what is now the former USSR and a few other people to do with Space. For years I wondered why photographs of them showed the letters CCCP, until I found out that was what the initials USSR were in Russian in the Cyrillic alphabet. I followed the exploits of these boldly going adventurers with whatever I could lay my hands on — television, newspapers, magazines, *The Observer's Book of Spaceflight*, even the PG Tips Tea collecting cards that made up *The Race Into Space*.

There were other people associated with astronauts who I looked up to such as James Burke, who would later to go on to make the wonderful series *Connections*, and Patrick Moore, whose work on mapping the Moon was used in the selection of the landing sites. Not that I knew it at that age. They were just Space People. People who I wanted to be, or if not be, then be like.

My most significant and longest lasting influence started when I watched the series *Cosmos* and discovered the astronomer/cosmologist/astrophysicist/astrobiologist (among other things), Carl Sagan. To an impressionable seventeen-year-old interested in all things to do with space, Sagan was a revelation. He was smart, he knew what he was talking about and could explain it in a way you could understand. He spoke out on issues that went beyond national boundaries. His reflections on the Pale Blue Dot — go onto the Internet and look it up if you don't already know about it — still profoundly move me each time I hear or read the words. Thinking about it, if you don't know about Sagan's Pale Blue Dot (it begins 'From this distant vantage point, the Earth might not seem of any particular interest. But for others, it's different') you really need to. I mean it. Stop reading this and go and look it up. Do not restart reading until you have done this. Do not pass go. Do not collect £200. Read it, watch it, have someone read it out to you — I don't care how you do it, just do it. You can continue with this tripe after you know about the Pale Blue Dot.

* * *

There will now be a short interlude.

If the Pale Blue Dot doesn't give you pause for thought I don't know what will. For me it is profound. I remember it when I see and hear what we are doing to each other and our world to help put things in context. I sometimes doubt we even realise we are living on a planet and it is the only one we've got. Sagan said, 'In our obscurity — in all this vastness — there is no hint that help will come from elsewhere to save us from ourselves'. I couldn't agree more.

In time I would go on to encounter other great minds, such as the inimitable Richard Feynman. If you don't know who he is I am not going to tell you. Don't just look him up, but get yourself down to a book shop and seek out his semi-autobiographical works. I recommend you start with *What Do You Care What Other People Think?* or *Surely You're Joking, Mr. Feynman!*

The third great influence to my younger self was Douglas Adams. I was fourteen when by chance I caught the first broadcast on BBC Radio Four of the first episode of *The Hitchhiker's Guide to the Galaxy*. From the opening lines I was hooked. There is no other way to describe it. It has appeared in other formats over the years — book, TV series, stage show, computer game, film, towel — but to me the original first two radio series are the definitive (if there can ever be anything definitive about *The Guide*) versions. I am not going to say go away and read/watch/listen to *The Guide* like I did for Pale Blue Dot as you would likely be gone quite some time, but put it on your list of things to read/watch/listen to if you haven't already. If you want to do it properly, start with the radio series and then go on to the books. You can safely skip the film if you've got the radio series and books under your belt.

There have been many other influences on me over the years. For a subjective, incomplete, definitely not definitive list please refer to the dedication at the beginning of this book. Prizes will not be awarded for any inaccuracies or omissions discovered, nor for guessing where I have deliberately been cryptic (although the first person to challenge me with the phrase 'You are Lobby Lud and I claim my five pounds' will indeed receive five pounds on the condition they are carrying a current copy of the *Westminster Gazette*)

Chapter 15

The Starbucks Obfuscation

I'm in London for a few days with work and on the way in I stopped at Starbucks to get a coffee to go. Talking to a colleague about it afterwards I said how I was asked my name when ordering, had my name written on the cardboard sleeve which fits around the cup to stop you burning your fingers because the cup is too hot (Caution: Very Hot; no pictogram warning for non-English speakers), and was then called by name when my drink was ready. You don't get that sort of behaviour in the coffee shops where I live. He said that it had happened to him many times before and when his name has been called out several other people have stepped forwards to claim his drink, which may or may not be the right one depending on what the other ones had ordered. This got me wondering, which is always a dangerous thing. What names could I get away with using when asked?

I decided to start a series of experiments the following morning to determine at what point the name I gave would be rejected. Since London is a cosmopolitan city I thought I would try the name 'Jupiter' out for size. It is not a common first name. I don't know anybody called Jupiter, but it seemed plausible enough for a first attempt. If you can have Venus, as in Williams, surely there is somebody out there called Jupiter.

'Peter?' asked the girl taking the order.

'No, Jupiter,' I replied.

She looked a little puzzled.

'Like the planet,' I added helpfully.

Without batting an eyelid she wrote it on the cup sleeve and passed it on for making up. I paid for the drink and waited for it to come.

Margaret had her name called and collected her drink. Then an actual Peter was called and he collected his. I was next. The barista looked at the sleeve and called out, 'Large cappuccino'. I am disappointed not to have had Jupiter called out, collect my coffee, and leave. Looking at the sleeve it does say Jupiter, but it isn't that clear, which is maybe why the barista didn't call it out.

I am going to give some thought to tomorrow's name. Ideas so far are foods, days of the week, rude words in foreign languages, and infectious diseases. Whatever it is will need to be plausible, short, and easy to spell. Possible names include varieties of cheese such as Stilton or Wensleydale; Tuesday or Friday, but not on the day the name falls. This may help spread confusion if people think it is Thursday because they've heard it called out, even though it is only, say, Wednesday; Fitta, Knulla, and Pattar; and Lassa, Marburg, and Hanta.

The following morning's visit to Starbucks is interesting. The name I have chosen is Paddington, after the bear named after the railway station. Large cappuccino for Padington, written down with one D, is duly ordered and paid for. After the person in front of me, Binita, it didn't raise an eyebrow. So, I'm waiting for my order to come through. First out is a David, who takes his drink and leaves. Then Carol. Then another David, only David isn't around. Then another David, then another, but no sign of any of the Davids. A fourth David is produced. At this point I am beginning to wonder about the David as a unit of measurement for how many people are in the queue in front of you when you are ordering coffee. By now David has appeared and is wondering where his fifth drink is. He has various drinks, including a frothy topped number, a whipped cream topped number, a clear plastic sided number, and an anonymous number in a regular cup. The fifth arrives, drizzled in a thick, sticky syrup, and David leaves. Then Binita gets called for her drink. Will I get Paddington/Padington or a large cappuccino?

Paddington gets called and I take my coffee, feeling quietly pleased that this time I've had 'my' name called. I'm wondering that if Jupiter, spelled not particularly clearly didn't get called, but Padington [sic] spelled clearly did, what name should I try next?

Chapter 16

The Story So Far

A fifty-year-old man is only a week away from his fifty-first birthday, wondering what the hell happened to all his hopes and dreams. One day he looks in the mirror and sees an old man staring back at him. One day he finds himself standing on a cold, dark, wet railway platform on the daily trudge in to work and asks himself if he is circling the drain.

Bridget Jones update: Units of alcohol this week: 24 plus or minus 96. That puts me somewhere between totally inebriated all week and zero. Weight: Still unknown, but being away all week and eating more than I usually do, plus all those cappuccinos ordered for Jupiter, Padington [sic], Glanders, Hackarl [sic], and Serrumen [sic] means that my belt is getting a bit tight and may need to go out a notch.

Adrian Mole update: Length not re-measured, but no reason to think anything other than still being comfortably above average. Have discovered that Pandora is also a brand of jewellery, and a quite expensive one by all accounts. No poetry written, let alone submitted to the BBC, in any coloured ink, green or otherwise.

As an aside, a number of people including the Mrs, the kids, my mum, and people at work have been asking me what I would like for my birthday, and to be perfectly honest I haven't got a clue. Actually I do have a clue, but what I'd like is a particular fountain pen and it is not going to happen as it is quite expensive, so it is easier to say that I don't know. That still leaves them with the problem of not knowing what to get me. It's not like I need anything. I am fortunate enough to be in a position where if I need something I can usually just go out and get it. Want? That's not the same as need. Like? Ditto. There is a big difference between need, want, and like. I have noticed that not everybody understands this.

If I am being really honest, what I *want* aren't things, but time. The things I would *like* are on the whole expensive and not likely to happen any time soon unless I win the lottery. Lotteries are a tax on people who don't understand statistics, and since I don't play any lotteries, winning one isn't going to happen. Not just any time soon, but any time full stop. The odds might well be overwhelmingly against you winning the jackpot, but you have to be in the game to win it and I don't have a ticket.

It is a funny thing about time and money. When you have got one you tend not to have the other — cash rich and time poor, or time on your hands and skint. In a worse-case scenario you are time poor and skint. I have never been, and don't think I ever will be, counted among the ranks of the idle rich. I don't think I would want to be either. Given a free rein, i.e., being accountable to nobody but myself and with a credit card with no limit that never needed repaying, I would travel the world and see all the things I would like to see. Deep down I know that I wouldn't want to do it alone, and deep down I know that however far I travelled and however long I was away I would still want to come home. And that's where the gift of time comes in. Time to be able to do the things I enjoy, and time to be with the people I love.

At some point the clock will run out for all of us, myself included, and it will be game over. I've already lost too many family and friends to accidents, illness, disease, old age, and all the other ways we check out and say goodbye to this arrangement of atoms, and I know that while I am still living and breathing I will have more goodbyes to say. Geez, I'm upsetting myself. I've got to get a grip and pull myself together. I am going to take a little while to give some people I have not spoken to for a while a call. There will now be another interlude. Feel free to make some calls yourself.

Chapter 17

THAT Birthday And The Naming Of Mealtimes

Thinking about it, I am wondering why people are asking me about my birthday so much. It was last year that was a milestone birthday, the Big Five-Oh. I even have a photograph of me having got the large pink sparkly helium filled '50 today' birthday balloon home from London. The balloon was a delightful gift from my colleagues who gave it to me on one of the windiest days of the year on the day when the weather caused major disruptions to the rail network because of trees blown onto the lines. I had to carry the wretched thing home through overcrowded station concourses, standing room only trains besides toilets which smelled of chemical sanitisers and desperation, missed connections, and prove through photographic evidence that I had brought it all the way back. In the end it became a matter of principle and grim determination that no matter what trials, tribulations, and challenges were thrown at me, I was going to get the bloody balloon home in one piece.

When I finally did get home, the dinner reservation at the restaurant we had booked had long since been cancelled as there was no way we'd make it, any chance of a late sitting had long gone, and the restaurant closed up for the night. It was a memorable 50th birthday, but for all the wrong reasons.

The timing of 'dinner' has been a constant source of confusion for me as the only time I have been fairly sure that dinner didn't occur was first thing in the morning. Growing up in the north-west of England, dinner was served at midday. This was confirmed by the fact that the people who served it up at school were called dinner ladies. The meal you had at the end of the day was your tea, which is not to be confused with the beverage which came in a cup and saucer if you were being fancy or had visitors, or in a mug if you were being practical. Tea, the meal, was confirmed by the presence of what was called tea time television.

However, some time after leaving home and going to college and meeting people from other parts of the country and the world, I became aware that there were a significant number who thought dinner happened at the end of the day, and the meal served at what I called dinner time was in fact lunch. Tea time was when the beverage was consumed, usually with fancy cakes served on a tiered stand with paper doilies, sometime in the mid to late afternoon, or in the morning, but if it was in the morning then it was usually without the cakes, but with biscuits*. Come to think of it, tea time was any time when tea was served, with the exception when you had a cup of tea with your breakfast.

*The biscuits** in question must be Rich Tea biscuits. Not Digestives, not Custard Creams, not Bourbons, or any other type of biscuit. Although these can be, and often are, consumed with tea they are not generally considered to be the definitive biscuit to be consumed with it.

Note to North American readers. Biscuits are what you call cookies, not those soft, flaky things that look more like a scone to a Brit. Under no circumstances get involved with a group of Brits on the pronunciation* of the word 'scone' for reasons that will become obvious if you ever do. It can get ugly.

***And while we're on the subject of the differences between British English (which came first) and American English, or Spelled Wrongly English as some Brits would have it, a Brit should in no circumstances allow an American to make them a cup of tea. While it is possible for an American to learn how to make tea properly, and many have, a jug of hot water into which a bag is added later is not tea. When in the States, it is generally safer to err on the side of caution and have coffee instead, although even this is not foolproof as some of the worst coffee I have ever drunk was served in the good old US of A. Still, a tea bag in tepid water is better than one well documented previous attempt to make tea with cold salt water which went disastrously wrong and caused a bit of a kerfuffle. The best coffee I have yet tasted can be found in a small restaurant, the name of which I can't remember, in a side street somewhere near the cathedral in Lund, southern Sweden.

* * *

It is now one week before my 51ˢᵗ birthday and I am on my way back home on the train after the week in London. I have a coffee with me, ordered under the name of Hastur — The Unspeakable One from the Cthulhu Mythos.

'Hester?'

'No, Hastur. H-A-S-T-U-R'.

The train is on time. The weather is behaving itself and there are no fallen trees on the line. All is going as it should until the train slows to a crawl somewhere in the Rugby area. There is an announcement over the tannoy. Kids have thrown rope onto an overhead power line and the train has to run slowly while engineers clear the problem. While we are waiting I think back to the Public Information films from the 1970s, and one about the dangers of playing on the railways and one in particular about a kid being electrocuted after breaking in to an electricity sub-station. Is the sign of getting old and cantankerous that for a moment I'd quite happily have let the little bastards fry for delaying the train? Thinking it through logically, dead or injured bodies on the line would lead to even longer delays, so maybe from a practical viewpoint, if not a humanitarian one, it could have been worse. In the end we are only about twenty minutes delayed, but even so I get home later than I would have liked.

I have now settled on the naming and timing of the various meals throughout the day. First off is breakfast, the first meal of the day which can still be called breakfast until sometime around late morning, at which point it starts to be called brunch. Too late and it becomes actual lunch, which is served from just before midday to early afternoon. Mid afternoon is the time for afternoon tea, at which time tea (the beverage, not the meal) is served. Coffee breaks, which can also include tea (the beverage, not the meal) can happen at any point after breakfast but before tea (the meal, not the beverage). Tea (the meal) is served at tea time, that is to say after afternoon tea but before the evening, and unless a substantial lunch has been eaten is the main meal of the day, which is the dictionary definition of dinner. Dinner is a meal eaten in the evening if you have not had your tea (the meal, not the beverage) that you either go out to a restaurant to, or have friends round for. Supper is a meal eaten later in the evening if you haven't had dinner and it has been a while since you had your tea (the meal, not the beverage) and you are still feeling peckish. Supper is to be distinguished from snacking, which is a bad habit and should be discouraged, along with grazing, picking, and nibbling. Scrumping is something entirely different altogether.

There has been much written on the subject of how to make the perfect cup of tea. Rather than repeat it here I will simply refer you to the 1946 essay by George Orwell *A Nice Cup of Tea*, although I disagree with him on the tenth point about the order to add the milk.

I've kind of lost where I was up to now. The two cups of tea (no biscuits, see point above about snacking) I had while writing about tea (the meal and the beverage) have not really helped me stay focused.

Where was I up to?

A short pause and nobody with a gun appears, and no younger versions of myself appear either. There is just me, a blank page, and a fountain pen (Parker Sonnet Red, Royal Blue Quink ink). Where to go next…?

Chapter 18

The Clock Strikes Fifty-One

Don't get me wrong, I enjoy the work I do, but I feel – I don't know, I'm struggling to find the right word here – I feel incomplete. That's not quite it. I've got a good job. I live in a nice house in a nice area. I have got a loving and supportive family. Shouldn't I be grateful? Shouldn't I be a bit more appreciative?

It's not that. Deep down something doesn't sit right. There is a grain of sand inside this oyster which is irritating me. That's how pearls get made. You might have the beginnings of a nice necklace, but you also end up with a dead oyster and that's not where I'm going with this. It is about unfilled potential, the 'what could have beens'. It is about wondering if you made the right decisions. It is about wondering if you are circling the drain. Fuck.

'I don't regret this, but I both rue and lament it'
– Philip J. Fry

And with that I turn fifty-one. There is no big ceremony or fancy to do. It is still three weeks until Christmas and for the rest of the world today is just another ordinary day. I get up the same time I always do when I am commuting to work. The Manchester Piccadilly to Sheffield train won't wait for me, even if it is my birthday. I still have to wait for it. There aren't many people in the office when I get there, and those that are don't know it is my birthday. I don't tell them. I do what I am there to do, then go home.

There is a nice meal waiting for me when I get back. On the table there are cards to open and a small collection of presents to unwrap. One of them is a small, squarish box, which makes a sloshing sound when I shake it. It contains a bottle of sepia ink. Another box is small and rectangular with a ribbon around it. When I open it I see it contains a black and silver fountain pen. I am delighted, not just for the fancy pen but the thought that has gone into each gift. I feel beloved.

I want to try the pen out as soon as possible, but that will have to wait for tomorrow. Tonight is a time for family and friends.

Sláinte.

Chapter 19

Kindling An Answer

I am wondering about the what ifs...? That can't be good. That way regret lies. I need a rethink. I need a plan. Damn it Marlowe, where are you when I need you? Does anybody have a gun and could just walk in here right now?

There is nobody with a gun. Just the Black Tulip standing in front of me, staring hard into my eyes. At least I think it is her. I am sitting in a dark room. Heavy curtains have been drawn, and as my eyes adjust to the darkness I can see light filtering round the edges. It isn't much, but is just enough to make out shapes. I can see dark squares and rectangles on the wall. Paintings. I think I am in Otto's apartment. I try to move but I have been tied to the chair, my arms to the arm rests and legs to the chair legs.

'Good. You're awake.'

I was expecting a French accent. This is more Home Counties.

'Where am I?' I ask and wince inwardly. That has got to be one of the most clichéd lines going. I would kick myself for writing it were I not tied up.

'On the receiving end of some questions I want answers to.'

That wasn't the response I was expecting. I'm the one with the questions.

'Why did you do it?' she asks.

'Do what? I don't know what you're talking about.'

'Yes you do. All these years.' She pauses. 'Why?'

Does she think I'm Otto? Or does she think I'm me? I don't think Anna is a killer, it's not her style. I should be okay if I play along.

'Who do you think you're asking?'

'The person who can answer my questions.'

Clever. Answer the question without answering the question. All she needs to do is make an unrelated point and she could be a politician, but that's not her style either.

'So what do you want to know?' I ask.

'Why have you done it for all this time?'

She's assuming I know what 'it' is, and I genuinely have no idea. I have a thought. If she is asking unspecified questions, maybe I can give unspecified answers.

'In the end, just force of habit.' There — nice and vague.

'And in the beginning?'

Fuck. What would Otto say? What would I say?

'What choice did I have?' That should cover us both.

'Everyone has a choice. It is what you choose that defines the consequences.'

This is starting to get philosophical. I am tied to a chair in a dark room with a crazy person in my imagination. That can be a scary place. Perhaps I should be getting worried after all.

'I'll ask you again. Why did you do it?'

There is more than just a hint of menace in her voice this time.

'I don't know.' I'm hoping the honesty might be the best option here.

'I am a patient person, bekannte, but my patience does have its limit and I am close to it now.'

Bekannte? I've never heard that word before, but I'm assuming by the way she said it she is not being friendly.

'I genuinely don't know what you mean.'

There is a long pause. Anna is thinking.

'Very well. Perhaps this might help persuade you.'

In the almost dark I can see her move away from me. It sounds like she is removing one of the paintings from the wall.

'I don't know what this is,' she says. 'It is a bit too dark to see clearly. Shall we find out?'

There is a spark in the blackness and a soft yellow flame flickers from a cigarette lighter. It is still dark, but I can see that it is Anna, and this time dressed from head to foot in black, but not a ninja cat burglar style outfit. She is in a black skirt, black tights and a black top, the kind of outfit you could walk past in the street every day without noticing. The only nod towards the unusual is that she is also wearing black leather gloves and a black balaclava with just the slit for her eyes showing any hint of colour other than black. I also see that just above the flame from the cigarette lighter she is holding a canvas painting. It is not a large painting, maybe around eight inches by twelve. I can't see what it is from where I'm sitting, but I can see the underside of the frame and a dark spot where the flame is beginning to char it.

'You wouldn't burn a painting just to find out?' I'm not sure if I exclaim that or just blurt it out. Either way, I didn't think Anna would burn a painting. Maybe I'm wrong.

'Let's try again. Why did you do it?'

I don't know. I really don't know. The frame is beginning to catch.

'Because…'

My words tail off. I don't know what to say.

'Because?'

She's coaxing it out of me.

'Because I compromised. Because I did what was expected. Because it was easier than taking a stand.'

There is now a flame licking around the edge of the canvas. It has caught.

'Go on…'

'Put it out. I'll tell you everything.'

'I don't want to know everything. I just want to know why.'

'Because… because…'

I'm struggling to accept what I'm about to say next.

'Because I didn't have the confidence to do anything else.'

The painting burns. The flames spread quickly across the picture, destroying it as it goes.

'And that, bekannte, is all I needed to know.'

She drops the burning frame on the floor by my feet and leaves. What do I do? Wake up and I'm out of the scene? Is that how it works? I try to imagine myself back at my desk, writing this, but those flames are still very real. The picture has fallen onto the carpet and I can smell that beginning to catch as well. There is an acrid smell to the smoke. Think. I'm tied to a chair, arms and legs. But what if I can slip the ropes on my legs over the ends of the chair legs? Would that work? I struggle to stand. It is not as easy as you might think, but somehow I get to my feet, half doubled over and manage to slip my left leg free. The right one is easier now that I can stand a little better. With my arms still tied I stamp the flames out, then waddle over to the curtains and pull one side open with my teeth. With more light in the room I can see that I am in Otto's apartment. This writing lark is starting to get dangerous. I'm still tied to the chair and have no idea when Otto will be back. I need to get out of here, but how? First off, I need to get out of this chair.

Although the ropes are tight, the chair doesn't look that sturdy. As a kid I was told not to tip back in chairs as it would weaken them. Now will be a good time to find out if it is true. I lean back heavily, straining against the ropes, and tip the chair back. There is a sharp crack, but it is not the chair giving way, but my head making contact with the floor. It hurts surprisingly more than I would have expected and I can't cradle the pain because my arms are still tied to the chair. Buggeration.

I roll onto my side, and the last thing I see before I pass out is what remains of the canvas, which was blank. There was no painting, just a prop. She had set it up.

So, the Black Tulip plays mind games. She is more dangerous than I thought, if you are on the wrong side of her. Since when was I on the wrong side? I'm one of the good guys. Or am I Otto? That thought doesn't last long as the scene fades to blackness and I pass out.

Meanwhile, back in the real world I keep going back to that sentence. 'Because I didn't have the confidence to do anything else.' It has touched a raw nerve. I don't like it. I can either back off, walk away from it like it didn't happen, like I didn't say it. But it is there, written on the page. I can't ignore it.

There is a seven-year-old looking straight at me. He says, 'Don't blink.'

The fourteen-year-old is staring at me. He doesn't say anything. Fourteen-year-olds can be like that. He has either not forgiven me for making seven-year-old me cry or he is thinking, 'Don't blink'. I don't know. Am I projecting what I'd like him to be thinking on him? Whatever it is I am doing, I'm probably overthinking it.

There is a twenty-one-year-old.
    'You know what I'm thinking?'
    'Let me guess. Don't blink,' I say hopefully.
    'No, I was actually thinking what I would do if I was your age. I can't imagine being that old.'
    'Get over yourself. You either hit my age or you're dead. Besides, I don't feel old. Inside I'm still young at heart. It's the body that is showing signs of wear and tear, not the spirit.'
    'Really? Where does "Am I circling the drain?" fit in with that?'
    'You wouldn't understand. Not yet anyway.'
    'Oh really.'
    'You don't, because I know. Because I was you at that age. Because I

108

know how it turns out. Live fast, die young. Isn't that the motto? Some do, but where does that leave them? Dead, and you don't get to do much in the grave other than lie there. Everyone else goes the long way round, a bit of a compromise here, a bit of the easy option there, and the next thing you know you're not raging against the dying of the light, you are going gently into that good night, and that includes you.'

'Not me. I've got plans.'

'Listen kid. I don't want to get all metaphysical on you, but I know that's not true because I am you. This is how it turns out.'

'As a sad act that lost the plot?'

'As someone who lost their way and needs help. Your help.'

'Hmmmm.'

Twenty-one-year-old me gives it some thought.

'What do you need?'

'Right now I need hope. Hope that it will all work out.'

'How can I do that?'

'I need your memories.'

'Don't you already have those if you are me?'

'Yes and no. They fade. You forget things. The details go, and then you don't remember that you've forgotten. Some chance thing, an object, a particular turn of phrase, a photograph, a piece of music, a scent, will bring it back and you are surprised you had forgotten.'

'Okay. You can have my memories.'

'Thank you. I will do my best to take good care of them.'

'I know you will because I would.'

I turn to leave. He calls me back.

'One more thing. No blinking.'

Chapter 20

Drawing A Blank

I am back at my desk. Several pages have written themselves and there is cramp in my hand. I don't remember any of twenty-one-year-old me's memories, but I know they are in there somewhere. They always have been. I didn't need the memories, I needed the confidence to ask for them. That's the part I need to confront, to work on.

Because I didn't have the confidence to do anything else.

'I'm not blinking' is all well and good, but unless there is a follow-through it is just so many brave words. If I am going to make it as a writer the first thing I need is to be a writer. And that means write. One word after another. Repeat until the end is reached, then start again. So far I've been doing that. Maybe I've not written as much as I'd have liked, but I have picked up my pen each day and written. As to the quality, we'll see about that.

'Don't judge it. Just write it. Don't judge it. It's not for you to judge it'
— Philip Roth

I take comfort from Hemingway that the first draft of anything is shit. What I've written is no exception. If this ever gets read by anyone it may still be shit, even after the first draft or the tenth draft. At this point I couldn't give a fuck. That's for other people to decide and right now there is just me in the room writing this. I'm the only one here when the page is blank.

So, here is some advice I give to myself. Something I never got from my teachers. Don't be so hard on yourself. It is easy to say, but not so easy to do when you're me. I am going to make mistakes. I will learn from them. I am going to write gibberish from time to time. Get over it. I am going to have times when I doubt myself and what I am writing.

Suck it up, Buttercup. There is only one person that can tell my story and that is me. Nobody else is going to write it. I am going to stop here now, but I won't dare leave the next page blank.

This page is intentionally left blank.

Only with the above words on it, it isn't blank.

Fuck.

Chapter 21

Nostalgia Is Not What It Used To Be

Well, I've learned something. Don't tell me what I can and can't do, even if it is me saying it. I reserve the right to make my own mind up and that time I chose to leave the page blank even if it didn't end up that way. I may decide to leave another page blank later on. I decide. Me.

I've heard it said that writing a story is a lot like crossing a stream, leaping from rock to rock as you pick your way across to the other side. But at what point does the stream become too deep? The distances between the stepping stones too far? Depth is only a problem if you fall in. It's the distance between the stones that is the problem.

The name Fred Fannakapan pops into my head from nowhere. I've not heard in a very long time. It was a name I was sometimes called by my dad to get my attention, as in 'Oi. Fred Fannakapan'. That takes me back. I wonder where the name came from? Something he made up? An incidental character from *The Goon Show*? I have no idea so turn to the Internet to do some searching and eventually trace it back to a Gracie Fields song, written by Reg Low, and later covered by Fivepenny Piece. I've not heard of them for ages. They were a local band from Stalybridge and Ashton-under-Lyne who at one point had their own TV series back in the 1970s. I had no idea they covered the song. I look them up on Wikipedia and am saddened to see that many of the original line up are now dead. It seems like more and more of the people I grew up with, well, not exactly with as that would suggest that I knew them personally, but many of the people who were part of my childhood are now no longer with us. Neil Armstrong is gone. Carl Sagan is gone. My first Doctor Who is gone. Adams is gone. It will come to us all one day. I am starting to get maudlin about it. Time for a change of direction.

Looking things up on the Internet and having a huge amount of information at your fingertips seems to be pretty much a given now. There is even a joke about Maslow's Hierarchy of Needs where someone has added 'Wi-Fi' at the bottom of the pyramid as the most foundational basic need of them all, before even food, drink, and shelter. Remind me to go back and edit that picture I put in earlier.

When I was a kid there was no Wi-Fi or Internet. In fact there are a lot of things that are now taken for granted that were either in their infancy or unheard of then. Video games were very new and very basic, and didn't show up until I was in my teens. There was once a time when *Pong* and *Space Invaders*, or my personal favourite *Tempest* were cutting edge. You didn't download a game as there was no Internet to download it from, or load a disk as the floppy disk, CD, or DVD as they hadn't been invented either. Games were typed from pages of code printed in specialist magazines. When cassettes with programs on them started to become available this saved a huge amount of time and, with hindsight, began the decline in programming and coding. How many people these days actually understand how the computer in their smart phone actually works? There are a lot of technologically illiterate people out there. Should the lights ever go out I wonder how we as a civilisation will fare. All it will take is one Earth crossing asteroid or one twitchy finger on the nuclear button and it is Good Night Vienna. The Fourth World War might well be fought with bows and arrows. Come to that, the Third World War might.

Back then TV had three channels, BBC1, BBC2, and ITV. Thinking it through logically there was a time without television, so what was part of just the way things were for me would have been cutting edge to someone only a couple of generations before, and wireless radio only a couple of generations before them.

Apparently you could tell a lot about a household by which channel they tended to watch. I was told that ITV was 'common', BBC2 'intellectual', and BBC1 'respectable'. I tended to flit about all over the channels, and back then you had to get up out of your seat and press a button on the television set to change the channel. There was none of this remote control business. You either watched the programme when it was broadcast or you missed it. There were no TV record/playback devices, video on demand, or iPlayer. If you were out playing you made sure you were back in time for a particular program if you wanted to see it, not that anyone had a watch or other means of telling the time other than asking or guessing.

When I was a kid you drank the water from the hosepipe in the garden. If you fell off a swing in the park you landed on concrete. Dog shit was white. There were no speed bumps and you could play in the road. Doors didn't know you were coming. Toothpaste did not stand on its cap and the tube was rolled up as you used it. It was called frothy coffee not cappuccino. Bottles were made of glass, whatever they contained, with the exception of washing up liquid and maybe one or two other things. Telephones had dials, which is why it is called dialling, and were attached to the wall by a wire. You couldn't choose a ring tone, you didn't know who was calling until you answered it, and if you dropped it on the floor it didn't break the screen because there wasn't a screen to break. Fireworks only happened on bonfire night. Trick or treat was what Americans did. We had a penny for the Guy. There was no such thing as a bike helmet. Roller-skates were metal and rubber contraptions you strapped to your shoes, not in-line skate boots. You would later go on to dismantle them and nail them to a plank when skateboarding was invented. Clothes were just clothes — things you wore — not branded, designer label status symbols. Old pram wheels would be scavenged whenever possible to make a bogie — I found out later that other people called them box carts — out of whatever else could be scavenged. The brake was always a piece of wood nailed to the frame to form a lever to rub against the tyre to slow the bogie down. It never worked.

In case you are wondering, dried snot was called a crow. I have no idea why.

Now I remember something else. Encyclopaedias. We had two sets. One was a really old Mee's *Children's Encyclopaedia* from the 1920s. It had a blue binding and brimmed with pride for Great Britain and the Empire. It stood in its own Bakelite bookcase. The other was a more modern set, but I can't remember which. It had a cream binding with burgundy covers. It wasn't the *Encyclopaedia Britannica*, that much I know, as I always longed for a set but never got one. Encyclopaedias were expensive. I have no idea why I wanted the *Encyclopaedia Britannica* other than I'd heard it was supposed to be the best and I really liked the name. It might be because I had discovered Asimov by then and thought it might be a bit like the *Encyclopaedia Galactica*, or at least the Earth edition. With the Internet, who buys encyclopaedias these days?

This brings me round to the alternative to the *Encyclopaedia Galactica* and a certain Mr Adams. I think I need to have a talk to fourteen-year-old me as there are a few things I'd like to clear up with him.

Douglas Adams had a massive impact on me when I first heard *The Hitchhiker's Guide to the Galaxy* on the radio. It was unlike anything I had ever come across before. It was thought provoking, with a different way of looking at the familiar in new and unexpected ways. And it was well written and very, very funny. And therein lies the problem. I was in awe of Douglas Adams, and rather than think, 'I could do something like that' and give it a go, I shut down. Fourteen-year-old me shut down.

Chapter 22

Another Conversation With Fourteen-Year-Old Me

I get two chairs and set them up facing each other. I sit in one and wait for fourteen-year-old me to show up in the other. He doesn't turn up straight away. Seconds turn to minutes. I'm still waiting. I try concentrating on fourteen-year-old me harder, then try relaxing and not trying so hard, and when that doesn't work I stop. I try counting down slowly from ten, nine, eight, seven, six, five, four, three, two, one, deep breath and relax.

Sod all.

He doesn't want to be spoken to and I'm wondering why. I need a different approach so I go and sit in fourteen-year-old me's chair. I think back to me at that age and close my eyes. I am back in my bedroom. There is the bed along the wall by the radiator. There is the wardrobe in the alcove beside the door. On top of it is the Heath Robinson cassette player. Next to it is Mee's Encyclopaedia. On the floor is the jazzy Axminster rug given to me by an aunt one birthday. Propped against the wall is a stack of mostly science fiction paperbacks, mostly Asimov, but not all. The book on the top of the pile is *The Dragons of Eden* by Carl Sagan. There is a half drunk mug of coffee on the floor and beside it a pad of paper and a biro. The coffee is still warm, so I can't have gone far. I look more closely at the pad of paper. A few sheets have been rolled over like this:

The uppermost page is blank. I can't pick up the pad and turn the pages over. It is like I am a ghost in this. A disembodied consciousness present in spirit, but not in body. Damn it, where is fourteen-year-old me?

He turns up soon enough, having only gone downstairs to get biscuits.

'What are you doing here?'

He doesn't seem too pleased to see me.

'I need to talk to you.'

'Yeah, well I don't want to talk to you.'

He points to the door.

For a moment I remember putting a sign up there. It was circular and around the size of a saucer and said, 'Go away'. It had originally said, 'Go away — with Endsleigh Insurance', but careful application of a layer of Tippex had taken care of the last three words and the hyphen. Now that typewriters are museum pieces does anybody still buy this stuff? Tippex I mean, not insurance. Anyway, that sign doesn't turn up for another five years or so. I digress.

'Please. It's about Douglas Adams.'

That gets his interest.

'What about him?'

'There is something you need to know.'

'Make it quick,' he says. 'I'm busy.'

I sit on the edge of the bed. He is sitting on the floor in an awkward looking way. Not exactly kneeling, and not sitting on his feet, but between them. That's how I used to sit when I sat on the floor.

I've just looked this up on the Internet. In yoga it is called The Hero Pose or Virasana. I wish I'd have known that earlier. It sounds kind of cool. I wonder when I stopped doing it. I'd probably break my knees if I tried it now.

'It wasn't the first thing he wrote.'

'What?'

'It wasn't the first thing he wrote.'

'You mean Hitchhikers?'

'Yes. You need to understand. It's important. He wrote other things before it. He got a lot of rejections. It hit his confidence.'

'Why are you telling me this?'

'Because I know how much you love Hitchhikers and because I know that without you realising it, it will also knock your confidence.'

'How do you mean?'

'You think that you'll never measure up as a writer. He set the bar so very high and you think that whatever you do, even if it is nothing like Hitchhikers, you will never come anywhere even close. When you do write you'll be racked with the belief that it's no good. When you do submit anything and get the rejection letters it will just confirm everything that you know. You'll beat yourself up about it. You will give up.'

'Thanks for the pep talk. Anything else you'd like to stick the boot in with while you are at it?'

'It's not like that. I'm trying to help.'

'Well, you need to try harder.'

This isn't going how I intended. I wanted to come across as supportive and understanding, to offer some guidance and insight to someone who needed it, to set some expectations that it wasn't going to be easy, but it could be done.

'What I'm trying to say is that it isn't easy. Hitchhikers didn't emerge fully formed out of nowhere. There was the stuff that went before, but you didn't see that. There were the drafts that got thrown in the bin. There were the drafts that got rewritten. You didn't see those either.'

'So why are you telling me this? You're the me from the future that knows that I don't know this.'

'I'm trying to help.'

'Who? You or me?'

That is an insightful question. Who am I trying to help? Fourteen-year-old me is long gone. He didn't die, but lives on in my memories just like seven-year-old me and twenty-one-year-old me, and all the other me's from birth right up to now. Tomorrow there will be another new me, and today will be a past I will remember, and so on until a day comes when there will be no more remembering.

'I'm trying to help the person you become.'

'What is it I need to know?'

'Just this — that you are loved.'

'That's it?'

'One day you'll understand what that really means.'

What I really want to say is that every writer gets rejected. It is an occupational hazard. A lot of writers get rejected a lot. Even successful and established writers get rejected. Neil Gaiman tweeted, 'Wrote a poem for an anthology of kids poems. It was just rejected by the editor for being too dark. (I thought it was funny)'.

I just need to accept that's the way it is. All I need is for just one editor to crack. If I put enough out there, one piece might find a way. I've tried being a sniper, carefully working on a single shot and missing. Reload, aim, fire again. Miss. Is now the time to try the shotgun approach? How about the pump action shotgun approach with caseloads of cartridges and blast everything in sight? Writing a lot of things in a lot of different styles will help me to develop my own style, my own voice. Who knows, I might even get a half decent with practice, and I might even have some fun. That would be a novelty.

Chapter 23

Mind The Clouds

I become aware that I am back in the real world at my writing desk. I've had an idea for a story. Scratch that. I've had two ideas and I don't know which to do first. I also want to go back over a script I submitted to the BBC Writersroom about a year ago and take another look at it.

There is also that novel from how long ago? Twenty years? That went through four drafts before being submitted and rejected. That scares me the most. Going back to something I wrote two decades ago and re-reading it. I can vaguely remember some of the plot and some of the characters. I think the thing that scares me the most is reading it after all this time and finding out that it really was crap after all. I spent a lot of time on that novel and really believed in it. Putting it in the drawer and forgetting about it was a defeat. My confidence took another hit. It was silly to even think it might even have stood a chance.

I catch myself. In one hundred and eighty words I have gone from being excited about two ideas to despondent. So much for 'I just need to accept that's the way it is' about rejection. It is going to hurt. I can either give in and not try or say sod it and carry on. The path forks. One way leads to Chinley railway station in the rain on a cold, dark morning with me thinking, 'Am I circling the drain?'

I don't know where the other way leads. I am somewhere in Dante's dark wood, but if anything from my childhood taught me, all paths lead somewhere. You are not really lost, you just don't know where you are. Except when you're on the moors and the weather closes in. Then not only are you lost, you are also in serious trouble.

I have a flashback to a hike I once did as a teen on the moors above Glossop, looking for a very particular location. It wasn't marked on the Ordinance Survey map. I had got the coordinates of where I was going from a book in the library. It was the sort of day where the weather was fine in the valley, maybe a bit overcast and maybe a hint of drizzle in the air, but nothing unusual. There is a local saying that if you can see the hills it is going to rain, and if you can't see them it is already raining.

A hike on the moors might sound like a pleasant stroll in the hills. It can be, but perhaps a little background is needed if you don't know the area. This is the Peak District, which sounds very pretty — all bumpy bits of geography with big lumps of geology sticking out all over the place. Stacks, summits, escarpments, and all the other words you will find in a text book to describe features on hills. It stretches between Manchester and Sheffield and is the southernmost end of the Pennines. The Dark Peak is the higher, wilder northern part. It is sometimes called the High Peak, but that is a borough and also includes part of the White Peak — so called because of the underlying limestone. The locals call it the Dark Peak because the underlying limestone is capped with a thick layer of Millstone Grit. Tough. Rugged. Course. The rock is a bit like that as well.

Daniel Defoe described the area as 'the most desolate, wild and abandoned country in all England'. That was back in 1725 and not much has changed since then.

Between the 1930s and the 1950s more than just a few aircraft flew up these valleys in poor weather conditions and simply ran out of valley. The engineers at Boeing were to coin a term for this – CFIT. Controlled Flight Into Terrain. An airworthy aircraft, under pilot control, is unintentionally flown into the ground. Aviation slang calls the ground in question 'Cumulo-granite', a usually fatal cloud formation.

Other than the towns and villages that huddle in the valleys, the land is a largely uninhabited moorland plateau. Any depression is filled with sphagnum bogs and black peat. Fast running streams cut down the sides of the valleys. If you know the area you will have heard of Kinder Scout. Even if you don't you may have heard of the Kinder Trespass or know it through the song *The Manchester Rambler*.

The ramble that day was up to Bleaklow, 2,000 feet above sea level. The name is in two parts. Low does not mean low. The natives were not being ironic. Low comes from the Saxon word 'hlaew' or hill. Bleak is exactly what its name suggests. Bleak. Extremely bleak. Think desolation. Think stark and inhospitable. Think stunningly beautiful. Think stunningly dangerous. The Bleak Hill.

Once you get up there it is a large flat expanse of empty, boggy peat moorland, cut through with groughs, water eroded channels in the peat. Navigation is tricky, even at the best of times, and this was pre-GPS and pre-Google Maps on your smart phone. I've not been back to test it, but I very much doubt you would get any kind of signal at all up there. I walked it with map and compass. Low tech, old school, dead reckoning. Back then it was Just The Way It Was.

The place I was looking for was close to Higher Shelf Stones. The name is typical of the accurate, if unimaginative, naming of features in the area. It is higher than the surrounding land, with the exception of the other summit, Bleaklow Stones, hence 'higher'. 'Stones' because that's what they are, and 'shelf' because that's what they look a bit like if you squint.

You don't so much arrive at the crash site, more sort of stumble into it. You start to see fragments of corroded aluminium in the open expanses of peat. Then larger pieces of wreckage become apparent. Spars that could be part of a wing; the leg of an undercarriage, or what is left of it; an engine, the propellors long gone. And then you notice something in the dirt that someone has made from part of the wreckage. Two pieces of metal crudely twisted together to form a cross. There are no names on this memorial. It is a small act of humanity to remember the people who died here. Boys not much older than me. This is the Lancaster crash site, which went down ten days after hostilities ended in World War Two. Close by are what remains of a Skytrain, better known to Brits as a Dakota, and a Superfortress. There were no survivors from any of these crashes. All the crews were killed. Twenty-six people in total in this one lonely corner of the middle of nowhere on the Bleak Hill.

They didn't get to walk down from this desolate spot and go home to their loved ones. In a different time, in a different life it could have been me. It could have been any of us.

I snap back into the real world and realise I'm stuck with my writing again. I am going to park looking at the old radio script and the old novel for the time being. I want to play around with the two ideas for stories I've had. The bit I'm stuck on is which one to do first. One, which I call *Pale Grey Dot* as a nod to the Pale Blue Dot seems to be a radio comedy in six episodes, or at least that's what it feels like. It is about the crew of a mission recruited to simulate the effects of living in a lunar base, only they are not on the moon, but in a mock up of a lunar base inside a disused aircraft hangar in the middle of nowhere. All they have to do is live there, inside the habitation modules, testing the technologies needed for a real mission for thirty days. The catch is that one of the crew hasn't realised that it is thirty Lunar days — the best part of two and a half Earth years — that he has signed up for.

The bit that is holding me back from doing this is that I've already had my first radio script rejected. How well received would six go down? That and the BBC script submissions through the Writersroom is one at a time. I can't think where else a radio script like that would find a home, so while I might well enjoy writing it, I don't think that idea would go very far. That and a radio comedy in six parts has the spectre of DNA hanging over it in the back of my mind. I'll take some notes and maybe write a few pages, and then put them in a drawer and forget about it for the time being.

The other idea is called *Spellbound* and I think it is this one I am more excited about. I haven't worked out the whole plot yet, but I've got some scenes in mind and the outlines of some of the characters. The names and faces are somewhat indistinct at the moment, but I'm hearing snatches of conversations in my head. Should I be worried? Hearing voices inside your head is supposed to be one of the signs of madness, except when the message is a religious one and then it is considered by some to be very holy. I suspect the two are closely connected. I'm putting it down to having an overactive imagination that writers are allowed to have and moving on. Nothing to see here people.

Chapter 24

An Entrancing Idea

Spellbound is set in 1830 and 1850, or thereabouts, and is about love and loss. A father-to-be strays into the Land of Faerie and is tempted to stay by the Faerie Queen. He believes he has only been there for a couple of days, but when he escapes and makes his way back to the real world he finds that twenty years have passed. The baby his wife was expecting is now a grown woman, and his wife is now twenty years older. Even though he is now back in the real world, something isn't right as he doesn't feel love any more. He has lost his heart, quite literally, to the Faerie Queen who has cut it out of his chest and is keeping it in a fancy jar in the Land of Faerie. He knows that if he goes back to retrieve it that time will pass more quickly for him than it will for his wife, but if he doesn't go he will never feel love again. I need a plot device so that the wife is unable to join him on the quest to get his heart back as I want it to be the daughter who goes into the Land of Faerie and gets caught up with all sorts of trials and misadventures.

After a climactic encounter with the Faerie Queen she retrieves her father's physical heart and returns back to the real world, only to find her father is now an old man tending the grave of his wife, who passed away many years ago.

There is a rich tradition to draw on for this story and I'll be able to weave all sorts of elements in. To me it has got the feel of a novel to it rather than a radio script or a screenplay. In a way that makes it easier because I don't have the BBC Writersroom to worry about or the submission window that goes with it so I can write at my own pace. I'm going to need to get some blank cards and Sharpie pens to storyboard it and get a better idea of the structure and plot turns before I actually start to write it. This feels right. I feel excited about it, but I am also a bit worried. I'm not getting a sense that the Big Boss is waiting in the wings. I'm not completely confident, but there is now a quiet hope, the flickering flame of a candle in the dungeon at Treasure Trap. Just don't wander off looking for monsters. Put the candle in a glass jar to protect it from the draughts and nurture it. Sneak out quietly when the monsters aren't looking. Use the candle to light a bigger flame, then go back and burn the place down.

Where did that come from? I'm not advocating the wholesale slaughter of innocent monsters by a pyromaniacal fantasist. That's where The Black Tulip came from and she turned out not to be anything like that at all. I wonder when she'll turn up again. Her and Otto have a story to be told too, but now is not the time. I need to write about Angharad. I don't know where that name came from, but the daughter is called Angharad. It's a Welsh name, and when I look it up I find it has a long association with Welsh royalty, history, and myth. It translates into English as 'much loved one'. I'm taking this to be an auspicious start. I will need the names of her mother and father at some point and these will need to be sympathetic to Angharad's name. I don't want to rush into giving them names so I will leave it for now and trust that something appropriate emerges at some point.

Storyboarding, or the Art Of Fiddling About With Bits Of Paper Until Something Resembling The Outline Of A Story Emerges. Also known as…

… and then the words stop and I don't write for the next three days. It's not that I don't want to, but three busy days back-to-back leave me tired and unable to face lifting a pen. It started innocently enough on a Saturday morning with a trip out to IKEA to pick up a new dining room table, the way you do. The journey is the best part of an hour there; an indeterminate amount of time following the conga line round the store, occasionally going back against the flow to check the details of other dining room furniture already passed; picking up two more dining room chairs of the same design as the ones we already have; picking out new bed linen; paying for the above, plus other odds and ends also picked up; gulping at the final amount to be paid; collecting the table from the collection point since it was an oversized/heavy/ some other reason item; playing three-dimensional jigsaw in the back of the car to load all of the above into it, still be able to sit in the car to drive, see out of the windows, and have to boot closed, all at the same time.

Then the best part of an hour back; unload; cook tea (the meal, not the beverage); wonder where the day has gone; turn in to bed. There may be bits missing from the above account. It was three days ago. I do remember that there was a discussion with the Mrs about additional items for the dining room, hence the back tracking to look at other cabinets, bureaus, and bookcases that would/might/could be needed to make the dining room less cluttered and provide more storage space. A second trip to IKEA the following day is decided. This is flat pack madness run amok.

An up and at 'em early start on the Sunday morning sees the new dining room table built and assembled. It is large and rectangular and the sort of table you could play ping-pong on. Six and a half feet long, three and a half feet wide — and that is before it is opened out and extended. It apparently sits six to eight people but looks like you could get many more around it, albeit with less elbow room. It has the kind of surface real estate you could play war games on at a scale not far short of 1:1.

A table cloth from the old table is put on it and barely covers one end. This is a seriously big table. Once assembled it is out to IKEA again, the best part of an hour there; more conga line shenanigans to get to the living space/storage examples to check they were what we a) remembered and b) wanted; down to the picking area to get the bookcase and doors; over to the information point to check the location as there was an empty space and a heavy duty trolley where the bookcases should have been; over to the new location given; back to the information point as this was also wrong; back to the original location with a member of staff to confirm that this was indeed the correct location and that it was empty despite the system showing ninety-three items in stock; then round the corner to the top of the aisle to find ninety-three bookcases sitting there; down to the checkout to pay for it all; gulp at the bill this time, which made yesterday's look like small change in comparison; over to the collection point to collect the other oversize/heavy/some other reason items; play three-dimensional jigsaw in the back of the car to load a bookcase plus doors, glass fronted cabinet, bureau and additional unit for the bureau, plus tablecloths and other assorted items into the car, still be able to sit in it and drive, see out of the windows, and have the boot closed, all at the same time; the best part of an hour home; unload; start assembling; wonder why it is dark outside and time for bed.

The following day, Monday, get up; go to work; come home; finish assembling the rest of furniture; go to bed.

According to the sage advice and wisdom of various writers down the ages regarding the protection of your writing time, making writing time in the first place, and actually writing during writing time, I can only assume these people did not have to go to IKEA twice in as many days and spend their evenings putting up flat packed Swedish furniture.

It is now day four. My writing time is *my* writing time. It is hereby re-instated. No furniture has been assembled in the writing of the above paragraphs.

The down side is I've lost the thread of what I was up to with Spellbound and Angharad. I pause for a few moments for a man with a gun or one of the various iterations of myself to show up. It is a no-show. A woman with a gun? Anybody? Okay, so that is going nowhere. I get out The Writer's Toolkit, set up the erratic hourglass, and pull out a First Sentence stick.

There she was, Amy Gerstein, over by the pool, kissing my father.

Really? He's seventy-eight years old. While I wouldn't put it past him, I wonder what Amy Gerstein's motives are. Hell, I don't even know who Amy Gerstein is. I also realise that I didn't start the hourglass off. I draw another First Sentence stick and set the hourglass running.

My mother was doing that thing she did. That thing with the rag in the sink.

That's disgusting. Rags are very unhygienic and should not be used for doing the washing up. But then I realise the stick didn't actually say what it was she was doing. I had made the assumption she was doing the washing up, but maybe she was using the rag to wipe down the oily piston of a motorbike engine she had stripped down. Maybe she was using it to mop up the blood from the latest victim she had just finished putting down the waste disposal unit. The hourglass runs out. I try and other First Sentence stick.

Your mother lied to you. That's the truth.

So what is it with my mother today? She has been an unhygienic, motorcycle restoring serial killer and now she's a liar? Maybe it was

Amy Gerstein she just finished putting down the waste disposal unit, having run her down on the motorcycle she just rebuilt. My mother that is, doing the running down and rebuilding. Amy Gerstein was just in the wrong place at the wrong time. The wrong place was by the pool attached at the mouth to my father. The wrong time was when my mother was there to see her. I'm wondering what Amy Gerstein's motivation was so I get out the 'Goals' wheel and spin it.

to save Mother.

No, that doesn't seem right. It also looks wrong with the lower case t and capital M.

I spin it again.

to get rich.

She clearly doesn't know my father. Perhaps he is the one that has been doing the lying, going round telling Amy that he is a multi-millionaire. Poor impressionable, deceased, and now reduced to a slurry Amy Gerstein.

Maybe I should try a Non Sequitur stick.

She may be young, but she's not stupid.

Excuse me? I beg to differ. She fell for the old 'I'm a multi-millionaire' line and I'm pretty sure that a puddle of pink slurry has a fairly low IQ. I draw another Non Sequitur stick.

You could make a living doing this kind of thing.

I suppose I could, but I had not thought about it until then. Anyway, that's beside the point. That's how the arsonist precursor to the Black Tulip got started. Next.

She may be young, but she's not stupid.

I just drew that one. Next.

Eloise was my half-sister, but everyone thought she was my cousin.

* * *

Er, no. Not everyone. Eloise didn't, I didn't, and presumably Eloise's mother didn't. That is everyone minus three, which by definition isn't everyone. This isn't getting me anywhere so I put the Writer's Toolkit away.

Chapter 25

The Hero With A Hundred Index Cards

Going back to *Spellbound*, perhaps I have to work out Angharad's parents names first and get a better idea of some of the other characters before I can start storyboarding them.

I sit and think quietly and throw around ideas for Angharad's mother's name. I'm quite taken with Carys so do some research on its suitability. The first thing I find is encouraging. The name derives from the Welsh word 'caru' which means love. I like that there is an echo of Angharad's 'much loved one', but the next thing I find out about Carys pours a bucket of cold water on the whole idea — it is a relatively modern name, only in common use since the middle of the twentieth century. First used in 1903 and very rare until the late 1940s/early 1950s. This is no use to me as all the action takes place in the 1830s and 1850s. I'd be about a hundred years out.

I don't even consider glossing over this and using it anyway. There might only be one or two pedants who would spot it, but stuff them. It doesn't feel right to me now, which is a pity as I think it is a really lovely name with the perfect meaning. I'm going to need another name and I'm all out of inspiration, so I take to looking through lists of baby names and meanings. I do this while listening to the Siouxsie and the Banshees back catalogue. It shouldn't take too long to figure out why if you know what is on the fourth studio album.

There is Caren, Carin, Caron, Caronne, Carren, Carron, Carronne, and Caryn — all variations of Karen — and meaning 'loving, charitable'. They would do, but I don't want to settle. There are variations on my late aunt Gwen's name, Gwynneth, but not Gwynneth itself. There is my daughter's name, Jennifer, which I'm surprised to see down as Welsh. I didn't choose it, the Mrs did and I'm not sure she realised the Welsh connection when she did. I don't remember talking about it at the time, so if it was mentioned I have forgotten. I go back to the A's and noticed that Angharad isn't listed. Hmmmm. This is clearly not a definitive list.

I continue scrolling through.

Rhiannon, plus variants thereof. That refers to The Great Queen. It doesn't say who The Great Queen is, but there might be some opportunities to make comparisons with the Faerie Queen. It is not a modern name either, so it would work with the period the story is set in. I keep looking and hello, we've gone from R to S to D, or Dd to be exact. I guess it has a thick 'Th' sound, but then we are in the straightforward D's — Dec, Decia, Deelys — and then into the E's. This list is clearly not in alphabetical order. There are variations on Elvira, great leader of there elven folk, but that doesn't seem right for Angharad's mum, unless she is not the ordinary person I thought she was.

What if...?

What if she was the Faerie Queen's daughter, banished to the land of the mortals? What if that is why she can't go back to the Land of Faerie? I'd better note the Elvira variations. There are quite a few of these: Elea, Elivina, Elva, Elvan, Elvea, Elveah, Elveen, Elvenea, Elviah, Elvinea, Elvinna, Elvyna, Elweena, Elwina, and Elwnya. Apart from the last three or four of these, they all seem a bit too obviously elf related.

Ah, now we're in the G's and Gwynneth is there after all, a 'fortunate and blessed girl'. Then we jump to the N's. Maybe Nerys, 'lady', could work. I eventually hit the end of the list. Nothing in particular has jumped out and screamed 'pick me'.

I go through the boys names for Angharad's father. As I do, I noticed the 'advanced search' option and see that one of the options in the language filter is for Celtic. I select that and re-run the search for girls' names. Five come up, none of which seem appropriate.

Right. Welsh boys' names. Apologies to Alun, Bryn, Caden, Dylan, and Euan, you're not what I'm looking for. The same for Folant and Gaven. There are no H's, I's, or J's. Kary, Lloyd, and Madoc. Then up comes Gawaine. That might be interesting with its shades of King Arthur and the Knights of the Round Table. Then I see it. Geraint, from a Latin origin meaning 'old'. Sir Geraint, Knight of the Round Table, married to Enid, which is also a Welsh name. I might be onto something here. Enid means 'purity'. Is this something to do with why she was banished from the Land of Faerie? It will be another thread to draw on.

How does this sound? Angharad, daughter of Enid and Geraint. Enid, the banished the daughter of the Faerie Queen. What did she do that was so bad? Does Geraint know her history? Is he the cause of her banishment? I need to do the first run through of the storyboard for this. I've got two black Sharpie pens (they were on a two for one offer) and a pack of 100 plain white 6" x 4" index cards. Before I start storyboarding I turn over the packaging card to its blank side and write Spellbound on it. I've got to admit I don't quite know why I do this, other than it might be fun. It looks something like this:

I start on the first few cards as I know how the story opens, jotting down an outline of each scene. Geraint and Enid are newlyweds. Enid is expecting a baby. All this is establishing the normal world in which they live. Then there's the bit where Geraint is separated from the Real World and Enid when he goes through an entranceway at an ancient barrow and enters the desolate Land of Faerie and encounters the Faerie Queen. This part goes quite easily. Then other characters get introduced. Angharad makes an appearance and the story starts to take off. Then I hit a blank. There is a whole middle bit missing and I have no idea what happens. I skip to the end because I know how that goes and write a few cards that wrap it up neatly.

But, and this is a big but, that gap in the middle isn't just a bit inconvenient, it is a gaping hole and I have no idea how to fill it.

The gap sits there for a week. I have a multitude of excuses: It has been busy at work; I have been tired when I got home; the train was late; the fire needed laying; the cat needed stroking; the ironing needed doing. Anything rather than face up to the fact that I have hit a tricky patch and I am just going to have to sit down with a pen and work through the chunk of the story that is missing. There is no mystery, no artistic 'aha' moment when inspiration strikes, just plain old-fashioned hard work to figure out what happens in the story between The Beginning and The End. I believe the technical term for it is The Middle and I am given to understand that stories are the better for having one.

Given that the index card approach didn't seem to work, other than to highlight that I had a whole section of story missing, I turn to the Internet for assistance. I quickly turn up a story telling plot storyboard and print out a copy. It runs to four pages of A4 and has twenty boxes to fill in to guide the story along. I get the cards I have done and start to transcribe the cards into the boxes.

Chapter 1: Protagonist's Normal World. The stuff about Geraint and Enid being newlyweds, and Enid expecting a baby goes in here.

Chapter 2: Inciting Incident That Forces Protagonist From Normal World. The stuff that leads up to Geraint going into the barrow and his entry into the Land of Faerie goes here.

Chapter 3: Secondary Characters Introduced; Setting & Tone Established Fully. It is at this point that I'm starting to have doubts about this approach, but I push on anyway. This is the bit where the Faerie Queen is introduced and makes her proposition to Geraint.

Chapter 4: Protagonist Must Make A Choice/Decision. Geraint wants out and to return to the Real World to be with his wife.

Chapter 5: Plot Point 1 — Protagonist Starts Journey As Result Of Choice/Decision.

It is at this point that I stop filling in the sheets. The reason? I have just realised that this is starting to look and feel an awful lot like the structure in Joseph Campbell's *The Hero With A Thousand Faces*, a book I had once started to read but made a conscious decision not to finish.

Why? It is a very good book, well written and well researched, and giving an insight into the structures that run through most of the world's mythic stories. It has been an inspiration to many blockbuster films and that to me was the first hint that it would be better not to finish it. If there was a template which guided a writer through the structure of the story which would follow this classic pattern, where was the scope for innovation, for coming up with something new and original? Sure it would follow in the well worn footsteps of epic tradition, but wouldn't it be formulaic? How many Hollywood stories follow the pattern of The Hero receives The Call To Adventure, refuses The Call, encounters a protective figure who assists the hero in crossing the First Threshold, and so on? There are trials, setbacks, the final conflict where The Hero is on the point of failure but at the last-minute rallies and beats the villain, claims the prize, and returns to the real world older and wiser. And, if it is Hollywood, they all lived happily ever after. The guy gets the girl, roll credits. Bleuch.

Don't get me wrong. At the right time in the right place I like these films, but is it just me or do others find this kind of thing a bit too samey? A bit too clichéd? If there is an archetypal structure to stories I'd like to find it out for myself. This goes against the advice of learning from the mistakes of others, but in this matter I'm going to be a contrarian. If I don't know what The Rules are, it is going to be so much easier to break them, and in breaking the rules there is a chance that something more interesting might emerge. It might only be interesting to me, but then I'm beginning to realise that is the whole point.

It is both a revelation and a statement of the bleeding obvious to me that I don't seem to be carrying the baggage of other people's expectations as I write this. I'm not writing for seven-year-old me, or a fourteen or twenty-one year old me either. No Marlowe, no Black Tulip. No worries about readers, publishers, editors, literary agents, or anyone. It is just me putting my thoughts down on paper and in the process clarifying in my own mind my own opinions, and slightly startling myself that I have them and am prepared to commit them to writing. I find it quite liberating.

I take the index cards again and spread them out on the floor, and the problem with The Middle hits me smack in the face. It's not that there isn't a middle, but I got it mixed up with the beginning, effectively making an over-bloated, overcomplicated start to the story. It is going to need another rewrite, but at least it is only a handful of index cards that need to be done and not however many thousands of words in the manuscript. Separating out what should really be in the beginning and putting other parts of it later should lead up to it joining the end in the right order, with no gaps, sudden jumps or anything else which would jar or disrupt the flow of the story.

There is just one thing which I can't quite put my finger on and that is just whose story is it? Who is the protagonist? Geraint for being the one to enter the Land of Faerie? Enid for being the one who was banished from the Land of Faerie? Angharad for being the one caught between two worlds? They each have their story. Maybe reading too much of the template storyboard is making me think in too conventional terms. They are valid questions, but for now I'm going to park them and concentrate on getting the storyline sorted out. When that's done it might give me more of an insight into how to tell the story. It might not, but I figure it is the next thing I need to do to make some progress.

Chapter 26

Where Is Everyone?

Fast forward three days. Actually, that is artistic licence. Christmas happened, but I have skipped over that bit and it is more than a week later. I have written a handful more index cards and while I may have the outline of the story more or less laid out I have hit a whole new different and exciting problem which is now causing me difficulties. I don't know what the Land of Faerie is actually like. I have pictures in my mind of a desolate wintry landscape with the ground frozen hard and a dusting of snow which has been blown by the wind, leaving barren fields uncovered, but white around the edges where it has drifted against dark stone walls. The sky has low, flat grey clouds leeching colour out of the scenery leaving it monochrome. It is bone numbingly cold. I look down and I see my open hand with a flower resting in the palm. My hand and the ground below are devoid of colour, but the petals of the flower are bright red. Blood red.

A stone circle stands in a field on a rise in the land. Twelve course outer stones encircle four roughly dressed trilithons in the centre. It looks something like this:

Twelve stones for twelve months. Four trilithons for four seasons. And now I realise that it isn't a portal in an ancient barrow that Geraint passes through into the Land of Faerie as I had thought, but he comes through the trilithon for winter. That's one card I need a rewrite.

Somewhere else in the same winter landscape lives the Faerie Queen. I want her to live in a fantastical castle, some kind of magical, tall, slender, pinnacle reaching for the sky, but that is exactly what all fantasy castles are like these days. Call it something like The Fortress of Ultimate Darkness, add a few jagged bits, and it is the kind of des res that the Dark Lord could quite happily claim as home sweet home.

So if not a cliché then where? I might be getting hung up on the shackles of winter thing, but she has to live somewhere. Change the season and Faerie Queens are about woodlands on a spring morning with dappled sunlight scattering through green leaves while butterflies flit from flower to flower across a rolling wildflower meadow. Or something like that. And that brings me to another thing. Where is everyone else? The whole Land of Faerie is depopulated, save for the Faerie Queen herself, the newly arrived Geraint, and possibly a pack of hell hounds that stalk the land. I want hell hounds stalking the land. I don't know why, I just do. But where are the villagers? Where are the courtiers? Where the hell is everybody?

At the risk of going off at a tangent, how did the Faerie Queen get to be a queen in the first place? Is it a line of succession? Is it an absolute monarchy? A constitutional monarchy? All these thoughts. Questions leading to more questions. Now I'm beginning to realise how difficult it will be to write about this world if I don't understand the rules of how it works, if I don't understand its internal logic. Fuck.

I stop to think it through.

If I were a proper writer what would I do? How would I approach this? Start at the beginning and see where the story led me? I'm dubious about this approach as I've got a feeling it could lead to a lot of dead ends and subsequent rewriting. Storyboarding isn't helping as it isn't the plot points I'm having difficulty with. Maybe trying out a couple of scenes and see where they lead might help — actually live in the world for a while and try it on for size. See what works and what doesn't. See where the seams need taking in and the hems need turning up. Or something like that.

I have half an idea already about the scenes I might try out for this. Geraint's arrival into the Land of Faerie is an obvious one. I want to experience his disorientation in this strange new land. More difficult, and perhaps more to understand what I don't know about this world, would be how Geraint manages to leave it. Right now I can see that this will probably take a few goes to get even some of it right. I'm hoping that what I learn will help to explain things a bit better to me. I also want to write something about a typical day in the life of the Faerie Queen to understand her better. What does she have for breakfast? Where does the food come from? Who prepares it for her? What kind of bed does she sleep in? Does she brush her teeth at night? Is there a fire in the castle to keep the place warm? If there is, how does it stay in? Who makes it up and who clears away the ashes? Is there a rubbish tip at the castle or do they cart it away or recycle? Thinking of other practicalities, where are the toilets? When it goes dark at night, what is used for lighting? Candles and lanterns? I'm not expecting to see electric lighting and switches on walls, but who knows? What would a steampunk Faerie Queen be like?

Tangents. Back to figuring out this world, not the details of how the plumbing works in it, at least not yet.

Tangents. Disorientation. Logic. Throw in perspective and I have an idea for the Faerie Queen's castle, only it's not a castle. How about it

148

doesn't have an outside, only an inside, like a Klein bottle or a Möbius strip? I'm reminded of the pictures of the impossible buildings and constructions done by the artist MC Escher. What if the castle was like the picture Relativity, where the normal laws of gravity don't apply and people appear to be walking across walls or climbing an upside down staircase? Instead of the stone walls of a typical castle, this could be whatever I wanted it to be — minimalist white walls, or glass, or crystal. It would also be something to further disorient Geraint — how would you leave such a building? Something as simple as opening a door and stepping outside would seem unlikely. What if there wasn't an outside? Lowering a rope made out of bedsheets from out of the North tower wouldn't really work either if halfway down it bent 90° to reality and you ended up lowering yourself back inside the West tower.

The plumbing would be a nightmare too.

So, where has this got me? A little bit further forward, but not much. I've now got a bleak, snow swept stone circle, not a barrow. I've got a starting point for a non-Euclidean castle with no outside, which will be a real hoot if anyone were to take up the option on the screenplay of Spellbound to see how they would figure that one out. I've also got some homework to do to try out some scenes and see if they will help me understand this world a little better, or at least better enough to make sufficient sense to start writing like I know what I'm doing. I'm still concerned with where all the other characters are. Hiding? Banished? Dead? Out of town for the annual Land of Faerie Wakes Week? No doubt they will turn up at some point, so if my unconscious mind would like to start to think about it and let me know sometime soon, I'd appreciate it.

Chapter 27

The Hills Are Alive

After writing the last few pages I had the oddest dream last night. Normally I don't usually remember my dreams. I assume that I have them, but it is only very rarely — and I do mean very rarely, like one every few years — that I ever recollect them, but last night was an exception. All I can remember is a single image — a raven standing on top of a crudely carved stone head. The stone head was placed on top of a gritstone column at about chest height.

Okay, I'll come clean. That's not what actually happened. The bit about not remembering dreams is true. I really don't remember dreams, except on very rare occasions. I think it goes back to when I was maybe thirteen or fourteen and had a recurring dream, the details of which I don't now recall, apart from the final image I always woke up with. It was a man, a soldier of some kind, from the past. It was a static picture, no movement and no sounds, but it was vivid, lifelike, and in full colour. It was like I was actually there, but frozen in time. The soldier was wearing an old fashioned uniform, a red coat. He was stood at the bottom of a steep slope, so was set against a grassy green backdrop. He never spoke or moved, and always looked straight at me. Or through me. And then I'd wake up. It happened night after night after night. It was always the same dream, always the same person. After more than a week of this it was beginning to wear thin as I knew how events would play out. I'd get in my pyjamas, have a wash and brush my teeth, go up to bed, read for a while and then turn in. I would turn the light out and drift off to sleep. The next thing to happen would be me seeing the red coat soldier against the grassy bank looking right through me, and then I'd be awake. It would be the early hours of the morning before dawn, and I'd not be able to get back to sleep. I was getting more and more tired each time it happened and

I'd had more than enough of it.

Then came THAT night, capitalised for emphasis.

It began as all other bedtimes began — pyjamas, wash, teeth, read, lights out, sleep. Only this time I was woken by a loud thudding, crashing, throbbing noise, and then another, and then another, and another. Wide awake now, the noise kept repeating, but it wasn't coming from outside. It was coming from inside my head. I clasped my hands over my ears to shut it out, but the deafening crashes kept happening. The walls of the room began to spin. I thought I would open the bedroom window to get some fresh air, and it was then that I got my next shock. I had no idea what the time was, but I'd guess at the early hours sometime well after midnight. It was dark and quiet outside with no cars or people about. The pounding in my head was continuing. Each beat came with the surrounding hills rushing at me, then drawing back, like some kind of visual echo to the throbbing in my head. I screwed my eyes tight shut but the sound kept going. I opened them again and the hills began rushing at me again. Terrified, I put my head under the pillow and pulled the bed covers up tight to make the hallucinations go away. I could no longer see the hills rushing towards me, but the deafening sound was still there, regular as a heartbeat.

Some time later I woke up. The sound had gone and it was quiet and still and dark. Everything was as it should be. I went to the window to check that the hills were static and behaving as hills were supposed to, and then it hit me again. The instant I saw their moonlit slopes, the pounding started up and they began rushing at me. I blacked out and collapsed on the bedroom floor.

The next thing I remember was waking up on the carpet, cold and uncomfortable. It was still dark, but silent. I lay there quietly without moving, making sure there were no sounds or hallucinations. I pushed myself up. There were still no sounds or hallucinations. Trembling, I went over to the window and pulled back the curtain to peer outside, and the moment I saw the hills, the pulsating sounds and the visions started again. I blacked out again.

I don't know how long I am out for, but when I come around again, I am as cold and uncomfortable as before. It is dark, still, and quiet, but now I am really scared. Still and quiet should be a good thing. Right now it is oppressive and threatening. I lie on the floor and weigh up my options. Stay here where at least nothing bad is happening? The downside is that it is very cold. It is winter and there is no heating on and dawn seems a very long time away. The alternative is getting back in bed. At least it would be warm, or rather it would warm up when I was under the covers, but the bed is close to the window, and the window looks out towards the hills.

I lie there a while longer, but the cold forces a decision on me. I will slide under the covers as surreptitiously as I can. But the hills beckon. Just one quick glimpse to check they are normal won't hurt, not if it was really quick look. I close my eyes, and, still kneeling, feel my way up the wall until I can feel the window sill. The curtains are closed. So far so good. Keeping my eyes tight shut I put my head under the curtains and prepare to look through the window. There is no sound other than my breathing. Now comes the moment of truth. Keeping as still as I can I chance one quick look and immediately regret it. While there isn't any sound, the hills are pulsating in time to some unheard drum beat. Ba-dum, ba-dum, ba-dum. Closer on the first ba- part of the beat, further away on the -dum. I watch in horrified fascination for what seems like an eternity, but was probably only a few seconds, before realising it is not only the world outside that is doing it, but also inside. My room is pulsating like a beating heart, but there is no sound, no sound at all. I try to speak, or moan, or shout, or make any kind of noise at all, but there is nothing. I can't even scream. This isn't quiet, it is the complete absence of all sound, a silent void. I climb under the bed covers, curl up into a foetal position with my pillow over my head and my hands over my ears. At least the rolling heartbeat drums have gone. At least I can hide in the dark, and maybe next time I wake up I won't be stuck inside this dream.

Time passes.

I gradually fall asleep and without noticing just slip under. Is this what death is like?

I wake up with a start and it is daylight. I feel an immense sense of relief, but I am so very tired. I have a fleeting memory of the grassy bank where the redcoat should be standing. The grass is pale, washed out, and the soldier is gone. There is no sign that he was ever there. The picture fades. I don't know why, but I know that it is all going to be alright. I don't dream again, at least not that I remember, apart from very rarely. The hills are hills, my room is my room, and life — and sleep — returns to normal.

But that is not how I thought of what I thought. It wasn't a dream remembered the following day. The raven standing on top of the crudely carved stone head were two separate thoughts which came together. There have been a few so-called 'Celtic' carved heads found in the Glossopdale area of the Dark Peak, and I have heard all sorts of stories about them. There are tales of surviving traces of practices from the past hanging on in the remote hills and valleys of the Peak. Ribbons are found tied to thorn trees beside lonely springs and pools.

The stone heads, with their blank, unblinking eyes keep watch. Over the years there have been many reports of a shadowy figure associated with them. If a head is moved to a different location, the figure moves with it. Oh, and the heads don't like to be moved. Bad luck follows their relocation.

Spellbound was always going to have a stone head in it, somewhere, but without a body it was either going to be on the ground, which didn't strike me as being a particularly good place for it to be, or built into a wall. But a wall would imply a building of some sort and that didn't seem right either. Raising the head off the ground and putting it on top of some sort of column at chest or head height seemed a better option. So, the stone head was sitting on a column. The raven perching on top of the stone head was the next step.

The raven came about due to the complete lack of other characters in the story so far. I had thought about it — or if not a raven then some other character — as a way for Geraint to get extra information about the Land of Faerie from someone other than its sole occupant to date, which was the Faerie Queen. If all other persons were missing from the Land of Faerie, it didn't seem right to have a human, or humanlike person as this supporting character. That left the hell hounds, but they didn't strike me as being the sort for polite conversation. Tearing you apart and devouring your entrails in front of you, yes. Casually mentioning that you could never eat or drink anything from the Land of Faerie if you were ever to leave again, no.

So, what would make a believable, talking familiar in this world? Parrots talk, but would be out of place. Ditto Mynah birds. A talking horse? Maybe, but a bit too Mister Ed, and my guess is that the hell hounds would long since have predated him. See hell hounds: pack behaviour, hunting techniques and diet. But a raven? There is some precedent thanks to Edgar Allan Poe and Norse mythology. I will just need to stay clear of 'nevermore' (which includes Arabella and Mortimer) and I should be fine. Oh, and eating a corpse's eyeball out of its skull — it has been done before. That then led up to where do ravens perch? Poe's bird was on top of a bust of Pallas Athene. Mine could have a Dark Peak stone head atop a gritstone column to sit on. As yet my raven doesn't have a name and I am not going to rush to give it one, but let it emerge when, or if, it is needed.

We are now back at the dream which didn't happen, and the rambling, half awake thoughts, which did. It began with Geraint stumbling through the Winter Trilithon and appearing on the other side in the middle of a storm. He left the Real World side of it in mist and fog, and emerges into a world of snow and ice. He turns to go back through it, but the angles are wrong and the stones aren't aligned exactly. In the driving snow, and it being night, he can't see that the trilithons are out of position from where he is. The Escher-like perspective is wrong. When he goes through the trilithon he is simply on the other side of it in but still in the Land of Faerie. This is where the raven makes its first appearance, to guide him through the storm to safety, or if not exactly safety, then at least to somewhere he won't die of exposure. The raven flies ahead and calls to him to follow. Caw… caw… to the Faerie Queen's castle without an outside.

This now raises the question of how do you get inside a building which doesn't have an outside? A door hanging in thin air is another cliché, and while I'm pondering that, the raven flies behind an old thorn tree — and doesn't reappear on the other side. Geraint goes the other way round the tree and the raven has gone. Disappeared. When he goes round the other way, the way the raven went, the angles change. The perspective is different and he is in the courtyard of the castle beside the thorn tree. If he stands in just the right spot he can see snow and darkness like he's peering through a crack in a doorway to outside. That is another big clue he is not in Kansas any more, not that he ever was.

I then have another scene come to mind. This time it is the raven pushing a note under the front door of Geraint and Enid's shop. It has held the note in its beak and is now delivering it. I can't read the note as it is folded up, but it is this which prompts Geraint to leave on his errand in the first place. In one version the note is for Enid to go, but Geraint won't have it since she is heavily pregnant so he goes in her place. In the other version he goes without having to dissuade Enid. Either way, the note is from the Faerie Queen, so I now know the raven is acting for her. I can see her writing the note and giving it to the raven to deliver. Only, the thing is I can't see the Faerie Queen directly.

She keeps shifting her shape. One minute she is an old crone, haggard and bent. The next she is thin and withered, then young and beautiful. I just can't settle on what she looks like, so she keeps shape shifting. Maybe it will sort itself out.

I go back to the note. What did it say? Who was it address to? Has the Fairy Queen already selected Geraint, and this is the mechanism how he is led into the Land of Faerie? But what if it was to Enid in her guise as the banished daughter of the Fairy Queen? I can't reconcile Enid's past in the Land of Faerie with a life in the Real World. The stuff about not eating Faerie Food and time passing differently just don't add up. I've become stuck again and I need to either have another half awake ramble inside their world, or find some time to daydream. I don't have work tomorrow, so don't have to be up early and out of the door to make the commute to Sheffield. I'm doubly glad because of the freezing temperatures and icy roads. Is this where I'm getting the snow and ice from, or from memories of childhood winters in the Peak District? I'm not sure it matters since it is setting the scene for the Land of Faerie. I just wish I knew more about Enid's back story. I've got Angharad, subject to any new disclosures about her mother. I've got Geraint – he is probably the most straightforward of them all. I'm kind of getting the Faerie Queen – even if I haven't quite figured out what she looks like yet what is driving her. I've got the raven. But Enid... who are you?

Chapter 28

The Conversation With Enid

The rambling thoughts while being half awake I had hoped for don't happen, and I go from being deeply asleep to fully awake in the time it takes for a cat to sit on your chest, bellow at you to demand food, then repeatedly dab you on the nose with its paw. Even with the claws retracted it is sharp enough to induce full consciousness very quickly. By the time I've got out of bed, fed the cats, made coffee, and gone back to bed, the twilight world I was hoping to roam has long since vanished. Instead I sit up in bed listening to the radio and drink my coffee. I try to imagine myself into this made up world to figure out more about Enid, but I don't get anywhere. All I see is her standing there, holding her pregnant bump with both hands and looking very tired and fed up. The harder I try to imagine her back story the more elusive it becomes, like the mystery of the missing folk from the Land of Faerie. I'm wondering if the two are connected, but if they are I can't connect the dots. Perhaps there aren't any dots to connect in the first place. I don't want to miss a whole day until the next time I'm likely to be half awake first thing in the morning (cats permitting), so I get on with sorting out breakfast and doing a handful of other jobs that need doing around the house. I'm hoping that while I do this I might come up with another way in which to find out more about Enid.

It doesn't happen. So, here I am, pen in hand, blank page in front of me, wondering how many cups of tea (beverage) it will take before inspiration strikes.

The answer doesn't come from tea (beverage or meal), but Marlowe. A familiar voice whispers in my ear.

'Why don't you just talk to her?'

'Good question,' I think. Why don't I?

As I have done before, I get out two chairs and put them facing each other. Then, and I don't know why, I draw the curtains closed to make the room darker. I close my eyes and to my surprise I'm not sitting in my room with Enid opposite me, but standing opposite her in the haberdashery shop. It all looks so old-fashioned with the heavy wooden countertop, stone flagged floor, and little brass bell ringing on a spring above the shop door. There are bolts of fabric on the shelves along the walls, and a mannequin in the bay window with its small panes of glass. Behind the counter with a long wooden ruler fixed to the near edge are pigeon holes filled with assorted buttons, ribbons, cotton reels, and other odds and ends.

There is a quizzical lilt in her voice as she asks me, 'Hello. Can I help you?'

The bell above the door goes silent, even though it is still moving. I am not quite sure what to say or where to start, so on the assumption that honesty is the best policy I begin to explain.

'I'm a writer and I need to ask you some questions. I hope you don't mind.'

'You're English aren't you?'

'Yes, but what does it matter? If it helps I have some Welsh ancestry, but that's not why I'm here. You are a character in one of my stories and I hardly know anything about you.'

'Aren't you supposed to ask a person's permission if you're going to make a story out of them?'

'It's not like that. This is fiction.'

'So, I'm a fictional character am I?'

'Not necessarily, but yes, I made you up, but I hardly know anything about you.'

'Well, I don't how I feel about that. I seem very real to me.'

'You are real, in a sense. I'm talking to you, aren't I? How much more real to you want to be?'

'I don't know how to answer that.'

'So is it okay if I ask you some questions?'

'You tell me. You're the writer putting words in my mouth.'

'I'll assume yes.'

Enid considers this for a few moments.

'Will it take long?'

'I really don't know. It's really just background stuff that I'm after at this stage to help fill in some holes I've got with the plot.'

'You won't mind if I sit down a while and take the weight off my feet to then. Carrying this one around is tiring me out.'

She pulls out a wooden stool from behind the counter and sits on it.

'How long now until the baby is due?'

'Another five weeks, but if I were to go into labour tomorrow it wouldn't be soon enough. This one is large enough already. I don't think there is any room left if it gets any bigger.'

She rubs her distended belly as she says this, but then she stops and fixes me with a hard stare.

'I'm not going to die in childbirth like some tragic heroine am I?'

'No, no. Of course not.'

It hadn't occurred to me she might ask such a question.

'You're going to be fine. I'll make sure you have a straightforward labour. No dramas.'

'And the child...?'

'... will be healthy. Mother and child will be fine. Do you want to know if it will be a boy or a girl?'

'No thank you. I'll find out soon enough.'

'As you wish. Now, I'd like to ask you about your childhood if I may.'

'There's not much to tell. I grew up in the village and have lived in this shop my whole life. My father died when I was nine, my mother passed away two years ago now. I visit their graves every Sunday after the service.'

And that puts an end to the daughter of the Faerie Queen theory.

'Do you have any brothers or sisters?'

'No. There's just me. And Geraint, and when this one arrives it will be the three of us in our own little family.'

'How did your father die?'

'There was an accident in the mine. Three people were killed, my father one of them. They brought them out in coffins, but they wouldn't let me look at him. They said it was better I remembered him how he was.'

'That must have been hard. What about your mother?'

'She got a chest infection. I sent for the doctor, but there was nothing he could do. She lingered for a few days, but in the end the pneumonia got her.'

'I'm sorry.'

'Don't be. She missed my father terribly after he died. They are at peace together now.'

Enid pauses.

'Do you know how I die?'

I hesitate before answering.

'Yes and no.'

'What does that mean?'

'It means I know you live a long life, but I don't know the specifics about how it ends. Old age I expect.'

'Well, that's more than most people will know.'

'Geraint is with you at the end.'

'I wish you hadn't said that. I don't want him mourning me and being left behind alone.'

'In the story you won't know that until it happens.'

'That's a good thing then. Like real life.'

'Like real life, with its ups and downs, good times and bad.'

'I'm glad Geraint is there. Did you know it was his father that found me as a baby?'

What? Where did that come from?

'How do you mean "found you"?'

'I was found abandoned in a blanket just outside the village. I thought everybody knew. I was just a few hours old, or so they say.'

'Maybe around here they know, but I wasn't aware.'

'Well, that's some more background for you. Geraint's father found me lying in the middle of the path, and mother and father took me in and raised me as their own since they couldn't have children.'

'Do you have any idea who your real parents are?'

'None at all. It wasn't anyone from the village or the ones hereabout, and since everyone knows everyone else's business it wouldn't have been possible to carry a baby for nine months and keep it a secret around here. Questions were asked and the authorities were informed, but nothing ever came of it.'

'Was there any speculation?'

'Of course there was. You don't have something like that happen and not have the whole village wondering. Gypsies or travellers were suggested, but there weren't any in the area at the time, and anyway they're supposed to take babies, not leave them behind. There weren't any other strangers known in these parts at the time either, so it has always been a mystery.'

'Was there anything found with you, like a note or any objects or anything?'

'Nothing. Just me wrapped tightly in a blanket.'

'No distinguishing marks?'

'None.'

'Very mysterious. How far outside the village where you found?'

'Not very far at all. Only a few hundred yards.'

'I thought if it was going to happen that children were left on the doorstep of the church or orphanage or some such place.'

'There is no orphanage here, and we don't have a church but a chapel. As to why I wasn't left on the doorstep you'd have to ask who ever left me on the path the reason.'

'Where is the path in relation to the Ringstones?'

'The path leads out by them, but it's quite a way out. A mile or more easily. Why do you ask?'

'I just wondered if there was any connection, that's all.'

'There's no connection and I'll thank you not to go spreading suggestions like that to other people. The place has an unnatural reputation and I don't want my name to have anything to do with it.'

'Sorry, I didn't mean to cause offence.'

'I think it is time for you to leave now.'

'But there are more questions I have to ask you.'

'I said I think it is time for you to leave now. Goodbye.'

And with that she is gone. The shop is gone and I'm sitting by myself back in my room.

Is she anything to do with the Faerie Queen? I can't say she is, but I can't say she isn't. All I can say is that it is a tantalising possibility I can't rule out. Or rule in either. Her being found abandoned as a baby with no clue as to her true parentage, now that is interesting. I'd say the balance of probability pointed in that direction. Perhaps I should arrange an appointment, or should I say audience, with the Faerie Queen herself.

I've got to admit that I'm more than a little apprehensive about this. I don't think she is a person to take lightly, and I don't want to get on the wrong side of her.

Chapter 29

Fine Dining With The Queen

Looking back at those last three sentences the day after I wrote them I am more than just a bit embarrassed about them. Apprehensive about meeting a fictional character I haven't developed or explored yet? What utter bollocks. However, meeting her and talking to her may well be helpful as there are aspects of her character I still don't understand.

Only... I'm still hesitant and I don't know why. I can see two ways of handling this. Take lots of preparation and carefully set things up, or just blunder in and see what happens. As I have still got the chairs set up I'll just start and see what happens. Here goes.

I close my eyes.

I am in darkness.

There is a stillness to the air. I'd say there was an other-worldly fragrance to the place, but that doesn't make any sense. What does 'other-worldly' smell like in the first place? I think it might be the scent of lavender, which isn't in the least bit other-worldly. Yes, that's it. Lavender.

It is at this point that I realise that I am lying in a bed, naked, and it is not my bed. This one has silk sheets and I can feel their coolness against my skin. I also realise that I am not alone. I remember the line, '"Will you walk into my parlour?" said the Spider to the Fly'. So much for just blundering in and seeing what happens. Result? I'm the main course at the Black Widow's banquet. Perhaps the Black Tulip will rescue me, but then I dismiss that thought. Wrong universe, and besides, she rescues looted works of art, not stray writers who get hoisted by their own prose.

There is movement in the bed beside me and the Faerie Queen rolls over and drapes an arm over my chest. I am acutely aware that she is also naked. I lie stock still, hardly even daring to breathe in case she wakes up. This is not how I was expecting our first encounter to go. It is still very dark, but my eyes are starting to adjust and I am beginning to see vague shapes in the darkness. The sheets are a light colour, as are the walls of the room we are in. Beyond that I can't make anything out as the shadows are too heavy, too deep. There doesn't seem to be a window to the room, or if there is, it is covered with a heavy curtain. Then again, I can't see a door either.

She seems to be settling back to sleep so I allow myself to breathe a little more easily. My heart is still racing and to me each beat seems deafeningly loud. Hill deafeningly loud? I put the thought aside. If my heart is still beating then I'm still alive. She murmurs in her sleep and snuggles up closer to me. I hold my breath again until she becomes still, then allow myself to breathe shallowly or else I will pass out from hypoxia, or terror, or a combination of both.

Although it is still too dark to see any detail, I can tell that she has fair skin and long, light coloured hair. I can't tell whether it is blonde, white, or even grey, just that it isn't dark. Odd, I think to myself. When I first imagined her she had long, black hair. I build up the nerve and chance touching her gently on the arm. Her skin seems smooth and warm. I lift my hand away carefully so as not to disturb her.

What do I do now? Lie here and wait until morning? Then what? Quietly creep out of bed instead and explore this, this… what? House? Castle? Whatever it is. In pitch darkness? How is that likely to work out? A stark naked stranger roaming an unfamiliar building at night? If that doesn't say prowler shot dead trespassing at midnight then I don't know what does.

Then it strikes me just how tired I am. Not just physically tired from staying up too late and getting up too early. I know only too well what lack of sleep tired feels like. Going-to-work-each-day-with-a-two-hour-each-way-commute tired is draining, but a good couple of sleeps over the weekend is usually just about enough to re-charge the batteries enough to make it through the week ahead. This is more like the-years-catching-up-with-you-and-even-a-couple-of-big-sleeps-isn't-enough tired. This isn't feeling drained, it is feeling — what is the word? Faded. Like a tapestry hung too long in a sunny spot. The colours are still there, but the vibrancy has gone.

I have a sudden realisation. How long have I been here? It is only a few moments since I closed my eyes, but it feels like I have been here longer. There was a golden haired girl in a glade in the woods. It was summer. She smiled at me. It is all dream-like. She held my hand. We kissed.

Wait? I'm a married man. Just what kind of erotic fantasy is this turning into?

She whispers in my ear.

'After the winter must come spring. I need you my love for the world to be reborn.'

The Rite of Fertility. The Rite of Spring. Call it what you will. The cycle of birth, death, and re-birth. It seems so obvious now. Hold on. What was that? Birth, death, re-birth? I am beginning to see where I fit into this now. The word isn't faded. The leaves on the trees turn the colours of autumn and fall. A day in the Land of Faerie is seven years in the land of men and women. Stay ten or eleven days and it quickly catches up with you. Still outwardly only ten days older, but inwardly I'm what? Seventy years old? Eighty? Ninety? Withered. Then dead. No wonder she gets through mortals so quickly. How long have I been here? I can't remember. Mere moments? Days? Too long, that's for sure. With each second the end is rushing nearer. I need to get out of here. I need to get back.

There was a line of poetry my grandma used to recite to me. It was just one line and she couldn't remember if she had heard it or read it somewhere, or had made it up herself.

'Who are we but mortal men to fly in the face of destiny?'

Is that how it works? We fly in the face of destiny and die like mortals, or fly in the face of destiny because we are mortal? The seasons turn. Soon it will be my winter, but not just yet. There is the rest of summer to go and I quite like autumn with all its mists and mellow fruitfulness. Keats, you know. I just don't want to keel over now, withered from too long a stay in the Land of Faerie. How would that go? A sudden heart attack and then next minute you're pushing up the daisies? A massive stroke and then Goodnight Vienna? I have that thought again. The thought I thought I was getting free of.

Am I circling the drain? Oh fuck. Here we go again.

I can hold it at bay by writing, but the last few pages have been hard to commit to paper. Each sentence has had to be forced out. Each word dragged onto the page. Am I wasting my time writing this? The doubts are coming back. I don't know if I should go on. But... but... I've come this far. To give in now would be the easy way out, the coward's way out, because deep down I know how it plays out. How it has always played out. The despair. The question. Am I circling the drain?

And the answer would come back, yes, and you always have been.

Always, apart from the dreams of the seven-year-old me and his companions. Who are we but mortal men? But it is so warm in this bed, the mattress so comfortable, the sheets so soft, and the Belle Dame Sans Merci so alluring, I don't want to leave. So what is it to be? The illusion and to wither and die? To put down the pen and succumb to the plug hole? Or...? Or...? Reality has a cruel way of being factual. It is not uncaring towards us, because that suggests the capacity to care, if it cared. No. Reality is far harsher. It is indifferent to us

I open my eyes. This is the real world, not fiction. People will die today. Real people. One day I will be numbered among them, but not today. Tomorrow, if I am still here, I will pick up my pen and write some more. And keep writing. One word after another until I can write The End. Then I will start all over again. My own personal cycle of the seasons, ever renewing, until one day... one day... when I don't pick up my pen, and the final sentence will be writ.

Chapter 30

The Population Explosion

It is New Year's Day. Units of alcohol consumed the night before: unknown, but somewhere between single and double figures. That makes it somewhere between one and ninety-nine units. I don't feel fragile so I am assuming it is towards the lower end of the range. I have decided that January will be a dry month for me in support of Cancer Research. This scourge of a disease has been end of too many friends and family. I miss them terribly. While supporting this charity won't bring them back, it will be a positive step I can take to help others out, and in some small way remember those that didn't make it. Plus it will give the old liver a break, and all the other health benefits that go with it. So, while it is not exactly a New Year's Resolution it is a nod in that direction. This year's real resolution is to submit a manuscript to a publisher — when I finally figure out the plot to *Spellbound* and start writing it. The resolution isn't about being published since that is outside of my control, but what I can control, what I can commit to, is sending a manuscript in for consideration. I am not going to do the whole 'Is it any good?' confidence wobble thing. I did that yesterday and where did it get me? Nowhere. So, new day, new start. New Year, new start too.

Where to pick up from though...? Perhaps I should go looking for the missing people from the Land of Faerie. Where are they all? So far the entire population is two: one Queen and one raven. In terms of a monarch to subject ratio I'd hazard a guess that it was too heavily weighted towards the monarch end, and I'm not all that sure the raven counts as a subject. Can you have a country where the only inhabitant is the ruler? At this rate that's the way it is going, but there must have been people at some point. Castles and stone circles, even ones that don't follow the normal laws of geometry that mathematicians usually bang on about, still need people to build them. They don't grow on trees. Well, the castle might if it is hidden in the angles behind an old thorn tree, but the stone circle didn't grow on a tree, so my point about people still stands. Right. People still missing.

I try a new line of thought. Maybe they are not missing after all, it is simply that I have not encountered anyone else yet. Geraint got to the castle, even made it in to the courtyard, but that is where it ended. Enid was in the haberdashery shop by herself. The Faerie Queen was tucked up in bed, which is hardly a noted social venue if you discount the succession of consorts she has entertained over the years. Given the limited exploration done so far there hasn't been much scope for meeting anyone else.

There is just one teensy problem with all this. The sense I've got is that the castle really is deserted. The surrounding countryside really is a wasteland, ravaged by... ravaged by what? Winter? It doesn't usually kill off an entire population. Maybe the weak, the sick, the frail, but everybody bar the queen? That sounds like what? Wasps? The hive dies off leaving the new queen to start a new colony in the spring. Is that what the Faerie Queen is, some type of giant humanoid wasp? It might explain the wings in some depictions of faeries. I have had half an idea that the Hell Hounds might have had something to do with it, but instead I'll run with the wasp analogy hypothesis. The worker wasps... wait, that's bees. Start again. The regular wasps have all died out because the cold weather has come. They're done buzzing around being a nuisance when you are trying to have a picnic or have a meal outside. The frosts have come and they are no more. Only the queen survives in her nest. The younger queens have left to start their own colonies and are hibernating, but what of the old queen? Does she survive to start a new nest the following year or does she die as well? I think she dies, but if that is the case what's with her trying to mate one last time to continue the cycle of the seasons? Is Geraint there to provide DNA or is he a tasty snack to tide her over the lean times? I solve one problem and get another one in its place.

The wasps nest idea could help explain Enid. She would be one of the young queens, but would that mean there could be others? And if she were a young queen, what is she doing in the Real World and not the Land of Faerie? This is creating more problems than I started with. I'm getting the impression that there is some kind of sense to this, if only I can figure out what the hell it is. It is probably going to be one of those things which is so obvious with hindsight, but right now it is as clear as mud. Let me try something out.

Once upon a time (isn't that how faerie stories are traditionally supposed to begin?) there was a beautiful Faerie Queen. She lived in a gravitationally irrational, non-Euclidean castle behind an old thorn tree. She was very kind and very beautiful and all her people loved her very much. So far so good, if not quite traditional in parts. One day, she met a handsome prince, and, er, no. One day, she left the Land of Faerie to find a handsome mortal to, er, well, she needed to make baby Faerie Queens as she knew that winter would soon coming and all her people would die and she needed to ensure the royal succession. So she 'married' the handsome mortal, who within two weeks of entering the Land of Faerie was dead. Worn out and happy, with a big silly grin on his face, but dead all the same. She gave birth to a beautiful baby girl.

Aha! One girl, not a clutch of young queens like wasps. That brings up the rather awkward question about biology. Where does the rest of the population come from? It is easy for wasps, not so easy for a single queen with a nine month gestation period. Damn. And I was this close [holds up fingers to show just how close I was]. Back to the drawing board again.

What is it with this story that I keep getting stuck on what should be easy things to sort out? Am I over-thinking it, trying to make this world so perfect in its conception that I can't fault it in the slightest? Just how much detail do I have to put in to make it believable? It is driving me crazy not being able to fathom it out. Yet, to me at least, it is such an important point that I can't fudge it. Correction. I could fudge it, but I won't compromise. I don't think it is 'artistic integrity' so much as sheer bloodymindedness about wanting to get something fundamental right.

So that's where I'm up to. Missing population explained. How they got there in the first place in order to go missing, unexplained. Enid's parentage explained. How she wound up on a path far away from the Land of Faerie, unexplained.

At this point I would go and get a cup of coffee and something to snack on while I mulled over the storyline, but as well as giving up alcohol for January I've also given up coffee. Well, caffeine, so I could have a decaf coffee, but what would be the point? Instead, I make a herb tea (technically incorrect since the one I make doesn't contain any herbs. It is a fruit tisane).

It does not help. Whilst refreshing, it does not lead to any insights or revelations that could help my predicament. Neither does a warm, relaxing bath, or long walk, which I get in the wrong order. I should have had a long walk and then a nice relaxing bath. Sleeping on it overnight doesn't help either. Fortunately, or unfortunately depending on how you look at it, the solution, or at least a partial one, comes in the form of a damaged tyre sidewall on the Mrs' car. An ominous looking bulge that wasn't there the day before has appeared. It clearly needs looking at. We are due to go away to a 50th birthday party for an old college friend later today, so I am basically sitting around idly at home waiting for her to return so that we can leave.

I'm sitting slumped in an armchair. There is nobody else in the house. No radio or television on, no cats around. Nothing. It is quiet. I sit and think, running through the plot so far and trying to think how to bridge the gaps. Nothing comes to mind. No flashes of inspiration. Nada.

Then I get to wondering about the raven. Was he — I've made the assumption it is a he, but there is no reason I can think of that it couldn't just as easily be a she — was he/she/it from the Real World or the Land of Faerie? Does it matter in terms of the raven travelling between the two worlds? Would time catch up with the raven in the Land of Faerie after x days (x to be determined based on the lifespan of an average raven)? If it is from the Land of Faerie, where exactly did it come from? Are there others? How do they breed? Like regular ravens or in some strange faerie way? It isn't helping the plot, but it is helping to pass the time until the Mrs comes back.

I start thinking about the Faerie Queen and the raven, and how it perches on top of the stone head. Then the Faerie Queen stands behind the stone head and reaches round and covers its eyes with the palms of her hands. When she closes her eyes she can see what the raven sees and hear what it hears. Then I understand. This is how she is able to follow Geraint back to his home. This is how she knew it was a haberdashery shop. This is how she knew what to write in the note and where to deliver it to.

What else would I see if I let the raven fly around? Not much as it turns out. The village is larger than I expected, more like a small town, which makes sense for the haberdashery shop to survive. I see the path to the village (I still want to say village) and how it leads out past the stone circle. I see the raven fly through the trilithon at just the right angle and disappear. I see it emerge into the blizzard that Geraint stumbles into, and then I realise the seasons are wrong.

The reasoning is like this. If the gestation period for the Faerie Queen is the same as a human, then in order for her to conceive at the right time to continue the cycle of the seasons, she would need to be conceiving some time in spring, say March, April, or May in order for a child to be born in December, January, or February. Taking the later date of May and a February birth, there is no way that Geraint could be arriving in a blizzard. He might leave the Real World in one, but it wouldn't be blowing when he got to the Land of Faerie. If he were to arrive in a blizzard it would still be winter, and with the nine month delay to produce a sprog, it would mean that spring would be starting sometime in autumn. That is plain wrong. Unless... what if the Faerie Queen had miscarried from her first, or previous, consort, or the baby had died, which was why she needed another one at short notice to get the ball rolling again, so to speak? At which point cue Geraint, but this doesn't seem right.

Then I get to thinking. How long would it take a young queen to grow up, or at least reach sexual maturity? If it were more than one season, with the old queen dying in autumn/winter and the new queen emerging in spring, that would mean two queens or potentially more kicking around the castle, and a whole nurturing mother/ daughter thing going on. This doesn't seem particularly wasp-like or Faerie Queen-like behaviour.

Perhaps she died? Perhaps the old queen gave birth to a new one, then died. Conceived May, born February. But... the New Year begins 1st January, or at least it does in the Gregorian calendar. So she would need to be conceived at the beginning of April. For a new queen every year that would mean three months to grow up and reach maturity. Well, there have to be some differences between the Real World and the Land of Faerie. The old queen gives birth, wraps the baby in a cocoon, then dies. The new queen emerges in spring, sees the dried husk of the old queen on the floor and proclaims, 'The Queen is dead. Long live the Queen.'

She goes outside the castle and scatters a handful of seeds on the ground. These seeds grow quickly and her new subjects step from behind them out of the angles. Voila — a population. Problem solved.

I'm on a run now. Keep going. Geraint enters the Land of Faerie around the beginning of spring, say from mid-March to mid-April, once the New Queen has been born and emerged fully grown from her cocoon. I have another thought. What if the Old Queen gave birth to twins? What if it were a girl and a boy, and male babies aren't needed? By the time she gave birth it would be winter. I can see her saying something to one of her subjects, say a chamberlain or some other official, 'Take it outside and leave it to die of exposure', before taking up the girl to cocoon her. The chamberlain lifts the boy baby and wraps it in a blanket

'As you wish, your majesty.'

Most of the servants have already died off, turning to dust and crumbling, or simply falling to the floor, withered. The old chamberlain is one of the few to remain, maybe even the last. He takes the baby outside, into the snows of winter and lays him down. He turns and walks away. He has only gone a few steps when he turns to look back at the baby. Maybe it is because he knows that his own time is short, maybe it is because he knows that the Old Queen will be dead soon too, but he feels compassion. Not everyone need die today. He picks up the baby, dusts the snow off the blanket, and strides purposefully towards the stone circle.

Walking through the trilithon at the right angle he passes into the Real World. It is summer and he can feel the warmth of the sun on his cold face and hands, but he knows he must act quickly. In the distance he can see a village and sets out towards it. It isn't too far away, but he can feel a heaviness in his arms and legs. He knows his time is short. He begins to stumble, but holding the baby tightly keeps going forwards. Closer, just a little bit closer. He falls again, but keeps the baby tucked in, protecting it. He falls to his knees, exhausted. It is not far to go now, he thinks to himself. Just a little bit further. He pushes up for one more effort, but his strength gives out and he collapses back to the ground. He lays the baby down and rolls onto his side. He can see the baby lying on the path. He can see trees in leaf, green fields, and a blue sky with white clouds. There is a warm, gentle breeze, but he feels cold. He almost made it. Almost.

And with that he dies, quietly and unseen. The ashes blow away in the breeze, leaving just the baby in the blanket on the path.

So, now I know there is a chamberlain in the Land of Faerie. I'll have to do some research to make sure it is an appropriate title. If it is, great. If not, I'll change it. It also suggests that if there is a chamberlain there are other roles as well. Other people for Geraint to meet. Other people for him to talk to while he is in the Land of Faerie. Will any of them help him? I have no idea. I suspect they won't, even if they know his heritage, which not even he does. Wait up. Something is beginning to dawn on me. If Geraint is the Old Faerie Queen's son, even if he doesn't know it, that would make the New Faerie Queen his sister, which would mean... But wait. That doesn't add up. Enid was the one found on the path, so Geraint can't be her long lost brother, can he? Wasn't Enid supposed to be the descendent, lost or otherwise, of the Faerie Queen? She told me she was, or at least laid a trail of breadcrumbs so obvious that she as good as said it.

I am going to have a long, hard think about the plot so far. Is it anywhere even close to complete? Are there still holes and gaps? I think another session with the index cards is called for.

Chapter 31

First Day Back Blues

Before I start on the index cards again it is back to reality on the first day back at work after the New Year. It has been good to have a break over the holiday period, but it is back on the treadmill today. Rather than feeling recharged and reenergised, ready to tackle new, interesting and exciting things, I feel only a burden of responsibility weighing heavily on me, one that crushes my spirit. I tell myself that I enjoy my job, but I know that is a lie I have been telling myself, or if not a lie then only the partial truth.

At least I have the good fortune to be working from home today. As long as I've got an Internet connection and a security token to generate the pass code to access the systems I can do that. I have already checked my company provided BlackBerry and seen there is a pile of email waiting for me in my inbox. How many of these will I just be able to delete? Not enough, that's certain. The clock is ticking and getting to the point where I can't put off starting any longer. I know I'll get through today like I always do, but I also know that tomorrow is a commuting day. And the day after that. And the day after that. To the building where you can't open the windows. To the job where I feel unsatisfied. Back on the treadmill, one foot in front of the other, and keep going. This isn't circling the drain. This isn't the rat race. This is plodding on, because that's what I've always done. This is quiet desperation. Ceaseless. Relentless. Never-ending. Until… until the sleep of the grave and the cold embrace of the earth. To the seven-year-old me — I am really sorry it worked out this way. I didn't plan for it to happen, it just sort of did. There is a saying in project management, which is 'Fail to plan, plan to fail'. I guess that about sums it up. I didn't plan anything. Life sort of happened and I got swept along. Swept into this dead end with no hope of escape. I now see the glimmer I usually get that whatever may happen there is always hope is the trap I seem to have fallen into every time. Hope. Things will work out. It will get better. Yeah? Well, look where that's got me. I've made my bed, now I've got to lie in it. The clock is coming up to nine a.m. Whatever else, I have got a job to do, even if right now I can't summon the enthusiasm. I'm envying my colleague who got out at the end of the year. She got out of the monkey trap.

If you don't know what the monkey trap is, allow me to explain. If you do, feel free to skip ahead a couple of paragraphs. The folk story about the monkey trap is this: There is a cage (or gourd or coconut depending on who is telling the story — take your pick) containing a banana. The cage has a hole in it just large enough for a monkey's empty hand to fit in. Unfortunately for the monkey, the hole is too small to allow it to take its hand out if it is holding a banana or a nut or some other morsel that has been placed inside the cage/gourd/ coconut to tempt it.

It is a clever trap used to catch monkeys who aren't smart enough to let go of the banana and run away, at least in folklore. In reality, my money would be on the monkey figuring out that if the hole was big enough to put a banana in, it is big enough to get a banana out. All you've got to do is shake it, but then that's the part where the hunter turns up while the monkey is thinking it through and bye bye, monkey pie.

The day passes pretty much as I thought it might, and I manage to whittle my inbox down to something approaching being under control. Most of the emails were automated system notifications. Most of the rest were replies to queries I'd sent out before the holidays, so it looks like someone was busy while I was loafing.

By the end of the day it is like I have not been off at all. I am right back in the thick of it. One foot in front of the other on the treadmill and we're off for another year. Now I can see the monkey trap and my hand jammed inside it grasping whatever metaphorical banana is in there. Do I have the courage, wisdom, fortitude — call it what you will — to let go? And if I did, would I swap it for another trap or gain some kind of 'freedom', which is deliberately in speech marks since I have no idea what it means in this context?

There is the first commute of the year coming up tomorrow. The drive in the dark on icy roads. Then the waiting on the platform for the train. You know the routine by now. One foot in front of the other.

178

Keep on going for another decade and a half until retirement. This is so depressing.

The first commute lives up to all its expectations. That it would be dark is a given, considering the early hour and time of year. It isn't icy, but it is cold. Heavy, grey clouds roll in from the west and although it isn't raining it is speckling with rain in the wind. The wind cuts through me. The usual faces are there on the platform waiting for the train, which arrives quickly like it didn't want to be out in the cold at this time in the morning either.

The train fare has gone up. Not by much, but it will add up over the course of a year. Chinley – Wakefield return is still less expensive than Chinley – Sheffield. This time the ticket conductor is letting passengers travelling to Sheffield know this. At least a little of the holiday spirit is lingering on.

'I'll tell you what. Wakefield is going to be a busy station today.'

Here I go again on the treadmill. One step in front of the other. This is so depressing.

Not everyone is in the office when I arrive, but I wish those that are there a Happy New Year. There are brief exchanges about how everyone's Christmases and New Years went. Then reality is resumed and it is back to work. One step in front of the other. More emails to clear, then on with the real work of the day. Queries have to be replied to. There are phone calls about the agenda for an off-site meeting. Details have changed. And so on. I have this to look forward to for how long? It is enough to turn a person to drink if I'd not sworn off the hooch for January.

The day passes pretty much as I thought it might, and when the clock hits that particular time I know it is time to pack up and walk down to the station. Again. Wait for the train. Again. Go home. Again. The only light relief is when the station announcer gets the platform wrong. 8B is changed to 6A just when a train clearly displaying Manchester Piccadilly as its destination pulls in to platform 8 and stops at the sign for 8A. Shortly afterwards an announcement is made that the train is in fact on platform 8A. It is not the first time there has been confusion over which platform it is due to arrive at. It won't be the last.

I get on it, take my seat, and stare out of the window at nothing in particular. The train is late arriving at Chinley. We have to stop while a goods train is manoeuvred into a siding. For some reason it takes longer than expected, as the ticket conductor explains as he walks down the carriage talking to everybody and nobody in particular. I get home twenty minutes late. One of the cats is waiting for me and I fuss her once I get out of the car. At least someone cares, or at least I like to think someone cares, even if she is just after food. I go inside and she follows me straight to the food bowls. The evening passes and I turn in to bed. Sleep. Sweet oblivion. Tomorrow will be a new day, most likely similar to the one just gone. The details will change, but the essence will be the same, just like it always is. One day after the other, and another, and another. Repeat ad nauseam, which is Latin for until you're sick of it, and if that isn't what it means it ought to be. I need something to shake me out of this malaise, but what? I recently heard someone say that we don't live to eat or make money. We make money and eat to live. It might have been an advert, or a TV programme, or a quote. I don't remember. The sentiment behind it seems sensible and to some it may even be profound, but to me all I wonder is what is life? What is it to truly live, when the reality is ongoing drudgery and monotony? In a hundred years none of this will matter. It probably doesn't matter right now. Still, tomorrow is another day, and you never know I might wake up dead. Now that would be different.

Another day comes and it is cold inside the house when I wake up, even though the central heating has been on for an hour before the alarm rings. It is even colder outside, with the wind chill making it seem colder still. At least it isn't raining today, at least not yet. That will come later as the clouds blowing overhead threaten rain is on its way. They are under-lit red from the oncoming sunrise. Red sky in the morning, desolation's warning. Red sky at night, desolation seems right. Get in to the office. Clear the emails, start the 'proper' work. Different details, but the same old thing, interspersed with a couple of teleconferences, one a progress update and one a team meeting. Not much real work is done in them, but at least everyone now knows the agenda for the off-site team meeting and has had a chance to call out any logistical issues they might have had. More emails to clear and that's the day gone.

Train back, which was on time and on the correct platform this time, and drive home in the dark, in the rain. Home to an empty house. No cat waiting this time. It is too wet and windy for that. Light the fire, start tea (the meal not the beverage). You know the routine. It is like some low budget version of *Groundhog Day* on the wrong day. An average, typical, run-of-the-mill, same-old, same-old day. With wind and rain. There are no prizes for guessing how tomorrow might turn out.

So what do I do? What can I do? Why am I even writing this? I don't know who my audience is. Me as far as I can tell. If I ever type it up and send it to a publisher, fuck knows what they'll make of it. Why am I writing? It is a selfish, solitary act, and yet each day I'm finding a little time for it. Half an hour one day here, maybe an hour there, sneak in a couple of hours at weekends when all the other chores have been done. Most of it is gibberish — you know, the language of the residents of gibberland. Have I written that before? I've certainly thought it before. If I have I must remember to edit it out or else you will think I'm being sloppy, or lazy, or both. Oh terrific. The cat has now jumped onto the table and is walking all over my notebook as I'm writing. Not the 'welcome home' cat, the other one. She has completely made me lose my train of thought, if I had one when I started writing tonight. I think it must be nature's way of saying whatever else you thought you might be doing, writing is not going to be one of them. Not today. I give up. Maybe tomorrow, after the usual early start, commute, routine day, commute back, light fire, get tea (meal) on, has been gone through.

Twelve hours from leaving the house to getting back, not including the getting up and getting ready, getting home and all that entails, knocks out most of the twenty-four hours a day you get, and sleep has to be fitted in there somewhere. There has got to be a better way. I give in and go and feed the cat for the second time this evening.

Chapter 32

Just A Shimmer Growing Dimmer In The Glimmer Of A Winter

Another day. This is getting repetitive. This time it is raining lazy rain that just drops vertically, but at least the wind has stopped. The train comes in to the station slowly, like it hasn't got the spirit to make the journey today. I know how it feels. The rest of the day goes like any other.

Around lunchtime the wind starts to pick up. For a short spell mid afternoon it looks sunny outside. When I look up from my work there is a bright rainbow outside and I watch it for a while. It is almost like a sign saying, 'Everything will be all right', but it soon fades, leaving a thin, watery ghost of itself behind that lingers about twenty minutes before disappearing completely. The clouds close in and the flat, steel grey Sheffield sky soon turns dark again. So much for encouraging signs. On my way home that evening I come across a quote from Honoré de Balzac.

'Vocations which we wanted to pursue, but didn't, bleed, like colours, on the whole of our existence.'

Is that how it goes? The bright rainbow of youth fades. Not dying immediately, but bleeding away slowly? The only difference between today and yesterday is that it is a little fainter, a little harder to see. Tomorrow will be more of the same.

There is one crucial difference, and it is only now that I notice it. I am still writing. Day in, day out, no matter how bad it has got, or how little time I have had, I have written. Sure, a lot of it hasn't necessarily made a whole lot of sense, but I have done it. There have been some days where I have not written much, but I still picked up my pen and sat down to write. Sometimes the words come easily, sometimes I have to force them onto the page, wrestling with each one in turn to string a reluctant sentence together. I'm even enjoying the ritual of filling the fountain pens, looking forward to unscrewing the barrel when I've finished to check how much ink is left. I am getting a quiet satisfaction when there is not much left. It means that I have had a good session, that the words have flowed.

I need to get back to *Spellbound*. It might be a flight of fantasy, but it is my fantasy, my creation. The characters are starting to become real to me. They are starting to talk to me. I can't leave them half formed on the page. I know that I still have a lot to do. I haven't finished working out the plot for starters. Having been away from it these past few days has meant that the problems I was having with the plot seem less daunting. They seem, what's the word? Less big. Less troublesome. Diminished. Faded, you might say. The problem isn't writing, it is thinking. If I can't get my thoughts straight, the ink doesn't congeal in my pen, the words congeal in my mind. The pen is merely the tool they don't come out through. It could just as easily be a typewriter or word processor that they don't come through. In past times it would have been a quill. Do people still write with quills these days? If they do, what do they write? I might have to get hold of one or make one some time. Then when I get stuck I can not write with it as well.

I am beginning to form a plan. Finish off the outline for *Spellbound* and see if it makes sense. I can't say I feel good about it. I mean, it feels like something along those lines but that's not it. It isn't confidence either, as I can't say that I am feeling particularly confident about it working out. It is more like an acceptance that if I fail and the outline doesn't work out, I will have learnt one more way it doesn't work. That wouldn't be a failure. Failure would be if I gave up and threw the towel in. It might take two, or three, or ten, or a hundred goes to get it right, but each time I'll learn a little more about why it is not working. I only have to get it right once to succeed.

Now if you'll excuse me I need to get those index cards and Sharpies out again. I'll be with you presently. Meanwhile, smoke 'em if you got 'em.

Chapter 33

And They All Didn't Live Happily Ever After

This time I make much better progress. Sure, there are some dead ends explored, ideas that lead nowhere, but it comes together. I make headway with the plot, with twists, turns, setbacks and triumphs beginning to emerge from the cards. After the doubts I had about whether it was Enid or Geraint that was the child of the Old Faerie Queen I now have an answer, and it turns out that it is Enid after all, for reasons I won't go into here. She was telling the truth when I spoke to her earlier.

I'm feeling good about the story now, apart from one teensy-weensy little detail. I can't get the ending right, or rather I don't know where it should end. Where I've got it to is a sort of ending, but the story doesn't seem right coming to a stop where it does. There is more unfinished business. Life goes on, and maybe that is the point. I can't write, 'and they all lived happily ever after' because they don't. There is death, and tragedy, and heartbreak, and in the midst of it all poor Angharad. I wonder if I am protecting her from a climactic finish where it ends badly for her, because if she loses she dies there and then, and if she wins she dies alone less than a year later. Either way it is not a Disney ending. It is altogether too miserable and wretched. At this stage all I can hope for is that if I let it sit a while an idea will form where I can work out a more satisfactory ending. Right now I can't think what it will be. I have sat over the cards, read them through I don't know how many times, and while the beginning and middle seem to have a nice flow, the end comes abruptly. It finishes a scene, but it doesn't neatly wrap up the story. Now I'm beginning to wonder if there is something else missing from the story, or if I've got the whole premise wrong. Maybe that's an overreaction, but it has got me thinking how there could be a happy ending, if you could call it happy.

186

At this stage anything less depressing would be a good start. Maybe that's the way to go about this. Not wait for an idea to hit me, but think it through from the end and work backwards. Time for a cup of tea I think.

I can't say the tea (herb, still on the caffeine free thing) helps particularly. It is pleasant and refreshing, but does not directly produce the end result I am looking for, namely an end. It does provide an opportunity to mull things over and is considerably cheaper than a new tyre. Unfortunately, all the endings I come up with are variations on well-established clichés or are just plain naff. The long lost Princess meets her Prince Charming and returns to the throne. It was all a dream. In some of them the villain wins. Can you do that? I suppose you can, but I can't for one minute imagine that it would go down well with a reader. Besides, who is the villain of the piece anyway? If you look at it from the Faerie Queen's point of view she is just doing what she is supposed to. That is just how she is. She's not a bad person. She is doing what is in her nature in the Land of Faerie. It's just the way it is. Then, through no fault of her own, things start to go wrong when Geraint doesn't behave the way he is supposed to. The lioness isn't wrong for killing the antelope. That's what they need to do to survive, otherwise there won't be any more lions, lionesses, or cubs, but that's no consolation for the antelope. Where is the happy ending there? The antelope escapes to live another day, and the lioness and her cubs go hungry. Keep that up for too long and you can change that to starve to death. Perhaps where I'm going wrong is not giving the Faerie Queen enough of an edge. Maybe she needs to be more nasty, more vicious. More true to herself. Maybe she's a bit too fluffy pink airy fairy twinkles and sparkles, not that I'd ever imagined her that way.

I lay the index cards out over the floor and kneel down to read them. It would be easier if they were blu-tacked to a wall, but there isn't any space on the walls of the room I am in so the floor has to do. Changing the nature of the Faerie Queen doesn't have any impact on the storyline. It makes some of the scenes play differently by giving them a different emphasis, but it doesn't fundamentally affect the story. More to the point, it doesn't open up a route to a more satisfactory conclusion, and by that I don't mean a happy ending. This story doesn't have a happy ending, but it does need to end properly. I just wish I knew how that was.

I re-read the cards again, and then it strikes me. I may have overshot the end and am trying to carry the story on to another ending. If I reel it back in then there is a conclusion. It is in going past this point that another story starts up, continuing from where the old one left off, which in a lot of ways is much like real life. It doesn't end. New stories pick up from where old ones leave off. There is a continuity. It just looks like an end because of the editing.

There is something else I notice, and I've got to admit this one is worrying me. The main character changes halfway through. The story is mainly focused on Geraint at first and his adventures in the Land of Faerie, but once he escapes he effectively can't return. At this point the focus switches to Angharad and what she gets up to. The ending, such that it is, happens when she returns to the Real World. As a storyline it works, but changing heroes midway? That's the part that concerns me. The constant throughout is the Faerie Queen herself, but she is not the protagonist. Am I falling into the trap of overthinking it and trying to twist it into the model of The Hero With A Thousand Faces? I think I am and I know that it is wrong. Okay, that was a wobble, but I'm left with a dilemma. I've got a story and now it has an ending. It might not be a satisfactory conclusion, but it is an ending all the same. All I need to do is pick up a pen and start writing it, but something is holding me back and I don't know what it is. I'm hesitant to begin, but why? I know the characters. I know the story. But what is stopping me just getting on with it and writing? Is it that because I now know the story and how it ends there are no surprises for me? All there would be are around 80,000 words to get down on paper and that's going to be a real effort with no guarantee of a reward at the end of it. That is a lot of time to put in and for what? Why am I doing this? Why do I write in the first place?

Fuck.

I'm going down this road again and I am going to put a stop to it. I am not a tortured artist. I don't do the whiny, neurotic thing. I write because I write. It is just in me. I write because if I don't it is like an itch you can't reach. You try to ignore it, but it won't go away. You've just got to scratch it. It is the same with me and writing. The only problem is that it is so bloody difficult when the words won't come. Maybe that is what is holding me back. The fear of the blank page. Finding the first words to put down that will draw the reader in to the story. The fear of not being able to come up with enough of a hook to start with. The fear of not being good enough. Maybe the question isn't why do I write. It certainly isn't for the fame and the money. Maybe the question should be who do I write for? If it is just me, then what is the big deal? I could just put any old rubbish down and nobody would care because nobody else is going to read it, but that's not me. There is something about having somebody else read it and enjoy it. The downside is somebody reading it and not enjoying it. Either way it means getting it out into the world so that it can be read, and that means literary agents and publishers, and that means rejections. Is that what is holding me back? The rejections?

I've had enough rejections in my time and I remember how it felt when the first one came back. I had spent a long time working on the manuscript. It was a novel called *The Flipside Of Somewhen* and was a sort of time travel and adventure to a parallel world where there were talking animals on a flying pirate galleon used to smuggle antiques into the future. It was quite surreal and I had taken great pains to revise it to the point where I thought it was ready. It has sat in a box unread for over twenty years now. I have never got it out for fear of discovering that it was rubbish after all. I have submitted radio scripts too. These were also rejected. At no point have I had even a hint that there was anything of worth in any them. I file them away. I stop writing, but then the itch returns. On reflection I'm now wondering if I have been rejected enough? What I have sent out didn't go anywhere, but then with hindsight did I really send it to that many publishers? It would be naive to think that anything would be met with success on the first attempt. Publishers must get loads, which go straight onto the slush pile. Lots of wannabes with second and third-rate stuff and worse I dare say. How do you make that breakthrough? How do you catch someone's eye just enough for them to think, 'I might have something here'. I don't know. If I did I would already be published and not agonising about it.

So where does this leave me, right here and right now? Alone in a room with a blank page and a pen, and no further forward. This is the point I despair. There isn't anyone I can turn to for help. Seven-year-old me wouldn't know anything about publishers. Hell, I don't know that much more, and what I do know hasn't been of any use so far. Marlowe won't be any use, and that's about it. I don't know anyone in publishing. I don't even know any other writers — published by a publisher ones that is, rather than self published. It is a very daunting challenge, but this time I can't give up. There has got to be a way. There just has too.

I decided to put the problem to one side for the time being and get on with writing. I can worry about publishers later when I've actually got something to publish. In the meantime there are ideas to be thought up, characters to explore, worlds to create. I'm still not sure about the main character changing halfway through in *Spellbound*, and to say I have reservations about the ending would be an understatement. The only way of knowing for sure will be to write the damn thing and show it to someone. Still, 80,000 words is a lot to write and if it is wrong that is a lot of wasted effort that could have been put into something else. I feel torn between writing the story and… and what? I've got other half formed ideas for stories I could be working on instead. Could I settle on one of these and develop it into something more promising? Come to that, do I bite the bullet and get *Flipside* out for a reading after all this time? On second thoughts no. I don't think I am ready for that, not just yet. But 80,000 words. It is a lot. Maybe I could do something between the twenty-two index cards the story currently inhabits and a full-length novel. Do a sort of summary of a few thousand words to put more detail in without writing the whole thing. That way I might get more of a feel for how it goes and whether changing the main character works or is a deal breaker. I suppose I ought to type up the index cards on my laptop, but that doesn't seem right somehow either. I think what I'll do is write them up longhand in the A4 spiral bound notebook I have got for writing *Spellbound* in. Then I'll write the summary version, then we'll see what's what.

I'm beginning to feel a bit better about this whole enterprise. Now all I need is the downside to smack me in the face to bring me back down to earth. Then I remember. Tomorrow is another commuting day, the first of the week. Just watch the weather be cold and pissing it down.

Chapter 34

Hope?

Just to be contrary it is not raining and there isn't much wind, but it is cold. Bitingly cold. The kind of cold where body heat drains away simply by standing there. The kind that makes your ears hurt if you're not wearing a woolly hat. I am not wearing a woolly hat. The train is ten minutes late. Ten minutes more to stand getting colder. There are only so many things you can say about how depressing Chinley railway station is in winter, especially at this time of the morning. Unless it is that time at night, but at least by then I'm on my way home and looking at it through the rear view mirror of a car with heating.

The train back today isn't the usual one. I've been on it before. How do I know? Some uncanny ability to memorise trains? A train spotters notebook giving the number of the train? Some distinguishing feature unique to this train? No, no, and yes. This is the train where someone wondered how many rows of seats you could get in and still have room for at least a few token passengers. Designed by a demented midget with a grudge against tall people. Built by someone who was just following orders, no matter how insane, which the Nuremberg trials showed was no defence. This is The Crippler. There are nine inches of leg room between seats. I know. I measured it. I can either stand or sit at a rakish angle unable to move, wedged in there. I opt to sit and thankfully the seat next to me remains unoccupied for the whole journey. Anybody attempting to sit there would have my knees to contend with and there's not much room in there to begin with. Thank you Northern Rail for the charming pleasures you inflict on unhappy commuters to make their journeys even more miserable. I don't ask for much, but surely the ability to sit without inducing a deep vein thrombosis shouldn't be too much to ask for. The one consolation I have is that the heating is on and is working. Just. Slightly warm is better than nothing and an improvement on how things have been. I have been cold all day. Another of the joys of working in an office where you can't open the windows is that you can't control the thermostat either. You can't even get to the thermostat. It is safely out of the reach of meddling fingers and set to vaguely warm, but not warm enough to run up a big heating bill, and not so warm that you really feel it, but not so cold that you need to put a coat, hat, scarf and gloves on either. If it is set to body temperature, I can only imagine the body in question is in a morgue. In Siberia.

When I get home the house isn't much better. The central heating has been on for a couple of hours. It has started to get warm, but it is only superficial warmth. Surfaces still feel cold to the touch, even if the chill has been taken off. Before I do anything else I light the wood-burning stove, but first have to clean out the ashes from the previous night. It doesn't take too long to get it going as I have become quite adept at this. As the flames lick around the kindling and get more established and I can put a larger log on the fire and at last I begin to thaw out properly. It has only taken all day. By the time that tea (meal not beverage) has been cooked and eaten I am warm enough to hold a pen comfortably and write. I begin transcribing the index cards into the front of the new notebook.

The next day the weather has outdone itself. There has been a fall of snow overnight, so I need to be out of the house even earlier to brush the snow off the car and scrape the windscreen and windows free of ice before I can set off. The main roads have been gritted, but the side roads haven't so I am having to drive carefully. It soon becomes apparent that while there may only be an inch or so at home, by the time I get into the hills it is a lot worse. Drifting hasn't helped, but the road is passable if a little scary in the dark on some of the more steep and twisting sections. By the time I reach Chinley I am not quite a nervous wreck, but I am relieved to be here in one piece and not in a ditch or wrapped around a lamp post in the Derbyshire countryside. It may not be Dark Peak level difficult, but the commute in snow isn't exactly a picnic. I just hope the forecast is right that it should be melted by the end of the day.

Chinley station looks almost picturesque in the snow, not that anyone is lingering on the platform to admire the view. Everyone is huddled in the shelter, out of the worst of it. Even so it is still cold. Surprisingly the train is on time. No wrong sort of snow on the lines excuses today. It is one of the regular trains, not The Crippler, so I am able to actually sit in the seat properly today. The regular trains are usually beat up affairs — functional, not pretty — and have seen better days. Trains on the Hope Valley line seem to come in a variety of different states of repair, ranging from the decrepit at the one end of the scale to falling apart at the other. It isn't so much that they are poorly maintained, but the running repairs inside the carriages look like bodges and an overall half-assed attitude seems to prevail. At least they keep going and get you to where you're headed for most of the time.

The Hope Valley line in winter has its own charm when the surrounding hills are dusted with snow or, like today, covered in the stuff. Dawn is breaking and the half-light adds to the drama of the scene. The stark dry stone walls seem even blacker against the snow. The landscape has turned monochrome apart from the occasional pair of red car tail lights or isolated yellow sodium lamp post. Is this the Land of Faerie in winter? The usual sequence of stations unfolds and before long we're on the outskirts of Sheffield. Past Dore station it all looks so grim today. Not 'grim up north' grim. The phrase is bollocks. It can be just as grim down south if you open your eyes and look. No, this is grim as in 'you don't want to be out there in this weather' grim. However, to get between Sheffield station and the office requires going out there, so I just have to get on with it. This time I have got a hat with me. Not a woolly one, but a warm one nonetheless. And gloves. And a scarf. And it is still bloody cold.

The temperature in the office today feels slightly warmer than usual, but it turns out that is just because the difference with the temperature outside is more pronounced. By the time I am partially defrosted it becomes apparent the heating is the same as it ever was — insufficient. The working day unfolds, starting with an unexpected call from the chap who headhunted me into the position I am now filling. He has changed companies and is rebuilding his network of contacts. After exchanging New Year's pleasantries and general chitchat about the Christmas holidays — now a very distant memory — he asks about how I'm getting on. I say nice things about how I am enjoying being here, how the work is interesting and varied, and how I am working on all kinds of exciting projects, but the reality is I'm paying lip service. I am guarded in what I say as I am in an open plan office, and while the people around me can only hear one half of the conversation, it wouldn't take a genius to figure out I'm unhappy and want out. There, I said it. I give him my personal email so he can stay in touch. I'll call him back another day when I can talk more freely and ask him to remember me if anything likely comes up.

The day soon collapses into a slowly unfolding a train wreck. It hasn't come off the rails yet, but it won't be long before it is sliding down the embankment and coming to a sickening, crunching stop. It will happen at the end of Quarter Two to be exact. That's the date that has been set for the project I'm working on to be completed by, as, due to the bizarre way in which performance is measured, anything that you are going to be recognised and rewarded for has to be done by midyear, even though the reward year ends in December. Everyone will go all out for six months to meet their objectives for mid-year and then coast for the rest of the year as there is no point. My issue (which is not a problem, because that would suggest something bad) is that even going flat out I can't get through everything that needs to be done in that amount of time, and that is working on to the exclusion of everything else. Add in other projects and pieces of work coming my way, plus all the other day-to-day stuff and the end of quarter two doesn't just look unrealistic but downright impossible. The option of pushing the deadline back won't happen because that's when the head of the department has drawn the line in the sand for all projects, and getting additional hands to help isn't going to fly either because they've all got their regular work and projects to complete by the end of quarter two as well. There is no chance of getting a contractor, as that idea would be shot down before getting halfway through asking. Dropping the other projects isn't an option either, because they are all on the priority list. So, whichever way you look at it I'm being set up to fail before the year has even got going properly yet. My challenge will be to fix this 'issue', and right here, right now I can't see how. Once upon a time, objectives used to be SMART — Specific, Measured, Agreed, Realistic, and Time-bound. This is SMIUT — Specific, Measured, Imposed, Unrealistic, and Time-bound. Not as catchy. Part of me would just love to say, 'Do you know what? I've had enough. I quit' and just walk out. It's not going to happen immediately as I'm on three months notice, so I'd still have to put up with three months of this crap. The reason I don't just walk out is that I still have bills to pay, a mortgage to keep going, and food to put on the table. Still, it is awfully tempting. Maybe now is the time to start looking around after all. There's no harm in looking, right?

The day passes with this black cloud hanging over me. Meanwhile outside the weather has changed. The snow has melted alright, but it is a very gusty, icy wind that is blowing. The kind some people call a 'lazy wind' because it doesn't go around you but through you. They'd be wrong about this wind because it isn't lazy but purposeful. It is going from point A to point B in the fastest, most direct way, and anything at point C (being a point someplace between point A and point B) is just in the way and going to get blown down or blown through. I make my way back to the station and am met with the sound of a piano being played. It is not piped music, but in actual piano with an actual person playing actual music on the station concourse. I must have walked past that piano I don't now how many times without realising it was there. I stop to look and listen for a while. You've got to take time out to smell the roses, otherwise what is the point of living? Sheffield railway station. The only station I know with an upright piano for the public to play freely on, though I dare say there are others. The song is *Smile (Though Your Heart Is Breaking)* and it is being played by a young woman wearing a thick coat and a woolly hat. Her gloves rest on the top of the piano. She finishes the piece, then picks up her gloves and departs. Everyone else just carries on like nothing has happened. The song seems oddly appropriate for the kind of day I've had. I make my way to the platform, only to find someone has collapsed and is lying on their side on the ground. There is a paramedic by his side and one of the station staff is standing over him. However bad I may think my day may have been, his is going a lot worse. Being ill while you're travelling is bad enough. Been there, worn the T-shirt, thrown up over it. But being passed out on a cold railway station platform floor when you're ill can't be good. There is some movement and they get the young guy sitting up, then on his feet. He looks pale and shaken, but the train ahead has just pulled in and he is bundled onto it. This, and the song, help put things into context for me. I had a bad day at work. Nothing went wrong and nobody died, just unrealistic demands being made around objectives. I'm still going to look around for a change though, that much is for certain.

When I finally get home, get the chores done and sit down to write it is getting late. I might not be able to get much done today, but I'm sticking with this writing everyday thing. It is now not so much a planned part of my routine, because I am snatching time whenever I can, but what I do. I think I am beginning to think of myself as a writer. Maybe not a very good one, certainly not published one, but a writer nonetheless and learning all the time. I am also finding that I am paying more attention to what I am reading, analysing its style, pondering what works and what doesn't. I've also read a few things that I have thought, 'I could do better than that', which either says something about the quality of what I was reading or I am developing an over-inflated opinion of myself. Whichever it is they have done something I haven't — been published. One day… one day…

I return to finish off writing up the index cards for *Spellbound*. Having written it up and re-reading it I am getting a much better feel for how the story progresses and I am a bit more relaxed about how the main character changes halfway through. It is more like making a movie and having the camera stay with the action rather than on one particular character. What I am now mulling over is whether to follow what happens to Enid and Geraint while Angharad is away on her adventures, and am thinking it wouldn't be right to follow them. Angharad has to come back to a surprise, and I don't want to spoil it for the reader. That brings me neatly on to the subject of sub-plots in *Spellbound*, or to be more accurate the complete lack of them.

Re-reading the story it is apparent how linear it is. Sure, there are twists and turns, high points and low points, and each character has their own motivations. I'm beginning to get under their skin, understand how they tick. It's just that, it is all so, don't know what the word is, superficial. There is no great depth to the story. It is a pleasant little entertainment, a nice diversion, but it is not exactly profound. I could hardly be accused of committing literature with it. It doesn't speak to our times, provide an insight into the human condition, or give a gritty insight into whatever the hell is in vogue on the bookshelves these days. It is the creation of a middle aged, middle class, reasonably educated white male. I guess that doesn't make me a minority, but it sure does feel like it some days. Maybe being tall is enough to make me a minority, but I doubt it. I've never heard of being tall-ist or tall-ism so that one is out of the window.

Chapter 35

Huffety Puffety Ringhenge Down

Now I've got a very short version of *Spellbound* written up, I am oddly reluctant to actually start writing the next longer version, even if it isn't going to be the full-length novel. I keep going back to are there enough characters in it? It feels too light on people — real people and faerie people — and I've got a scene in my head which doesn't fit anywhere. It doesn't have any of the main characters in it, I don't even understand what the point of it is. Still, it is in my head and I need to get it down somewhere. The scene is inside an ancient tumulus. The tumulus is called the Ringhenge, and it is a large, grassy mound on the top of a hill. It looks across to the other hill where the Ringstones stand like broken teeth against the sky. There is an opening on the side facing the Ringstones. Three large, heavy stones set into the side form an entrance to its still, damp recesses. The huge stones lining the passageways to the chambers deep inside are cold to the touch, almost clammy. Sound is deadened. There is no movement in the air away from the entrance. Nothing stirs here, not even beetles or spiders. If you stand in the half light near the entrance and let your eyes adjust to the dark you can see patterns engraved into the flanks of the stones. Large spirals and concentric circles are all over the stones covering every surface. This is a special place.

You go deeper, slowly and carefully moving forward into the darker shadows, one hand on the wall, the other reaching out into the emptiness in front of you. Whatever you thought you could hear outside is now silent. The only sound you can hear is your own breathing. You become aware of the beating of your heart inside your chest, faster than normal, ready for fight or flight. But fight what? You hold your nerve and step forward again, going deeper and darker. The terror is beginning to build inside you, a primal fear, not of the dark, but of the things that live in the dark. It isn't the dead you fear, it is the living. But the living what? Visions of bloated, white, amorphous things enter your mind. Eyeless horrors that claw at you. They are hungry. They are always hungry. Food is scarce down here and tasty food is scarcer still. For a moment you imagine them gathered over your lifeless corpse, fighting among themselves over some scraps you once called you, but you catch yourself. It is just your imagination. It is just your mind playing tricks on you. There is nothing down here. It is just you. You and the dark. The all encompassing, enveloping, smothering dark. Is this what claustrophobia feels like, that choking in your throat? You swallow hard and take another step forward, then another step, forcing yourself deeper and deeper, forcing yourself further and further away from the outside world, the world of warmth and light.

Your hand reaching out in front of you touches something. Cold and unyielding, an enormous slab of stone blocks this end of the passage. You have come as far as you can down this way. You stand there motionless with your hand on the stone in front. Although your eyes are completely dark adapted it is black in here. Not night black or pitch black or darkroom black. This swallows you. This is the blackness of the void. Airless, starless, lifeless. You run your fingers over the rock in front of you. It isn't smooth. This also has patterns carved in it. You begin to feel for them, trace them out. Concentric circles. Then something else. Some kind of hatching or grid. Then lines running together, side-by-side, curving. This is another spiral. You start to trace it round, going from the edge inwards, the spiral getting smaller and tighter, until you reach the centre and pause, your fingers still touching the stone.

There is a movement in the air, almost imperceptible, but you notice it. You strain your hearing, your other senses being useless, but there is no sound other than your breathing. Even when you hold your breath there is nothing. Is it your imagination again, or...? Is that a dim light coming from the stone, from the centre of the spiral beneath your fingers? No? It was hardly perceptible. It must have been your mind playing tricks on you. You stare at the blackness where your outstretched fingers are touching the stone just in case. Nothing. But you keep looking. There is something, something very faint, but it is there. It fades, comes back, fades again, almost like an ember being blown on to coax it into life. It is not your imagination now. This is real. The light is growing, but still weak. Each time it is getting stronger, spreading, reaching out into the spiral. A weird, dull, orange-red coal ember colour is coming from within the rock and getting brighter, pulsating. It is not just the stone you are still touching. You notice the circles and dots on other stones beginning to glow and pulsate too. There is also a sound, faint at first but timed with the pulsations, a sort of humming noise like some distant massive electrical equipment. There is great power here. The spirals, circles, dots, and other symbols on the stones lining the passageway are glowing brighter and brighter. Orange-red becomes orange, then yellow. The sound is loud now.

You try to move your fingers away from the spiral you are touching, but they are stuck fast to it. The light is now blue. A coldness is spreading up your arm from your fingertips. Is it the coldness of the rock or is it draining something out of your arm? The chill spreads into your shoulder. Desperately you wrench your arm, trying to get free. The sound is deafening. Again and again you pull, harder and harder. You can feel your neck and side beginning to freeze. The light is now blinding. You give one last pull with all your might and your hand comes free. The noise stops suddenly and the light fades to blackness. Your arm hangs limply by your side and you reach to lift and cradle it. It feels cold and dead. Deep inside you know that something has been woken. Something almost got out, or across, but from where you don't know. You feel the overwhelming need to leave this place.

Turning on the spot, you attempt to retrace your steps, trying to touch the walls as little as possible. Inch by inch you shuffle forwards in the dark. How long have you been in here? How much further to go? There is a gloom, a hint of light in the passageway now. The entrance lies some way ahead. You move forward a little faster now, still trying to avoid touching the walls. Then you see it. The thin sliver of the entrance and you quicken your pace. The relief as you reach it and step into the world is immense. There is sensation starting to come back into your arm, and you can move your fingers again. The world is bright and airy, full of smells and sights and sounds.

Without looking back you walk away from the barrow. In the darkness the consciousness from beyond the chasm of time and space begins its long and lonely wait again.

There. I told you I had no idea what it was about or where it fitted. The barrow overlooking the Ringstones is just window dressing. I have no idea if it does overlook the Ringstones or not. The barrow could just as easily be on its own somewhere in a different story. I can't put my finger on it, but it doesn't feel like *Spellbound*, it feels darker, almost alien. 'Faeries and aliens' might be an interesting, if unusual, new genre, but I think I'll leave it to other people to explore that particular avenue. Yet somehow, there is a connection that I can't place. It has a meaning, but I'm buggered if I know what it is.

Maybe if instead of sending you into the barrow, I go instead. Better yet, why don't I send the Black Tulip, Anna Gallis, down? She knows how to take care of herself. Or Marlowe. He's good in a tight spot. I know that neither of these suggestions are appropriate. I'm the one that is going to have to go down if I am going to get any answers. I'm not looking forward to this in the slightest. Something bad is down there and I am going to poke it with a stick. Whichever way you look at it, it is not a sensible idea, but fools rush in and all that.

I try and get myself in the right frame of mind for this, what exactly is the right frame of mind? I decide to go in with a blend of inquisitiveness, curiosity, self-preservation, and a healthy dose of scepticism.

Okay, here goes. I'm outside the barrow facing the three stones which make up the entrance. Grey, heavy, and flecked with lichen, they have stood here down the centuries, guarding the way in to this netherworld. When I touch them they feel the way any stone would feel. There is no magic here and yet… I hesitate at the threshold. It is just a story, right? I mean, it's all made up. Nothing can happen because I'm writing this, but is it fiction or autobiographical? Could I be writing my own death scene? Foolish thoughts, surely, but still I hesitate. Maybe sending Marlowe down would be a better idea after all, but I doubt he'd do it. He's got his own agenda and whatever fee I offered I don't think it would be near enough for him to take the case.

'All you've got to do is go down in the dark without a torch and touch the wall of the passage at the far end.'

I can hear him asking, 'What's the catch?', and I don't think I could lie to him.

So it is down to me then. The answer to my question is at the centre of that spiral. I suppose I'd better get it over with. Here goes nothing, and with that I step inside.

A few steps in and the light quickly fades. I let my eyes adjust to the dark and while that happens I look at the stones lining this end of the passageway. They are rough, with natural surfaces, and more to the point unadorned. The patterns must appear further in. I begin to see shapes in the darkness ahead. The passageway goes off in different directions, but I know it is the one straight ahead which I need to follow. Putting one hand on the wall to steady and guide me I start to move forward. Step by step it gets darker and I pause again. Was this really such a good idea? The answer, no, but I have got to do it. There is something at the end and I need to know what it is. I've got to keep my hand held there no matter what happens.

I wait for my eyes to adjust further and I begin to make out the spiral and concentric circle patterns on the stones. The more I look the more I see. They are everywhere. The concentric circles and spirals vary from a hand width to an arm span. Some tightly coiled, others lazily open, some single spirals, some double. I trace my finger around one from the outside to the centre, but nothing happens. I wasn't expecting it to, not with this one. It is the one at the end of the passage that is special.

I move forward again, deeper into the passage, further into darkness. I begin to edge my way, one hand on the wall, one hand reaching into nothingness. The blackness is suffocating. I notice that my breathing is very shallow, muffled. I keep edging forwards for what seems like an eternity. How long have I been in here? Five minutes? Five hours? Time seems meaningless. I can feel patterns in the rock under my fingers, and cracks and crevices where stones meet, so I know I'm making some sort of progress. I keep moving forward. At some point I will touch the stone at the end of the passageway, and then? I'll worry about that when I get there. Until then, another small step, and another. Ever closer. I can feel the panic starting to rise in me. I pause to suppress it, but it is hard. I want to scream, a long, soul wrenching primal howl in the darkness, but fight the urge. I take a few deep breaths to recompose myself. I know that I can leave at any point, just turn around and back my way out, but if I did that I'd be walking away from the answer I am looking for. The answer I don't even know the question to. I have come too far to turn around now.

I resolve to keep going forward. Step by step. Ever onward. And then I touch it. I snatch my hand back. Am I ready for this? As ready as I ever will be. I reach out purposefully and put my hand onto the stone. I concentrate on what I can feel, my sense of sight being useless. There is a roughness to the stone, but that could be said of any of the stones. It is cool to the touch rather than cold. I try to compare it to the stone on the other side of the passage. They feel about the same. I thought they felt cold when I first entered the barrow, but now I am not so sure. I can feel the ridges and furrows of the carvings beneath my fingertips and start to explore the surface more. It is not concentric circles. This is a spiral — the spiral. I find the edge and the point the carving begins, and place my fingers on it. This is where it happens. I steel myself.

I begin to trace my fingers in the groove, following the spiral inwards, slowly at first. The coil gets tighter. I'm getting closer to the centre. My heart is beating fast and my breathing is getting ragged. Then I reach it. The point where the spiral originates. The dead centre. I keep my fingers pressed tight against it. Where is the glow?

I strain my eyes in the blackness to see the first glimmer of anything. Nothing comes. I wait. Talk about an anti-climax. I trace out the spiral again. This time more slowly, more carefully. Still nothing. I try it quickly. Then from the centre to the edge, then back again. There is not even the faintest hint of a glow. The stone stays inert.

Maybe there is another spiral higher up or further down. I feel over the rock, but only concentric circles surround it. Maybe it is at the end of another of the passageways. I turn in the darkness and feel for the way forward, for the way out, and touch another stone. That shouldn't be there. I reach out again, this time more to the side in case I hadn't turned around far enough. There is still stone there. Maybe I turned too far and I am touching the passage wall. I reach out in front of me. There is a stone. I reach out to the side. Stone. Behind me then. It must be behind me. Stone. If only I could see. If only I had brought a light. Instead only darkness and a rising sense of panic. Calm down. Get a grip. I think I am probably just turned around. All I need to do is get my bearings and figure out which way I am pointing.

I reach in front of me and feel the surface of the rock. It is the spiral rock with the concentric circles around it. This is the end of the passageway. I feel across the surface to the right, feel where another stone joins it. That must be the passage wall. There are a mixture of smaller spirals and concentric circles on it. I keep feeling towards the right and there is another join. Maybe this is the passage wall. Spirals in circles, but different this time. I reach again to the right, and there is another stone. I can feel spirals in circles on it. With a growing sense of dread I feel my way to the right again. There is another stone. It seems familiar. My fingers find the beginning of the spiral again. I have the sinking realisation that I am trapped. I don't know how it happened, but the passageway has somehow closed up behind me. There is no way out. I finally let out the scream which has been building up inside me.

So this is how it ends. I sink to my knees. Both hands are touching the spiral stone. I rest my forehead against it. Alone in the dark, I wonder how long I will last before I die, and what it will be like. Time passes, but how long I cannot say. I am now cold and hungry. I can expect more of that before I… before I… I don't want to use the words. Before I die.

I start shouting. 'Hello. Can anybody hear me? Help.'

There is no reply. The silence engulfs me again.

'Nobody here but us chickens.' I give a small laugh at my own joke, but it isn't funny.

This isn't how it was supposed to end. The spiral was supposed to open, but then what? That was the point. I didn't know.

I stand up again and find the beginning of the spiral. With a single finger I start to trace it out. Who were the people that carved this out? Who dragged the stone from where ever it came from? Who pushed it upright to form the barrow? Who covered it with earth? What was the purpose? What was it for? My finger moves forward.

'The Moving Finger writes; and, having writ,
    Moves on: nor all your Piety nor Wit
    Shall lure it back to cancel half a Line,
    Nor all your Tears wash out a word of it'
    – Omar Khayyam

Is this what it has all been about? My finger reaches the centre of the spiral. I hold it there. There is still no glow, no sound. I contemplate what this means. It means what it is. There is no subtext, no hidden meaning, no conscious forethought. Just a man in the dark with his finger pressed against a rock carving. And yet, what if…? What if I let my hands drop to my side? What if I closed my eyes? What if I just step forward into the rock?

I take a deep breath, close my eyes even though it is dark, and step forwards. Then another step. Then another. Wherever I am it is not in the barrow. There is a different feeling. There is some movement in the air. It is not cold or damp, but warm. I can smell the scent of, what is that, flowers? Something sweet and heady, like honeysuckle. I open my eyes. It is still dark, but there is starlight. The moon's silvery light casts shadows on the ground. Compared to the barrow it is ablaze with light. I am in a garden. There are lawns, wide sweeping borders crowded with shrubs and flowers, and specimen trees, all ghostly in the moonlight. I can see a telescope on a tripod in the middle of the lawn. It is a fairly large amateur one and there is someone standing beside it.

Chapter 36

The Old Man And The Me

I walk over to the telescope and stop short, not wanting to startle the old man looking through it. He is wearing a grey fleece with the collar turned up and he doesn't seem to have noticed me. I cough gently to let him know he is not alone.

'I know you are there. I've been expecting you.'

He doesn't look up, but keeps his eye to the eyepiece.

'Where am I and who are you?' I ask.

'I thought you might have worked it out by now, but I'll give you the benefit of the doubt and give you a few more minutes to think it through.'

'I was inside an ancient barrow. There were spirals carved in the stones. Tracing one was supposed to make it glow. I was looking for an answer...' My voice trails off as I realise how feeble this sounds.

'I know. I was there.'

'But how? I was alone, unless you mean you were there at a different time or watching somehow. Infrared cameras?'

'I was there at the same time as you. Of course, I was quite a bit younger then.'

He is still looking through the telescope.

'No, I was alone,' I protest. 'I was trapped inside the passageway. The stones had moved behind me. I know it was dark and I couldn't see, but I could touch all four sides without moving. There couldn't have been anyone else in there with me. I'd have known.'

'And yet there I was. With no way out I closed my eyes and stepped forwards and was surprised to find myself in a beautiful garden at night. I do hope you think it is beautiful. I've put quite a bit of effort into making it nice. You should see the flower beds in the day. I'm quite pleased with the way they've turned out this year given the

208

weather we've been having.'

The penny drops and it dawns on me. 'You're me.'

The old man looks up at me and I recognised his face immediately. It is my face, only older.

'Give the man a cigar.'

It is not like looking in a mirror. The years have had their toll. More wrinkles, less hair, and what there is, is white. The eyes are the same, but different. Older. Wiser. Sadder. Those eyes have seen things I haven't seen, yet.

'You've seen and read enough science fiction in your time to know the rules,' he says. 'Rule One. No asking about what happens in the future.'

'Not even any hints?'

'None. Crossing timelines and temporal paradoxes and all that other mumbo-jumbo. Dangerous stuff to mess about with.'

'So why am I here?'

'You're supposed to be smart. You figure it out.'

'I've met younger instances of myself while I've been writing this. I suppose it was obvious I'd meet an older me at some point.'

'And where better than at the end of the book?'

'Why didn't you appear earlier? I could have done with some help when I was struggling.'

'Because that's not how it works. You should know that by now.'

'It is a journey I need to make by myself. No one else is going to write the words, think the ideas, tell the stories.'

'Exactly.'

'Do I stick at the writing?'

'That is a question I am not going to answer. Refer back to Rule One.'

'Do I get published?'

'You're really not getting this Rule One business, are you?'

'Well, you can't blame me for trying. I know you did it too, because I just did it.'

'Which is why I reminded you about Rule One in the first place because I already knew you were going to ask.'

'Is there any advice you can give me?'

'Yes, there is. Don't keep buying fountain pens. You only need one. Two if you want to alternate and you've got enough already.'

'No, I mean proper advice.'

'That was proper advice. It will save you a fortune in pens, only I've already got loads so you probably didn't listen.'

'Tell me something useful.'

'I don't need to. You know as much as you need to know right now. Just keep writing, learn from your mistakes, find your own voice, and stay curious.'

'That's it?'

'Of course not. There is a lot more advice. There always is and quite a bit of it is contradictory. The secret is to say what is useful to a person at the time. You know, point them in the right direction and then shut up and let them work it out for themselves. If I gave you all the answers you won't learn to think for yourself, and that's what it's all about.'

'So what do I write about?'

'Rule One on the specifics notwithstanding, write about what you're passionate about, what interests you. If you don't care about your subject, neither will your reader.'

'But I don't know who my reader is.'

'Best way.'

'So says someone who has written…?'

I wait for the older me to finish the sentence.

'…far more than you.'

'Okay, so can you tell me anything about the barrow scene? Where does it go?'

'You've already found a place for it.'

'Have I?'

'Yes, here. You've written it. Now move on. Find something else to write about.'

'But I thought it might be in *Spellbound*.'

'Well, it isn't. You use it here, otherwise we don't have this conversation.'

'So can you tell me about *Spellbound*? Are there more characters in it? What about sub-plots?'

'I've got two things to say about that. Firstly, hello? Rule One? Secondly, it's been a long time since I wrote it. I can't remember all the details.'

I want to ask more specific questions about it, but I know that I'll get Rule One thrown back in my face.

'Do I finish it?'

'When is anything ever finished? You can keep polishing it and tweaking it forever, but there comes a point when you have to let it go and move on to the next thing.'

'How do you know when that is?'

'I'm dammed if I know. I just do the best I can and guess like everyone else.'

'You know, I thought that if I ever met an older version of myself I would be more insightful, more helpful, more... what's the word?'

'...circumspect about what he says. Listen kid, I've probably said more than I should have already. If you're going to write, then write. Don't worry about what, just do it. One word after another and keep going. It is very simple. Some of it is going to be shit. I mean truly awful, and some of it will be quite good, but all of it will be a first draft to begin with and you don't have to show that to anybody. It was Terry Pratchett who said the first draft is just you telling yourself the story. You'll make mistakes, lose your way, miss bits out and all the other stuff that happens when you're telling a story for the first time. Then you'll refine it, re-work the bits that don't work quite the way you want them to, fix words which don't sound quite right, cut out stuff that gets in the way. Then you'll do it again, and again, and again, and if you do it enough you'll end up with something that someone else might just want to read. Then you reach the point where you have got to be brave and send it out into the big, wide world. They are a lot like children in that respect. You bring them up as best you can, but at some point you've got to let them go.'

'Thanks, I'll bear that in mind.'

There is a pause. It goes on for long enough to begin to get awkward.

'You want more?'

'No, I think that's enough for the moment. Like you said, give them enough to figure the rest out for themself. I think I've got enough now to make a start.'

'Good. You're starting to get the hang of it. We might make a writer out of you yet.'

'I'd like to think so. There is one last thing I'd like to ask you.'

'Sure, go ahead. Just remember Rule One.'

'I will. It's this. How do I get back?'

'Easy. The same way you got here. Close your eyes and step backwards.'

'That's it?'

'Try it.'

With that I close my eyes and step backwards. Immediately I know

I'm somewhere else. The air is cool and damp. The blackness envelops me. I open my eyes and it is still pitch black. I reach out and know what I'm going to touch even before I touch it. Stone. On all four sides. I'm back in the barrow again.

Bastard.

Okay, don't panic. I got out of this before. I can do it again. I close my eyes and step forwards. This can go one of two ways. Either I walk into the wall or I'm back in the garden again.

'Back so soon?'

'Very funny. When I asked how do I get back, I meant how do I get back to the real world, not back to where I was before?'

'You should have been more specific. Sloppy use of language.'

'But what if I edit it out?'

'Then I'll edit it back in and being older than you I will always win. Chalk that one up to experience kid.'

'Fine. So how do I get back home to my home in my time in the real world?'

'Are you ready now?'

'Yes, I'm ready.'

'Then close your eyes and click your heels together three times and say to yourself "there's no place like home".'

'Seriously? You want me to do a Dorothy from *The Wizard Of Oz*?'

'Yeah, why not. It'll be fun.'

'Who for? You or me?'

'Me of course.'

'You're not really going to make me do it, are you?'

'Look, do you want to go home or not?'

'I do.'

'Then get busy with the heels. Remember, three times.'

I sigh, then close my eyes and click my heels together three times.

'There's no place like home... There's no place like home... There's no place like I'll get you for this...'

'No, you won't. I get the final edit...' and the voice fades out.

Chapter 37

Room Disservice

Without even opening my eyes I know I am somewhere different. When I open them I am sitting at an unfamiliar desk in an unfamiliar room. There is a hotel key beside my notebook and then it comes back to me. I'm writing this while on another business trip. I had become so engrossed in what I was doing that I forgot where I was. Damn. I really do wish I was at home, but tapping my heels together won't cut it this time.

I sit back in my chair and try to gather my thoughts on what just happened. It is at this point that I realise I haven't eaten (tea the evening meal), and I am getting hungry. There is a menu on the table, which I had earlier moved to the side, tucking it behind the tea tray (for beverages, although the tray also has instant coffee (regular and decaf) and those little pots of UHT milk, two mugs, and a kettle) together with the directory of hotel services as they were in the way. I look through menu to see what is on offer. It is the usual hotel fare and includes Great British Fish and Chips, and something called The Brian Burger. After explaining that it is an 8 ounce Aberdeen Angus beef patty served in a toasted brioche bun with French fries on the side, it goes on to say that you can add streaky bacon or Monterey Jack cheese for fifty pence each. It does not explain who Brian is. Brian could be anyone, or anything. Brian could be the name of the chef who came up with the groundbreaking idea you could add bacon, or cheese, or — get this — both to his burger. It could just as easily be the name of the hotel chain's CEO's dog. It could even have been the name of the Aberdeen Angus cow now making up said burger, but if they are going to sell a lot of these there must be whole herds of Aberdeen Angus cows all called Brian.

It could be the name of the typesetter who printed the menus who thought he would have a laugh by slipping his name in there. There are so many possibilities. Nowhere else does Brian's name appear on the menu. It is as if he is taunting me. Brian needs to come forwards and explain how his name got on a burger, unless he can't because the burger is made from the recently departed Brian. Until then I will not be partaking in any Brian Burgers. In the end I decide to go with something a bit fancier — steak and fries. It would have been nicer if it had been steak and proper chips, but this isn't a top end hotel. I also decide not to go down to the restaurant to eat, but order it as room service. That way I can do a bit more writing while I wait for the food. Plus it is dropping cold outside and I don't fancy going out to eat as I don't know what other restaurants are in the area. I'm not expecting the food to be wonderful, but it should be nice enough. I dial down for room service, place my order, and am told that it will be with me in twenty minutes.

I start to think through the next part of what I will be writing and how best to word the next few sentences, and get lost in thought. Before I know it there is a knock to the door of my room and I get up to let whoever it is in with my food. It is at this point that I instantly regret not looking through the little peep hole set in the door to check who is there. Instead of someone carrying a tray with a cloth and one of those shiny metal covers to keep the food warm, there is someone carrying a tray with one of those shiny metal covers with their other hand under the cloth and just enough of a gun barrel sticking out for me to be under no illusions what it is. It is not the first thing to catch my attention though. That easily goes to the fact that the person carrying the tray and holding the gun is identical to myself, even down to the same open necked white shirt and dark grey suit. The gun barrel is merely an 'Oh by the way you might want to notice what I am pointing at you', indicated by the other me making eye contact, then looking down to the gun in question, then back up to me. The other me gestures me to back away to let him into the room. The door closes behind him and he gestures again for me to step back further. Without breaking eye contact I sit down by the desk again.

'You might want to put that tray down,' I suggest. 'It will be getting heavy and I don't want you dropping my meal.'

The other me rests it down on the bed. The gun stays pointed in my direction the whole time. It is odd watching an exact double of myself. He looks older, more tired than I expected, but then I guess that's how other people see me.

'You know who I am and why I am here.'

It isn't a question, it is a statement.

'The Big Boss. Now I finally meet you, don't you think the name is somewhat presumptive?'

'I don't call myself that. I leave it to other people. I'm just me.'

'What happened to the person who was supposed to be bringing my food up?'

'They're taking a little nap. They had a bump on the head and had to have a little lie down. Now, if you please, the manuscript.'

He gestures to the open notebook on the desk beside me. I reach over to it and pick up the fountain pen resting on its open pages and slowly and deliberately put on a performance of putting the cap back on. Then I carefully put the pen down on the desk beside the notebook. Taking my time to make sure the pen is lying square to the notebook, I then carefully fold the book shut. I pick it up by the corner and hold it up.

'You mean this old thing?'

'That's the one. I can't have you writing anything down which would embarrass me.'

'You do know I'll just keep writing.'

'And I'll just keep taking what you have written. It will be safer with me after I put it in a drawer or a cupboard. We don't want it getting into the wrong hands.'

'You mean the hands of anyone other than you.'

'You get the idea.'

'And if I refuse?'

'Please…'

He makes an apologetic shrug, with more than just a hint of non-apologetic menace.

It is at this point that I see the door to the bathroom behind him slowly open. Twenty-one-year-old me looks right at me and puts his finger to his lips to indicate to keep quiet. I need to keep the other me distracted for long enough to not notice whatever plan is being put into place.

'I've got to say I'm reluctant to hand this over so easily. Give me one good reason.'

'Because I have a gun.'

'That might be a motivating factor, but it's not a reason.'

'It's all you're going to get.'

As he is saying this I can see seven-year-old me move silently from the bathroom to the side of the bed, getting dangerously close to the edge of Big Boss me's vision. Fourteen-year-old me, followed by much older me both emerge and take up position. It must have been pretty crowded in that bathroom, and that raises the question about when and how they all got in there. I need to keep the Big Boss talking.

'When you say, "That's all you're going to get", do you mean that from a philosophical or metaphysical point of view?'

I have no idea what that means, or even if it makes any sense. It doesn't have to as long as I keep stalling Big Boss me. He doesn't understand it either.

'Just give me the book.'

I go to hand it to him, then stop.

'I've got a better idea.' I pause for dramatic effect. 'Get him boys.'

Nothing happens. The others don't jump him.

'What's that supposed to mean?'

Seven-year-old me speaks up. 'Now?'

The Big Boss turns to the voice and then back again to train the gun onto me as I get up to rush him. He loses his aim as he is grabbed round the neck by twenty-one-year-old me and by the gun arm by fourteen-year-old me. I also grab his gun arm and the four of us crash into the wall. Twenty-one-year-old me is throttling him, and I can hear the Big Boss gasping to breathe. Fourteen-year-old me is prying his fingers off the gun one finger at a time. Seven-year-old me is joining in whenever he can to land the occasional opportunistic kick or punch. I am trying to keep his non-gun hand out of action while the others do their bit. The Big Boss chokes and sinks to his knees and there is a loud bang. The gun has gone off. Seven-year-old me holds his stomach and has a startled look on his face. Blood spreads between his fingers. He falls to the floor.

I have never seen anyone shot before, I mean not for real. It is not like it is in the movies or on TV. There is blood spattered on the wall behind him. Gun smoke hangs in the air.

'You fucking idiot. What did you do that for?'

I punch the Big Boss hard in the head and fourteen-year-old me wrests the gun from his limp fingers.

Older me crosses to the seven-year-old and holds him in his arms.

'It wasn't supposed to happen like this.' The Big Boss' face is ashen. 'I didn't mean to… honestly I didn't mean to…'

As he saying this, the body of seven-year-old me begins to go see through and fade.

'What is happening?' I ask.

Older me replies.

'I wrote about this once. He is disappearing. Just vanishing away like a fading memory.'

'No, he can't. Bring him back.'

'Sorry, I can't.'

And with those words, seven-year-old me fades into nothingness.

Fourteen-year-old me speaks next. He is holding his hand up and looking at it intently. It is starting to become see-through.

'It's happening to me too.'

It happens quickly and the rest of him fades away as though he had never been there. The gun falls to the floor.

Twenty-one-year-old me lets go of the Big Boss. There is a strange look in his eyes — curiosity and horror. Twenty-one-year-old me is looking through his hands. They too are fading. There is panic in his voice.

'I don't want to go. Please, I don't want to go.'

But his pleas are of no use. It happens just as quickly as the others and he too is gone.

Older me is now looking at the Big Boss version of me.

'He is starting to go too. Being older it will take a little bit longer to catch up with him, but he'll be next.'

'But what is happening?'

'When he shot and killed seven-year-old you he also killed off all the older you's too. Without the seven-year-old there was never an eight-year-old, or a nine-year-old, or a ten-year-old. He also killed himself, and me. It is just a matter of time before it catches up.'

As he is saying this, Big Boss me is fading. It is strange to watch as the room becomes visible through him. One moment he is there and the next he has ceased to exist.

Older me is talking quickly now.

'Listen very carefully. I don't have long and this is important. Apart from the time they were alive, like you are right now, they lived on through what you wrote. They were only here because you wrote them here. I'm only here because you wrote me here. When that other you, the one filled with all the negativity, all the baggage, shot seven-year-old you, he stopped everything else from happening, because the other you's weren't there for it to happen to.'

Older me pauses. He can see me looking intently at him. He is starting to fade.

'It's happening. I can feel it. A sort of blankness washing over me.'

'Is there anything I can do?'

'Yes. You've got to write. You've got to keep writing like your life depended on it. They lived on through your words. You can write them back in.'

'But they are dead. They never existed.'

I can see the walls appearing through the older me.

'They did exist. They always existed. Once when they had their day in real life, and once again in stories.'

'But the story is over.'

I say that into emptiness. There is just me, alone, in the room.

From nowhere I hear a disembodied voice, or I maybe imagine it.

'There is always another story. You've just got to tell it.'

And then I really am alone. There is no tray on the bed. There are no blood marks on the wall. Just me. Alone. In a hotel room.

Is this how it ends?

No. The story isn't over until I say it is over. None of them will have died in vain. There is still the time when I fell in the disused canal at Stalybridge having canoed up to the Standedge Tunnel and back. I'd be about seventeen then. Or the time I fell in the sea at Penrhyndeudraeth as a kid. Or in the pond at Uncle George's house. Or the drainage ditch in the back garden at home. I have fallen into a lot of things in my time.

And I got my wellies stuck in the mud when I was out playing one time and had to walk home barefoot.

And looked at the stars and dreamt.

This is not how it ends. I open the notebook to a blank page. The page is unwritten. I unscrew my fountain pen to check the level of ink. It is about half full. That's enough for now. I screw the pen together again and rest it on the open page. There are words in that ink. I just need to coax them out. Just put the nib to the page and tease them out, like pulling a thread from a ball of yarn.

There are so many stories to be written.

I pick up my pen and start to write.

* * *

~~THE END~~

THE BEGINNING

'Everything is not always as it seems. Assume nothing. Assumptions readily close the door to all that is and might be. The open mind sees beyond the breaking wave to the distant shore. It takes the longer view and sees more'

— Song of the Old Tides
   Barry Brailsford

CHAPTER ONE

IN WHICH WE FIND THE PRESENT TENSE

There is a sickening moment when you realise the crash is going to happen and nothing you can do will stop it. You are completely helpless. This is the point you realise that from now on you are simply an observer.

It was a regular journey, the mundane kind you make every day. Uneventful. The kind you forget as soon as you have made it, but not today. The scene unfolds in slow motion. The car appears out of nowhere, coming at you head on. It shouldn't be on your side of the road overtaking another car. Not just before a blind summit. That would be stupid. You brake hard, not that it will make any real difference to what you can see is about to happen. Not at this speed and distance. There isn't enough time. There isn't anywhere for you to go. Do nothing and you crash head on. Closing at over a hundred and twenty miles an hour between you is going to be messy. Swerve over to the wrong side of the road and you collide head on with the other car being overtaken. They don't deserve that. You're pretty sure you don't either, but you're not in a position to discuss the point. Swerve off the road and you miss the collision, only off the road is a long, steep drop down the side of a hill. It can't be worse than a head on, can it? Or is it merely swapping one problem for another and delaying the inevitable? You think this as your car is already going through the wooden rail marking the side of the road and over the edge. The rail isn't there to stop you, more to indicate there is a right side and a wrong side to be on, and you are now quite definitely on the wrong side and there is no going back. The laws of physics are in the driving seat now.

There should be noises — car horns, screeching tyres — but everything is silent in free fall. The silence hangs in the air. Then comes the crunch. Once heard, never forgotten. Airbags go off. The car rolls. How blue the sky is. Then there is green. Grass. Then blue again, then green. Repeat. Windscreen shatters. Then stillness. There is a haze. Smoke from the airbags? I am upside down. Nothing hurts, or can't I feel anything? Is that a good thing? Car upside down. Air choking. Then feeling. Pain. Upside down. Got to get out. Fingers fumble for seatbelt. Fall out of car. Out. Hands and knees. Sparkling diamonds lying in the grass? Fascinating. Can't think straight. Stare. Important. Why?

Colour starts to drain out of the world. Eyes blur. There seems to be a person standing beside the crash. Is it a girl? It is hard to tell. I feel cold. Numb. Oblivion comes.

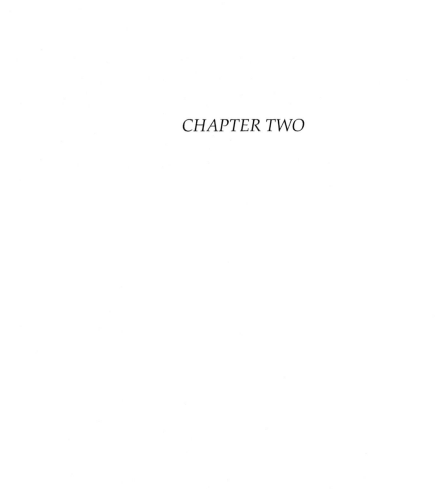

CHAPTER TWO

IN WHICH WE FIND THE PAST IMPERFECT

I start with a jolt and find myself sitting in my car in the car park at Chinley railway station. I have no idea how I got here. You get journeys like that sometimes where you are on autopilot. You remember leaving the house and getting to where you were going but have no recollection of the bit in between. Apart, that is, from the idiot who almost caused an accident. I practically had to stand on my brakes to avoid hitting him. What kind of moron tries to overtake on a road like that anyway?

Luckily he was able to nip in before he ran out of road with me in the way. He will have cut up the car he was overtaking though. I'm saying he but it could just as easily have been a she. I didn't notice the other driver or what kind of car they were driving. I was too busy trying to avoid being killed in a head-on collision.

I let that sink in.

I could have been killed.

A split second the other way and it could have ended very differently. I realise that I am shaking.

I am only halfway on my journey. Driving to the railway station is only the first part. I still have to catch the train to Sheffield before I get to work. From leaving the house to sitting at my desk takes the best part of two hours. At the end of the day I've got to do it all over again, only in reverse.

'Get a grip,' I tell myself. 'It was a close call, but nobody died.'

I feel really unsettled, but I've got things to do and the train won't wait. I grab my bag, lock the car, walk down to the station, and try to put what just happened out of my mind.

Chinley is a quirky little village set on the western edge of the Peak District In Derbyshire. It Is the sort of place that looks like it has always been there, a sleepy backwater nestled in the foothills of the Pennines, but appearances can be deceptive. The original settlement was a handful of scattered farmhouses. Most of what is here now was built in the Victorian period, apart that is from the houses clustered around the railway station. They are much more modern, 1980s at a guess, and are suggestive of a developer who had a patch of land and cashed in during the housing boom around that time.

After my bit of excitement this is what I need — a dash of suburban normality. I walk slowly down to the station, admiring the view and taking time out, quite literally, to smell the roses growing along the path leading up to the footbridge over to the platform. Their scent is heavy in the early August morning air. They remind me how good it is to be alive. I have a flashback of a car coming straight at me and feel the panic rising again, but I take a few deep breaths and it passes.

Not today. I don't die today.

I am taken out of the moment by the sound of a train passing through the station without stopping. I don't see it, but I know it is the Cleethorpes train. It always goes through before the Manchester to Sheffield train stops. That's the one I need to be on so I leave the roses, cross the footbridge, and wait on the platform with the handful of other commuters headed for Sheffield.

The sun is warm on my back even though it is still quite early in the morning. The weather has been good the past few days and I'm in shirt sleeves, although knowing the fickle nature of a British summer I've got a waterproof jacket rolled up in the bottom of my bag. I don't think I'll be needing it today though as it looks set to be a fine day.

There is a platform announcement.

'The next train on platform two will be the 07:48 Northern service, calling at Edale, Hope, Bamford, Hathersage, Grindleford, Dore, and Sheffield.'

For those unfamiliar with the place, Chinley is an unattended station. There is not much more to it than a platform and a shelter from the weather. And a footbridge. To call the shelter a waiting room would be like calling a bus shelter a waiting room. It isn't, and wishful thinking won't make it one. There is no station master, no ticket room, no nothing apart from said platform, shelter, and footbridge. There isn't even a ticket machine. There is a very nice wooden planter containing a variety of herbs and a printed sign inviting passengers to pick a few leaves, but not too many, for their own use. It's a nice touch, but I don't think I've ever seen anybody pick any. Rub the leaves and smell them, yes. Pick them, no.

A train appears from around the bend and trundles into the station. This is the local stopping service calling at all stations along the line. If you want a fast train to Sheffield you get another one, and you don't get it from Chinley. This one trundles. There is a pause while the doors open. There is always a pause.

I get in and take a seat by a window. Whatever you might say about the train, the Hope Valley line is counted in the top ten railway journeys in the country, particularly on a summer morning like this with hardly a cloud in the sky. It makes you quite glad to be alive. I shudder again as I think about what could have happened, but put it to the back of my mind. Not today.

We have hardly pulled out of the station when the conductor reaches me. He is a somewhat rotund gentleman stuffed into an ill fitting lilac Northern Rail shirt. The buttons are pulled tight across his chest and he is already looking uncomfortable. Give it a few hours while the heat of the day builds up and the hint of sweat showing under his arms are going to turn into large patches. He looks at me with eyes that say, 'Let's get this over with. I've had enough already.'

'Chinley Sheffield return please.'

'That's thirteen twenty.'

I have the exact fare ready in my hand — a crisp ten pound note, three pound coins, and a twenty pence piece. I always pay cash, always the exact change. The first few times I made the journey I paid by card, but gave up after the number of times the ticket machine gave up while going through the tunnel shortly after leaving Chinley. Cash was just easier.

Even though the windows are open and there is fresh air blowing through the carriage it is going to get ridiculously hot by the end of the day. This is the voice of experience from having made the same journey yesterday. It will be suffocating going back home, but at least tomorrow I can work from home so won't have to do the commute. That's one of the benefits of doing a job which only requires a laptop and an Internet connection. I don't even need a telephone as there is a software phone on the laptop. As long as I can get a connection I can pretty much work anywhere. At home I can open the window and put the fan on, but it won't be anywhere near as cool as the air-conditioned office where the windows won't open in Sheffield. Swings and roundabouts.

The conductor hands me my ticket. Before I can say thank you he has already moved on.

'Any more tickets from Chinley?'

I check my ticket before putting it in my wallet, then put the wallet away in my bag. As I do, the train enters the Cowburn Tunnel. I know it is called the Cowburn Tunnel as there is a sign giving its name at the entrance. I've seen it often enough while I have been staring out of the window. There is another tunnel further up the line just after Grindleford called the Totley Tunnel. It has a sign by its entrance with its name on as well. I wonder if I spend too much time staring out of train windows.

I reach inside my bag to get the book I have been reading on my commute. I open it at the bookmark and settle back to read for a while. As we pull in to each station I look up to keep track of where we are up to. Edale becomes Hope becomes Bamford and the train slowly fills. By the time it reaches Hathersage most of the seats are usually taken, but not in the summer holidays. The carriage is nowhere near as full as it usually is. Even the cyclists who typically stand near the bike racks are sitting down. Perhaps it is because there is space, perhaps it is the heat. Who knows.

I turn my attention back to my book and realise I've lost my place, so restart from the top of the page. It's funny how books have the power to draw you into different worlds where you can experience things you never thought you could or would, see places you never dreamed of seeing, meet people you wouldn't otherwise have met. These word portals can provide fresh insights, challenge accepted wisdom, ask awkward questions, and most dangerously all, get you to think for yourself. No wonder books have been banned, suppressed, and burnt by those whose authority is threatened by free thinkers.

We pull into Grindleford and more people get on. As well as commuters there are also a few walkers among their number. They are easily identifiable by their rucksacks and walking boots, but why they are headed to Sheffield at this time of the morning and not off for a ramble in Padley Gorge is their business. I know which way I'd be going given the choice. Only one more stop now before Sheffield, then a short walk from the station and I'll be in an air-conditioned room for the rest of the day.

I sit with my book open in my hand and look around the carriage. It is a mixed bunch on the train — the cyclists in their fluorescent tops and Lycra, the walkers in their outdoor gear, and the commuters with none of the above. Their tribal outfit is more varied, reflective of the different jobs they are heading to, and most are focussed on smart phone screens, isolated from the real world. It being August, the student and lecturer crowd from the University are nowhere to be seen.

I go back to my book as the train leaves the station. You can tell when you're in the tunnel without even having to look up as the soundscape changes noticeably. There is still the clack of the tracks, but it is closer, louder, and there is the noise of the train's diesel engines and the rushing of air. It is even more apparent with all the windows open as they are in summer. The electric light gives the inside of the carriage a harsh quality compared to natural daylight. It makes everything look mass produced, characterless, tired, and worn.

The lights flicker. It looks like one of the strip lights is on the blink. Then the whole carriage is plunged into darkness. It isn't just dark, it is pitch black. Tunnel black. The sounds of the train seemed to be amplified without any light. The track seems noisier, the train louder, and if I didn't know any better I'd say there was an odd smoky smell like a coal fire. The lights momentarily flicker again, but what I briefly see inside the carriage seems wrong. Something is different, but I can't put my finger on it.

One of the other passenger speaks. It is a woman's voice.

'I see they've not fixed the lights yet. The same thing happened yesterday. It's a disgrace.'

She must have been on a different train to me as the lights were working perfectly when I was on it the day before. There's one thing puzzling me about the darkness. Why isn't there any light from the mobile phones being used? A dim circle of light emerges from the dark, but it isn't the harsh blue white light from a screen but the warm yellow flame of a lit match. A young man with a neatly trimmed moustache is holding it up.

'I don't suppose anyone's got any candles?'

There are mutterings of 'sorry' and 'no'. I suppose I could get my phone out, but we've been going through the tunnel for a while now and even though it is a long one we will be out and back into daylight any time now so there's not much point.

While the match is burning down I begin to see the passengers next to him. There is a middle-aged chap to his left. It looks like he's wearing a jacket and tie. I don't remember him sitting opposite me before, but then I wasn't really paying attention and in my defence I did have my head in a book. Maybe he got on at Hathersage and I didn't notice. The jacket and tie look out of place with this weather, and anyway, who wears a tie to work these days? I thought it was 'business casual' unless you were in one of those jobs where a suit and tie was expected. Maybe he has, but that's not a suit jacket he's wearing.

Next to the middle-aged chap is a woman in her late 50s or early 60s. It is hard to say in this light. She is wearing a hat some sort. I don't remember seeing her get on either.

The man with the match blows out the flame as it has burnt down close to his fingers. Just before it goes out I can't help but notice that the overhead luggage rack has moved. It used to be all along the length of the carriage. This looked like it was above the seat opposite. That can't be right.

We are back in darkness again.

'Shall I light another one?'

'No point. We'll be out of the tunnel soon enough.' It is the woman's voice.

There is something very wrong with this. A faint light starts to seep into the carriage and then bursts into daylight. That is when I realise something is desperately wrong. I am not in the carriage I was in before. Somehow this has turned into a carriage from the olden days. It looks like a museum exhibit with its wooden panelling and heavily upholstered seats. The people sitting opposite me are dressed like they would have been a hundred years ago, and the carriage isn't an open carriage with seats down the sides and an aisle in the middle. It is a compartment with seats facing each other all the way across the carriage. There is a luggage rack above the seats and a door on either side of the compartment.

The other passengers in the compartment don't seem to have noticed anything untoward.

'What just happened?'

'The lights are on the blink. I told them about it, but they've not done anything.'

It is the woman with the hat. She looks a bit like an older version of Mary Poppins, which for some reason I find unsettling.

'I mean about the carriage.'

'What about the carriage?'

'It's different. Old.'

'Don't look no different to me.'

It is at this point I notice my clothes, or rather I notice that they have changed too. I am no longer wearing an open necked white shirt and black trousers, and sitting with a navy blue backpack on my knees. The shirt is still white and open necked, but my trousers are now brown and my backpack has transformed into what I can only describe as a large brown leather briefcase-like bag with some kind of metal hinge opening and a handle at the top. I think it is called a Gladstone bag. It has my initials embossed in gold letters on it. I leap up with a start and I am not sure whether I drop it, throw it down, or push it away, but either way I am out of my seat and it is on the floor before I realise I might just possibly have ever so slightly overreacted. The other passengers give me the kind of stare usually reserved for madmen.

'Are you all right dearie? You look like you've seen a ghost.'

'The train. Where is it going?'

'Sheffield,' she says, looking at me with concern. 'Are you on the wrong one?'

'No. Yes. Kind of. I mean it's the right one, but the wrong one.'

'You're not making any sense. You either are or you aren't.'

'In a manner of speaking I am on the wrong train.'

'You'll be best changing at Sheffield then. Stop after next so not long now.'

I pick my bag up and return to my seat next to the window. As I do so I notice the train starting to slow down. We must be getting close to the next station, Dore. Then I notice the smoke blowing down the side of the train.

'We're being pulled by a steam train,' I say out loud without realising it.

'What were you expecting?' says the match guy. 'A team of horses at the front?'

He laughs at his own joke and looks around the carriage to see if anyone else heard his quip. I ignore him and watch out of the window as we arrive at Dore.

It occurs to me that the block of flats behind the station isn't there, and that the station is, well, a station. The building is there, but instead of the blocked up windows on the platform side they have glass in them and it's not a restaurant in a converted station building, but an actual station complete with ticket office, waiting room, porter with a sack trolley, and a station master in a uniform and peaked cap. In fact everyone seems to be wearing a hat of some description. Of the small crowd waiting there I can see an assortment of cloth caps, bowler hats, boaters, trilbies — at least that's what I think they are — and that's just the men. I am no expert on the names given to different types of hat although I recognise a top hat or a baseball cap when I see one. There are no definitely top hats or baseball caps among the crowd. There is another peaked hat, but this one is khaki and there is a young soldier wearing it. He doesn't look much more than a boy.

The train stops and the door to the compartment opens. All but two of the seats in the compartment have already been taken and six people get in. I smile wryly to myself. There was overcrowding even back then. I check myself. Back when? If I am back then, whenever it is, then I am out of time. Somehow I'm in the past, but that's crazy. And yet here I am, or here I think I am. It all seems very real. Perhaps this is all some sort of dream and I will wake up soon and remember what a strange dream I had.

I am jostled back to reality by the soldier's kitbag bumping my head as he struggles to lift it onto the luggage rack. I stand to help him up with it.

'Thanks mate.'

'It's all right. Anything to help one of our boys.'

I'm not sure why I use those words. They sound like something I'd hear in an old movie about 'our brave boys'. Then I have a chill. Is this before, during, or after the First World War? Have I just been talking to someone who gets killed in the fighting at Passchendaele, Cambrai, the Somme, or one of the many other battles? Either way it will only become the First World War when the second one breaks out. Until then it will be the Great War. The war to end all wars. If only they knew. I will have to be mindful of what I say as I'm likely to come across as some sort of maniac if I start talking about what to them will sound like crazy things. And this is a time when there are insane asylums and the workhouse, and they weren't shy about throwing you in there.

I sit back down again. I've already attracted attention to myself so I'd better try to blend in while I get my bearings. Looking out of the carriage window would be the best option, but I can't help looking over at the newspaper the man sitting next to me is reading. I try to do it without making it too obvious I am reading over his shoulder. It's not the articles I am interested in, it is the date at the top of the paper. It is difficult to read because the train is on the move again and the paper is moving about. I can see it is the *Manchester Guardian*. That makes sense if the train has come from Manchester. I'm assuming it is today's copy. It takes a few surreptitious glances before I see the date — Thursday, August 10, 1911. That's over a century ago. By coincidence, today — my today — is Thursday 10th August.

What do I know about 1911? I quickly realise it is not a lot. It was before notable things like the First World War and after others, like the death of Queen Victoria. I don't know who is on the throne. It must be one of the kings, but I have no idea which one. I don't know who won the FA Cup, or even if there was an FA Cup in 1911. The money will be different too. This is pre-decimalisation so it will be pounds, shillings, and pence. Twelve pennies in a shilling, but how many shillings in a pound? And what was a guinea? A pound and a penny or a pound and a shilling? Or was it a pound and a half? I don't know. I'm really going to have to take it one step at a time.

I sit quietly for the rest of the journey looking out of the window. The usual landmarks I see coming into Sheffield aren't there. There are streets and houses and factories, but nothing modern looking. No business parks, retail outlets, supermarkets. It all looks so, well, old, and yet it looks fresh and new. Well, newish. Even really old things had to be new once. A building that has stood in the same spot for a hundred years was once pristine and new. It was once just foundations, and before that it was just a field. The same applies if it is a thousand years old. At one time, probably not all that long ago, all this would have been fields with a few farms scattered about. Welcome to the sprawl of the city.

The train slows again as we come into Sheffield station. It passes under the same bridges it does in my time, forcing the smoke from the steam engine down, and stops at the same platform. With a final squeal of brakes we come to a halt.

Someone else is already helping the soldier boy down with his kit bag, while match man has lowered the carriage window and is reaching out to open the door. I sit tight as the other passengers get off until I am the last one in the compartment. The man who had been sitting next to me has left his newspaper on the seat, so I fold it up and tuck it under my arm to read later.

I don't really know what my plan is. I had been on my way to work before all this occurred. Since I am here I might as well go and find out what has happened to my workplace.

Stepping down onto the platform I am again struck by how oddly familiar everything seems. It is busy, like it always is at this time in the morning, but everyone is dressed differently, and what is it with the hats? Everyone, and I mean everyone, is wearing a hat. Apart for me that is. It is a beautiful, warm sunny day, and I don't look too out of place in just a shirt and trousers, even though everyone else in a shirt has the collar buttoned up and is wearing a tie or a dickie bow, even in this weather. I've been used to wearing a shirt to work tieless and open necked for that long it feels odd to fasten up the top button, but if it helps me blend in I'll do it.

I walk down the platform in the same direction as the other passengers, and as I pass the locomotive which had been pulling the train I pause to take a closer look. I'm no expert on steam trains, but this one is much smaller than I'd been expecting. Then again it wasn't pulling that many carriages so I suppose it wouldn't need to be massive. It stands there hissing quietly to itself, smelling of smoke, steam, and coal, and seeming almost alive. It looks quite fetching in its deep red and black livery with details picked out in a creamy yellow trim. Think Thomas the Tank Engine, but with a better paint job.

I can't stand here looking at trains all day I've got things to do, so make my way towards the footbridge to take me over the tracks and out to the exit. I can't get over how many railway staff I pass as I am leaving, and they all seem busy doing something or other, such as checking tickets. It is at this point I realise I can't just stroll out of the station. There is the small matter of a ticket inspection at the exit. I bought a return ticket when I was on the train — my original train — but what do I do here? I stand out of the way to think. I put my ticket in my wallet, which I put in my bag. Perhaps I have a ticket if there is a wallet in this bag. Then I have a sudden thought and start patting my trouser pockets. I had mobile phones in them — one that was mine and one that was for work. It has always galled me that I've needed to carry two. I relax slightly as there is something in each pocket, but when I take them out the phones have become a pocket notebook and a pocket diary. I put them back in my pockets.

I do better when I open the Gladstone bag as there is my wallet sitting at the top of my stuff. Correction. There is a wallet sitting on top of what was approximately my stuff. My laptop appears to have turned into a thick notebook of the paper and not computer variety. My lightweight waterproof green jacket is now a light brown raincoat. I'll look more closely at my other things later. For now I need to concentrate on leaving the station. I open the wallet and sure enough there are rail tickets. There is also paper money, but not like anything I've seen before. I'll look at that later too.

I take out the tickets. They are a different size and shape to the originals, but are marked Chinley — Sheffield Midland and Sheffield

Midland — Chinley. I've never heard of Sheffield Midland before. It has always been plain Sheffield, but I'm assuming the Midland bit means here. I walk towards the ticket inspector and give him both tickets. He looks at them, clips one, then gives them both back to me. I tuck them back inside my wallet — I'd better start calling it my wallet — as I walk away.

My next surprise is that the station concourse isn't a concourse any longer. I mean it is there, but it is not the marble floored, enclosed space I was expecting with coffee shops, sandwich bar, convenience store, and Cornish pasty stand. The arches, which in my time are glazed, stand open to the weather and it is full of horse-drawn carriages, carts, several vintage cars, and a charabanc. The cars are vintage in the sense they are old looking, only they are new or look nearly new. This is so weird.

I cross the what I can't call a concourse any more and leave the station. It is very different out there as well. No gently sloping walkway away from the station with its steel wall sculpture with water running down its curved surface. No fountain at the bottom of the cascade of water on the other side making rainbows in the sunlight. I do recognise the pub on the other side of the road and make my way over to the Howard. I've never been in before and don't plan to now, but it is a good landmark to stop at and look back to what is now known as the Sheffield Midland railway station.

The station looks so familiar with its distinctive stone frontage of large, open arches. It is like looking at a photograph of somebody you have only ever known as an old person from when they were younger, and being surprised by how, well, young they looked.

I walk up the hill away from the Howard, noting the absence of the university buildings, particularly the large one with the Andrew Motion poem on the end wall. I can't remember what the poem is about now — something about leaving Sheaf Square and clouds — but there was a refrain in it.

'What if…?'

What if this started making some sort of sense? I struggle to get my bearings. I know I need to be further up the hill and somewhere over to the right. I know this route like the back of my hand I've walked it so often, but there are no landmarks to recognise. Where there should be a distinctive Novotel hotel there is a distinct lack of a Novotel. I keep walking and see the tip of the spire of the cathedral. It is the spire of the Catholic cathedral, not the Anglican one. The Anglican one also has a spire, but it is short and dumpy. This one is tall. I know roughly where I am now and soon find myself on Surrey Street, which leads to the top of Fargate. There is no sign of the Winter Gardens or the Crucible Theatre.

I'm disappointed when the pen shop I walk past on my way to work isn't there. It is a wonderful little place, quirky, and full of all sorts of treasures. I once bought an old Typhoo Tea fountain pen from there. I thought the place had been going for donkeys years, but apparently not as far back as 1911, or if it was it wasn't at that location. I head onto Leopold Street — this bit is recognisable — then Orchard Lane and Vicar Lane. This area has been extensively redeveloped. Not redeveloped. What is redeveloped backwards? Not un-modernised. Not deconstructed. I settle for 'built differently' and leave it at that. Then on to Lea Croft.

I know I wasn't expecting there to be a 1970s office block. The Three Tuns pub opposite looks much as it does today, but that's it. No office block, and, I realise, no idea what to do next. I don't have a clue what is going on. I am completely out of my depth. I can't call anyone, not with my phones having turned into a pocket notebook and diary, and even if I found a public telephone box how could I call forward to the present?

I have a flash of inspiration. What if I wrote a letter to be delivered on a specific date in the future to a specific place or person? That way I would get a message through from the past. Then I think through the rest of that thought properly. Even if they received it, so what? It isn't like they could do anything about it so I'd still be stuck here. I'm going to have to live through the First World War if I can't find a way back. That's a sobering thought.

I check my watch, which is no longer a wristwatch but a pocket watch on a long silver chain. It is just after nine. Seriously, what do I do? Going to work isn't an option. I might as well go home, but I'm pretty sure home won't be there either. As I can't stay here it makes sense to at least check it out to know for certain.

I pick up my Gladstone bag containing, for all I know, all my worldly goods and walk back to the station. This time I try to take in the detail. For one thing the roads are cobbled and although there are cars the traffic is mainly horse drawn. The streets have a certain farmyard quality to them as a result of the horse powered horse power.

There are no traffic lights, and in fact road signs of any kind seem thin on the ground. There are lots of advertising signs though, painted on the gable ends of walls and on enamel panels, colourfully drawing attention to the need for liver salts for health, washing powders for whiter than white laundry, beef tea for the dyspeptic or anyone with a weak stomach, and since when was Skegness anything other than bracing?

I continue back to the station, noticing what is no longer there because it hasn't been built yet and what is there which has since been knocked down. More has changed than has stayed the same. When I get to the Town Hall I stop on the opposite side of the road to the police box standing outside. It is the wrong colour because this one is green and white and the shape is different, but what if it was a TARDIS? What if this is a dream where I'm in Doctor Who? The policeman who emerges and pulls the door shut behind him soon disabuses me of the idea. He fixes me with a 'What are you looking at?' stare. I pretend to check my watch for the time and turn away. I don't want to attract the attention of the authorities as I don't know what I would be able to say or explain.

Back at the Sheffield Midland station I don't know what time or which platform the train will be leaving from. When I'm going home I always check the display board in the concourse in case there has been a platform alteration, which there sometimes is, but more usually it leaves from the same one. In 1911 there is no display board. Instead I see large printed timetables displayed on the wall and find the one which covers Chinley. As luck would have it, the next train is leaving in about fifteen minutes.

I show my ticket to the inspector and he lets me through.

'Platform eight,' he says.

Same platform it's usually leaves from, I think to myself.

The train is already there when I get to the platform. Some carriage doors are already open and people are getting on. The engine driver seems to be doing something to the engine, but I have no idea what. He looks exactly like an engine driver should, with blue overalls, a cap, and a red scarf tied around his neck. It must be roasting dressed like that in front of a coal fired boiler all day in this weather. But then, when the train is going and it is an open sided cab, maybe not. In the depths of winter it must get really cold.

I choose an unoccupied compartment and climb in. I can't help but notice that there are no allowances made for anyone who isn't fit and able. I have my pick of which seat to take, so choose a window seat facing the direction we will be travelling in and put my bag beside me. While I'm waiting for the train to leave I look around the compartment. If this is a dream it seems very real. The attention to detail is quite remarkable, even down to the grime on the glass in the window frame where it hasn't been cleaned right into the corner. I look for the symbol which should be somewhere saying it is safety glass, but can't see one. When was toughened glass invented? Maybe I could invent it and make my fortune. Is that how it could work here? Use my knowledge of things from the future to rake in the cash? There is only one drawback to this otherwise fantastic plan. I have no idea how you would go about making safety glass.

A whistle is blown and I hear carriage doors being slammed shut. I pull my door shut to save whoever is doing the door closing the effort. There is a plaque on the door.

'Notice. In order to aid in the prevention of consumption you are earnestly requested to abstain from the dangerous and objectionable habit of spitting.'

When was penicillin discovered? With no antibiotics even a minor infection could be fatal here. There is no NHS either. It started in 1948 so it is either private health care or nothing. This world is so different to the one I came from. It is so similar in so many ways and yet so alien. It truly is like a foreign country and things are done differently here.

Another blast on the whistle, which is quite clear with the window open, and the train departs. The day is getting hotter and we're nowhere near midday yet. The breeze will be nice and cooling. There is something about the sound of a steam locomotive pulling away I find deeply satisfying. There is a hiss and a chuff that starts slowly and gets faster as the train picks up speed. You don't get that with diesel or electric trains. They might be more efficient and more economical to run, but steam is alive. These engines have character. Passing under the first bridge just after leaving the station comes a choking reminder they also have smoke as it blows back down and into the carriage, filling it with a thick haze. I close the window, leaving a crack at the top to clear the air and not let smoke back in. Nostalgia has its place, but so does modern engineering. Electric trains may not have the same appeal, but they don't leave you choking.

While I am alone in the compartment it occurs to me to investigate what I have on my person and in my bag. I start with what I am wearing. Long sleeved white shirt, same as I had on before. I'm not taking it off to read the label, but it feels like it is all cotton. There isn't a breast pocket on this one. Trousers no longer a comfortable black poly cotton, but brown and some kind of wool mix in the fabric. Socks, brown, ankle, pair of. Formerly black, ankle, pair of. Shoes previously black brogues, now brown. In my pockets are a notebook and a diary, not the mobile phones I had before, neither of which have been written in. Unchanged is the folded white cotton handkerchief. I'll have to pick up a tie and a hat if I am really going to blend in. I quite like the idea of a fedora, but haven't seen any yet. I don't think I am a bowler hat sort of person, whatever one of those is.

Enough about hats. What is in the bag? I open it up and there is my wallet, or rather what is now my wallet. It superficially resembles my old one. Inside it are train tickets and paper banknotes, which I count. One hundred and twenty pounds sterling. I had taken some money out of an ATM a couple of days ago to cover the train fares, coffees, and lunches for the next couple of weeks. This must be a lot of money in 1911. I've no idea what the average weekly wage is, but I'd better not go flashing this much cash around in public. I notice that my bank cards have all gone, not that I could do anything with them here so it is no loss. There is no point reporting them missing so that they could be cancelled. Who would I tell and what could they do?

I dig down into the bag for the coin wallet I have, or had. This is now a leather money bag. I loosen the cord and tip the coins into my hands. There is an assortment of copper, silver, and gold. They are big and surprisingly heavy compared to today's coins. I put them back in the money bag and put it away. I don't know exactly how much is there, but it looks like quite a bit. If I need to buy anything I think it would be best to use the coins.

Also in the bag is a large case bound foolscap notebook. I think this is what my laptop has become. It too is blank. There is a fawn coloured raincoat. I check the pockets. My keys are still keys, but won't fit any lock I would need them to open. My car key is now something that looks like it opens a padlock. I put them back in the pocket.

I wonder what happened to the staff ID card I use to get into the building at work. There is something in the pocket I keep it in, but it is not a pass. It is an envelope. The typing on the front has my name on it, care of The Manager, London, City & Midland Bank, Threadneedle Street, London, England. It has already been opened so I take out the letter it contains and read it. It turns out to be a letter of recommendation from the Chief Manager of the Hong Kong and Shanghai Banking Corporation introducing me and saying that I am 'a most capable clerk' whose work was 'always done to our complete satisfaction'. All very flattering but what am I supposed to do with it?

I put it away and keep looking at the bag's contents. I had an assortment of ballpoint pens in black, blue, red, and green. What can I say? I like to use different colours. These are now an assortment of fountain pens. I will look at them more closely when I can, but not now on the train.

We stop at Dore and a few people get off. I haven't made the return journey at this time of the day before, and certainly not in 1911. It seems fairly quiet. Shortly after Dore we go through the Totley Tunnel. I sit looking at the lights in the compartment waiting for them to flicker and go out and when we emerge in the daylight on the other side being back in the present, but no such luck. They stay on the whole time. When we pull into Grindleford immediately by the tunnel exit it is still 1911 and the train is still being pulled by a steam engine. As we go down the line the familiar stations come along as expected, each one the same but different — newer, busier. The Hope Valley itself is much the same and beautiful as ever. There are still farms scattered throughout, which look like they have been there for hundreds of years. Perhaps they have. We go through Bamford, Hope, and Edale, and I feel a rising sense of anticipation the closer we get to Chinley.

As we go through the Cowburn Tunnel I try to clear my mind in preparation for what I will do when I get there. What was my car key won't work, not that I am expecting my car to be there. I don't want to think about what I will do then, but in the back of my mind I know I am going to have to.

Leaving the tunnel I know there are only a few minutes before we arrive. I make sure everything is put away in the bag and get ready to get off. When we get to Chinley it has clearly changed a lot since I have known it. It looks like a good part of the station is on land where now there are houses. As we come in I can see no sign of the car park where I had left my car. There must have been a redevelopment to have wiped all this away. Instead of a single island platform there are many more. There are station buildings and station staff all over the place. It is buzzing with activity. There is another train in the station, a long one with a large maroon locomotive at its head which loads of people are getting on. What happened for all this to become a sleepy little station with nothing there in my time?

Now that I am here I have no idea what to do next. There is a tea room so I figure I will do what the British do when there is a crisis — go and have a nice cuppa. I go to the counter and place my order. It comes the way that tea served properly should come — in a china cup and saucer. There is a time and place for builders' tea served in a mug, and this isn't it. Looking around I can't see any sign of a paper cup or a plastic lid anywhere. It looks so much more, well, civilised. Less throwaway. Less disposable.

I remember I have the newspaper that I picked up on me. Now might be a good idea to read it to get an idea of what is going on in the world. I look at the front page. I still can't get over it that it is Thursday, August 10, 1911. Leafing through the pages it would seem there is trouble brewing on the railways. Disputes are breaking out between workers and railway companies, and there has already been some unofficial action. There is talk of a national strike. In other news the heatwave, which has been going on since July, looks set to continue. I also find out that the Prime Minister is Asquith and the king is George V.

By the time I finish my cup of tea I have decided on a course of action. There is no point checking on my car as I saw from the train window it isn't there. Instead I'll go home and see what is going on there. There isn't a queue at the ticket office so I go straight up to the ticket counter. The ticket clerk is in full uniform and looks hot and bothered. He looks up from fanning himself with a timetable as I approach.

'Excuse me. How do I get to Macclesfield from here?'

'You're best going to Manchester and changing there. Great Central run a service from London Road, so you won't need to change stations.'

I've never heard of London Road or Great Central before, but no matter. As long as it gets me to Macclesfield I don't particularly care.

'Single to Macclesfield then please.'

'I can only sell you a ticket through to Manchester. You'll need to get a separate one for Macclesfield when you get there. Different company.'

'Which one was it again?'

'Great Central. We're Midland.'

'In which case I'd like a single to Manchester.'

I put enough coins to cover the cost of the ticket into the hollow in the counter. The ticket clerk counts them before sliding the ticket across.

'It leaves from platform two at twenty-three minutes past, so you've only got a short wait.'

I thank him and take the ticket. As it is such a lovely day I go and sit on a bench on the platform until it arrives. It is one of those days when there isn't a cloud in the sky, the air doesn't move, the sun is getting higher overhead, and you can feel the heat rising. I can even see the tracks shimmering in the distance.

A train whistle sounds and a locomotive comes into view. It is a magnificent sight as it hurtles towards the station, smoke belching from its chimney. It doesn't appear to be slowing down any. There is no tannoy announcement advising passengers to stand well back. Instead it sounds its whistle again, a long blast followed by two short ones, before it passes through. It is incredibly noisy, not just the sound of the engine, but the rattling and rushing of the carriages and the clack, clack, clack, clack as they go over a joint in the rails. The smoke hangs in the air and only slowly dissipates.

My train arrives a few minutes later. I find a place in an unoccupied carriage and take a seat. I spend most of the journey looking out of the window and before I know it we are in Manchester. The train pulls into a large, vaulted building — cast iron and skylights — where it terminates and I get off. The signs on the platform confirm that this is indeed Manchester London Road station.

I make my way to the ticket office and get a single to Macclesfield. The train won't be for another hour, so I figure I'll get something to eat while I'm waiting. In a large railway station in my time there is no end of fast food concessions to sell you a burger, pizza, noodles, pasty, or any number of other cheap and cheerful foods which are neither cheap nor cheerful. In 1911 there isn't a golden arch to be seen, no finger lickin' colonel, no nothing. There is another tearoom, much larger than the one at Chinley. I take a seat at a table and am soon attended to by a waitress, recognisable in standard issue maid attire — black dress, white pinafore, and white cap. She stands poised with a pencil and pad to take my order.

'I'd like a coffee please, and what have you got to eat?'

'It depends what you want. We've got lots of different cakes, sandwiches, or if you wanted something hot there is soup, crumpets, Welsh rarebit.'

'The rarebit sounds good.'

'Anything else?'

'No, just that and the coffee will be fine thanks.'

'If you change your mind let me know. I'll bring over your order when it is ready.'

While I'm waiting for it to come I look around at the other people in the tea room. I can't get over how well-dressed everyone appears. Shirts and jackets are pretty much standard for men, and there are quite a few waistcoats as well, which in this weather must be unbearable. The women wear long dresses, and everyone has a hat. I don't know how they're coping in the heat.

My food doesn't take long to arrive. The rarebit is good — two thick slices of toast covered in a grilled cheesy sauce. The bread is proper bread too — fresh, hand cut, and not out of a plastic wrapper. Although there is a small jug of milk to go with the coffee I don't pour it. I like my coffee black, and this coffee is exactly how I like it — full and rich, but without any bitterness. If this is what dining in 1911 is like I could get quite used to it.

After I finish I settle the bill with the waitress and make my way to the platform. As I am walking there I notice a WH Smith bookshop. Have they really been going that long? I suppose they must have. I'm tempted to go in to see what books they have in stock, but I'm keeping an eye on the time and don't want to miss my train as the next one isn't for another hour.

The train is already waiting for me when I get there. It is another Thomas the Tank Engine type, only this one is more rounded and has a large brass dome in the middle. It too doesn't have a face on the front of it and is a rather fetching apple green, not blue. I wonder when the Reverend W. Awdry began writing the books? Maybe I can give him the idea. The carriages are varnished teak. They are not like modern carriages where you can walk through the length of them and cross into another carriage. These have individual compartments and the seats go across the full width of the carriage. The doors are all wide open.

I check with the guard that this is the Macclesfield train.

'Yes, but I wouldn't get on as it isn't leaving yet. You're better waiting out here as it is cooler.'

By cooler I can only imagine he means less hot. The sun is directly overhead, there is no breeze, we are inside a glass roofed building not too dissimilar to a greenhouse which contains steam engines which run on boiling water powered by coal fires. This comes from someone whose only concession to the heat is to loosen his tie and undo the top button of his shirt.

A few other people turn up for the train and mill around the platform while they wait. I have taken up position on a bench and fan myself with the newspaper. It doesn't do much other than waft already stuffy air around. These people really need to get a move on and invent an air conditioning.

As it gets closer to the time to depart people get on the train. The carriage doors remain open until the last possible moment. I take a place in the last carriage at the rear of the train, figuring it will be furthest away from the engine and hence the smoke, so the window can be left open without smoke blowing in. This is a fine idea in principle, but not in practice. The window remains mostly closed for the journey and I sit in the hot, sticky compartment thinking about air at a nice, crisp temperature instead of one that would be good for growing bananas or ripening tomatoes.

It takes less than half an hour to get to Macclesfield from Manchester. When I depart the train I am struck by how much the station has changed. The bridge across the platforms is different, there are no overhead electric cables, the station buildings are different. The signal box looks like it is in more or less in the same place, but it too is different. Outside the station is a mixture of old and new. New in the sense of old that isn't around in my time, and old in the sense of new in 1911 and still there in my time. The hotel opposite the station looks more or less the same.

Right. Time to find out what has happened to my house. I turn left out of the station and set off on foot down Sunderland Street towards Park Lane. Takeaway Alley, the stretch of fast food take-out restaurants by the railway station, isn't there. Instead there are other shops in their place. Same buildings, different fronts.

I walk up Park Lane slowly, partly because I'm not in any rush to reach where I am going because I already have half an idea what I'm going to find when I get there, but also because it is also so damned hot. I don't have the energy to walk quickly. The houses along here are the same as I remember them. The only differences I can tell are the stone they are built from looks fresher and the hedges at the front are much smaller and neater. There are iron railings on some of the walls, presumably before they were sawn off for scrap as part of a war effort to come.

Park Lane is quite a long road. By the time I get to the top where it ends and Ivy Lane begins, the sinking feeling which has been getting heavier with each step has sunk with the loss of all hands. What I suspected would be the case is confirmed. The Flower Pot pub is there, but that's it. Ivy Lane is an actual lane and the place where my house should be is fields. I cross over the road and lean on the stone wall looking out to where my house will be built in around fifty years time. The fields are picturesque, but a fat lot of good picturesque is going to do me now I don't have a home.

I run through the events that have happened since I left home at seven o'clock this morning. I drove to Chinley and parked my car. I got on a train. Halfway through a tunnel the world turned into 1911. All the stuff I was carrying has turned into its 1911 equivalent, or closest approximation. My place of work has gone. My house has gone. Everything I knew or had or could rely on has gone, leaving me with my wits, the clothes I am in, and the contents of the bag I am carrying.

CHAPTER THREE

IN WHICH WE FIND THE FUTURE CONDITIONAL

I don't know what happened for me to have ended up where I am now. The 'gone back in time' hypothesis is what I assumed happened, but there might be other explanations. I might have always been in this period, gone mad, and hallucinated what I only think is my former life. Or, I have gone mad in the real present and this 1911 business is the hallucination. If it is the latter then it is a hallucination that will involve me sleeping out under the stars tonight in my hallucination. Even though in all probability it will be a warm evening I think I would prefer hallucinating the comfort of being in a proper bed. If it is the former I would still prefer the comfort of a proper bed and I will see about getting myself checked out by a doctor.

I decide to stay at the Queens Hotel opposite the railway station. I have more than enough money for a room and if I stay there tonight it will give me time to think things through and figure out what might be going on and what I can do about it.

The walk back down to the station is slow because of the heat. The sun is unrelenting and the pavement is baking. Maybe getting a hat isn't such a bad idea after all. It's not just about keeping your head warm in winter, it is also about keeping the sun off in summer. When I get to the Queens, the front door is propped open to catch what little breeze there is. The air inside is hot and stuffy and smells of stale tobacco smoke and beer. I don't intend to sit inside on a day like this. This is the sort of day for sitting somewhere outdoors in the shade with a long, cold drink and watch the world go by.

The reception desk is unattended when I go in. On the polished mahogany counter is a brass bell with a sign beside it saying 'Ring for attention'. I press it and moments later a large lady in a long black dress emerges from a room to the side.

'Good afternoon. What can I do for you?'

'I'd like a room for tonight if you've got one.'

'Do you have a reservation?'

'Sorry, no. I'm here unexpectedly.'

'Very good, sir. Do you know long you intend to be staying with us?'

'I'm not sure at the moment. Tonight for certain, maybe a day or two after that. It all depends.'

'I see, sir. That won't be a problem. We've got a few rooms that aren't taken so you should be all right.'

'Thank you. I'll let you know when my plans become clearer.'

'I just need you to sign the register.'

She opens a large leather bound volume, bookmarked at the next blank space to complete, and writes in today's date.

'Name?'

I give it to her.

'And what address is that?'

I can't give my Macclesfield address. The place hasn't been built yet and if she ask where that is I won't be able to tell her.

'Twenty-two Acacia Avenue,' I say, remembering the address from an Iron Maiden song. 'Reigate,' I add, remembering a line from a Monty Python sketch. I omit the part about the Reigate in the sketch being in Mozambique.

She writes it down without batting an eyelid. Why would she? The cultural references are way before her time.

'I just need you to sign here,' she says, turning the book round and handing me the pen.

I signed my name and hand the pen back.

'Breakfast is included with the room and starts at seven. Will you be dining with us this evening?'

'I'm not sure yet. I thought I might go for a walk first. Look around the area.'

'Very good, sir. If you change your mind the restaurant opens at six and we would be happy to see you.'

She reaches to the rack of keys on the wall behind her and takes one off.

'You're in room six. Up the stairs to the left and third door on the right.'

She hands me the key , which is attached to a large wooden fob with the number six painted onto it. There is no danger of accidentally wandering off with it. If I go out of the hotel it will be far better to leave it with reception and collect it on my return.

'Will you be wanting any help with your bags?'

'No thanks. I've only got this one.'

I hold up the Gladstone bag for her to see.

'We are travelling light, aren't we sir.'

'My journey wasn't expected.'

'So you said, sir. Well, if you need anything else just let me know.'

I go up the stairs and find my room. I unlock the door — it is strange to be doing it with an actual key rather than a plastic card that you swipe — and go in. The room is basic. There is a bed, a bedside table, a chair, a wardrobe, a chest of drawers, and a sink. There is no sign of an en-suite. I go back downstairs and ring the bell again.

'Hello again. Sorry. There doesn't seem to be a bathroom.'

'I should have said. It's at the end of the corridor you're on. The WC is the door next to it in case you're wondering.'

I wasn't wondering, but I am now. I can remember there being outside toilets. Is this the height of luxury to have one indoors, and an actual bathroom instead of a tin bath in front of the fire in the parlour?

I go back upstairs and find the WC. I may have gone back a century or more, but there are things relating to human physiology that haven't changed and what is euphemistically called a 'comfort break' is one of them. When I have finished I check the bathroom. It contains a cast iron clawfoot tub.

Comfort restored I go back to my room. The window is open, but even so the air is stifling. I sit on the edge of the bed and take my shoes off. It feels good to kick them off. I lie across the bed looking up at the ceiling.

'Now what?' I think to myself. Alone in a strange place, far from home, nobody I know, nothing to do, nowhere to go. I decided to go through my stuff again and start to lay it out on the bed.

Wallet, coin bag, raincoat, notebook, fountain pens, newspaper. I empty the pockets of the raincoat. Letter of recommendation. Keys. I then empty my trouser pockets. Pocket notebook, pocket diary, pocket watch, handkerchief. That's it. That is the sum total of everything I have. Oh, and the bag itself.

I check the wallet in case it has anything else inside it that I may have missed. Other than the train tickets and the £120 in banknotes there isn't anything else. It is the same with the coin bag when I tip that out.

I turn my attention to the bag and quickly find I had overlooked the book I had been reading. *Anansi Boys* by Neil Gaiman has transformed itself into *The History of Mr Polly* by HG Wells. I've not read *Mr Polly* before so I'm curious to know what it is about. And why that book? I have read *The War of the Worlds,* but I doubt it is anything like that. I'll read it later when I've got nothing else to do. There is no television and I don't think radio was a thing back in 1911. I check myself. There is no 'back in 1911'. This is 1911. There was cinema — Charlie Chaplin and Buster Keaton and Harold Lloyd. Will they be around? Maybe I could go and see one of their films. I've not been to a silent film at the cinema before, so it would be an experience.

First things first though. Just being practical there are things I am going to need if I'm going to be stuck here for any length of time. Off the top of my head I can think of toothbrush, toothpaste, a change of clothes, pyjamas, and a shaving kit. I very much doubt that electric razors have been invented yet.

As there is still quite a bit of the afternoon left, the room is hot, and I did say I was going to go for a walk, now is as good a time as any to get these things. I don't want to be walking around with this much cash on me so I hide the wallet on top of the wardrobe. It should be safe enough there. I put the handkerchief, pocket notebook, and coin bag back in my pockets, put my shoes back on, and leave the rest of my things on the bed as I won't be needing them just yet. I lock up the room and go down to reception.

'Can I leave this with you?' I say as I hand the room key over.

'By all means, sir.'

'There is one thing. Could you point me to somewhere that sells men's clothing, toiletries, that sort of thing?'

'There are some places on Chestergate you could try.'

'How do I get there?'

'Out of the front and turn left. Take the first left up to hell and keep going until you reach the top. Turn right on Mill Street and go along for a bit and Chestergate is on your left opposite the Town Hall. You can't miss it.'

I follow the instructions and soon find where I am looking for as it isn't far. Many of the shops have window canopies on them providing much-needed shade. I walk down the street and haven't gone far when I notice a hat shop. Looking in through the window with its small panels of glass — I haven't passed a single plate glass window — there is one that catches my eye. It looks a bit like a fedora and will do nicely.

I go in.

'Good afternoon. Could I look at one of the hats you have in your window?' I say to the shopkeeper, a stout man with receding hair.

'Certainly. Which one is it you're interested in?'

'The brown one with the brim and a crease down the middle. Here, let me point it out to you.'

He gets it down from the stand it is resting on and hands it to me. I turn it around in my hands, examining it like I know what I'm doing.

'Do you know what size you are?'

'I don't, no.'

'I think that one may be too small for you. I've got it in a larger size if it doesn't fit.'

It perches on the top of my head.

'One moment while I get the other ones.'

He disappears into the back, only to emerge a few moments later carrying three different sizes.

'Try this one.'

This is too loose and I am left peering out from under the brim.

'Way too big.'

'Some gentlemen prefer a larger size and pad the headband for wearing. Try this one for size.'

I put it on my head and it fits perfectly.

'That sits better.'

'It is a good fit. I'll take it.'

While I am paying I ask if there is a men's outfitters nearby.

'Opposite side of the road, four shops down.'

I wear the hat out of the shop feeling slightly self-conscious, but I'm not standing out quite so much. It doesn't take long for me to acquire another shirt, pair of trousers, socks and underwear, so that I'll have one to wash and one to wear. Or one to rinse out in the sink back at the hotel and leave to drip dry and one to wear to be more accurate. I have put on and am now wearing a tie. I've also got a *Gentleman's Travel Kit* containing toothbrush, tooth powder, shaving kit, comb, nose hair trimmer, tweezers, manicure and pedicure tools — everything the well groomed gentleman might need. What is more I'll be able to get all this new stuff into the Gladstone bag. I think I am now set for wherever all this takes me, which for the time being is back to the hotel.

Before I head back I go for a wander around. I still can't get over how strange it all looks — old-fashioned yet new, or newish, like someone took an old, grainy black-and-white photograph and made it into high definition, 3-D, full-colour, surround sound, and you stepped inside it. It is all so real.

After an hour or so I realise that I am more or less wandering aimlessly, but I have found a doctor's surgery and made an appointment for tomorrow. No harm in getting checked out, just in case. I have also thought of a third scenario. I have amnesia and what I thought was my former life are false memories. It is a bit more reassuring than being mad, but it is still unsettling. Maybe because I am thinking these thoughts it means I am neither insane nor an amnesiac, but if I'm not, then what am I?

It can wait until tomorrow. Meanwhile, what I'll do is keep a journal of everything that has happened since this morning so I can refer back to it if I need to.

I take a leisurely stroll back to the hotel. I've worked at quite an appetite so I think I will dine in the hotel tonight after all. I collect my room key from reception.

'Did you have a nice walk, sir?'

'Yes, thanks. I got the things I needed.'

'So I see. You're looking very dapper if you don't mind me saying.'

'Thank you,' I say, raising my new hat. 'By the way, I think I will be dining this evening.'

'The restaurant will be opening in a few minutes. Just take a table whenever you're ready. We're not very busy this evening. The boy will see to you.'

'Thanks. And can someone give me a wake-up call in the morning?'

'I can get someone to knock your room door if that's what you mean.'

Of course. I wasn't thinking. There isn't a telephone in the room. Looking more closely, there isn't even one on the reception desk. When was the telephone invented? I thought they'd have them by now. I try to cover my mistake.

'Sorry yes, that's what I meant. I, er, was travelling in America for a while and that's what they say over there.'

'I thought you'd been abroad from the way you were talking. Esme, I said to myself, that's an accent from not round here and no mistaking it. Still, we get all sorts in here, no offence, sir.'

'None taken. Now, if you'll excuse me I would like to freshen up before dinner.'

'Before you go, you didn't say what time you'd like to be woken.'

'Could you make it around seven?'

'Certainly, sir.'

I take my leave and go up to my room. I put my new shirt and trousers on a coat hanger to hang out the creases. I'll try out the shaving kit in the morning. For now I just splashed cold water on my face. Even though the water is tepid as it comes out of the tap it is still refreshing. I dry myself on the hand towel at the side of the sink. I wonder how long they have had running water. How long ago would it have been since it would have been a jug and a basin with water fetched by a bucket lowered down a well or out of a hand pump?

No matter. It is a tap now. I check myself in the mirror and look passable. Time to go down to the restaurant. I've eaten alone many times while travelling and am thinking of taking my 'new' book down with me to read. Instead I decide that I will take the large notebook and start to write my journal. I pick one of the fountain pens — an attractive gold nibbed, mottled black and tan one which makes it look like it is made out of tree bark — and go downstairs.

The dining room is empty when I get there. As nobody is around I have the pick of the tables and choose one in the corner where I can see the whole room. I open the notebook at the first page, uncap the pen, and begin to write.

Thursday 10th August 1911
The Queens Hotel, Macclesfield

I have barely started when a boy comes into the dining room from the kitchens. He looks to be about fourteen and seems startled to see me. He goes back into the kitchens and a few moments later returns with a cloth draped over his arm and comes over to my table.

'Cook is just getting organised. Can I take your order or get you a drink while you wait?'

'Do you have a menu I could look at?'

'I'd have to go in get it. Just tell me what you want and I'll let you know if we have it.'

I don't think this kid has much grasp of the concept of customer service.

'What do you usually serve?'

'All sorts of things really. Pork chops, cottage pie, sausage, gravy and mash.'

'I'll have the cottage pie please.'

'We're out of cottage pie.'

'How about the chops?'

'I'll have to check with cook.'

With that he walks away from the table and goes back inside the kitchen. It is just possible that I am not dealing with the sharpest knife in the drawer here. I can hear some sort of discussion taking place in the kitchen. He emerges holding a sheet of paper and starts reading from it.

'For starters there is soup and the mains are... '

Before he gets into his stride I jump in.

'What kind of soup is it?'

'I'll have to ask cook.'

He goes back to the kitchen, only to emerge a few moments later, take three steps, stop, look puzzled, then turn around and go back into the kitchen. There is more talking. I can't quite make out what is being said. He comes out again and over to my table.

'Vegetable.'

'Any idea which vegetables?'

I ask not because I really want to know, but because I am curious to find out what his reaction will be. His face falls.

'I'll have to ask cook.'

'Tell you what. You go and get me a drink and I'll have a word with cook myself, save you running backwards and forwards all the time.'

'What would you like?'

I keep it simple because I know if I ask for anything even slightly complicated or a little out of the ordinary it will cause problems.

'A pint of beer would be nice.'

'I'll be right back.'

He is trying to be helpful, but needs a few pointers on what that means in practice.

I leave my table and put my head round the kitchen door. It is like stepping into a scene from the downstairs bit of *Upstairs, Downstairs*, or the kitchens at *Downton Abbey* — large wooden tables, copper pans hanging up, things that would look more at home in a mediaeval torture chamber than a 'modern' kitchen, and an enormous black cast iron range for cooking on. Various pots and pans are simmering on top of it. In the middle of it all is an amply bosomed woman with bright red cheeks, wielding a cleaver. Whatever was on the chopping board in front of her is now cubes of red meat.

'Sorry to interrupt, but I thought it might be easier to ask you direct what was on the menu tonight.'

'Soup, steak and kidney pie, and in about quarter of an hour a shepherd's pie. There were some chops, but they've gone off. It's this weather. Can't keep anything fresh for long.'

'Some soup and the steak and kidney pie will be fine.'

'If you didn't want anything cooked there's some cold cuts and I could rustle up some salad and tomatoes. There's a bit of pork pie that should still be okay.'

'No, no. Don't go to any trouble. The soup and the steak and kidney pie will be just the thing.'

Even though this is more the weather for salad I've got quite an appetite, and besides, anything 'that should still be okay' sounds a bit too dodgy for my tastes. At least if it is hot it stands a chance of killing off any bugs before they can harm me.

I go back to my table and as I do the boy comes through with my pint of beer. He puts it down on a coaster and leaves.

I start to write down my thoughts in the journal. It feels a bit strange writing with a fountain pen after years of using a biro, but it soon comes back to me. I had a fountain pen years ago when I was a kid, but it had a scratchy nib and I never really got past that. The ink cartridges would run out and I'd not replace them. I had better things to spend my pocket money on. This pen feels different. The nib glides smoothly across the paper, and it is more flexible than my old pen, with a nice bit of give to it.

My bag didn't have any ink to refill the pens with, so I make a mental note to get some. I doubt ink cartridges have been invented so it will have to be a bottle of ink. Old school, or here, just school.

I haven't got far, only up to the part where I am going through the tunnel before everything changed, when the boy brings my soup out. I push the notebook aside and he sets the bowl of soup down in front of me, together with a plate of thickly sliced, crusty bread. There is a pat of butter on the side.

There is something nagging at me. Something I can't quite put my finger on. If I am in the past, how did I get here? I mean really, how would it happen? You don't just go to sleep and when you wake up it is the past. If it happened, people would have written books or letters and we'd read them and know. What would be so special about going through a tunnel that it would happen? If it didn't and it is 1911 and I've lost my memory, how come I know so much about this other world where I have apparently been living my whole life up until now? How come I know about credit cards, mobile phones, the

Internet, and television? Something isn't right.

I pick up my spoon and try the soup. It is really good. Again, it is made from fresh ingredients and tastes so much the better for it. I'll bet the cook used stock she had made herself. I could get used to soup like this. It is so much better than anything that comes out of a tin or packet.

I go back to my journal and make a few more notes in it while I'm eating, covering the events on the train. Why here? Why 1911? I am lost in thought when the boy comes to take away the empty bowl and plate. I do a quick calculation. If he is about fourteen now and it is 1911, that means he'll be seventeen when war breaks out. If he doesn't volunteer he'll be conscripted before too long. I wonder if he will make it through to 1918 and back home, and if he does, what he'll have gone through.

Before I have a chance to start writing again he brings over the main course — a large plate of steak and kidney pie, mashed potatoes, peas, and gravy. The pastry is lovely and flaky. The food smells delicious. When I get back to my time, assuming there is a my time to get back to and I figure out how to do it, I'm going to do my best not going to eat anything that comes out of a packet or tin again. It will be fresh and tasty, not processed, mass produced, and full of additives.

I don't write in my journal as I am enjoying this meal too much and want to savour every mouthful. If I could get away with licking the plate I would do, but it is not the sort of thing you do in polite company, even if I am still the only one in the dining room at the moment. I do have some standards, but it is awfully tempting.

When he comes to clear the plate, the boy says, 'Cook said to let you know she has done some spotted dick and custard if you'd like some.'

I'm already full from the soup and the steak and kidney pie, but I'm sure there is a bit of room I could squeeze it in. It is a decision that my waistline might come to regret later, but it is a risk I am prepared to take. Besides, how could anyone refuse a pudding with a double entendre for a name?

I have hardly picked up my pen when he returns with a bowl of the steaming dessert. It is a hearty pudding at the best of times and I can only get halfway through it before admitting defeat. When he comes to clear the table I ask him to tell cook that it is no reflection on her cooking, but that I'm absolutely stuffed and couldn't eat another mouthful even if you held a gun to my head and told me my life depended on it.

I take the pint I have been nursing through to the saloon bar where I can hear a piano being played. It is much busier in here and I find a table to sit at by the fireplace. It isn't lit, but it looks like it would be very snug and cosy on a cold winter's evening.

The pianist plays a few tunes I've heard before, but had long forgotten. Music hall songs from long ago.

'Here's a new one for you,' he says as he opens out a sheet of music and starts playing. 'Honey dear, when you're near, just turn out the light and then come over here, nestle close, up to my side…'

It is a few moments before I realise he is singing *Oh! You Beautiful Doll*. Is it that old a song? I decide to leave as the group standing round the piano join in a lively rendition of *Down At The Old Bull And Bush*. I am suddenly feeling very alone. I'm in a crowd, but I'm not part of the crowd. I am a long, long way from home and I want to be by myself.

I go up to my room and sit on the chair. I am still sitting there as it starts to go dark.

I get undressed and fold my clothes over the back of the chair. I didn't get pyjamas as there weren't any, or the nightshirt that was the only alternative. As it is a warm night I lie naked on top of the bed. Sleep comes quickly. I dream of blue skies and green hills and diamonds in the grass and a girl in a dress holding a bright red balloon on a silver thread. She holds it out for me to take. I hesitate. Something isn't right.

Suddenly I am wide awake and sit upright. Sweat is dripping off me and I am in fear for my life. My heart is pounding and I realise I am trembling. I go over to the window. The moon is up and there is a gentle breeze in the night. I take long, deep breaths to try and calm down. It has been a long time since I've woken up like that from a nightmare. This wasn't scary so much as chilling. I check my pocket watch. In the pale light I can see that it is half past three in the morning. I go back to bed, but I can't sleep, or don't want to sleep. I lie there with my eyes closed.

CHAPTER FOUR

IN WHICH WE FIND THE PRESENT PROGRESSIVE

Day 2. Friday 11th August 1911

I get woken by the sound of knocking on my door. I must have fallen asleep at some point, but I don't remember when.

'I'm awake, I'm awake,' I call out groggily.

The knocking stops, and I hear footsteps away from the door.

I rub the sleep from my eyes and swing my legs over the edge of the bed and sit. Even at this early hour I can tell it is going to be another hot day. I get up and run cold water into the sink, then splash it on my face to really wake me up. Time now to try out the shaving kit. It is more of a rigmarole than a quick shave with an electric razor, and no doubt it will get easier with practice, but before long I have a smooth chin again. Thankfully the safety razor has been invented. If this was back in the days of the cutthroat razor my face would have been a bloody mess by now and I would be seriously thinking about growing a beard. No wonder those Victorians had mutton chop whiskers — it means less surface area to have to look after.

I pat my face dry with a towel and look at myself in the mirror. Not too bad a job, if I do say so myself. I empty the sink and run fresh water in to rinse through yesterday's socks and underwear, leaving them to dry on the windowsill. I dress and go down for breakfast. There are already a few people down there. If I didn't know better I would say that they were business types, maybe sales reps or middle management, judging by their clothes.

I find a table to sit at and wait for the waitress to come over.

'Good morning. Would you like the full breakfast, kippers, or the kedgeree?'

I'd forgotten that kedgeree was eaten at breakfast.

'The full breakfast sounds good to me,' I reply.

'Tea or coffee?'

'Tea please.' If I'm having a full cooked breakfast then a cup of tea seems only appropriate.

She goes away and comes back shortly after with a pot of tea and a small jug of milk, which she lays on the table. A few minutes later she returns with a plate piled with fried eggs, bacon, sausages, mushrooms, tomatoes, fried bread, black pudding, and toast. There is also a slice of orange on the plate. I'm not sure if it is a garnish or to be eaten.

'What's the orange for?'

'It's traditional.'

'But why orange?'

'Scurvy,' she explains. 'I mean, to prevent it, not give it.'

'Oh,' I say, not quite sure what to make of this. In the days before vitamins I guess it makes sense.

The breakfast tastes as good as it looks. You can say what you like about 1911, but don't knock the food. So far it has been delicious. I take my time eating so that I can savour the meal properly. Having said that I do have one eye on the clock as I have an appointment I don't want to be late for — my checkup at the doctors. I don't know if it is the quantity or deliberately eating more slowly, but I can't finish all of the breakfast and admit defeat, pushing the plate away. I check my pocket watch. I need to be making a move soon, so go up to my room to collect my coin bag before heading out.

I take a leisurely stroll to the doctors. Like yesterday the heat is beginning to build. Today is going to be another hot one.

The surgery is in what from the outside looks to be just another town house on the street. The only thing that distinguishes it from the other houses is the polished brass plaque beside the open front door. It reads simply 'Dr. R. Kenworthy, MB ChB'.

I go in and am asked by the rather severe receptionist behind the desk to take a seat until my name is called. There are others already waiting, and one by one they are called through. It seems to take an age before my name comes up. There aren't any magazines or newspapers to browse, so I sit quietly minding my own business and wonder when the first *National Geographic* turns up in a waiting room.

When the receptionist does eventually call my name I go through to the doctor's room and close the door behind me. He is a white-haired old gentleman sitting at a desk against the wall. The shelf desktop organiser in front of him is crammed with papers and folders.

'I haven't seen you before, have I? What seems to be the matter?'

'I'm new here. Just visiting really, but I need a check up. Just to make sure everything is all right.'

'Hypochondriac, eh?'

'No. It's just that something strange happened to me yesterday and I need to put my mind at rest.'

He refers to a manila folder with some notes in it.

'Ah yes. You're the one who lost his memory or thinks he's travelled from the future and needs his marbles checking.'

Blunt and straight to the point. No messing about with any niceties.

'Well, more or less, yes.'

'Right. Let's get started. Take your shirt off so I can have a look at you.'

I take off my shirt while he gets his stethoscope ready. After being prodded and poked, told to cough, breathe deeply, stick my tongue out, say aah, had my eyes and ears examined, had my reflexes tested, and been prodded and poked some more I am told to get dressed again.

'There is nothing physically wrong with you,' he says. 'Overall you're in good shape.'

'That's something, but it doesn't explain how come I just seem to have popped up in 1911 without any idea what happened.'

'You haven't been hit on the head or been under a lot of stress lately, or anything like that have you?'

'Nothing like that.'

He asks me some more questions about my medical history, my family's medical history, anything that might give a clue.

'Hmmm,' he muses. 'This is getting outside of my area of expertise.'

'What do you suggest?'

'I get some rest if I were you. Can't hurt.'

'But isn't there anything else you can do?'

'You're not showing any physical symptoms, so I don't think it is physiological. I know someone who is a specialist in this sort of thing in Manchester. I'll write you a referral to him.'

'Do you have any idea when will be the earliest I can see him?'

'I've no idea what his waiting list is like, but we were at medical school together so I'll see if I can pull a few strings to get you seen sooner.'

'Thanks. That would be appreciated.'

My consultation being over, I leave the surgery having settled the bill with the receptionist. Welcome to healthcare before the NHS, where if you were poor and couldn't afford it you went without.

I am at somewhat of a loose end now I've had my check up. With nowhere to go and nothing to do it is a bit like being on vacation. I didn't exactly jet off to somewhere warm and sunny, but it is warm and sunny, the currency is different, and I'm definitely not at home. I have, to all intents and purposes, gone on holiday by mistake, to steal a line from *Withnail and I*.

I have an idea to get a copy of today's newspaper and read it in the park. Finding a newsagent isn't difficult as there is one on the corner by the surgery. It is hot and stuffy inside despite the door being open, and smells of tobacco and newsprint. It reminds me of the newsagents I worked for when I was in my early teens and had a newspaper round after school delivering the *Manchester Evening News*.

I amble down to the park and find a bench in a shady spot beneath a tree. The news is fairly mundane. There is more about the railway workers being unhappy with the way they are being treated over their wage claims. No change there then. I could have been reading that article in a newspaper in my own time. I pause to reflect on what 'my own time' means these days. This is now something open to interpretation. I'm disappointed to realise there isn't a crossword or sudoku in the paper. I'm not usually one for doing puzzles, but it would have been a pleasant way to while away some time.

It occurs to me that although this isn't exactly *Groundhog Day* – I woke up this morning and it was a different day, not the same one repeating — I could take a leaf out of Bill Murray's character, after he'd done the whole trying to seduce the girl and then trying to kill himself routines, and try to improve myself in some way. I could learn to play the piano or become fluent in a foreign language. Right now that seems too much like hard work, so instead I decide to go and look for an ice cream. I reckon this is a suitably impossible task given the lack of refrigeration, but it seems like an eminently sensible pursuit given the weather. Besides, it is lunchtime and even though I am still full from breakfast I do think I'd like something. If that something was nice and cold on a hot day like this then so much the better.

I can hardly believe my eyes when, moments after leaving the bench, I see a cart selling Granelli's ice cream in the park. The name is blazoned in colourful letters across the side. For anyone from Macclesfield the name Granelli is synonymous with ice cream. The cart is shaded by a canopy — not enough by itself to stop the ice cream from melting — and when I get right up to it I can see ice and salt packed into the wooden tubs the zinc cylinders containing the ice cream are sitting in. According to the chap pushing the cart, the ice comes from the Bosley Ice Works a few miles down the road. Who knew?

I buy a vanilla cornet and take it back to my bench to eat. Once again, the food in 1911 is really good. This is proper ice cream made with real vanilla and real cream. At this rate I'm going to have to watch my weight or the pounds will start piling on.

Even though I take my time to enjoy its rich, creamy flavour, the ice cream is gone far too soon. I toy with the idea of getting another one, but with great reluctance decide against it. Treats should be spaced far enough apart so that they remain treats. I can always have another one another day.

What to do now though? I've read the paper, seen enough of the park for one day, and don't feel inclined to go back to the hotel to get my book — which gives me an idea. I will go to the library and see if they have a copy of HG Wells' *The Time Machine*, assuming he has already written it.

I head back into the centre of town to the library. It is another of those buildings that has seemingly always been there. This though is not the 'new' new of the library in my time, but the 'old' new of the one before it moved. I go in and feel immediately at home surrounded by books.

I go up to the desk where the librarian is checking through a pile of returned books and ask in a quiet voice, 'Excuse me. Can you show me where I would find books by HG Wells?'

The librarian, a bespectacled middle-aged man with a faintly distant air to him, takes me to a bookcase filled with what I take to be contemporary authors, but it looks like I'm in the classics section. There is L Frank Baum, Hilaire Belloc, Ambrose Bierce, Algernon Blackwood, Frances Hodgson Burnett, GK Chesterton, Joseph Conrad, DH Lawrence, Gaston Leroux, and that is just A to L.

I find a copy of *The Time Machine*, which turns out to have been first published in 1895, and take it to a table to read. Looking at the dates stamped inside the front of it, it has been loaned out on a good many occasions.

I open it and start reading, and have only gone a few sentences when a character called the Psychologist is introduced. I don't remember this from the 1960s film starring Rod Taylor as the Time Traveller. Given that the doctor I saw only a few hours ago is referring me to a psychologist, even if he didn't use that exact word but talked about 'a specialist in this sort of thing,' I continue to read with interest.

'"All the wild extravagant theories!" began the Psychologist.'

I am beginning to think he might be right. When you hear galloping hooves, expect horses not zebras. Maybe the simplest explanation is the correct one after all. 1911 certainly does seem very real. Perhaps amnesia is what happened. It doesn't explain why I know so much about the future, but then if it hasn't happened yet how would anyone know it was really true and not what I had made up. What if the real future of what I thought was my time had flying cars and spaceships and colonies on other planets and they were the reality? How would I know what I had was a false memory?

I put the thought aside as doubting my own sanity is a deeply disturbing prospect.

I go back to the book and keep reading and get so absorbed in it I completely lose track of the time. I am jolted back into the real world by the librarian tapping me on the shoulder.

'I'm sorry sir, but you'll have to finish now. The library is closing.'

There is no point protesting and I close the book. I don't have any form of identification so I can't become a member and borrow it. Besides, closing time isn't the best time to join a library anyway, although it could be argued that any time is the right time to join.

He takes the book from me and walks me to the door, closing and locking it behind me. Time to go back to the hotel I suppose.

When I return I find a telegram waiting for me. Who would send me one? Nobody knows I'm here and yet it is my name on the envelope. I open it up and read it, curious to know more.

= APPOINTMENT 2 PM MONDAY 14TH = DR ANDERSON ST JOHN STREET MANCHESTER++

Well, I have to say I am impressed with the speed the doctor got a message to his old colleague and set this up. I don't know where St John Street in Manchester is, but I'll find out I'm sure.

I take a lighter meal in the dining room in the evening — eggs and gammon — and forego the soup and the dessert. Afterwards I look in on the saloon bar, which is much more packed than it was last night. There are music hall songs being banged out on the upright piano, but it looks like it is a different pianist tonight. Then it occurs to me that of course it is busy tonight as it is a Friday evening, the end of the working week and time to let off some steam. I could join in, maybe make some acquaintances, but like last night I don't feel inclined to. It's not that I want to be antisocial, I just feel kind of out of it. Disconnected. I'd rather write more of my journal or read than drink alone in the midst of strangers. I get a bottle of red wine and a glass from the bar and take them up to my room. The evening passes and with the fading light I turn in to bed.

In the early hours I wake up from the nightmare with the little girl and the red balloon. My hands are shaking and I am covered in sweat. The room is really stuffy so I get up to open the window wider to let more fresh air in, but it is already as wide as it will go. I stand looking through the window, trembling slightly. Outside it is still and quiet as the town sleeps beneath the silver moon.

CHAPTER FIVE

IN WHICH WE FIND THE PRESENT INDICATIVE

Day 3. Saturday 12th August 1911

When I wake up next morning I come to the conclusion that it is quite definitely not *Groundhog Day*. As it is the weekend and I don't have to be anywhere I treat myself to a lie in. It would have been better if it had been my own bed at home, but my present situation rules this out.

When I eventually get up I wash and dress and go down to breakfast of a boiled egg, toast and marmalade, and cup of tea. It will be enough to set me on for a while.

I head over to the library to look at a map of Manchester so I can work out where I am going on Monday. St John Street turns out to be off Deansgate and a bit of a walk from the railway station, which I realise is the Manchester Piccadilly of my time. Now that I know roughly where I will be going I feel happier, not that I was unhappy before. I am glad there are libraries and librarians. In this day of the Internet, with all the information you can think of within such easy reach you don't even have to get out of your chair, there is still the need for them. Not everything is online, and what there is isn't necessarily reliable. You still need people who know what they are doing to intermediate. Here in 1911 there is no World Wide Web, but there are libraries and they are worth their weight in gold.

I find *The Time Machine* back on the shelf and take it to a table to continue reading it from where I left off. When I get to the end I haven't found any insights in it into my condition or how I got here, but it is still a good read all the same. I return it to the shelf and think about joining the library but two thoughts strike me. I presume I would need some form of identification and I don't exactly have any, and temporarily living at a hotel probably wouldn't qualify as being a resident. Besides I won't be staying so there is no point. When I go for my appointment I may as well take a room in Manchester as there is nothing special keeping me here. Until I find out what happened to me, nowhere is really home.

On my way out of the library I see a poster pinned to a noticeboard giving details of brass band concerts in the park on Sunday afternoons. I don't have any other plans and it will be a pleasant change so I might stop by.

Meanwhile, what to do? This loafing around doing nothing but waiting is beginning to drag. I like to be busy doing something. Anything. There is no indication there will be anything other than more loafing and waiting ahead.

I leave the library and go to the park, picking up a newspaper and ice cream along the way. I need to move on from here. There is Manchester coming up, but where after that I don't know. If I'm being honest with myself I don't even know what the specialist will have to say will make any difference. If there are going to be any changes, I'm going to have to be the one to make them. I could reinvent myself here. I've got enough money to last me while I do. There is the slight matter of what to reinvent myself as, but there is no rush to decide.

Is this what relaxing and not having anything to do does? Gives you time to think? To ponder the bigger questions about what you are going to do with the rest of your life? Right here and now on a warm, sunny afternoon in the park it doesn't seem to matter. The day drags on.

Come dinnertime I am getting ready for something substantial, just not first night substantial. Rather than eat in the hotel again I look for somewhere different and find a small, family run place near to the Theatre Royal and eat there. Looking out of the window across to the theatre I can see there is construction work going on next to it. After I have finish eating I go over to see what they are doing, but the foundations and partly built walls aren't giving anything away. It does seem odd to see wooden scaffolding on a building site.

I go next door to the theatre to see what is on and get a ticket to a mixed evening's entertainment with a little bit of everything. It opens with a one act drawing-room play which can't decide if it is a comedy or drama, or at least that is how it appears to my mind. The audience seems to like it and it gets a good round of applause when it comes to an end. There is an intermission while a screen is lowered and a black-and-white silent film is shown. I can hardly believe my eyes when the title 'Macbeth' appears on the screen followed by 'William Shakespeare'. They are about to show a silent film of *Macbeth*. The lack of dialogue is going to make it interesting, and yet just a few minutes in and it all becomes apparent. There is a lot of use of titles put up between scenes to explain what is going on, and the actors are doing a lot of overly dramatic arm waving, swooning, and contorted facial expressions to get the story across. Despite how hammy it looks they actually manage to tell the story. It is Shakespeare's shortest tragedy, but even I am surprised when they managed to fit the whole thing in from start to finish in about quarter of an hour.

At the end of the film the screen is raised and behind it the set has become a music hall, which is how the rest of the performance goes. There are some variety acts, including the improbably named Nelly Noodles And Her Amazing Dancing Poodles, and a lot of singing. Most of the songs I don't know, but recognise a few classics like *Champagne Charlie, Boiled Beef And Carrots, Down At The Old Bull And Bush*, and *I'm Henery The Eighth, I Am*. I am in a good mood when I leave and go back to the hotel to sleep.

In the early hours I wake up covered in sweat with my heart racing. It is the nightmare with the little girl again. Maybe nightmare isn't the right word, but by no stretch of the imagination is it a pleasant dream. I am in a field. I'm not lost, or at least I don't think I am lost. In my hand I am holding something. I open it and there are diamonds, each one catching the light and sparkling. They must be worth a fortune. Then I see the girl. She's not old, maybe nine or ten, and it looks like she's going to a party. Her blonde hair is tied back with a blue ribbon that matches her dress. She walks towards me holding a bright red balloon on the end of a silver thread and offers it to me. I supposed to take it? Does she want the diamonds in return? I close my hand on the diamonds. A trickle of red appears between my fingers, its colour matching the balloon. A drop falls onto the grass. It is at this point I wake up. This isn't good. This has happened three nights in a row now. Every night since I arrived in this miserable place. I miss my old life, my family, my friends. I don't want to stay here. I want to go back. I want to go home.

CHAPTER SIX

IN WHICH WE FIND THE PRESENT CONTINUOUS

Day 4. Sunday 13th August 1911

I feel groggy and worn out as I rub the sleep from my eyes. The heat really got to me last night, and what with that and not sleeping well I take a while to get going. The transition from horizontal to vertical goes through several slow stages as I take my time to get up. There's no rush. It is Sunday after all.

Sitting on the edge of the bed with my socks in my hand I wonder how many times I can rinse through them before they will need a proper wash. In this weather, not many is my reckoning. Same goes for the underwear.

When I am finally dressed and ready I go downstairs for breakfast, taking a more modest version of the full cooked one — just bacon and eggs, but with a serving of mushrooms. There is the obligatory slice of orange on the side of the plate.

After I leave the hotel I am glad to have my copy of *Mr Polly* with me as I find the newsagents shut. In fact, now that I look around, all of the shops are shut. Then it sinks in that it is a Sunday and in the old days everything closed on Sunday. The only places open for business are places of worship and I steer clear of those. Until someone can explain why their particular religion is the one true one and all the others are wrong, and then apply their reasons for excluding all the others to their own and still have it hold up, I'll be in the 'come back when you can prove it' camp.

I take myself off to the park to find a shady spot to read my book. Lunch is an apple from the fruit bowl on the side at breakfast which I put in my pocket on the way out.

As the afternoon wears on I make my way over to the bandstand for

273

the concert. Chairs have been set up around it and people have already started to arrive. I find a place towards the back and continue to read. However, it is in the open sun and soon a bead of sweat begins to trickle down my neck. There aren't any chairs in the shade, so I give up and walk away from the bandstand to sit under a nearby tree. I can listen from here without being parboiled.

At length the band turns up, looking smart in matching uniforms of red jackets and black caps and gold brocade. I think it is an all male band, at least I think it is as I can see any women in it from this distance. They set up in the shade of the bandstand, whose usual purpose is to keep the rain off when the weather of a more typical British summer returns, and begin to play. The first tune is a lively one, maybe a military march or something. Whatever it is, it gets the show going and there is a good round of applause at the end of it. More tunes follow, some longer and slower, others brisk and energetic. It strikes me that this is embryonic stadium rock, albeit an early 20th-century version on a much smaller scale using very different instruments, but the principle is the same. Kick off with something buzzing to get things going, move on to the next piece to establish the tone, but a bit slower, then something to get the audience on their feet, then take it down, next one turn it up, all the while building to a grand finale. For me the tone gets completely ruined when they play *The Liberty Bell* and all I can think of is the theme music to *Monty Python's Flying Circus* and making the raspberry splat sound at the appropriate point. The crowd enjoys it and clap when it finishes. They don't notice the chap sitting a distance away under a tree laughing at his own joke and reciting lines relating to dead parrots, being a naughty boy, and someone with a speech impediment talking about his friend who ranks as high as any in Rome. Enough. This is getting far too silly...

I stay around after the concert ends as there is still a bit of my book to finish. Between the book, the concert, and walks round the park I while the day away. I eat at the hotel that night — nothing fancy just a pork chop, veg, and buttered new potatoes. I write up my journal in the bar afterwards. It is quiet in here this evening — no piano and not many people. With it being the start of the working week tomorrow and business travellers sensibly being at home, I sit by myself with a pint of beer not bothered by anyone. At one point I have to go up to my room to get a different pen as the one I am writing with runs out of ink. That's the second one to do that now. I'll have to get ink when I'm in Manchester tomorrow.

When I have finished writing I down the last of my pint and go up to bed. I put off turning in for as long as I can by rinsing through the clothes I have been wearing and hang them to dry overnight.

Eventually I accept that I can't put off going to bed any longer and lie down to go to sleep. The embrace comes swiftly and the now familiar course of events plays out again. I am in the field holding the diamonds in my hand. I notice details I didn't see before — how blue the girls eyes are; that she is wearing patent leather shoes that match the dark blue ribbon round her waist; the way she holds the silver thread of the balloon by twining it round her fingers. She offers it to me again. I look away.

I open my hand and study the diamonds. They sit in my palm in a pool of bright red liquid. I can't feel anything, but I know it is from where I have gripped them too tightly and they have cut into my hand. They glisten in the light and I am fascinated by how the blood runs off their facets. I am not ready to give the girl any of them and she scowls and pulls the balloon back.

I wake up with a start. My heart is pounding and the cotton sheet I was lying on top of it is soaked with sweat again. I feel cold in the night air, even though the room is hot and stuffy. Somebody really ought to get around to inventing air-conditioning and if not that then an electric fan wouldn't go amiss. 1911 is not the year that ventilation and climate control comes into its own.

I pull off the sheets and find a less sweated part of the bed to lie on. I am tired and soon fall asleep again. As I drift off I wonder if I can have the same dream twice in one night.

CHAPTER SEVEN

IN WHICH WE FIND THE CONDITIONAL PROGRESSIVE

Day 5. Monday 14th August 1911

Time for a change today, in more ways than one I hope. After the usual morning regime of wash, shave, and get dressed, I pack my belongings into my Gladstone bag, remembering to take down my wallet from off the top of the wardrobe, and go downstairs for breakfast.

I have already let the hotel know I'll be checking out today, so it is just a matter of getting something to eat and settling the bill before I leave. In some ways I'll be sorry to go. This has been the nearest thing to home since I washed up in 1911, but it is not my real home. My real home is just a field at the moment, but somewhere out there is the time and place I call home, and the people I know and love.

Still, it is time to move on. I have an appointment with a specialist and I'm going to stay in Manchester for a while. I'm not in any rush to get to Manchester, but there is no point hanging round Macclesfield either, so when I finish my breakfast I go back to my room to collect my things and make sure I've got everything, go down to reception and check out. I hand my room key back one last time, leave, and cross the road to the railway station to catch the next train. I haven't planned on a particular time, but at this time in the morning they run fairly regularly. I'm not waiting long.

I can't get over these noisy, smoky engines. Each time I see one I feel like I am on a heritage steam trip or on holiday in Wales taking a ride on the Ffestiniog Railway. I keep forgetting these are working machines, designed to get people and goods from one place to another quickly and cheaply. What is now vintage was once cutting-edge. There was a time when steam engines were just a dream. Before the railways were the canals, and before that the horse and cart, and before that was Shanks' pony. The canals weren't leisurely pleasure cruises either. They were working waterways carrying bulk cargo. It was a hard life. I expect in 1911 it still is.

I get in a carriage with three people already in the compartment and take a vacant seat by the window. I haven't bothered to buy a newspaper today as it seems to be the same stories over and over at the moment — how much longer will the hot weather last; how it looks like being the hottest summer on record; how badly affected the grain crop will be with the drought; the labour dispute on the railways; the King visited somewhere or opened something. However, I do like that it is serious if somewhat staid reporting. There is no D-list celebrity tittle tattle, no cult of sport spouting, no soundbite click bait headlines, no women on page three hanging out of their tops, and best of all no astrology columns. I can't take any newspaper seriously if it has an astrology column.

With nothing to read I settle back and look out of the window. It isn't long before my fellow passengers have their noses buried in newspapers and books. Give it a hundred years or so and they will swap the papers for mobile phones and become zombies checking Facebook or Instagram or whatever it is they turn their brains off for.

When I get to Manchester Piccadilly, or London Road as it is now called, or then called, I am surprised by how the area around the station has changed. I know from the short time I was here on my first day in 1911 how different the station is, but then I didn't go far beyond the platforms on the ticket office. Outside is a whole different Manchester. I know roughly where I am going and the main roads shouldn't have changed that much, even if the buildings have. Piccadilly Gardens is sort of en route so I head there first. I find it disorientating that what should be familiar, isn't. What I should recognise, I can't see. Even Piccadilly Gardens doesn't look like Piccadilly Gardens, or any sort of garden, just a wide open space. From there I walk down Market Street, then turn left onto Deansgate. It is a long road even now.

I have hardly gone any distance when I notice a stationers on the opposite side of the road so cross over. There is no waiting for traffic lights to turn red or a pedestrian crossing to let me across. It is not that busy, the horses and carts don't go that fast, and the trams soon pass. Each time I go into a shop in this period I can't get over how old-fashioned everything is. The tills, when there is a till, is a sturdy typewriter-like contraption with the amount to pay appearing out of the top with a 'cha-ching' each time an item is rung up. There aren't stickers with the price on and there isn't a barcode in sight. There aren't any plastic carrier bags. Things are wrapped with brown paper and string. There is no Sellotape. Bottles are returned for the deposit on them. I'm getting to really like it. They seem to have invented recycling before its time, but not called it that. Most of the stock seems to be either in the window or behind the counter. A bell rings as I open the door.

'Good morning, sir. How can I help you?'

'I'm after some ink for my fountain pens,' I say to the man behind the counter. He doesn't seem to be wearing a name badge. Nobody does, not in 1911.

'Certainly. We carry a wide range of colours. Did you have anything in mind?'

'Just blue or black. Nothing fancy.'

'We've got blue and black, and also a royal blue if you wanted something midway.'

'Regular black will be fine.'

'What size would you like?'

I have no idea. 'A small bottle will do.'

'We have two and three ounce bottles.'

'Two ounces will be enough,' I say. 'I don't need much.'

I have no idea how much two ounces will be. It turns out to be not unlike the bottles of ink you can still get today. I pay for it and leave the shop. I am about to walk away when I notice a young sailor looking in the shop window. Although Manchester is about forty miles inland it is still a port because of the ship canal leading in from the Mersey estuary and Irish Sea. It doesn't look like a Royal Navy uniform he is wearing, so I assume he is something to do with the Merchant Navy. It's the first time I've seen a sailor in Manchester. I'm curious to know what he's doing here.

'Have you just got in?' I say, gesturing towards his uniform.

'No. I've been here a few days now. Today is my last day before we sail again.'

'And you're spending it window shopping?'

'I'm looking for a pen to write home with, but these are all outside what I can afford. You don't know anywhere that sells them more cheaply do you?'

'Who will you be writing to?'

'Mainly my mum and my sweetheart.'

'Are you engaged to her? Your sweetheart I mean.'

'Not yet. It will take a few more trips before I have anything like enough to think about getting engaged, let alone married.'

'Where are you going?'

'Japan.'

'Whereabouts in Japan?'

'A place called Hiroshima. Nobody's ever heard of it.'

I've heard of it, but I can't tell him why.

'Have you been before?'

'Three times now. I've got a friend that I stay with when I'm there.'

'Another Brit?'

'Nope. One of the locals. Mr Sakata. He is very interested in Britain and we talk at length when I'm visiting.'

There is something about this young chap that I like and I'm struck with a fit of generosity.

'You know, I've got several pens and I don't need all of them. You can have one of mine if you like.'

'I couldn't.'

'I've got more than enough and I can spare one.'

'Are you sure? I'll give you something for it.'

'I wouldn't hear of it. Besides, you've not seen what I'm giving you yet.'

I open my bag, reach inside and pull out the pens I have.

'Take your pick,' I say holding them out.

'I don't want to take your best pen,' he says.

'Just take one. Any.'

He puts his finger on a plain black one with a gold clip and band on the cap.

'Would it be okay if I had this one?'

I give it to him. 'It will need ink. That one's out. I'd give you some, but I've only got one bottle. That was what I was in there buying.'

'I'll get a bottle myself. You've already been more than generous. Would you let me buy you a drink as a thank you?'

I check my pocket watch. By appointment is ages away.

'Sure. Why not.'

After him getting a bottle of ink for his new pen we retire a short distance to the Wellington Inn, which I immediately recognise by its distinctive half timbered frontage, even though it is in the wrong place. I vaguely remember it being moved when the Arndale Centre was developed, but that won't be for quite a while yet.

I find a table to sit at while my new companion goes to get the drinks.

'There you go,' he says putting a pint and a whisky chaser in front of me. 'Thanks for the pen.'

'Don't mention it. Just you make sure you write home when you can.'

'Try and stop me.' He takes a sip of his beer. 'So, what brings you to Manchester?'

'What makes you think I'm not already from here?'

'For starters your bag has clothes in it and your accent isn't from round here.'

'You're a regular Sherlock Holmes.'

'So I'm right, aren't I.'

'You are. I'm travelling and I have an appointment here later this afternoon.'

'Where are you travelling from?'

'That's why I have an appointment. I don't know.'

'How do you mean you don't know?'

'Just that. I think I have amnesia, but I don't know. I'm seeing a doctor to get it checked out.'

'Must be terrible losing to memory. Can you remember your name?'

'Oh yes. Name, address, everything. Just not how I came to be here.'

'But if you can remember everything how come you've got amnesia?'

'That's the rub. The things I can remember might not be real. I might have made them up. I can't be sure.'

I can tell he is working things through in his mind.

'You could always check up on what you think is real. If they are then you don't have amnesia. If they're not then…'

He hesitates.

'Then I've probably gone mad.'

'No. Not mad. That wasn't what I was going to say.'

'What were you?'

'That you've just got confused. You can't be mad if you think you might have gone mad. It's not how it works.'

'And you're an expert on this how?'

'I'm not. It just stands to sense.'

'I like your thinking.' I raise my glass to propose a toast. 'Here's to sense.'

'And all those who sail in her,' he adds.

We finish our drinks.

'Would you like another?'

'Thanks for the offer, but no. I need to keep a clear head for the doctor. Can't go and see him half cut.'

'You're probably right.'

He reaches out and shakes my hand. 'Well, thanks again for the pan.'

We go our separate ways and I make my way down Deansgate. I pass by a book shop and pick up a copy of *The Time Machine*. I know there isn't anything of interest in it to help my situation, but it will give me something to read again in the evening, and I might spot something new the second time around.

I find St John Street and Dr Anderson's practice easily enough, but don't go in as it is still quite a while until my appointment. Instead I seek out a nearby cafe and nurse a cup of tea and a cream cake until it is nearer my time. Cometh the hour, cometh the me, and I present myself to the receptionist.

'I have an appointment with Dr Anderson at two.'

The receptionist, an amply bosomed woman who looks distinctly matronly, checks her list.

'Take a seat. The doctor will see you shortly. He is with someone at the moment.'

Whoever he is, this Dr Anderson is doing all right for himself. The whole place looks like no expense has been spared, down to the deep buttoned leather Chesterfield sofas in the waiting room, the luxurious if somewhat ostentatious red and gold damask wallpaper, and the large potted palms scattered liberally around.

I'm not waiting long when a grey haired older gentleman appears from behind a panelled mahogany door. He is wearing a neatly fitting charcoal grey suit with a thick gold chain across the front, which disappears into a very fancy waistcoat. He has the appearance of an industrialist who has done very nicely, thank you very much. The sort that can afford to come to a place like this. I didn't think to ask what the appointment was going to cost me, and for the first time I worry about money. Sure I've got enough, but it is a limited resource and I don't want to go throwing it around like there is no tomorrow. As far as I know there will be a tomorrow, and one after that, and another one after that.

The industrialist turns and speaks back into the room he has just emerged from.

'Will I see you at the club later this week?'

I don't catch what is said in reply, but he waves and pulls the door to. Before he goes, he has a quiet word with the receptionist, who notes something down and then hands him a card. Another appointment I presume.

The receptionist goes through, then reappears.

'Dr Anderson will see you now.'

I go into the room. It is as richly furnished as the reception and waiting area.

'Come in and take a seat.'

The doctor, wearing a crisp white shirt and a bright yellow bowtie, gestures to a chair next to his desk. He looks around the same age as my Macclesfield doctor, someone in his early sixties at a guess. I sit down and put my bag on the floor by my side.

'So what seems to be the problem?'

'I don't how to put it. It's complicated.'

It's one thing to talk to a stranger you will not see again, but he is a doctor and my case is a little unusual to say the least. It's not that I don't know if I can trust this guy, it's more about the consequences of being open to someone with the power to have me committed to an insane asylum. At least, I think that's what he can do.

'Why don't you start at the beginning and tell me about it?'

I decide to go for broke.

'Okay. Well, last Thursday I went through a tunnel on a train and when I came out the other side I was in 1911 and I've been stuck here since then.'

'Interesting. Go on.'

That's it? He didn't even bat an eyelid.

'Well, that's sort of it. I don't know if it is really 1911 or I am imagining it. I have memories of life before now, but that is over a hundred years in the future from here. I don't know if I've gone backwards in time for real or am having some kind of breakdown.'

'What do you think?'

'I don't know. That's why I came to see you.'

He picks up a letter from his desk.

'I see from this that you've had a full physical examination. There doesn't seem to be any issues there.'

'Physically I'm fine and mentally I feel fine too. It's just that I don't fit here. It is like I've found myself in a foreign country with no idea how I got here and no idea how to get home. Can you see my problem?'

He doesn't answer straight away. I feel an awkward silence coming on so start talking again.

'There is also a girl.'

'Who is she?'

'In my dreams. I've been waking up at night with the same recurring dream. It's not exactly a nightmare, but I wake up shaking, my heart racing, and covered in sweat.'

'What happens in the dream?'

'I am in a field and there are diamonds in the grass. I'm holding some in my hand and they're covered in blood. The girl is there looking at me and she is trying to hand me a balloon.'

'Why does she have a balloon?'

'I don't know. It looks like she has been to a party.'

'What else can you tell me about the dream?'

'It seems very vivid, like I am actually there.'

'Is it in 1911 or your other time?'

'I don't know. Do you have rubber balloons in 1911?'

'Yes, we have rubber balloons in 1911.'

'Red ones?'

'Even red ones.'

'Then it could be either. That reminds me. When I got here all the future things I was carrying or wearing all turned into 1911 things.'

'Or they were 1911 things all along.'

'Exactly. You understand how I am experiencing this.'

'I think I am beginning to.'

'But what does the balloon mean?'

'What do you think it means?'

'I don't know. That it is symbolic of something?'

'Or just a balloon. Only you will know.'

'So what do I do now?'

'We'll get to that. What can you tell me about the time you think you might have left?'

'It was a complete life. I had a family and friends, a house, a car, a job, and it was a world where things in 1911 haven't been invented yet. Telephones you can carry around inside your pocket, computers that connect you to other computers wirelessly, machines that fly through the air...'

'I think you will find that we have invented the aeroplane in 1911.'

'It all seems so real, like I was actually there, but this time and place I find myself in also seems so real. I don't know what to believe or what to do. I feel very out of place.'

'You said you were on a train and went through a tunnel. When you came out the other side you found yourself in what you consider to be the past. How do you think that happened?'

'I've no idea. The lights in the carriage went out and it was pitch black. When we were back in the daylight everything had changed. The carriage, the people in the carriage, the clothes I was wearing. Everything.'

'When you say the people had changed do you mean it was the same people but in different clothes, or different people altogether?'

'I don't know. I wasn't really paying attention. I think they were different people. They weren't surprised to be there, unlike me.'

'What have you done since you arrived?'

'Not much to be perfectly honest. The first day I went to where my house was, only it hasn't been built and was just a field. The next day I went to the doctors to get checked out. I spent the weekend sitting around the park, and today I came here. Oh, and I did go to the library and read *The Time Machine* by HG Wells.'

'Had you read it before?'

'No, but I had seen the film. I don't think either has been of any use to me here.'

'I wasn't aware there had been a film of it made.'

'Not in 1911 there hasn't.'

'So what do you propose to do now?'

'I've no idea. I've got enough money to last me for a while. The exchange rate with 1911 has been very favourable, but beyond that I don't have a plan. Try and figure out how I can get home I guess.'

'How do you propose to do that?'

'No idea. Maybe I'll go and find HG Wells and ask him.'

'I'd like to consult with some of my colleagues. Yours is a most intriguing case and I'd like to get some other opinions. Would you be able to come back in a week's time?'

'If I'm still here I will. If I don't make it you can assume I made it home. I'll make an appointment on my way out, and leave a forwarding address in case you want to write to me. Of course any letter will have to go the long way round and you won't get a reply.'

'I will assume I'll see you next week.'

* * *

Finding out where HG Wells lives turns out to be surprisingly easy. A quick visit to the library and a look through *Who's Who* puts him at Spade House in Sandgate, a stone's throw away from Folkestone in Kent. Should I catch a train down now or leave first thing in the morning? I might as well go down now as there's nothing keeping me here and I'd rather be on the move than waiting around, even if I arrive there late. There's bound to be a hotel near the station and I'll be able to go and look for Wells in the morning.

I head back to the station and get a ticket for the next train down to London. The journey is unremarkable. When I finally get to Folkestone it is getting on in the evening. One of the porters gives me directions to somewhere to stay, and a short walk from the station towards the seafront finds me outside a typical British seaside hotel, where I get a room.

Folkestone seems a nice enough place, with narrow, steep, and irregular streets. You can almost imagine smugglers quietly moving contraband around in the dead of night, not that I'll be listening for them. I'm too tired and need to sleep.

'Five and twenty ponies,
    Trotting through the dark —
    Brandy for the Parson, 'Baccy for the Clerk.'
    — Rudyard Kipling

CHAPTER EIGHT

IN WHICH WE FIND THE FUTURE RELATIVE

Day 6. Tuesday 15th August 1911

It is as hot and dry in Folkestone as it has been in Macclesfield and Manchester. The main difference is that here there is a cooling sea breeze. My room looks out to sea and having the window open last night meant I got a good nights sleep, apart from the recurring dream about the diamonds and the girl. Still, I wake up in a cold fear. There is something chilling about her, but I can't work out what. I mean, it's only a little girl, but I'm becoming really scared of her. On a beautiful sunny morning like this, with the not so distant sound of waves breaking on the beach, it is hard to remember the terrors of the dark.

The walk to Sandgate from the hotel takes around half an hour at an even pace and goes along the seafront. It isn't difficult to see why Wells has chosen to live here. The views through the trees down to the beach and across to the countryside and the steep wooded hills are simply beautiful. Spade House itself isn't difficult to find. It is an imposing mansion with white roughcast walls set back from a bend in the road and overlooking the sea. I feel nervous walking up to the front entrance, which has a doorway with an arch shaped like a spade from a deck of cards.

I knock on the door and wait for an answer. I am about to knock again when it opens. The woman who opens it looks like she is a housekeeper or maid. Only now do I realise I should have thought about what I was going to say before I got here. Turning up unannounced and expecting him to see me seems unrealistic. I could kick myself for not thinking ahead and at least sending a telegram.

'Are you just going to stand there or are you going to say something?'

'Oh, sorry. I, er, well it's a long story. Is Mr Wells in?'

'You're wasting your time asking. He's not here.'

'Do you know when he'll be back? '

'No time soon.'

'Ah.'

'Ah indeed.'

'Do you mean he has gone for a walk or gone to see his publisher or something?'

'Neither. He doesn't live here any more. He moved about two years ago.'

Now that's something I wasn't expecting. He is not receiving visitors or he's busy were more along the lines of what I thought I'd get.

'Ah.'

'Ah indeed again.'

'Do you know where he lives now?'

'I don't rightly know.'

'I've had a bit of a wasted journey then.'

'Not my problem. Now if you don't mind I got things I need to be getting on with.'

She closes the door, leaving me standing on the doorstep. This has not gone at all how I would have liked. As I walk back into Folkestone I am struck with an idea. In my bag is a copy of *The History of Mr Polly*. On the title page it has the publisher's name — Thomas Nelson and Sons. London, Edinburgh, Dublin and New York. If I get back to London I'm sure I can track them down.

As I make my way to the station I half consider staying here for a few days holiday, but no. As nice a place as this is and as glorious as the weather is right now for an English seaside holiday, I want to go home — my proper, real home. Right now my only lead is HG Wells and that means finding his publisher so I can get a message to him.

It is the middle of the afternoon by the time I am back in London when I have a brainwave. Although Nelsons had published *Mr Polly*, *The Time Machine* was published by Heinemann. My first port of call needs to be a bookshop to find out who else has published his books and if possible get an address. Either that or find a library and go looking in trade directories for publishers. As it happens the first I find is a bookshop close to the station by London Bridge. There are a few books by Wells and they all have been published by different people. Finding him this way is going to get me nowhere. I need a plan B. Actually I need a plan 2. If plan B fails, as do plans C, D, and E, then I am limiting myself to twenty-six attempts. With a plan 2 I can keep going until I find one that works. So, what is plan 2? Right now I have no idea. How do you go about finding where famous authors live in early twentieth century London? Not by hanging around bookshops looking at the names of publishers that's for sure.

I have a thought. Books aren't the only thing to be published. Newspapers are as well and in London that means Fleet Street. I only have a sketchy knowledge of the geography of London so get a map of the city while I am at the bookshop. My request for a copy of the London A to Z is met with a blank look. Too early I guess.

As I cross London Bridge — the one that was later sold to the Americans and re-built in Arizona — I start to form a plan. Newspapers have reporters and if the stories are to be believed, the reporters of the old Fleet Street would be in the pub. Reporters know how to find stories and people, so if I find one and get a few drinks in, then I might be in with a chance of finding Wells.

It takes about half an hour for me to get to Fleet Street on foot. While I am passing by St Paul's Cathedral, which looks the same now as it will do in my time with its immediately recognisable dome, my legs remind me how much walking I have been doing lately by beginning to ache.

Halfway down Fleet Street I find just the place. It doesn't look much from the front — squat and dark with bullseye glass in the window. The lantern hanging over the street front is trying too hard to make it look 'Olde Worlde', but Ye Olde Cheshire Cheese turns out to be the real deal. I go down the alley at the side and enter a tangle of scattered rooms. The absence of natural daylight gives it a gloomy brooding atmosphere. Time saturates its ancient walls and sawdust covered floors.

As I thought there would be, the place is heaving with journalists. Some are propping up the various bars, some are sitting round tables, others standing, and others still are huddled in snugs, deep in private conversations. This is where the news comes from, where it pools together, where it breeds.

I spot one chap by the bar who might be a good prospect. His glass is headed towards empty, and while his tipped back hat doesn't have a press card tucked into the hat band he looks every bit like what I would expect a Fleet Street journalist to look like. More than a hint of shabby, more than a suggestion of dangerous to know. I'd better be careful. I stand beside him at the bar and order a pint of bitter. When it arrives I take a deep drink, then rest it down on the counter.

'Aaah, that's hit the spot. Nothing beats a nice long drink on a day like this.'

I don't want to make it too obvious I am trying to strike up a conversation.

'I hear you,' he says raising his glass.

'You look like you're getting a bit low with that one. Can I get you a refill?'

'Don't mind if you do.'

I order two more pints and pay for them.

'It's been a hell of a day. Totally wasted journey.'

'What were you doing?'

'I came down to interview HG Wells — you know, the author. I came down from Manchester yesterday and went to his place outside Folkestone today, only it turns out he moved two years ago. I'll have some explaining to do when I get back without a thing.'

'What paper are you with?' he asks.

'I'm not,' I answer honestly. 'I was doing a piece for a literary journal. *Northern Literary Gazette*,' I add less honestly, making up the title. I've no idea if there is such a publication.

'Never heard of it. How come you went to the wrong place?'

'My editor said it had all been arranged and told me it was at Wells' house and gave me the time to be there. I just needed to go to his house and do the interview. He didn't give me the address so I looked it up in what I guess is a now out of date book. More fool me.'

'I might be able to help you out. Get another round in.'

I order two more pints while he slips away from the bar. I am beginning to think that he has disappeared when he comes back a while later holding a torn strip of paper with writing on it.

'He lives out towards Regent's Park. The house number might be wrong so you'll have to knock on a few doors, but at least you'll be on the right street.'

'How did you get this?'

'Trade secret. It's not what you know, but who you know. Trite but true.'

'But my interview was supposed to be today.' I'm making this up as I go along, but want it to sound believable. I know there was never an interview in the first place, but he doesn't.

'So? Blag it. It's not like it would be the first time there's been a cock up over an appointment.'

'That's true. That's very true. I'll go and see him tomorrow and make out like it was the right day. Blag it, as you say.'

'That's the spirit. We wouldn't get anywhere without bending the actualité a bit to make the facts fit the story.'

'Assuming he is in, of course. He might have gone somewhere.'

'If he has you either wait or doorstep him. You might not want to hang around too long though if you're planning on getting back to Manchester anytime soon.'

'Why's that?'

'A little bird told me it's looking like there's going to be a strike on the railways in the next few days. The talks aren't going well and the unions are getting stroppy.'

'That's useful to know. Thanks for the heads up.'

We finish our drinks over small talk. When it is time to leave I shake his hand.

'Thanks again for bailing me out. I owe you one.'

'I'll hold you to that.'

I leave the pub and walk out onto Fleet Street. The combination of fresh air and three pints of beer drunk more quickly than I am used to go straight to my head and I feel distinctly woozy. I make my way back the way I had come as I remember passing a hotel on my way here and I need to get a room and lie down.

The room is small, cramped, hot, stuffy, and overpriced. I can overlook the small, cramped, and overpriced. It is the hot and stuffy I have a problem with. Having the window wide open doesn't help. Now even I am beginning to wonder how much longer this heatwave will carry on.

I do my usual routine of rinsing my shirt, socks, and underwear before turning in to bed and leaving them to dry, which in this weather means they are ready to wear again by morning. Even though I am alternating what I wear I'm not sure how much longer I can keep doing this before my clothes are going to need a proper wash. The shirts don't look quite as freshly laundered as they first did and are beginning to get a hint of greyishness to them. I don't think it is too noticeable yet, and the socks and underwear don't have to be too spotless as long as they don't smell. I don't know what is in the carbolic soap I've been using, but whatever it is seems to be doing the trick.

Although it is not late I feel exhausted so lie back on the bed. It is an

292

odd combination of soft and hard, or maybe a better way of describing it would be to say the mattress is unyielding, but thin on the saggy bedsprings. The blanket is course and prickly against my skin, so I take this off the bed and lie on crisp cotton sheets. I am so very tired — a combination of fatigue and alcohol — but I know that if I sleep I will have the dream again.

I run through my appointment with the specialist again. He said something about the dream having a meaning and being symbolic, but only I would know what it meant. Right now I have no idea. Why didn't he ask more about the girl or the diamonds? What do the diamonds represent? Wealth? But holding them in a bloodied hand? Does that mean doing unspeakable things to get rich, maybe even killing for them? Blood diamonds?

And what about the girl? I mean, who is she really? I could try talking to her in the dream. She looks like she's been to a party in that dress and balloon. Why her? I don't know what it means. I could start by asking her name and where she comes from, only, only… I don't want to. To sleep won't be perchance to dream, it will be terrifying like it has been each time I've had it. How did the rest of that quote from Shakespeare go? 'To sleep, to sleep perchance to Dream; aye, there's the rub, For in that sleep of death, what dreams may come.'

I struggle to stay awake, but it is a losing battle. As I drift off I remember other words. Were they from a song? 'Someone take these dreams away, that point me to another day.'

In the dark hours of night it happens again. I try to remember to ask her name. I move my mouth, but no words are come out. It is completely silent in the dream. I ask her, 'What is your name?' My lips move, but there are no sounds. She moves her mouth, replying to me, but I can't hear anything. Is it a long word or a short phrase? I can't tell. I ask her name again. She keeps saying the same thing, but all is silent.

Then I am wide awake again, heart palpitating, covered in cold sweat and shivering. Is this how it is going to be each night? What do I have to do to get past this? What do I have to do for the dream to go away so I can sleep through to morning? I am frightened and alone. I don't know what to do.

CHAPTER NINE

IN WHICH WE FIND THE IMPERFECT PROGRESSIVE

Day 7. Wednesday 16th August 1911

Memories of the dream fade in the light.

There is no point rushing this morning, because although I have to get across London to Regent's Park, Wells will be going about what I expect is his normal routine. Even so, it is not long after nine o'clock when I am outside the address given on the slip of paper, or, rather, opposite the address, separated by a road, wide grass verge, and an iron railing fence. The house, if it is Wells' house, is a rather fine Regency building. I am assuming Regency since it overlooks Regent's Park, but I'm no architect. It is in a terrace of cream coloured three-storey houses, if you include what seem to be rooms in the roof, each house with a balcony on the first floor looking out towards the park.

I pace up and down, checking my pocket watch every few minutes, trying to work out when would be a good time to knock on the door. Nine o'clock seems too early, and in any case it is now after nine so I would have been late. Nine thirty is plausible, but I reckon ten o'clock will be more like the time an appointment would have been made for.

Then I stop myself. I haven't actually made an appointment. That was just the line I span the journalist to get Wells' address. When I was at Sandgate I went up to Spade House at a not unreasonable hour on spec so why shouldn't I do the same here? I walk around the road and stop outside his door. It would be handy if there was a blue plaque outside that said, 'HG Wells lives here', but that will only turn up several decades after he is dead with the tense changed to 'lived here'. At the moment he is very much alive and therefore ineligible for a commemorative plaque. I knock on the black gloss painted front door and wait.

It opens and there is a sour faced maid wearing the regulation black dress with white pinafore, scowling at me.

'Excuse me. Would this be the residence of Mr Wells?'

She looks me up and down. 'He lives next door. The tradesman's entrance is round the back.'

'I'm not a tradesman.'

'Maybe you are and maybe you're not. Either way he still lives next door.'

She closes the door on me.

Okay, so Wells is next door, but which side? I knock the door again.

'Sorry. Next door this side or next door that side?' I ask, pointing up and down the road.

'That side,' she says and closes the door again.

I get the impression I may not have been all that welcome, not that it matters. This is not the house I want so she can be as sour faced as she wants. I go next door and stand outside an almost identical black gloss painted door. My stomach tightens into a knot. This is it. I knock three times on the polished brass door knocker. There is a pause which seems to last an eternity. Eventually I hear movement on the other side of the door. It opens and standing before me is the man himself. At least I think it is him. It is a man in his mid-forties with a thick moustache, but much shorter than I was expecting.

'Mr Wells?'

'Yes. What of it?'

His voice is a lot higher pitched than I was expecting, almost squeaky, and while he is smartly dressed in a shirt and tie, waistcoat and jacket, he looks somewhat dishevelled. Surely this can't be the man who wrote *The Time Machine* and *The War of the Worlds*, can it?

'I was wondering if I might have a word with you.'

'You're not selling anything, are you?' he says, eyeing the bag I am carrying suspiciously.

'No, nothing like that. I was going to ask your opinion about something.'

'I'm just on my way out, but you can walk with me if you like.'

'Where are you going?'

'Only round the park for my daily constitutional.'

We cross over the road and head towards one of the entrances. For a short guy he can walk quickly.

'So what is it you want to talk to me about?'

'I find myself in a situation that I could do with your advice on.'

'If you're after money you've come to the wrong man.'

'No, no. It's not about money. I have money. It is about time travel.'

'I've written a dozen and a half books since *The Time Machine* and I am moving away from my scientific romances. I'm sorry, but I have other interests now.'

'I think I may be from the future.'

'You seem uncertain on the point.'

'That's where I could do with your advice. How can I tell if I am really here, now, having travelled from the future, or here now having always been here and only imagining I travelled from the future?'

'There is at least a third possibility if not more, where you are still in your future, imagining you are in your past, but as I think that and you look like you're here and now in my present it is probably safe to rule that one out.'

'So this really is 1911?'

'All year. The questions are if you did travel to this year how did you get here, and if you didn't, why do you think you did?'

'That's the part I don't understand. I have a detailed memory of a life before I got here, but I don't know what happened. One minute I'm on a train in the future and the next the whole world has changed and I'm on a train in the past, which is here, now.'

'I only write stories. I have no idea how a real time machine would work.'

'But that's just it. I didn't use a time machine. I got on the train. A regular, run-of-the-mill, ordinary train on a regular, run-of-the-mill ordinary day, with regular, run-of-the-mill ordinary people. There was nothing unusual about it. No time machines, no magic portals, nothing.'

'That would suggest you have been here all along and your memory is playing tricks on you.'

'But the past, my past in what was my present, seems so real, like I lived it one day at a time like it actually happened.'

'Have you met anyone here who remember you before your train journey?'

'No. I went home, or where I think home is, or will be, but it is just a field. Everyone I have met since I've been here has been new to me.'

Wells keeps walking as we talk. We have passed a boating lake and are now strolling down a long, straight tree-lined avenue.

'I am sure in my own mind that this is the year 1911. If I pinch myself I feel pain so I am satisfied that I am here in what I regard as the present. If I were to pinch you I am fairly sure you would feel pain too, from which I conclude that you are also here in the present with me.'

I could say something, but decide to keep quiet so as not to interrupt his train of thought.

'This leaves us with the possibility that your belief to have travelled backwards in time is mistaken, or that you really have. The points against this are that you have no idea how it happened, or more to the point, no evidence that you have.'

'Which is pretty much what I said to start with.'

'But what you haven't said is what you propose to do about it.'

'Which is why I came to you. I figured that the man who wrote *The Time Machine* would have a few ideas.'

'Oh I've got several already. The first is that like it or not you are here. If I were you I would go about securing a means to support myself financially. Whether you have travelled backwards in time or have always been here you'll find yourself starving soon enough without an income. Poverty is a harsh reality to live in. Trust me, I've been there.'

'What you say makes sense, but I've enough to last me for a while until I figure all this out.'

'Which leads me to my second thought. Without a means to travel in time, you might not figure it out, so preparing for the possibility of being here indefinitely might be a good idea.'

'I've been doing my best not to think about it.'

'Now would be a good time to start.'

We walk on in silence while I think about this. I don't know what I was expecting, but my encounter with Wells isn't going how I hoped it might. I get the impression he doesn't really believe me.

'I'm pretty sure you don't have a time machine to drop me off in my own time in, but just supposing it really was possible to be transported backwards in time, how would you go about getting back if you didn't know how it had happened?'

Wells thinks about this while we walk. At last he speaks.

'If it were me, I would go back to where it happened, where it all began, and thoroughly investigate the scene. Look for anything out of the ordinary, anything unusual. I would then arrange to meet with the finest scientific minds who were open to the idea to get their thoughts. As I said, I've only written scientific romances. I didn't build the machines within them.'

'That's a really good suggestion. I've been so busy chasing after what has happened since I got here, I haven't thought about how it might have happened to begin with. I need to return to the scene of the crime, so to speak.'

'If you do find anything of interest I'd like to hear about it. You can drop me a line if you like.'

'I will do. Now, if you'll excuse me I need to catch a train before they all go on strike to get back to where it all started.'

'Of course. Don't let me hold you up.'

'Thanks for listening and not dismissing me as some sort of nutter.'

'Oh, I think you'll find we are all nutters in one way or another. Look at me, I make up fantastical stories and people believe them.'

'Just you wait until you hear what Orson Welles does with one of your stories. I won't spoil the surprise, but remember you heard it here first. If that doesn't prove I'm a time traveller then nothing will.

'A wise man proportions his belief to the evidence. David Hume, I believe.'

'It has been a pleasure to meet you, Mr Wells.'

I leave Wells to continue his walk around Regent's Park and make my way back to the railway station to catch a train north to Sheffield, or Grindleford and the Totley Tunnel to be more precise.

It takes some enquiries at the wrong railway station before I find the right railway company and the right station to take me back up the country. Part of me — the part that has never grown up — is delighted to be travelling by steam train again. Another part of me — the one that is hot and uncomfortable — understands why they were replaced by diesel and electric locomotives and hankers after air conditioning, modern carriages, and an at-seat trolley service.

Leaving from St Pancras, with its soaring red brick clock tower and imposing facade, gives my venture to go back to where it all began a suitably impressive backdrop. Before long, the reality of travelling kicks in and I begin to get bored. The train is busy and the compartment I am in is full, and as I am not by a window I spend most of the journey reading the assortment of newspapers I have bought. What I read and hear about the rail dispute doesn't sound hopeful. The talks between the railway workers and the rail companies are rapidly deteriorating. The unions have issued an ultimatum: accept direct negotiations within twenty-four hours or a national rail strike will be called.

I don't fully understand what the problem is — something about "conciliation boards" — but it would appear there has been some unofficial strike action already. The train I am on might be one of the last ones out of London, which would explain why it is so busy. I just hope I can make it to Grindleford before anything happens.

Arriving at Sheffield it is apparent the strike will be going ahead tomorrow. The newspaper hoardings are all clear on that point. The trains are still running normally for now, but not for much longer. I take the next available one out to Grindleford, making sure to get a seat by the window so that I can keep a lookout as we go through the tunnel.

I'm not really paying attention when we stop at Dore. It had all happened by the time I'd got here. Whatever happened took place in the tunnel. It is there that I am most interested. Then it occurs to me. Tomorrow there will be a train strike. A national train strike. The first one ever and no trains will be running. I will be able to walk down the Totley Tunnel without having to duck for cover every few minutes as one went past. It is almost like fate has led me to this point.

As we enter the tunnel from the Dore end I press my face to the glass of the window and shield my eyes from the light of the carriage and start counting. One Mississippi, two Mississippi... I can't see much in the feeble light from the carriages, just enough to see the tunnel wall rushing past through the smoke from the engine, but even then there are long stretches where it is simply blackness. We emerge at one hundred and fifty-eight Mississippi's, which at a rough and ready guess would make the tunnel a bit less than three miles long if we were doing sixty miles an hour through it. This is allowing for the train slowing down before we exit the tunnel. Immediately outside the tunnel the track goes under a bridge, and immediately after the bridge the train stops at Grindleford where I get off with quite a few other passengers.

I walk up the path from the station towards the road and quickly realise there isn't very much here. A few station buildings, but that's about it. The passengers who got off the train with me walk away to the right, but that way just looks like open countryside. Left doesn't look any better. Where the hell is Grindleford? I go back down to the platform and find a porter. He is busy moving wooden crates onto a cart.

'Excuse me. Is there a hotel or a pub that does lodgings anywhere nearby?'

He rests the crate he is holding down.

'There's the Commercial Hotel and the Maynard Arms in the village, or Fox House on the turnpike.'

I'm quite taken with the idea of staying somewhere on a turnpike road and a name like Fox House sounds intriguing, so decide on the Fox.

'How do I get to Fox House from here?'

'Out of the station and take a left and keep following the road. The Commercial is a lot closer though.'

'Thanks, but after being sat down since London I could do with stretching my legs.'

I walk up from the station. At the junction the road joins sharply from the left and curves around towards the right. There are some very fine looking new houses and just round the bend think I can see the Commercial. However, my mind is set on the Fox so I go left.

The walk is pleasant enough along the road, which runs through woods. The shading of the leaves does a lot to lessen the heat of the day. Through the breaks in the trees the sky overhead is an unbroken blue. How long has it been since there was any rain? I know from the newspapers it was before I got here. When it breaks there is going to be one almighty storm. There is no sign it will be happening any time soon.

Half an hour later and with no sign of the Fox I am beginning to think that maybe I have made a mistake and should have stayed at the Commercial Hotel, but decide to keep going as it can't be much further. It is. Another ten minutes puts me at the junction with what I presume is the turnpike road. A short distance away I can see a building through the trees. As I get closer I can see a sign with the words 'Fox House' on it outside what turns out to be a cluster of stone buildings. They look old even now. At a guess they were built around the time the turnpike opened. All the doors and windows are wide open and there is a bit of a breeze, so hopefully the rooms here should be comfortable.

I go inside and up to the bar. There doesn't seem to be anybody about, but there is bell on the counter. I ring it for attention.

A woman's voice calls out from the back.

'Now what you want?'

In my politest voice I reply, 'I was hoping for a room for the night.'

A ruddy faced woman comes through. She looks flustered. If I was to imagine a stereotypical farmer's wife it would be her.

'Oh, I'm sorry. I thought you was someone else. Now, what was it you were after?'

'I'm looking for a room for the night, maybe longer, if you've got one.'

'I'm sorry dear. We're full at the moment.'

Considering that I haven't seen anybody outside and it is empty inside I find it a little hard to believe.

'Are you sure? It doesn't exactly look busy and I have come a long way.'

'It don't look busy now because they're all out right now. You wait to this evening and you'll see.'

'Could you check in case there has been a cancellation? I've walked all the way up from the station and I don't want to have to walk all the way back again.'

'I don't need to check because I already know we're full.'

'Isn't there anything? I really just need a bed for the night. It doesn't have to be anything fancy. I wouldn't mind if the room had a broken tap or something else wrong with it so long as it had a bed.'

'Well, I suppose there is one room. It's small and it's not made up and the window sticks.'

'It sounds perfect. I'll take it'

'It'll be at least an hour before I can get round to making it up. I've got a lot on and we're short staffed at the minute.'

'That's okay. I'm in no rush. I can wait outside with a beer while it is got ready.'

She pours me a pint, which I take out with me. There are a few benches scattered around. I choose one against the wall in the shade, looking out towards the road. It is one of those rare, perfect moments sitting by myself with a cold drink on a sunny day, and for a moment I forget I have any cares in the world. The breeze gently ripples the leaves in the trees, but other than this it is still and tranquil. It could be any year —1911 or 2011 or 1811 — for all I care. I run my finger down the condensation on the outside of the glass. How do they get it cold without refrigeration? I doubt it is ice from the Bosley Ice Works. Cold cellars I suppose. This looks the sort of place that would have cellars buried under its heavy stonework. If there are cellars there will also be lamps. I'll have to ask if they will let me borrow one for when I go exploring the tunnel. I don't fancy stumbling around in the dark. If they don't have a lamp I'll have to find some candles and something to put them in to keep them from blowing out. Treasure Trap tip.

Other than having something to see my way by, I don't think I'm going to need anything else to go exploring. I can leave my bag and things here, and as long as there isn't a last-minute deal the rail strike will go ahead, which means no trains to contend with. This is almost going too easily.

I take my time finishing my pint. By the time I am on my second there are people starting to arrive. I watch the various comings and goings while I write up my journal. I'm glad I thought to keep one as rereading it shows I am making some progress towards figuring out not so much what happened, but adjusting to how things are now. I've not sat back and let things happen to me. I've been the one getting up and doing things.

A lot longer than an hour since we first spoke, the landlady comes out to find me to lets me know my room is ready. I follow her inside with my bag, up some narrow stairs, and along a corridor. My room is right at the end round a corner. She opens the door for me. She wasn't kidding when she said it was small. The room is scarcely big enough to hold a single bed and no other furniture, but it will serve the purpose. Even if the window does stick the sun isn't on it and the room feels comfortable temperature-wise.

'This will do fine.'

'Like I said, it's small, but if it's just a bed for the night you're after it will have to do. It's either that or the barn.'

'Honestly, it will be fine.'

'If there's anything else you need you've only got to ask.'

'Actually there is something. Do you have a lamp? I was going to be asking anyway, but I notice there isn't a light in the room.'

'I'll fetch you one later. Is there anything else?'

'Not right now. I'll be down in a bit for some dinner.'

She leaves me with the room key, which I rest on the bed as there isn't a bedside table. This is one very snug room. When I go to open the sticking window it is immediately obvious why it is sticking. It has been painted shut. There is a right way and a wrong way to paint a sash window, and whoever painted this one did it the wrong way. It is sealed shut and no amount of pulling it or pressing against the window is enough to crack it open. I just hope that the room stays like this, otherwise it is going to be an unbearable nights sleep if it gets warm, even on top of the covers.

With nothing else to do in the room I go back downstairs into the pub. There are a few people inside, but most are sitting outside. My spot in the shade has been taken, so I find another one and sit and reread *The Time Machine* again, this time with a glass of ginger beer for company. I don't know why I keep going back to it as I know the story well enough now. It's not as if I am expecting to find any clues as to my situation in it. I do regret not thinking to get HG Wells to sign it for me, but the moment has passed and I'm not going back to London just for an autograph.

When I start to feel hungry I go inside to order something to eat. The menu is limited, but I quite like the look of the steak and mushroom pie with flaky pastry that one of the other guests is tucking into.

While I am waiting for it to be brought out to me I go back to my book. I want to be exploring the tunnel now rather than killing time until tomorrow, but without knowing when the strike will actually take effect it is probably best I leave the tunnel to tomorrow.

After a while my food comes out. It tastes as good as it looks. I nurse another pint of beer, bitter not ginger, through the rest of the evening before turning in.

It isn't fully dark when I go to my room, but dusk is falling and it is getting harder to read in this light. As I'm going through the bar the landlady calls out to me.

'I've got a lamp for your room.'

On the end of the bar is an oil lamp with an ornamental glass cover, not exactly designed for exploring railway tunnels, but it will do if I am careful with it.

'I've filled it, but not had a chance to take it up.'

'That's okay. Do you have any matches to light it?'

She produces a box from her apron. I thank her and take it upstairs with me. The lamp gives a warm glow when lit. It isn't exactly a bright light, but it will do. I get undressed and realise I don't have anywhere to rinse through my things this time, so fold them and put them at the bottom of my bag. After lying on the bed I blow out the lamp and close my eyes. I can hear the sounds from the pub filtering up, but it isn't intrusive. I drift off into sleep. I don't know how much time passes before I have the dream again. This time it seems different to begin with as I am falling backwards. My arms and legs flail. I am looking up into a clear blue sky. Then my back slams into the ground and knocks all the wind out of me. For the first time I feel excruciating pain in this dream. Tears well in my eyes. I've got to get up. I roll onto my side, then push myself up onto my hands and knees. I am trembling. The grass is scattered with diamonds again, sharp crystals glittering in the green. I don't want to look up. She will be there, with her dress and her balloon, and she is. Her eyes bore into me, compelling me to look up.

'What do you want?'

This time the words come out, but they are hoarse and stick in my throat. It is the first time I have heard sound in this dream.

She holds out her hand.

'You want the diamonds? Here, take the diamonds.'

I reach into the grass and start to pick some up for her. There is something at the back of my mind I'm trying to remember. Something I was supposed to do. I stop and try to think. There are diamonds in my hand, fragments of crystals tinged red with... with...

There was a word. The red means something. Rose red. Ruby red. There is a connection with... a name. I am supposed to ask her name.

She puts down her hand.

It is the early hours of the night and I am wide awake. Sweat does not drip off me, my heart isn't racing. Despite it being a warm night in a room whose only window does not open, I feel deathly cold. I climb shivering under the sheets and pull the blanket over the top of me.

CHAPTER TEN

IN WHICH WE FIND THE PAST DISCONTINUOUS

Day 8. Thursday 17th August 1911

Sunlight shining through a crack in the curtains wakes me. I lean over the side of the bed and fumble for the pocket watch on the floor. My fingers eventually find it and I check the time. Almost half past six. I lie quietly while I run through the dream from last night in my mind. Despite waking up chilled to the bone from it, I feel a normal temperature now. I don't have any aches or pains, and while it was another interrupted nights sleep I don't feel fatigued.

The dream is unsettling. I mean, the dream has always been unsettling as long as I have been having it. The difference this time is how real the pain from falling on my back felt and the rasp in my throat as I tried to talk. If the dream is changing, how will it change tonight? It would be nice to have one night's sleep without it happening, but that seems too much to hope for.

I get dressed and go down for breakfast. It is nothing fancy — bacon, eggs, sausage, and a slice of toast — which I eat in the bar with the other early risers. More toast arrives with another cup of tea, which I have with orange marmalade. The jar has a handwritten label on it which says, 'Seville Orange Marmalade June 1910'.

With breakfast over I go back to my room to get the lamp and matches. I can't think of anything else I need to take with me, other than something to cover up the lamp. Yesterday's newspapers come in handy for that. I decide to take my jacket with me. Even though today looks like it is going to be another hot one, I expect the tunnel will be cool and it is a long one and I don't know how long I will be exploring it, given that I have no idea what I am looking for.

I leave my room key behind the bar as I don't need to have it on me and leave the pub. I follow the road back the way I came yesterday down to the railway station.

The station buildings are quiet and shut up. The time is not quite half past eight. There should be people about, but it is strangely silent. I'd have thought if it was a strike there would be a burning brazier with people stood around it on a picket line. Here it looks like they have simply locked everything up and gone home. Mind you, I don't think I'd want to be standing beside a roaring fire on a day like today whether I was on strike or not.

I walk down towards the platform where the trains to Sheffield stop. I had wondered if the gate would be chained up, but it is open. There aren't any passengers about on either platform. I sit on a bench and wait. When I check my watch again at quarter to nine there have been no trains. It looks like the strike is happening, which is ideal for what I need to do.

I stroll down to the end of the platform away from the tunnel and look down the line. There are no signs of any trains. Going all the way to the other end of the platform there are still no trains. I'll give it until nine o'clock before I make my move to be on the safe side. On the hour I leave the platform and walk back up to the bridge over the line. The tunnel, with the stone facing to its entrance, is right in front of me. I listen carefully and the only things I can hear are birds in the distance. I check to see if there is anybody about, and satisfied I am alone and not being watched I climb over the stone wall on the bridge and pick my way down the embankment towards the track and the tunnel.

I go a short way inside the tunnel to get out of sight, and while there is still light I take out the lamp and light it, leaving the newspaper I had wrapped it in folded and weighted down under a few pieces of ballast to stop it blowing away. I'll need it later to smuggle the lamp back into the pub. The lamp casts a circle of warm yellow light in the tunnel. I walk slowly at the side of the track for trains coming from Sheffield. This way I will see them coming. If I walk on the side for trains to Sheffield they will come up behind me. This is a precaution. There shouldn't be any with the strike.

As I walk I can see the stone blocks that make up the tunnel walls. It must have been quite a feat of engineering to have built it. How long did it take and how many people were involved? It is strangely silent in the tunnel, except for when I catch a piece of ballast with my foot and send it skittering along the track. The echoes die away. The darkness hangs heavy in here. I turn to look back to see how far I have come. The entrance is a dot of light in the distance. Looking at my watch it has only been twenty minutes. Am I a quarter or a third of the way through? It is hard to judge distances in here. So far I have seen nothing out of the ordinary.

I keep walking. In the distance ahead I notice a faint patch of light. As I get nearer I can see it is a ventilation shaft. With all the trains that run through the tunnel belching smoke and steam it is obvious why they are needed. I take a few moments to look around it for clues, but it is apparent there is nothing out of the ordinary here so I press on. Now there's a thought. How long the lamp will last? It was full when I came in, but I have no idea how long it will stay lit. If it does run out I can feel for the tunnel wall and use that as a guide to get out.

I keep walking.

I have been going for a while now and think I can make out another faint patch of light in the distance. As I get closer I can see that it is another ventilation shaft, but this one isn't the same as the one I saw earlier. That one was directly above the tunnel. This one seems to be coming in at the side. I quicken my pace and soon see that the light is coming from a cleft in the side of the tunnel. As I stand inside it I can make out a huge cavern. There is a ventilation shaft in the ceiling and a column of light in the centre. Even with this light it is hard to make out the walls of the cavern. It is enormous. Also streaming from the ventilation shaft is a steady trickle of water. It pools below the shaft. If this is how it is after a month or two of drought on the surface, what must it be like after heavy rain?

I go inside the chamber and walk around the edge. This couldn't have been part of the original tunnel design. I mean, it doesn't seem to serve a purpose. It is just here, as if they hit a natural cavern and figured that since it was here they might as well put another ventilation shaft in. I go towards the pool below the shaft. Water drips constantly into it, sending ripples across the surface. I can see there is something else in the pool in the centre, a rock or something. It is hard to see. I walk around the edge to get a better view. It looks squarish, black, and I want to get a closer look at it.

Since I haven't come equipped to go paddling, the easiest thing to do is to strip off so that my clothes and shoes don't get wet, then go in and drag whatever it is out. The air is cold to my naked skin, but not as cold as the water I step into. It isn't as deep as I thought it might be. As I get closer I can see that whatever it is, it isn't a rock. If anything it looks like whatever it is, it is wrapped in a black bin liner.

It isn't that heavy, and lift it out of the water and carry it across to a dry spot by the lamp. It is wrapped in a bin liner. There weren't bin liners in 1911, were there? I mean, this is plastic. Inside I find a plastic crate with a lid. This is so not a 1911 artefact.

When I take off the lid I have to do a double take. Inside the crate is the bag I was carrying when I went to work. The one that changed into the Gladstone bag currently residing in a cramped room with a sticking window at Fox House. Underneath the bag are my clothes and my coat. The same ones I was wearing when I came back to the past. This doesn't make any sense. It looks like all my stuff is here, but why? I get dressed back into my 1911 clothes and leave the cavern. It isn't easy carrying the crate and the lamp at the same time by myself, but manage it well enough. I want to get this lot back to my room and go through it.

I start walking back down the track, this time facing any trains that would be headed to Sheffield. It is hard keeping track of time in the tunnel. My watch says it has been an hour and a half, but it seems like much longer.The crate gets heavier the longer I carry it. Then it dawns on me. I am carrying my backpack which contains my laptop inside the crate. It gets a whole lot easier when I sling the backpack over my shoulder.

The lamp is holding out well enough, and I can see the tunnel entrance in the distance. Not that far to go now. I press on, but go only a few steps when I hear the distinctive chuff—chuff—chuff of a locomotive. The tunnel entrance has dimmed and there is a light headed towards me. I hastily cross over the track to get to the other side of the tunnel and lie down against the tunnel wall. I fumble as I try to open the lamp to blow out the flame. Somehow I get it open and extinguish it. The train is nearly upon me as I cover my head with my arms and lie face down until it has passed. I've never been inside a tunnel with a steam train going through before. Well, I have, but I was inside one of the carriages being pulled so it doesn't count. The ground shakes and the noise deafens me as it thunders by, but the worst is the choking smoke that burns my throat. When it is still again I push myself up in the darkness and cough and splutter until I can breathe again.

That definitely wasn't a passenger train — there were no lights from any carriages. It must have been a freight train of some kind, but what it was doing running when there is supposed to be a strike on is anyone's guess.

I reach inside my pockets for the box of matches, and feeling to make sure I have got the box the right way up, take out a match and strike it. It sparks into flame and I relight the lamp. Time I wasn't here. I pick up my backpack and the crate and cross over to the oncoming side of the track. I walk with a renewed sense of purpose now as I don't want to have to go through that again. The tunnel entrance seems to take an aeon before it gets nearer, but soon enough I am out of the tunnel and climb part way up the embankment. I sit for a moment with the warmth of the sun on my face.

When I have rested long enough I put my backpack over my shoulder and pick up the crate again. It is easier to carry now I don't need the lamp, which I put inside the crate. It is another three quarters of an hour before I am back at the Fox and in my room. I put the crate and the backpack on the bed and start to unpack them. The crate has my clothes from when I disappeared from my present — shirt, trousers, shoes, socks, and handkerchief. Belt, work mobile phone, personal mobile phone, coat, wallet, staff ID card, house keys, car keys. It's all there. I try to turn on both the phones, but nothing happens. They have been on for over a week and the batteries are dead.

My wallet has the money I had when I left with it, and the train tickets, receipts, and bank cards. Fat lot of good these will do me here. I take my laptop out of my backpack and turn it on. The screen comes to life with my login prompt. I type in my password and I'm in. Then it occurs to me. There is no Wi-Fi. Not just that, but even if there was, there is no Internet. I can't use anything here, except for the clothes and the bag and the pens. Everything else is outside of its technological ecosystem. The laptop has nothing to connect to. Same for the phones. The keys don't have locks to fit; the bank cards are simply flat rectangles with writing on. Even if their technology was around they wouldn't associate with any account, even if the bank was around in 1911.

I sit on the bed beside my collection of assorted twenty-first century useless junk, not that it is broken or obsolete, it is simply too far ahead of its time for where I am now to be useful. I slump off the bed into the narrow gap by the wall and sit on the floor. This is not going the way I wanted it to. I still have no idea how I got here, and even less of how my old stuff was neatly boxed up and hidden in the same tunnel I fell through time in. I mean, what is the point? Is it some kind of sick practical joke or an initiation test of some sort? Whatever it is, it looks like I am going to be stuck here for a while longer.

I need another plan, another idea. Wells said go back to where it all began and I have. I found the crate with all my things in it, but not how I got here. Maybe there is another cavern further up the tunnel with a time machine in it. I didn't go all the way through the tunnel to the other end. I came back when I found the crate. Perhaps there is more to be found. I will need to check it out, but if I am being honest with myself I think it is a false hope.

I get up from the floor to stretch and notice that there is something else in the bottom of the crate I hadn't seen before. It is a white envelope. I don't remember having an envelope on me when all this happened.

I pick it up and turn it over. On the front it has the words, 'Not to be opened until Death'. It looks like my handwriting, but I don't remember writing it. I would remember something like that. The envelope is sealed. Should I open it? I mean, it is my handwriting and it is in with my things.

I hesitate. It doesn't say whose death. Is it really mine to open? After everything that has happened I decide it is. There might be a message inside which will help me, or at least give a bit of information which might be of use. I slide my finger under the flap at the back and open it. It comes away without tearing. Inside is a card. There is a picture of a red balloon on the front of it. I open the card. The printed text reads, 'You are invited to the after-wake party for [blank] at [blank]. Wear something cheerful and come and celebrate their life.' There is a smaller picture of a red balloon at the top.

My hand trembles and the card falls to the floor. I feel strange, lightheaded like I got up too quickly. The room slides sideways as I slide down the wall.

CHAPTER ELEVEN

IN WHICH WE FIND THE TENSE INDETERMINATE

Day 9? Friday 18th August 1911

When I come to I am on the floor. I ache all over and struggle to stand up. I end up sitting on the edge of the bed. My head is pounding. I don't know what the time is, but it is daylight. When I check my pocket watch I find that it has stopped at two twenty-three.

I am still in my room at the Fox and all of my things are still on the bed. I sit quietly and try to remember what happened. I must have blacked out and banged my head. Being unconscious on the floor for I don't know how long would explain why I feel so stiff and achy. I stand up, unsteadily at first, and stretch to ease my joints. I can go downstairs to the pub and find out what time it is. There is a clock in the bar which I can reset my watch by.

It is odd how quiet it seems.

I go over to the window to look outside. A heavy fog or a mist has fallen. Maybe the run of hot weather is finally coming to an end. I can't see very far, basically just the immediate area outside before the world fades into a soft greyness.

I go down to the bar. There isn't anybody around. I suppose that's not unexpected. It was quiet when I first got here. Still, this seems unusually quiet. I go over to the grandfather clock and reset my watch. Nine twelve. Funny. I'd have thought there would still be some people around having breakfast at this time. If it was evening the bar would be busy. I ring the bell on the bar for attention.

Nothing.

I ring it again. Still nothing. I call out.

'Hello. Is anybody here?'

There is no reply. I listen carefully and can't hear anything apart from the grandfather clock marking out time to itself with its ponderous tick tock tick tock.

I go around the bar and into the kitchens. There is nobody here either. Looking more closely I can't see anything being prepared, cooked, or cleared away. It is as if everybody had finished whatever it was they were doing, put everything away neatly, and left.

I call out again.

'Hello? Can anyone hear me?'

There is no reply.

Despite my headache I feel hungry. The last thing I had to eat was breakfast which was what, yesterday morning? In the kitchen I find a cold chicken and ham pie which has had some slices cut from it already. I find a plate and a knife and cut another slice. I also find a crate of lemonade bottles, the ones with a marble in the neck, and take one of these. It is an odd breakfast, but then so far it has been an odd day and it is still only morning.

With breakfast over I leave some coins on the plate to cover the cost of what I have eaten. I still haven't seen or heard anyone and I am getting concerned. I walk around the pub looking, but there still isn't a soul to be seen. Where has everyone gone?

I go outside. Maybe someone is here. The fog has got heavier. I can hardly see my hand in front of my face.

'Hello,' I call out. 'Anyone?'

My voice doesn't carry far in the mist. Looking around I can hardly see anything at all. I can just about make out the pub behind me, but other than that everything else fades out really quickly. This is a real pea-souper.

'Is there anybody here? Hello?'

There is no reply. It is eerily silent. The fog seems to be smothering all sound. There's got to be someone around. People don't just disappear en masse. I go back inside, calling out for anyone. Still nothing. Repeatedly ringing the bell in the bar does nothing either. Where the hell has everyone got to?

I go to my room to get my jacket and hat. I'm going to need them in this. Going outside again the fog has got thicker still. I cross the road in front of the pub to go down to the station, and if there is nobody there I'll walk down into Grindleford itself. I have only gone a few steps when I notice that something is not right. The trees on the opposite side of the road which should now be visible, aren't. I take a few more steps. The other side of the road doesn't seem to be there. It just fades out into nothingness. There should be a grass verge and then a stone wall and then some trees. There isn't even a grass verge. I take several steps backwards onto the road. It is still here, and turning around I can just about see the pub. Something weird is going on. I cross the road again, pacing out how far I think the other side will be, but it doesn't end. The road simply fades away. There was no grass verge, no wall, no trees. It is like there is nothing beyond where I am and the pub. This is not a dream, but it isn't reality either. If I haven't time travelled, what have I done and where am I now?

Then I see her. Standing in front of me. The little girl with blonde hair and the blue party dress, holding a red balloon on a silver thread.

'Would you like this now?' she says, holding the balloon out to me.

'I don't understand.'

'Are you ready to take it?'

'Take the balloon? What do I want a balloon for?'

This isn't making any sense.

'So I can cut the string, silly. I've got some scissors.'

'What? Who are you?'

'I am your Death.'

'I thought Death was a tall, hooded fellow in a cloak with a big scythe. The Grim Reaper and all that.'

'That's just one of the Deaths. Everyone has their own. Yours is me. Now, are you going to take the balloon so I can cut the string?'

'Why would I want to do that?'

"Because the string is the thread of your life and you opened the invitation.'

'I didn't. Oh...'

There are times when you realise you've made a big mistake and you get that terrible feeling deep in your guts. Guess what I've got.

I turn and run back inside the pub and up to my room, locking the door behind me.

Think. Think. I need to think. I can't run because I have nowhere to run to. The world just fades out. It doesn't exist much further beyond the building I am in. I have a horrible realisation. I am going to die at the hands of a little girl with a balloon and a pair of scissors. It would be comical if it wasn't so serious. Think.

I hear movement outside the door. It must be her. The handle moves, but the door doesn't open because it is locked.

The invitation. Where is the invitation? I find it on the floor where it must have fallen when I passed out. I open the card again. There is writing starting to appear in the blank spaces, but it is fuzzy and indistinct.

'Aren't you going to let me in?'

I don't reply. How long can I stay holed up in here? For the rest of my life I expect, which won't be long if she gets in. She asked me why I opened the card. No, invitation she called it. If I put it back inside the envelope and seal it up again will I be uninvited? It is worth a shot.

I look around for the envelope. I can't see it. Where has it got to? I panic and start going through the things on the bed. It's not there. Think it through. It can't have gone far. If it's not on the bed try on the floor or under the bed. I get down and look under it and the envelope is there. I reach it out and put the invitation back inside, then lick the envelope and seal it as best I can.

Nothing happens.

She tries the door again.

'Don't you want to be my friend?'

This little girl is seriously scary. I put the envelope between *The History Of Mr Polly* and *The Time Machine* to keep it pressed closed while the glue dries, and rest them on the floor.

She is still outside the door. What was I thinking? That she would disappear in a puff of smoke?

I sit on the edge of the bed and wait. It seems to drag on, but eventually I hear footsteps moving away from the door.

I go to the window and, trying to stay as hidden as possible, look out. I can't see the front of the pub from here, so don't see her leave. It is still dense with mist, but it doesn't seem to have got any worse.

What do I do now? I don't want to go downstairs in case she is still there. I pack my present-day clothes and bag back in the plastic crate and rest it on the floor, then get into the bed. My head hurts, I ache, and I feel so very tired with the interrupted nights sleeps and whatever happened yesterday, or today, or whenever now is.

Sleep comes swiftly.

CHAPTER TWELVE

IN WHICH WE FIND THE SIMPLE PAST

Possibly Day 9 or 10. Friday 18th or Saturday 19th August 1911

I wake up in the clothes I went to sleep in. It is daylight. I get out of bed and go over to the window. The mist has gone and it is lovely and sunny outside. There are sounds coming from downstairs, so it would seem things are back to normal. Well, normal if you think that being back in 1911 is normal.

I pause by the window. Although the view is the same it somehow seems different. I can't quite place what it is though. It's probably just my imagination. When I go to check on the invitation pressed between the two HG Wells books my blood runs cold. The books aren't there. I'm sure I left them on top of the plastic crate. The crate isn't there either. Then I notice other things have gone, or, to be more precise, have changed. The Gladstone bag has been replaced with a brown leather satchel. My Fedora has gone too. I liked that hat.

I empty the contents of the satchel onto the bed. My wallet is there, but it is not quite the same. The bank notes are different too. I count up the total. One hundred and twenty pounds. The same amount I started with. The keys I had have changed, as have the notebooks and pens. The notebooks are blank. The journal I have been writing is blank. The pens I have are now dip pens, but there is no ink. The ink I bought has gone. In fact everything I bought in 1911 is gone.

I look down at the clothes I am wearing. They aren't the same either. They are still brown trousers and a white shirt, but the fabric and designs are different. Looking around the room it superficially looks the same, but it too is subtly different. I go back over to the window to look out again and notice that the frame isn't painted shut any longer. This one opens.

I go downstairs to the bar. It too is the same, but different. There are people getting their breakfasts. They don't look dissimilar to the people who were down here yesterday — the yesterday without the mist — but I don't recognise any faces, not that I was paying that much attention.

A wiry young man comes through from the kitchens carrying two plates and takes it over to some diners. I catch his eye.

'With you in a moment. Take a seat and I'll be over.'

I sit at a table for two, even though it is just me. He comes across when he has served the other guests.

Before he has a chance to say anything I blurt out, 'What year is this?'

'Eh?'

I would have expected a slightly more eloquent response, but if I was asked a question like that out of the blue it's probably what I'd have said in his place.

'The year. What year is it?'

'Eighteen fifty-nine.'

'What day?'

'Friday.'

' I mean the date and month.'

'September. Second of September.'

I lean back heavily in the chair. Not again. Not this again.

'Are you all right? You look pale.'

'I've been better,' I say, regaining my composure. 'If it isn't a stupid question, how long have I been here?'

'Just a few minutes.'

'No, I mean staying here.'

'I don't know. I only do mornings. You wasn't here yesterday. I'd have remembered you if you were. I don't forget a face.'

'Is the landlady around?'

'There isn't a landlady. Do you mean Effie?'

'Who is Effie?'

'Tom's wife. He runs the place. I suppose she's the landlady if she's married to him.'

'Can you get her for me?'

'I'll see if she is around, but I've got other guests wanting their breakfasts and I'll be in the doghouse if I don't see to them first.'

'I'll have whatever is going while I wait. And a pot of tea if it's not too much trouble.'

There is no point rushing this. If I was stuck in 1911 for over a week, goodness knows how long this will last.

'Not too much trouble at all. I'll bring it over.'

He detours to clear away one of the tables before disappearing into the kitchens. I sit watching the other diners. They look like they are more of an outdoor type than the 1911 crowd. Not the weekend rambler kind. These look more like they live on the road. Probably something to do with the turnpike, I expect. The grandfather clock is still in the same place. The room looks like it could do with a lick of paint though. The 1911 version, although well lived in, did look a bit more cared for, not that this place looks uncared for. More sort of rustic. Antiquated. My pot of tea arrives.

'She'll be out in a short while,' the waiter says before disappearing back to the kitchens.

I pour milk into the bottom of the cup before putting the tea strainer over the cup and pouring. So, like 1911 there are no tea bags. Perhaps I could invent them and become very rich, but if I was only in 1911 for a week and a bit, that doesn't give much time to build a business empire, does it. I abandon the idea and have another thought. What if I keep falling backwards in time in stages? What if I'm only a week in 1859 and the next thing I'm back in the 1700s, then the 1600s? How far back will I keep falling before I stop? My thoughts are interrupted by a ruddy faced woman. She looks a bit like the 1911 landlady, but it is another person. Similar, but different. She puts a plate of bacon and eggs in front of me.

'The boy said you forgot what year it was.'

'Are you Effie?'

'As I live and breathe. He says you were asking for me.'

'Yes I was. Look, I know it might seem like a daft question, but when did I check in here?'

'Late last night. You arrived talking about lights in the sky.'

'What lights?'

'You should know. You got us all outside to look at them. The Northern Lights. All over the heavens they were, leaping and swirling. I've never seen anything like it before in my life.'

'Oh, yes,' I feign.

'Can't remember what year it is, can't remember when you got here, can't remember the lights. You'll be telling me you can't remember your name next. Just you make sure you remember to pay your bill before you leave.'

'I think I'll be staying one more day. Something unexpected came up.'

She leaves me to eat my breakfast. I need a plan. There is no point going to look for HG Wells again. I doubt he has even been born in 1859. I need to go back to where it all began again. I have to go back inside the tunnel and to the cavern. Hopefully my things will be there.

After I have eaten I borrow a lantern and a box of matches without causing too much suspicion. I already seem to have picked up the reputation for being a bit odd, so apparently this is in character for me. I don't need anything else, and set off down the road towards the station and the tunnel.

It is another pleasant sunny day even if it is a different year, but I notice there are fluffy white clouds in the sky and the ground doesn't look so parched. There has been no heat wave and drought. As I get to the part of the road where the bridge over the railway track should be, there is no bridge. The road simply dips down a little and carries on. There is no tunnel, station, station buildings, track, or anything even remotely resembling a railway. I had taken it for granted it would be here, but quite clearly the Hope Valley line has not been built yet.

Buggeration.

Up until now my concern was about how to stay out of the way of trains since there wouldn't have been a strike on in 1859 and they'd have been running. Now my concern is how do I get to the cavern in the first place? I stand in front of where I think the tunnel entrance is going to be and estimate the direction I need to start walking in. Maybe there is an opening on the ground I can find and climb down on a rope. I'll need to mark the opening with a marker or a pile of stones or something and come back with more equipment.

I set off up the hillside through the trees and try to stay as true as I can to the line of what will become of the tunnel. It isn't easy and despite trying to walk towards the landmarks and looking back to where I started from and how far I've come I am already unsure if I'm on the right track. The trees clear and I start walking across fields. Ahead of me I can see more trees. I'm going to have to come back with a compass to do this properly. After leaving the field I walk through the trees and the landscape opens up into rough grassland and then onto open moorland. I have been climbing steadily all the way. Somewhere around here, below the ground in a hidden cavern, are my things. I look around at wide expanse of bleak empty nothingness that is the moors. This is futile.

Even if, by some miracle, I am standing where the air shaft is going to be with the cavern directly below, there is no way there is going to be an opening. Even if there was a fissure up to the surface, it is going to be blanketed by peat and hidden by heather. I have to face it. I'm not going to be getting my things back.

I stand and silently contemplate the scene of my failure. I am so close and yet so far away. A lifetime away. Several lifetimes. This is so unfair. This is so bloody unfair.

I make my way back slowly, back across the rough grass, through the trees and the fields, until I am on the road again. When I check my pocket watch — a different one to the 1911 version – I see that it is late afternoon. I have been out wandering a lot longer than I had realised. I also realise I haven't had anything to eat since breakfast and I'm hungry.

The Commercial Hotel should be just around the corner and I should be able to get a bite to eat and drink there. As I round the curve I can already see that the houses which were there in 1911 aren't there now. As I go further on I see that the Commercial isn't there either. There is nothing for it but to go back to the Fox.

I return the lantern and the matches unused.

'You seem of heavy heart,' the man behind the bar says as I order a pint of beer. I can only assume it is Tom the landlord.

'It's been one of those days. It started out strangely and went downhill fast.'

'I know what you mean. Can I get you anything else?'

He doesn't seem too interested in what I've been doing and I'm happy to keep it that way.

'I don't suppose you could rustle up something to eat? I'm starving.'

'We're not serving food yet, but I could put together a quick ploughman's if you'd like.'

'That would be perfect. I'll just be a couple of moments while I get something from my room.'

When I left my present, I was carrying a book which turned itself into *The History of Mr Polly* by HG Wells. I want to get whatever it has turned itself into now. I leave my pint on the bar and go up to my room. When I tipped the things out from the bag earlier I didn't pay any attention to the book. It is still on the bed. When I look at the title on the spine I can't help but laugh at the joke which fate has played on me. *Hard Times* by Charles Dickens. At least I will have a good book for company.

I go back to the bar and there is a plate with a chunk of bread, lump of butter, thick wedge of cheese, and dollop of pickle waiting for me. The barman, landlord, Tom, or whoever served me doesn't seem to be around. I take my pint and food outside to eat.

So, here I am again sat outside the Fox eating, drinking, and reading a book on an idyllic English summer day. Apart from being completely the wrong year it is an otherwise lovely day. That and not being able to retrieve my things. Apart from that it is lovely. I need to have an idea. I need another plan and I don't think going in search of Charles Dickens will be it.

I mull over what Wells said. His exact words, and I remember them distinctly, were, 'If it were me, I would go back to where it happened, where it all began.' Coming back in time happened in the tunnel, but what if it began somewhere else? Where something begins and where something happens aren't necessarily the same thing. Without the railway I can't catch a train home or even get to Chinley. Instead what I will do is walk the route back. I know the villages the train stopped at, so I will simply follow them back to Chinley, then walk the road back to Macclesfield. All I need to do is turn right out of the front of Fox House and head for Hathersage. I've no idea how long it will take, but I'm not in any particular rush. I can stay at the inns along the way, and if there isn't one I'll sleep in a field beneath the stars as the weather is so nice.

That's it then. That's the plan. I have another pint and watch the world go by and while away the rest of the day reading. I've not read Hard Times before, but it is a really good book.

As the evening wears on I have a proper cooked meal — Shepherd's Pie. As the light begins to fail I stop reading and turn in for the night. I want to be on the road early, so a good night's sleep, nightmares permitting, and a hearty breakfast and I will be on my way in the morning.

It seems strange to be lying in this bed in this room again. I have the window open and there is a cool breeze blowing. I drift off into a reverie and fall asleep. I dream of flying, of soaring through the air. I effortlessly glide to wherever I want to go by thinking it. I fly through clouds. I can see the ground far below me, with the fields a patchwork of green, the houses as little dots. I float. I swoop. I see a red balloon hanging in the air and everything is in slow motion. I am falling, falling from so high. My arms and legs flail helplessly. It is too far away to grab. The balloon recedes away from me, an ever smaller red dot in a wide blue sky before it vanishes.

Before I hit the ground I wake up. I push myself up on the bed and sit in the darkness. Shadows flicker on the walls and an odd light comes through the window. This had better not be part of the dream. I pinch myself to see if it is real and convince myself it is.

I go over to the window and look out. The Aurora Borealis, the Northern Lights, are back. Dancing across the whole sky, brighter than a full moon, but of an indescribable softness and delicacy. There are greens and reds and violets. At times it looks like the reflection from a large fire beyond the horizon, as though some distant city was going up in flames. At other times it looks like rays from the sun reflecting upwards from the back of a cloud. The aurora changes again and the sky looks like it is suffused by a pink vapour, then takes on a dark roseate hue.

Beneath the silent spectacle taking place above, the world sleeps. The spectral lights continue to shimmer, to fade, to brighten, to arc, and I watch them with quiet awe. I don't know how long I have been watching them, maybe an hour, maybe two, but eventually they die down the sky returns to the stars in their familiar patterns, slashed through by the hazy band of the Milky Way.

I go back to sleep again.

CHAPTER THIRTEEN

IN WHICH WE FIND THE PAST CONTINUOUS

Day 2. Saturday 3rd September 1859

It isn't the earliest of starts, but it isn't the latest start by any stretch of the imagination either. I am up for a little after seven, breakfasted, picnic lunch packed, bill settled, and on the road for eight.

I'm not exactly prepared for a long walk. I have shoes instead of boots, but they look strong enough and it isn't as if I will striding purposefully over hard moorland. This will be sticking to the road and putting the miles in.

I sling my satchel, with all my worldly possessions in it, over my shoulder and set out towards Hathersage. It is a beautiful summer morning with a hint of dew on the grass. It feels good to be alive on a day like this. Walking down the turnpike road I have to say how well maintained it seems to be. Even though it isn't asphalted — that will come later no doubt — there aren't any large potholes on the stretch I walk. This is just as well as the drivers of a couple of horse-drawn carts I pass coming the opposite way wouldn't be best pleased if there were.

After about an hour I reach Hathersage and keep going. Bamford is another forty-five minutes, but I don't go into the village. Instead I am trying to keep my route as close to the bottom of the valley as I can as that is where the train line will one day run, so I effectively bypass it on my way to Hope. I am reminded of the John Shuttleworth song *She Lives In Hope, But She Used To Live In Barnsley* and sing a few lines I can remember to myself. It is getting on for eleven o'clock by the time I reach the village. I remember seeing it from the train when I travelled this route on my commute. It was set back from the station so I didn't really get to see it, just some house roofs and a church spire standing beyond a stand of trees.

There is an inn in the village and I stop there for an early rustic lunch of bread and cheese, washed down with a pint of bitter. I love its name — the Cross Daggers. Why can't pubs have proper names like this and not jokey but lame names like the Slug and Lettuce, no doubt dreamt up by some marketing company hired by a corporate chain who thought it would be a good way to bring in customers. It might work on some, but not me.

Talking to the landlord he says it will be a good three or four hour walk to get to Chinley, so my plan is to get there today, or possibly Whaley Bridge if I make good progress, and stay there overnight before heading onto Macclesfield tomorrow. I'm glad to sit down and rest for a while. My legs are holding up and my feet aren't suffering. Even so, I kick my shoes off to let some fresh air get to them while I eat. I take my time over lunch.

After a comfort break, a euphemism for relieving oneself, which is itself a euphemism, and another pint, the proverbial and in this case the literal 'one for the road', I set off again. The route isn't the more direct one recommended by the landlord which goes through Castleton, with the castle it takes its name from perched high on the hill overlooking the village. Instead I make my way towards Edale as this is the route the Hope Valley railway follows. At first the landlord didn't know where I meant by Chinley. He'd never heard of the place and he'd lived in the area and knew all the localities hereabouts all his life. He knew where Buxworth, which is the place I drove through just before getting to Chinley, but even that took some explaining before he got it.

'Oh, Bugsworth you're meaning. I didn't understand you the way you were saying it.'

I can't believe that Chinley wasn't there before the railway. I keep walking. I find the route getting harder as I walk as there is more up and down than I had realised from the comfort of a train seat. Edale is at the end of the valley. The train goes through the Cowburn Tunnel, but I know there will be no such tunnel when I get there. I will have to climb up out of the valley and head across the tops to get to where I am going. Even though it is mid-afternoon and I have already eaten I stop again when I have gone through Edale and sit on a stone wall to eat my picnic lunch. It will make my satchel slightly lighter and to be honest I have worked up an appetite again. I unwrap the brown paper parcel prepared for me at the Fox and eat the ham and mustard sandwiches they packed for me, the English mustard giving it that extra bit of zing.

Although I enjoy the rest I don't want to take too long and I still have another seven miles to go, according to the milestone I am sitting by. Getting going again takes a bit of effort. While I am getting used to walking it has been quite some time since I have done this distance. As I have more of the same tomorrow I think I will knock getting to Whaley Bridge on the head for today. Chinley is where I am going and Chinley is where I will stay overnight.

Not far outside Edale the land starts to rise. It gets progressively steeper the further I go and I find myself taking short rests to get my breath back before doing the next stretch. At last I reach the crest and it eases off to a relatively flat, open landscape. I am back on the moors again. Fortunately the road keeps going even though it is now a track. The ground is firm beneath my feet and there are indications — wheel tracks, hoof prints, and the occasional pile of manure — that horses and wagons pass this way. I wouldn't want to come this way in winter. The moors are treacherous and lethal in bad weather, but on such a warm, sunny day as this, they are staggeringly beautiful in their bleakness and ruggedness. However, I am not here to admire the scenery and I press on towards my destination. What started out as a pleasant walk is now becoming an effort and I give a big sigh of relief when the land eventually begins to slope downwards. I can see Chinley in the distance. Not much longer now. Even so, it is a good half to three quarters of an hour before I finally get there in the early evening. Chinley is a lot smaller than it is now, or in 1911 come to that. It must have expanded when the railways came. Here in 1859 it is a quiet backwater of the Peak District.

There isn't actually an inn in Chinley, and I am directed to the Red Cow at nearby Whitehough, which is a short distance outside the village. It is another stone built building typical of the area. I secure room for the night, and after freshening up in a bowl of warm water from a pitcher brought up for me — there doesn't appear to be any running water here, either hot or cold — I go downstairs for a well earned drink and what I hope will be a very hearty meal. The accommodation is basic to say the least. The bar area has sawdust strewn across the stone flagged floor, the seating is hard wooden benches, and the ale — 'we don't serve beer here' — comes in a heavy brown pottery mug. The ale is as heavy and brown as the mug it comes in. You couldn't get any more olde worlde if you tried, except perhaps to nail horse brasses to the beams. The difference here being that there aren't any horse brasses hung up. If they are hung anywhere it will be on horses doing a hard days work.

The meal that arrives is as hearty as I had hoped — steak and kidney pudding, potatoes, carrots, peas, all in large amounts, with a huge chunk of bread and butter. To follow, custard tart, equally large. If I were writing a review I would give this place five stars and a highly recommended in the comments. One or two more ales, together with *Hard Times* help the evening to pass most agreeably. When I turn in for the night I am more than a little bit tipsy. I don't know what proof those ales were, but they weren't weak, that's for sure. As soon as my head hits the pillow I am asleep.

Then comes the dream. This time there is no flying. It begins by falling. Instinctively I reach out and grab something. It catches in my hand. A thin silver thread. I look up and attached to it is the balloon. I fall backwards. The blue of the sky contrasts with the red of the balloon. Everything seems so serene. If I am going to die in the dream I don't want it to be holding a balloon. Anyway, it's not like it is large enough to support my weight and float me to safety. I let go of the balloon and watch as it becomes smaller and smaller as it rises and I fall, until it is just a speck in the sky, and then nothing.

I am standing in a grassy meadow. Tall grasses sway in the breeze and butterflies flit from flower to flower. I look around, but there is nobody else here. I am wearing the clothes I was in when I set out to work. At my feet are my bag and a plastic crate. I open the lid of the crate and put the bag inside. Then I take the phones from out of my pocket and put those in the crate on top of the bag. Next, I unbutton my shirt, folding it neatly, and put it inside the crate. Then I take off my shoes and put a sock inside each one. I lift up the shirt and put the shoes and socks in, then rest the shirt on top of the shoes. Then I take off my trousers and boxer shorts. I fold these as well and put them in the crate, then replace the lid. Naked, I walk across the meadow carrying the crate.

I don't wake from the dream, I stop dreaming.

CHAPTER FOURTEEN

IN WHICH WE FIND THE PRESENT

I feel a bit stiff when I wake up in the morning. Although comfortable, the bed was softer than I like. I sit on the edge of the bed and straighten my back before standing and completely stretching it out.

I get dressed and go downstairs without washing or shaving first to find something to eat. Breakfast is ham and boiled eggs, which makes a pleasant change from bacon and fried eggs, and is accompanied by what seems like a never ending supply of cups of tea. When I get back to my room the water in the pitcher has been changed. It might once have been hot, but now it is somewhere between lukewarm and tepid. I wash my face and rub my finger round my teeth to clean them as best I can — this is what you are reduced to without a *Gentleman's Travel Kit*. Before long I am ready for the road again. I leave the Red Cow and make for Whaley Bridge, which takes less than an hour to get to. I keep walking until I find the turning for the Macclesfield Road.

As I turn onto the road and start walking up the hill there is a sudden stabbing pain behind my eyes, but as soon as I feel it the pain goes. That was strange.

I keep walking and a few minutes later the pain comes again, then goes. I stop and rub my eyes and the sides of my head around the temples. I'd better not be coming down with anything. If I am I'll have to turn around and find somewhere to stay in Whaley Bridge. When the pain recedes I start walking again.

I don't feel ill in myself or under the weather. If anything I feel rather good. Apart from the stiffness first thing this morning I'd say I was in fine fettle. I keep walking. The hill out of Whaley Bridge is long, steep, and just seems to keep going and going. I plod on uphill, first rounding a sharp right bend and then an even sharper left as the road changes course to run along the side the hill rather than straight up it.

It still climbs as it goes, but now has a steep drop off the side.

As I round the second bend I begin to feel lightheaded. After a few more steps I feel distinctly dizzy and stumble. I sit at the side of the road until it passes. The road is a steep climb, but surely it's not that steep and I'm not that unfit. Even so, I sit a while longer until I am sure the dizziness has gone. I stand up and press on again.

I've driven this route many times, but hadn't really noticed just what a drop there is at the side of the road. It is not precipitous like a cliff, but you still wouldn't want to fall off it. There is a lot of down to fall into and the landing wouldn't be gentle when you did.

As I make my way up this stretch, which is long and fairly straight, I hear a voice calling in the distance. I turn round and look, but there isn't anyone there, or if there is I can't see them. I keep walking.

I have only gone a few paces when I hear calling again. I stop and look, but still can't see anyone. Maybe it is my imagination. If someone is trying to get my attention they will call again.

I turn to keep walking again and that is when lights start flashing in front of my eyes. I close my eyes and rub them and they go. What with the shooting pains and the dizziness maybe I should turn back if I am coming down with something. I sit leaning against the wooden railing at the side of the road, this time looking across at the wide expanse of countryside in all its greenery. After about ten minutes, with no recurrence of flashing lights or dizziness, I begin to feel like a fraud. I need to keep going if I'm to get to Macclesfield.

Best foot forward as they say. I start walking again. About three or four minutes up the road I stop dead in my tracks. The road ahead leads to a crest before levelling off and then rises again. A cold chill runs through me and I feel very weak. My head starts to spin. There is ringing in my ears. I stagger to the side of the road, but before I get there I lose my footing and fall heavily to the ground. My vision is blurred. My ribs hurt. My head hurts. Something wet trickles down my face. I touch it, then look at my fingertips. Red. Blood.

The flashing lights before my eyes come back. Then the stabbing pain behind them comes back. I'm scared. Through the ringing I can hear a faint voice, but I can't tell what it is saying. It sounds far away.

Lying on my side I draw my knees up and wrap my arms around my head. I feel dreadful. I should have turned back soon, found somewhere to stay, been nearer to people. Instead I am by myself, alone on a road outside of town, with no one to turn to and nowhere to go. I need to get up and get back to Whaley Bridge somehow. I force myself to my knees, then somehow get myself upright. I stagger forward one step, then two, then lurch sideways over the wooden railing at the edge. I am falling, falling down the hill, tumbling out of control. The ground rushes up and knocks all the wind out of me. It is a blur of green and blue as the sky and the ground rush past. I am living in a world of pain as I am flung ever downwards. Seconds turn into minutes turn into hours.

I remember a car on the wrong side of the road. I was driving to work. I had to swerve.

I am still falling.

I went through a barrier to miss it. There was no noise. Everything was silent until my car hit the ground. Airbags went off.

I lie motionless, half on my side, half on my front. I can't feel anything. Maybe that's for the best. There is a car by my side. It is on its roof. The driver's door hangs open.

I close my eyes. When I open them there is a girl standing there. She looks young. She is wearing a blue dress and carrying a red balloon, which floats on the end of a silver thread. She also holds a pair scissors.

I try to push myself up, but fall back to the ground and close my eyes. There is something gravelly beneath my hands and I close my fingers around it. When I open my hand and look it is fragments of shattered glass from the windscreen. They look like diamonds, glinting and sparkling as the sunlight catches them. I let them fall from my hand. I feel so very cold.

I feel something being twined around my fingers.

The world fades.

Too weak to wake this time.

Printed in Great Britain
by Amazon

67446524R00193